A Private Reason

A STORY OF LOVE, LOSS AND REDEMPTION ACROSS A GENERATION

Janet Warran

A Private Reason

A STORY OF LOVE, LOSS AND REDEMPTION ACROSS A GENERATION

Janet Warran

MEREO
Cirencester

Mereo Books

1A The Wool Market Dyer Street Cirencester Gloucestershire GL7 2PR
An imprint of Memoirs Publishing www.mereobooks.com

A PRIVATE REASON: 978-1-86151-283-3

First published in Great Britain in 2015
by Mereo Books, an imprint of Memoirs Publishing

Copyright ©2015

The address for Memoirs Publishing Group Limited can be found at
www.memoirspublishing.com

The Memoirs Publishing Group Ltd Reg. No. 7834348

The Memoirs Publishing Group supports both The Forest Stewardship Council® (FSC®) and the
PEFC® leading international forest-certification organisations. Our books carrying both the FSC
label and the PEFC® and are printed on FSC®-certified paper. FSC® is the only
forest-certification scheme supported by the leading environmental organisations including
Greenpeace. Our paper procurement policy can be found at
www.memoirspublishing.com/environment

Typeset in 10/15pt Century Schoolbook
by Wiltshire Associates Publisher Services Ltd. Printed and bound in Great Britain by
Printondemand-Worldwide, Peterborough PE2 6XD

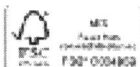

With thanks to the poet and novelist Laura Kasischke,
who encouraged me to continue with this novel and to keep
my faith in the vision of it.

In loving memory of Jane Annakin, who tucked me (and a first
draft) under her wing because she always believed in both.

For Simon

At last the secret is out, as it always must come in the end,

The delicious story is ripe to tell to the intimate friend;

Over the tea-cups and in the square the tongue has its desire;

Still waters run deep, my dear, there's never smoke without fire.

Behind the corpse in the reservoir, behind the ghost on the links,

Behind the lady who dances and the man who madly drinks,

Under the look of fatigue, the attack of migraine and the sigh

There is always another story, there is more than meets the eye.

For the clear voice suddenly singing, high up in the convent wall,

The scent of elder bushes, the sporting prints in the hall,

The croquet matches in summer, the handshake, the cough, the kiss,

There is always a wicked secret, a private reason for this.

W H Auden

The inquest has been held into the death of local artist Christina Hopwood, whose body was discovered on the beach at St Margaret's Bay in February. Ms Hopwood had been missing from her home for several days. Following a police investigation and the disclosure of medical records, the coroner has recorded the death as 'suicide while the balance of the mind was disturbed.'

CHRISTINA

I am drifting. I am ash on water. My edges crumple and curl. I am the woman in the burning photograph, flaking and floating away on the wind.

My vista is a canvas and all the paints have run. The colours are fading. Now a crimson darkness, as if a hand has reached across to shield my eyes from all of this. A reel of images slips onto a spool. The pictures start to flicker into a life. My life.

Look.

This is the playground at St Luke's School. I'm sitting on a bench. It's wood and the splinters have snagged my skirt. Claudia, my sister, is here, chanting something with the other children. My scarf is over my ears, so I can't hear what they say. My mouth is full of fluff and tears. But there is Harriet, my grown-up daughter, standing on a sea wall. I

1

don't understand. She is waiting to confront me. Again. But she's out of her time. She's always been out of my reach.

That's my mother standing in the garden of my childhood home, Hunter's Lodge. Mother looks very glamorous in that fur coat and matching hat. She's very beautiful, isn't she? What thin calves and ankles she has. She must be smiling up at my father, she's saying something but still I can't hear.

Hunter's Lodge is such an ugly Victorian house. Pointed arches and fussy brickwork. There are three broad semi-circular steps and a rockery right at the end of the garden. They are made of Welsh slate that has thick white veins running through it.

There's the greenhouse, there behind the apple trees. I am ducking into it; there's a strong, peppery, chemical smell that pricks my nose, not unpleasant, quite seductive, like petrol. And the heat, argh, it feels so thick and sticky. It's claustrophobic in here, even though it's glass and I can see all about. I am having trouble getting my breath. I must be still and stop fighting this.

There's a better view of the house. It looks very imposing, all those steps sweeping up from the lawns. It's perfectly symmetrical, I didn't realise. That bay on the left is the drawing room and the windows on the right are the library.

Shh! I am in there. I am in the library. What am I doing here? It smells of my father - sandalwood and old cigars. So many books. All those words that people have laboured over for us to discard by a chair or drop as we drift to sleep. Boxes and papers and some chocolates in big glass jars, the tops too wide for my small hands to twist off. The chocolates are wrapped in coloured foil, all different colours, and I'm excited by the abundance of all that sticky sweetness. No. It's dark in this corner and there are shadows here that frighten me. Daddy says if I'm a good girl, I can have some chocolates.

Father's desk is a mess: rolls of paper, notebooks, rulers, a setsquare; pencils and pens and a bottle of Royal Blue Quink. In front of the hearth is a fireguard which has a tapestry Aunt Margaret stitched on the front, I know it's a hunting scene but I can't see it quite clearly enough. So many shadows in here and I must be very, very quiet. Daddy says so. There's the set of brass fire tools, the poker and the grate brush we play soldiers with, and the toasting fork. All tarnished. Oh, I can taste tea-time toast and warm butter and sharp homemade marmalade with too-thick rind. The butter runs down my chin.

That's Frederick, in that photograph. There, look, look, on the mantel. He's my big brother. So handsome in his airline uniform, smiling and proud. Wait - this picture's in the wrong time too. He dies. He died. I can't remember. Oh, Freddie. That's Jesse in the picture with him, Freddie's spaniel, sitting to attention at his feet. The picture reminds me of something. Old tombs in a church where schoolchildren come in droves to make brass rubbings.

Listen! Freddie's here somewhere, I'm sure of it. Yes, I can hear him in the drawing room and Jesse's claws click-clicking on the parquet. Freddie? Oh, my beloved brother, how I have missed you.

Wait. This is me and my father. Somewhere. My hair is very long. I'm sure I could sit on it if I tried. Sometimes it gets tangled. My mother cuts the tangles out with kitchen scissors. Everything is tangled, muddled up. I don't know if I am looking at pictures or if I am in them.

Father and I again. Me in my best frock. I'm outgrowing it. The elastic at the bottom of the sleeves is too tight and leaves marks on my upper arms. I hear Mother saying, "Sometimes you just have to put up with things, Christina". The roses on the bodice of that dress are made of a piece of crimson silk that was once a slip of my mother's. Everything is rationed, you see. My mother's love is rationed. But Daddy says he loves me.

Father and I again. He's holding my arm very tight, just above my elbow. He whispers in my ear, I feel his breath. There is perspiration running down my back. My scalp prickles. He won't stop talking. It's too close. He's too close. Breath on my neck. My heart is racing. Go away, please go away Daddy. Go away!

Emmy? That's better. This is Flint Cross, the garden at the back of Jim and Emmy Reed's bakery shop. I am young again here. Look! I'm right there, sitting under the pear tree. I'm drawing. I draw with wax crayons. There's that funny old flowerpot that says "Dymchurch" in tiny pearly shells. I can smell the wax from the crayons. The red crayon is really stumpy because red is my favourite colour. It's an angry colour and I use it all the time. I keep my crayons in a tin from the bakery. The tin has a boy sitting on a fat horse, on the lid. It smells of stale cake and wax inside. I like horses.

See, there's Emmy again, there, waving to me from the scullery window. Emmy is more of a mother to me than my own. For a minute there she suddenly looked old, she was suddenly a very old lady. Time keeps slipping.

Emmy is with me here, right here, beside me, walking up the lane to St Clare's. It's the convent school. I go there because I like drawing and my teacher at the other school said I'd be better off with the nuns. It's better being away from my sister Claudia. There are older girls here; some of them board at the school. They don't talk to me much.

Isn't it misty in the woods behind us? The trees are so still they don't look real. Their leaves are made of paper and crayon wax.

Winter. It's damp and I think I can smell snow in the air. I can feel the damp and the cold in my bones. Claudia and I are buttoned up for the weather. I've got a long thick plait down my back, I feel the weight of it and it swings like a pendulum as I walk. Our mother is here with us, wearing that fur coat again, it reaches almost to her ankles. I can smell the cakes that Emmy has put in a box for my mother to take back to London. The cakes are wrapped in brown paper and inside the box I've put a drawing for my daddy, rolled up and tied with a piece of tapestry wool.

This is my parents' holiday bungalow. It's on the coast, near the marshes. I hate it here. This is after the war. There's streaky pink lino in the passageways that makes me think of fatty ham. I can hear children shrieking. We are washing shells in the huge, Belfast sink in the kitchen. That's Claudia and Fred on the beach, eating sherbet dip. Half a Crown for three canary yellow tubes with the liquorice stick poking out the top. I can feel the weight of the coin in my hand, I'm holding it up to the lady with the sweet cart. She doesn't see me because she's smiling at my father, saying something, and my father is touching her. I hate her. She has very red lips and big yellow teeth. I kick the side of the cart and father smacks me hard behind the legs. His hand is sandy and it stings. The marks of his fingers are there for the rest of the day.

Apple trees. Lopped off branches, crudely cut. I'm trying to duck beneath the broken bits to avoid the sharp ends of their severed limbs. Someone's dragging me here, behind the old wooden garage at the bungalow. I can feel my face now, hard against the splintered slats of the garage. The smell of wet wood. And the musky smell of my fear.

What's happening? No, don't. I want to see, but something's pulling me down. A roaring sound. I'm trying to keep my chin above the water. There's Claudia, standing on the bank of the drainage canal that runs by the bungalow. I'm in the canal, its thick green water filling my mouth. I have to get out. Claudia has told me there are eels in here that will bite off my feet. She's standing on the bank with her hands over her ears. Help me, Claudia! Why won't you help me? Can't you hear me? Claudia?

Arms under me, pulling me up. A man's chest against my back, holding me tight to him. And now my father's voice, all choked up saying, "Chrissie, Chrissie, my little princess. What have I done, what have I done? Please breathe, please breathe". And his lips on mine, like dried-up worms.

CLAUDIA

I remember my sister Christina so clearly as a little girl, sitting on the school bench at St Luke's. Just sitting there, watching us, tapping her feet because she said her toes were numb with the cold. God, she was always cold, always muffled up with scarves and extra socks and vests. Her hands were always blotchy in winter, purple and orange patches flaring up from under that pale skin of hers. She always had chilblains. Really and truly, she was such a bore about them.

Ooh, I loved school. That was the first school we went to, St Luke's Primary. Funny that I only think of the playground being in the winter, mostly I just remember my childhood as sun and games and laughing, really and truly. It was a little school, just a main hall with four small rooms along each wall and a church across the courtyard. It was at the bottom of the hill, below Hunter's Lodge, our house.

Oh, the school closed down years ago. There's a new, modern primary school a mile further down into town. St Luke's still stands empty and derelict. Until the council decides what to do. Such a waste. You'd think they'd use it for something. I don't know, a youth club? Silly. There aren't youth clubs any more, that's old-fashioned, kids just hang about on corners now, don't they? The ones who are better off just sit at computer screens all day. Or those awful computer games. That's why they are so many social problems, now the kids don't develop social skills. And no sense of family any more. Family is everything, don't you think?

Yes. We once went back to visit, Christina and me. St Luke's I mean. Harriet, Christina's daughter, was with us, she must've been ten or eleven, unruly and wild as ever. She never stopped talking. Making up for lost time! She didn't speak at all until she was about ten. She was an odd little girl, really and truly. After that you just couldn't shut her up. Such a noisy child.

Of course, I wasn't very happy about it, we were trespassing, going in there. There were signs up and lots of wire. She knew I didn't approve but Christina had found a gap in the wire and the three of us sneaked through all the same. It was all Christina's idea, of course. She had one of her notions that if we stood there, long enough and quietly enough, we would be able to hear all the children's voices from all those years ago. Singing, chanting rhymes. I got fed up standing out in the cold and said I'd take Harriet for a cup of tea somewhere and come back later. Of course Harriet didn't want to go but as soon as her mother said she didn't have to, she changed her mind. Harriet has always been a contrary miss with her mother. But it isn't really surprising, is it?

I pushed the boat out and took a black cab into the West End. We had tea at a cheap little place on the Strand. We sat at a table in the window watching the people in the street scuttling about in the wind. It was near Christmas, so even in the rain and the wind, the streets were very busy. We counted the number of umbrellas that turned inside out and watched their owners struggle with them. Harriet said that it was like the people were battling with a flock of scavenging blackbirds. Or some such thing. She was always an imaginative child. Sometimes she'd scare herself silly with the things she made up in that funny little noggin of hers. Poor Harriet.

We had to wait ages for a cab to take us back to Hunter's Hill and the school. When we finally got there, Christina was still just sitting there, on one of the mossy benches, hugged into her coat, her hands pushed up into the sleeves, left into right, right into left, like she had one continuous loop of arm from shoulder to shoulder. She really did look as if she was listening to something. *Hearing* something. Oh, I don't know. It was a bit of a funny day all round.

Hunter's Lodge? It wasn't a lodge, there wasn't any other mansion or anything nearby. I don't know why it was called that. It *was* the big house, set in a couple of acres. It had huge wooden gates at the entrance, set slightly back from the road and a gravel drive that curled round behind rhododendrons. You couldn't see the house itself from the road, just the gates. It was really something, quite stately. Christina always said it made us seem very grand and that we weren't, it was all one big lie. Rubbish. She always had to put the family down, put Dad down. Later on, when she had all her posh friends, she definitely thought we weren't good enough for her.

Hunter's Lodge. Well it had a drawing room, a library, five bedrooms, and grounds which included a walled vegetable garden with a greenhouse. There was a huge ornamental rockery with semi-circular steps in the middle which were made of Welsh slate and led down from the back of the house to the lawns. The house had mains gas, which was really something before the war. There were servants' quarters, but we didn't have anyone living in, although Mother did have a daily help, and a sort of cook-housekeeper called Mrs Rice. And we had Aunt Margaret who did the laundry on a Monday – in a wonderful old tub in the scullery. I loved washing day, the windows all misted up and the smell of washing soap. What would it have been? Oxydol, that was it! I loved helping Aunt Margaret to put the sheets through the mangle. That was my favourite bit.

Aunt Margaret was Dad's older sister. She lived in a little terraced house down the road that she rented from Dad. Poor Aunt Margaret, it wasn't much of a life. We were told she had lost her sweetheart in the first war. She'd trained as a milliner but her sight had deteriorated by the time we were born. Look, I don't want to speak ill of the dead, but Aunt Margaret was a bit, well... sometimes she gave me the creeps. And sometimes she smelt. She mumbled. Nowadays we'd say dementia. Alzheimers or something like that. One minute smiley and happy and wanting to play with us, the next shouting at us to get indoors, not get our clothes dirty. Mind you, she never shouted at Christina. Never raised her voice around her. They were thick as thieves, Aunt Margaret and Christina. It says a lot, really and truly. Pair of loopy loos.

When she was growing up, Christina used to spend hours with Aunt Margaret. Now it makes more sense, of course; kindred spirits. Both quite bonkers. Though I can't fathom what they can have talked about. But they'd sit together for hours on end, *sewing* together, mending something probably. Aunt Margaret made clothes, too, things for us. A pair of trousers for Frederick out of one of Dad's coats. Or she'd unravel a sweater and knit it into something else. Real wartime type scrimping and saving. But clothes were still rationed, remember. People forget.

Sometimes she and Christina would be out in the garden, Christina sketching some still life she'd set up and Aunt Margaret doing one of her dreadful tapestries. I don't know how she saw enough to stitch so intricately, you know. She used to hold the thing right up close to her face. Some of her tapestries were William Morris designs, which she copied from a book. Or she did shooting scenes with ridiculously clean spaniels with far too restful-looking pheasants in their mouths. Awful things. I gave the last one - a fireguard - to a church raffle. I pity the poor person who won it.

When I went to work for Dad - I worked for him from

the age of sixteen, you know, after he'd sent me to Pitman's to learn shorthand and typing - I found out that he'd actually bought Hunter's Lodge for the land but our mother liked it and the war came, so he never did anything with it. Well, yes, I suppose it was a bit of a funny-looking house, but beautiful in its own way. Mother lived there for a while after Dad died but it was ridiculous having her rattle around in that great big place so I moved her nearer me, to a nice little bungalow. Eventually they demolished the whole place, the house, the outbuildings. They built fifty-odd homes - little execu-boxes - on the plot. I drove up a couple of times, watched them smashing the house to bits. My ex-husband said I was being morbid. Holding on to the past.

For a long time, the contractors left the gates at the entrance to the site. I had this fancy that I'd buy them, as a keepsake. They finally bulldozed them one Monday morning. This tiny chap in a monster machine gouging out the posts. The end of an era, really and truly.

Our father? Oh, that's a real rags-to-riches tale. He became quite a local celebrity, you know. There were articles about him. When he died so tragically, his obituary was in all the papers. He had left school at twelve to apprentice as a bricklayer. It was only when he came back from the first war that he had his break. A foreman fired him for being cocky, told him go back to college to learn the building trade properly before he started answering back. So he did. He ended up running his own company. Mansfield Ltd. He taught at Woolwich Poly later in life. His name's still up there on a plaque somewhere. He'd had a hard life. He used to tell us how he had to crawl under the stairs to study because his father drank and he would beat him if he found him with his face in a book. Aunt Margaret would sneak him something to eat. She was the woman of the house. Their mother had died, but I never found out when or of what. Dad never spoke of it. But he always said he pitied his own father. We didn't ever know him, our grandfather, *he* died of cirrhosis of the liver, about the time our parents married. Of course, that was why Dad never drank; he said he had no difficulty signing the pledge with the memories of his childhood in that rotten house.

Dad was a brilliant draughtsman, drew wonderful plans, real works of art. I've got some of his original plans, for the first houses he built. I had them framed. They're in my hall at home. They're something a bit unusual, they often get remarked on. Anyway, when he finished his training, Dad went into business with a carpenter. And really and truly it went on from there. The business just grew and grew. He got a lot of local council work through his connections, on municipal buildings, repairs, alterations, that kind of thing. Then during the war he was in charge of bomb damage. And afterwards he bought up a lot of land on the cheap - plots of rubble where rows of houses had been wiped out. Freddie, our brother, said our Dad always had his eye on the main chance, like it was something a bit immoral. As I see it, it was a business opportunity. Nowadays, of course, he'd be admired for his business acumen and foresight. He'd be one of those business troubleshooters you see on the box, going in to sort out little companies.

He was our hero, our father. Even to Freddie, though in a different way of course. But we all adored our Dad. None of us really got over him being killed. He died in a car accident when he was sixty-three. Things seemed to take a real turn for all of us then. Freddie went to France, my marriage started going downhill. And Christina, by then she'd taken up with all her fancy friends. Living the high life. She'd pretty much cut herself off from us all. Didn't visit Mother, never came home. Now I look back, of course, I can see that it was the first sign that things were not as they seemed, really and truly.

You know, even after all this time and everything that has happened, I'm still quite cross with her. So she had her issues, but really, it was just so selfish.

Of course, Christina was always Dad's favourite. I suppose the baby of the family usually is, usually the one who's spoilt rotten. And then of course there was the fact that Christina had contracted pneumonia when she was little and everyone thought she'd die. We had a fever nurse in the house for three nights. We were going through what they called the Phoney War then and nurses were hard to get because they were being trained for war work. So I suppose Christina being so ill when she was little made her all the more special. Dad used to call her his princess. I didn't have a nickname. Sometimes he called me Claude. Because I was a bit of a tomboy, really. I was quite tubby when I was young. I had freckles and my hair was cut short for a girl in those days. My daughter Sarah says that in pictures of me at that time I definitely look like a boy. She says I look like Mickey Rooney in that film with Elizabeth Taylor... about the racehorse and the girl jockey. Oh, you know. *National Velvet*, that's the one.

Christina was born on my birthday, I can remember *that* extremely clearly. I wasn't very pleased. It was meant to be *my* day. I was having a little birthday party; we hadn't even got to the cake and the candle-blowing when all the other children's mummies started running about whispering. Then Mother was being helped upstairs and my friends and I were sent out of the house to play in the garden. It started to rain, so Freddie took us off to play in the old greenhouse, where it was warm and muggy. Fred was our elder brother - did I say? He died young. So much sadness in our family, seems the men never made it. He was forty-nine. He had a heart attack on the golf course. Incredible really, because he'd just had a medical - he was a pilot for a French airline. Such a waste. He used to look so handsome in his uniform. Tall and dark. He had wonderful blue eyes, stunning, just like Dad's, with lashes a girl would have died for. What an expression. Christina had very dark brown eyes you know, not a bit like either of our parents. When she was born, everyone remarked on them, they were so dark they were almost black.

So we were born on the same day, my sister Christina and I. But we were complete opposites. Always. That's why I can't believe any of this astrology, star-sign nonsense. In fact, it's a wonder my sister and I came out of the same mould. Christina was always skinny and I was always curvy. Christina liked her own company and spent hours alone, playing on her own or with mad Aunt Margaret, of course. Whereas I was always off playing, usually with the boys, getting filthy somewhere. My friends now can't believe I was a tomboy. Well, people change, don't they? But I was a really roughty-tufty child and to me, Christina's weediness was like a red rag to a bull. It makes me smile to think of it but I was a bit cheeky with her at times. Well... she was a nuisance. She'd have been quite happy on her own but Dad used to shout, "Don't forget your baby sister!" He was always calling after me to take Christina. Well, not just me, Freddie and all our friends. So we were always trying to think of ways to get rid of her for an hour or so. I mean it was just games, of course, nothing grisly like you sometimes hear today. Kids doing terrible things to one another. Oh, it was just harmless fun, really and truly.

PUPPETS

Eleanor sits in the studio. There's a plaintive song on the radio. The stretched, reedy voice like thin snakes, side-winding on bare boards. It suits this space. Dust. The stink of oil paint and turps. Is Willard still upstairs? Willard was a cartoonist, made a fortune. He's very old. He's Eleanor's best friend. She smiles and tilts her head on one side when she tells people that. She says there are nearly forty years between them but they are like peas in a pod, truly the best of friends. Thing is though, she doesn't really know what he does upstairs in his studio now. He probably sleeps, but it doesn't matter, she just loves it that he still wants to be here. That something is warm and constant. Her friendship with him has always been that, warm and constant. True. A true thing.

Willard knew her father from when they were young

men, when they were both starting out working for a London newspaper. Her father had been a trainee print manager and Willard, a little younger, quite talented as an amateur caricaturist, had been apprenticed in the graphics department, long, long before her father had upped sticks to start his own little print business in this sleepy seaside town, right here in this rickety old building full of memories. By then Willard had begun drawing political cartoons and had earned himself quite a reputation. After a couple of years he had gone freelance and had followed her parents down from London, renting space in the upstairs mezzanine from her father, then after he died, from her mother, and now from her. He doesn't work much now, just the odd bit of illustration, but he is here every day and all day, Monday to Friday. Snoozing. Sleeping deeply. Dreaming. A presence any which way. She thinks she can understand why he still needs this quiet, sunlit space. This building seems to hold her in its embrace and perhaps Willard has a sense of that too. He says he likes being near the young people. He likes routine. It's very near the pub. For Eleanor, well, she doesn't know life without Willard really. She can remember him as a middle-aged man when she was a toddler. He would swing her round by her arms in her parents' little garden, round and round, her mother's smiling face at the kitchen window.

Eleanor turns a wedding ring on the third finger of her right hand. Her mother's ring, a very orange gold. Twenty-two carat. A soft gold. The funeral director had told her this. Just yesterday. He had passed it to her in a crisp white envelope. As you know, he said, there was no engagement ring, no other jewellery, just the wedding ring. Somehow it had seemed like a criticism. Maybe he thought she had taken off her mother's other rings in the hospital. But her mother hadn't been the type to wear much jewellery, she had replied, just a wedding ring and a watch. She had been looking directly at him.

The funeral director had quickly moved on to the subject of the service. Hymns. He had handed her a hymn book, *Songs of Praise* embossed on the front in gold lettering. She fingered the letters. She'd had a Songs of Praise volume at school. They were given them in the second form. They were encouraged to cover them in bright fabrics. Her mother had sorted through her needlework box and given her half of an old striped pillow case. She had stitched her name on the front in pink chain stitch, her mother had shown her how to do it. 'Eleanor Joan Ashfield'. 'Eleanor' was after her grandma. Joan her mother's name. Joan. When Eleanor was little, she had thought the word sounded rich and syrupy and golden, like a tiger's eye stone or a summer sunset. Her mother, Joan.

Eleanor hadn't recognised the names of any of the tunes for the hymns. The funeral director said that if she hummed a melody she knew, he might be able to tell her which tune it was. *Love divine, all loves excelling*. It had been one of her mother's favourites. She started softly, in a broken hum. The funeral director smiled and joined in, waving his arms like a conductor. *Joy of heav'n to earth come down*. She felt her voice deep in her chest and started to belt the words across the room. *Pure unbounded love thou art, visit us with thy salvation, enter ev'ry trembling heart.* The last line had made her cry. Not just gentle sobs, but proper wailing. The funeral director said he would give her a moment and left the room. There had been a box of supermarket brand, man-sized tissues on the table beside her.

Eleanor takes a breath and looks out the window. There's the pub, across the road. It's recently been taken over by a brewery. When she was small, the men who worked for her father here used to call it the Filo, First In Last Out. It wasn't the pub's name, she can't remember what it was. Now it's called the Four Horseshoes. Philip's there, waiting to go in, hunched into his coat. He's beginning to look really sick now. Zip, his little terrier, is at his heels, like he's listening. He cocks his head, left to right, like a clockwork toy. He is His Master's Voice. Philip drinks at ten-thirty in the morning but he has cancer of the throat and he will die soon, so no one feels they have the right to say anything. All these characters in her life. An old cartoonist. One man and his dog. Crazy world.

The windows in the studio where she sits are small and the panes have thick, uneven glass. One of the artists her mother rented some of the space to last winter had nailed the ground floor windows shut to stop drafts, but now it gets so stifling and humid in the summer that even the watercolours she uses to paint her illustrations won't dry properly. Crazy. She'll do something about it. And the old yellowing newspaper on the floor, curling at the edges. She twists on her stool to read a headline. The *Sunday Sport*. 'ALIENS TURNED MY SON INTO AN OLIVE'. Crazy world.

Looking left, she sees the old writing bureau that served as a repository for all her father's paperwork over the years. Patrick Ashfield was never tidy, never organized, though the business seemed to do well enough. The bureau has been like that - so full of papers the drawers won't close - for as long as she can remember. She can't imagine there would be anything important in it, her mother would have sorted through any important papers after her father died.

Tom, who also rents studio space from Eleanor – the other side of this ground floor - had once spent a drunken afternoon with his boyfriend Martin, speculating about what they might find in the drawers if they cleared it out. 'Bills of lading, I've always liked the sound of them', Martin had said, giggling, a little stoned or drunk or both as he had passed through the room to the back kitchen to make sobering coffee. Tom had said 'Who Bill, darling?' There had been more laughter. Eleanor said it could be love letters, call-up papers for the war, a photograph of a soldier with 'Soon be home, sweetheart' in copperplate on the back. Tom wanted a secret diary, something revelatory and sensational, that Eleanor could sell for a fortune so she could buy them all yachts in different colours and they'd sail in convoy to Cannes. But she had suddenly become serious and said she didn't want them going through her father's things, she'd do it by herself, thanks for the offer and everything. And now she doesn't want to go through the things in case she is disappointed. Or in case she finds things she isn't ready to find.

Tom - officially her tenant, more of a friend-in-need

really - makes puppets, mannequins, proper ones out of wood, with pinned joints. Like Pinocchio without clothes on, Martin says. 'Smaller noses, darlings'. Tom does puppet shows too, as a sideline he says. Eleanor hasn't had to try hard to guess what his main line - his main source of both income and amusement - might be. Willard disapproves of Tom as one of her renters. He says he is fickle and irresponsible. Tom makes a bit of a living for himself, enough to pay for this workspace, as he has a job part-time teaching. English as a foreign language. In the summer, this seaside town is full of chattering voices with unfamiliar vowel sounds and intonation. But Tom also has Martin who has a private income. So really, working is just a way for Tom to have more of a social life.

Tom and Martin sometimes move in questionable circles – 'too much money and nary a scruple', says Willard. Sometimes Tom and Martin tease Willard but they're careful not to go too far. Martin often jokes with Tom about them 'being lampooned by Willard in the pages of some silly antediluvian chronicle' but Eleanor knows that they'd probably rather like that. None of it matters - they make her laugh and Tom always pays the rent on time; and they only go so far; oh, they know that Eleanor and Willard are close and they know better than to upset their discreet landlady.

Tom sometimes sells his puppets to some of Martin's wealthy Russian, so-called 'friends'; he says they are quite the thing with some of the wives. Eleanor thinks the puppets are creepy, if she's honest. A pair of unfinished, unvarnished puppets hang down by their slender, shaved heels from the beam above her head. Tom climbed up and put them up there when he arrived. He said they would keep an eye on them all. Crazy.

Would you keep an eye on little Harriet? There's a good girl. My mum, gently pushing us through the hotel kitchens where she worked. Harriet. God, I haven't thought about her for years. Harriet always had very brown skin because she lived somewhere hot and exotic. She always came with her father, for a week at a time, over several summers. That's how I remember how brown her skin was, because my skin was so pale next to hers even in the height of summer. And she was a redhead like me so I couldn't understand why she was brown, not pale and freckly like me. They stopped coming after a while. I wish I'd thought to ask Mum more about them, where they went back to, where home really was for Harriet. I wish, I wish. So many little things I never thought to ask mum about. At the end, there was so little time.

There was supposed to be something wrong with Harriet because she couldn't talk. That was why she and her father kept coming to England, to go to London to see a specialist. But actually there wasn't anything really wrong with her at all, she was perfectly able to speak. And I knew all along but I never told anyone, not my mum or my dad, not a soul. I wonder if she ever grew out of pretending? She must have done, surely it was some childhood thing? It wasn't just talking, she actually didn't make any sounds at all. So when anyone spoke to her, they talked loudly, over-enunciating, as if she were deaf. They would go right up to her face and shout. I think people felt embarrassed around her because of this. But I wasn't embarrassed. Besides, I knew. I just accepted it, just accepted **her**. I suppose, in that wonderful way of children, I simply thought, well, she just doesn't want to talk. And because I was a child and none of the grown-ups said anything, never talked to me about Harriet or asked me, I just didn't bother about it. Besides I was a frightful chatterbox so I easily said enough for two.

We were in the gardens, Harriet and I. It was a dull day, with a little drizzle. My father was there. He'd come to pick up my mother after work. Harriet didn't have a coat to put on when it started drizzling so he had put Harriet into mum's mackintosh. She was so little and so shy, she almost cowered from him. My dear, soft, father. He made it a game, putting the mac on her. He put her arms in the sleeves and they hung down. 'Oh, look, Eleanor, we've lost Harriet's little paws, now what shall we do? Are they up there? Let's see.' He had to roll the sleeves up, over and over until there were thick wide cuffs, and then he found her hands. She just stared up at him, great big greeny brown eyes.

At the end of the vegetable garden the gardener had planted a row of buddleia to attract the butterflies, so I thought I'd take Harriet up there to look at them. I was chattering away to her, the way I always did. The sun had just come out and we were watching the butterflies, there were loads. And I was saying, my-daddy-says-this and my-daddy-says-that and I told her that my daddy says that butterflies are happiness and if you rush about after them they'll keep flying away but if you sit still they'll come and sit on your *shoulders and then you will be happy. And Harriet tugged at my sleeve and said as clear as anything, "Can I take one home for my mummy to make her happy?" I expect I didn't even bat an eyelid that she had said anything, I probably answered her with some bossy remark about them being the hotel's butterflies and not being allowed. It's only now, all these years later that I am puzzled. Why are these odd things coming back to me? Is it the shock of Mum's death?*

A clumping of boots on the stairs. Willard is shrugging himself into his old waxed jacket. He puts a hand on Eleanor's shoulder.

"Burning the midnight? Not off to Peter?"

Willard always talks in like this, abbreviated, in short sentences. Tom says it's because he thinks in boxes an inch and a half across and three down, a cartoon strip. Martin says Willard talks in Braille, you have to feel your way around the words to get to the rest of the meaning.

Eleanor thinks that since her mother's funeral, everyone has seemed so far away, even funny and dear and beloved old Willard who talks in his odd, staccato way. She has sensed some distortion in the space between them, like having one eye shut, so you are unable to judge depth. She knows that Willard is grieving too but a grief shared is not a grief halved.

"No, I was just daydreaming. Peter's in Dubai, researching some stuff."

Eleanor smiles. Willard imagines he sees a little of Joan about the eyes, but it has to be imagination because he knows that she is not Joan's daughter by birth. It is partly the knowledge of her mother, Eleanor's real mother, that makes the air between them distorted, but Eleanor doesn't know this yet. She doesn't yet know anything about her birth mother, she has only ever been a name in a file. Christina Mansfield. When she was sixteen, they had told her. She had taken in the information but part of her had chosen not to process it, not to really believe it. And she had never wanted to know more, never really thought about it. Not while the woman she loved as "Mum" and the man she loved as "Dad" were still alive. At least, not til now; she recognises there has been a shift, somehow, that for the first time she is fixating on the word 'adopted"; that thoughts of her parents, of Joan and Patrick, seem slightly off-kilter and she wants to refer to them as her 'adoptive' parents, not Mum and Dad. Perhaps she regrets not asking before it was too late; she doesn't want to meet a random social worker with a buff-coloured folder sitting behind a desk in a council office. But Joan's death and Eleanor's curiosity and her grief and her loneliness – and fate - will change this. It will.

"Everything's all right."

Willard says this as a statement. He doesn't want her asking. Not yet. He needs a bit more time to think through a plan.

"It is, Willard. Nightie-night, then."

Willard smiles back at her. They both hear it. *Nightie-night, pyjama-night.* Joan used to say it. Willard nods and turns to walk out through the back entrance. She calls after him as he opens the door.

"Willard," she says, "do you remember when I was a child, there was that little girl who came and stayed at the Crest Hotel when Mum worked there? With her Dad. They lived abroad somewhere." She looks down idly at what she is drawing. It's a sketch of a group of rabbits having a picnic, for a children's storybook but it's flat and charmless and she knows she hasn't been able to concentrate at all this week. She has her back to Willard. She doesn't look up or around when she continues, "Harriet. Her name was Harriet. Do you remember? I know it's a funny to be thinking of, after all this time, but it's been bothering me who she was."

Willard kicks the door closed again with his foot, the force making the windows rattle. He takes a breath and turns to her. He thinks, *after all this time, it's time.* He is almost relieved. There is a pressure in his chest that needs to be released. It is love and it is grief and a secret that has felt like a betrayal ever since Patrick died, and now with Joan gone, too, there are characters that he must outline for whom Eleanor will determine the colours and contrasts.

High up, in the rafters, above Eleanor and Willard, the two wooden puppets gently swing.

CLAUDIA

I remember Dad coming home and saying war had been declared. And some of the men who worked for him coming up to the house to give in their notice. Everything happened very quickly. But you know, it didn't really mean anything to us as a family, as children - nothing seemed to change at first. It didn't seem to affect *us* much - I mean, I don't remember things being very different at the beginning. Dad's company started converting some of the dockland warehouses so they could be used for making munitions. We didn't see so much of him I suppose but we were used to that really, he was always at the office or on site. When the bombing started, though, he'd be away night after night and sometimes we'd wonder what had become of him. I remember Mum and Aunt Margaret putting up blackout in the dining room, and Mum's friends coming round to tell her the latest tale of devastation. Really and truly, it never felt real. No, I don't remember ever being afraid.

And then we were evacuated to the country. 1942. Now that *was* a shock. Just Christina and I were sent away, Fred stayed with Mum and Dad in London. I suppose he was just that bit older - he'd have been fifteen - and was company for Mother. I don't remember being upset by this but I probably was at the time. I was usually quite annoyed if I couldn't do what the boys did, if I couldn't be with Freddie and Dad doing more interesting things.

By the time Christina and I went to the country, most of our friends had long since left London and so classes at school were down to just a few of us. For Christina and me it was all very civilised, none of that terrifying scramble onto trains to unknown seaside towns with just a satchel and a label round your neck and thin-lipped spinsters who were mean with the food and meaner still with their affection. We were lucky girls. Besides, Dad wouldn't have let that happen to us. Mrs Rice, our daily, had a sister who lived in this little village called Flint Cross, in Sussex, and Dad arranged for us to go and stay with her and her husband down there. I was pretty excited about living in the countryside. Perhaps that's why I didn't mind having to go with my sister, be a girl for once. Cos I'd never been to the country. It would be my own adventure I thought.

The Reeds had no children of their own. They were older than our parents. James Reed was the village baker. You know, I only recently discovered that the bakery had originally belonged to Emmeline Reed's side of the family. They'd been the bakers in the village for generations.

They were an odd couple really, like Mr and Mrs Spratt, he thin and gaunt, she a real caricature of a baker's wife, fat and floury and always jolly. I never saw her without an apron on. Her aprons were white, always heavily starched, with embroidered butterflies round the edges of the bib. They were very kind to us. If you ask people about those days now, too often you hear the sad cases, terrible memories of billeting. But the Reeds were kind, simple people. They led this wonderfully gentle life in their sleepy village, with parish meetings and church cleaning rosters and all that lovely village gossip floating in and out the cottage and the shop.

They made wonderful breads and cakes, and the bakery had quite a reputation with people as far away as Hastings and Brighton and London. They made bread for hotels too. Mr Reed was also a confectioner, he made sweets - peppermint creams, pralines, hazelnut fondants - all decorated with tiny flowers made out of sugar. Mrs Reed said people would come from miles around to buy them by the quarter, nestling in dainty paper bags with purple string in the top. But by the time we were living there everything was rationed so there wasn't the sugar.

We loved to watch them in the bakery making the bread, it was one of our treats. Sometimes Mrs Reed would give us each a piece of bread dough to make something with. I loved the taste of raw dough so I'd always be eating mine. The bits I had left would be grey because I had forgotten to wash my hands and I would have squeezed them and folded them and pulled them apart again. Christina always made a perfect little something for the oven, rolling and moulding the dough until it was all plump and smooth. She liked to make animals, and dough people with currant eyes that popped off in the oven and fat limbs that would drop off the minute she lifted them off the baking sheet. It always upset her that they never stayed in one piece.

Jim Reed had such elegant hands, long, tapered fingers and dainty pale nails, more suited to a concert pianist than a baker. But he'd never have been that because he'd lost a thumb on his right hand, in an accident as a boy. He had terrible lungs; he used to wheeze like a squeezebox and when he laughed he'd always start to cough. Mrs Reed told us he'd been gassed in the first war. But flour does things to your lungs, doesn't it? He lived into his early seventies though, so perhaps it wasn't as bad as it sounded.

Of course it took quite a while for Christina and me to get used to being away from home, stuck out in the country. But after the initial shock of damp beds and no inside loo, I got to quite liking it really and truly. Christina loved the animals. Mrs Reed kept chickens and a bad-tempered old goat called Amos and a ginger cat called Mouser because that was what he was meant to do. We used to collect the eggs every morning before school and give Amos any kitchen scraps. And there was so much space, so many places to explore. I wasn't homesick for long and then of course we started school there so I made lots of new friends. But Christina was whiney for months. She always felt things much more keenly, she was always much more sensitive, my sister. I think she missed Dad a lot. Even though he visited us often, usually once a fortnight or once a week if he could. Of course I missed Mum - and Dad and Freddie too - but I was much better at controlling my emotions than my baby sister. Really and truly, Dad's visits made Christina worse, more homesick and whiney rather than less. For days after he left she'd be pale and distant, hardly speaking. To this day I remember Dad clutching her to himself, her face buried in his jacket. Sometimes she'd smell of his sandalwood shaving soap where he'd held her so tight to him to say goodbye. He really tried with her.

I missed Mum the most. I cried when she came down. She only came a couple of times. Or maybe it was just the once. Yes. It was winter. She came on her own, on a train from Charing Cross, and I can remember the slippery feel of the front of her fur coat when we hugged at the station. She wrote to us, though. Lovely letters telling us what it was like, living in London. She'd write about going to a dinner where they'd served jelly made out of carrots for dessert, or how Dad had sneaked some champagne from the Savoy during an air-raid, funny stories that used to make me laugh. I don't suppose they were all true, although our brother Frederick used to insist they were. Really and truly he was rather disapproving of some of Dad's larks, our brother. He was more like Christina, so serious about everything. He didn't get on with Dad. Dad and Mum and me, we were much more easy going, we liked to have a bit of fun from time to time. Christina and Frederick, well, they were always so worried about things, every little thing was always so important. Drove me potty, really and truly.

School life was pretty wild down in the country. I was always getting into mischief with the village boys or on the bus to and from school. It was such fun. There wasn't a primary school right in the village so we started going to the school in Boars Head which was a couple miles away. It was either a walk across the fields or a bus ride if we were in time to catch it from the top of the lane. Children would faint at the thought now, wouldn't they? Walking all that way.

Christina didn't start school until a bit later, and then she only stayed there for a term because she was unhappy. She got to be a right misery. Typical Dad, he came down and sorted it all out and as usual indulged her. So Christina got to go to the private convent school just up the road. The truth of it was that she just wouldn't make the effort to get on with anyone. Perhaps it was a bit of a rough school I suppose, but it didn't help that she was such a pale, skinny little girl, so weedy and weak and drippy. Really and truly she was just the sort to get picked on. And I certainly wasn't going to make it worse for her by standing up to the bullies. I just kept quiet and got on with it. Anyway, there were lots of tears and tantrums, so when Mrs Reed told father, he arranged for her to go to the convent. He had to pay of course. Oh yes, Christina was their 'expensive child' - Mum was always saying that about my sister.

Christina could really sulk sometimes, you know, put on a real show. She was quite a manipulative child. Very moody. Poor Mrs Reed, she'd get so upset. There was that terrible time when Christina lost Dad's watch. His wristwatch, not the fob, thank goodness. I've got the fob, it's a bit of a treasure. I have it upstairs. No, we had just started at the school in Boars Head, in fact. Dad had left his wristwatch with Christina on one of his Sunday visits, telling her she could count the hours until the next Sunday, when he'd been back again. And that it would be her lucky charm. He made a hole in the strap with the corkscrew bit on his penknife so Christina could wear it on her tiny wrist. Of course it was heavy and clumsy and for the whole week it made her left arm hang down like a useless limb. Honestly, she sat staring at that wretched watch growing paler by the day, as if she really was counting away the hours and minutes and seconds. And then she went and lost it. I ask you! Just typical.

You can imagine, Dad was absolutely livid. I remember him marching Christina off across the fields and when they came back her face was all red and shiny where she'd been crying and her dress was all dirty - she'd obviously had a jolly good hiding. Well, really, she deserved it. But as if that wasn't enough, goodness me, did she sulk about it. Wouldn't speak to me for weeks. It really upset Mrs Reed, she wanted to telephone our mother, but I kept telling her it was just Christina's usual sulking. Mrs Reed fussed and fussed, like it was the end of the world or something. As that was probably the only real telling off Dad ever gave Christina she certainly made the most of it. I suppose that's what made Dad put her in that other school. Crying and wailing and refusing to eat or even drink. Ridiculous. Really and truly, if Dad had told her off a bit more, it might have toughened her up. I tell you, it doesn't hurt being strict with children, they need to know the rules.

Oh, yes, I kept in touch with Emmeline Reed for years of course, I used to pop down there to see her all the time. I haven't been for a while now, she isn't quite all there these days. She has proper professional care and everything but she still lives in the cottage at Flint Cross. Really and truly, she's pretty amazing for her age. My daughter Sarah still goes from time to time. It's funny how you stay in touch with some people through the generations, isn't it, how they become fixtures in your family.

It was strange, because Christina became very chummy with Emmeline Reed in later years. When Christina was married and living abroad, she actually stayed there with baby Harriet when she came home on leave. We saw her there in fact. Really and truly, I don't know why she did that, put Mrs Reed to all that effort and fuss when she and her husband had so much money - I mean, she could have stayed in a hotel anywhere she liked, the Savoy, whatever. She could have had her own car and driver to take her there rather than having to be put up. That would have been much more Christina's style to be frank.

Oh, yes, when my ex-husband Joseph and I were first married we used to visit the Reeds and then when Sarah was little, it became a regular family outing. We'd go the last Sunday of every month, whatever the weather and whatever else was going on. We had an old shooting brake that Joseph's father had helped us buy. It was quite something to have a car then, lots of our friends didn't. Some of them had motorbikes and sidecars but most people relied on public transport. Anyway it was on one of those Sundays that we found Christina there, with poor little Harriet, quite a tiny baby, ridiculous bringing such a small baby all that way on a plane. I had no idea she would be there. It was quite a shock. Because by then, Christina and I were not on speaking terms. So it was all *very* awkward.

Oh, well, Christina and I had had this falling out when Dad died. But there's no point in getting upset about it now, it was years ago, all in the past. No point in dragging that up all over again.

Well, perhaps I do tend to think about my siblings a bit more now. That's what happens really and truly, when you get older and lose family members. Sometimes the memories pop up right out of the blue, little things, sometimes things I can't remember exactly.

I hope the Reeds both knew how grateful we were for looking after us so well. I never talked about how I *felt* with them, of course, you didn't with people like that, you never breached emotional seas.

Yes, like I said, Emmeline Reed still lives there. Of course the shop all closed down years ago, but she's still there in that old cottage. I worry about her being there, of course, especially alone at nights. I told her I'd help her find somewhere suitable, where she'd have some company, but she wouldn't have any of it. She said she has all the company she needs. Like I said, she has a girl from some agency, but that's not the same as company of your own age like she'd have in a nice home somewhere. She's a private carer person, the agency girl. *You* know what I mean; comes in every day, cooks her meals, sees she's all right, keeps her company in the evenings. I don't know how it's all paid for, I really don't, I keep telling Emmeline that savings don't last forever. The girl doesn't tell me anything, says I'd have to talk to her boss. Really and truly, that's why I have to wonder if Emmeline Reed really knows what goes on. I mean, she might be all there in lots of ways but at that age they are so out of touch with how the modern world works.

Oh, I don't know, it was about three years ago perhaps, the last time I went. She was very quiet, the dear old thing. She said something about expecting a visitor. She seemed very excited about it. The carer said she didn't know of any visitors that were coming.

For all I know, she still sits in that old chair in the scullery, looking out at the garden, smiling - really and truly, who knows what she even hears half the time, she's definitely pretty hard of hearing now. I phoned after Christina – well, you know – but Mrs Reed couldn't hear me. And the carer girl said that recently she'd be sitting in her chair, looking out of the window and then she'd start waving, like there's someone in the garden she's waving to. But there's nobody there, nobody at all.

EMMELINE

It was simple. One was very good and sweet and one was a very cheeky little madam. A nice one and a naughty one. Like the song goes, the one about Santa Claus coming to town. You'd better watch out, you'd better not cry. Bing Crosby. He was lovely. Claudia was the cheeky one, she must've been just eleven and she was a big girl, quite chubby, full of it. Her little sister, Christina, she was seven. Tiny little thing. Like a little dolly. Tiddler.

Very different girls. There was a boy but we didn't get him, he stayed in London right through the war. I think Jim would've liked to have the boy but we didn't have room. Jim was my husband. He died twenty-three years, four months and three weeks ago. I still miss him. Never mind, eh?

We were lucky. Dear me, you heard such stories about all them evacuees; bedwetters, little tikes eating you out of house and home, bad-mannered ragamuffins with necks black from lack of washing, stealing your bits. At least we knew something about ours before they arrived. My sister Mary was living in London and she did a bit of cleaning and such for their mother. Mind you, we had no children of our own so me and Jim weren't sure what we were letting ourselves in for. Still, we liked children well enough. Jim always said he'd have fancied a baker's dozen of our own if we could've had 'em. But I lost the first and we were never blessed that way again. Still, never mind, eh? We couldn't have wished for better little ones to look after for the war. Oh, there wasn't any shortage of love in this house. I only wish I could've kept the littlest one, little Christina. It might've all been a different story then, eh? I never dared tell Jim. Perhaps he knew. Mind, if he did, he never did anything about anything. I dunno. He'd just tell me to mind my own beeswax, that people like us didn't meddle. Argh!

Mr Mansfield brought the girls down himself. He had this big black car, an old Lagonda, very smart. We felt very posh with it sitting outside the shop and everything. I remember it as if it was yesterday, these two little girls sitting up in the front with their Daddy; Claudia, chubby and covered in freckles, with a mop of thick auburn hair, short like a boys, all smiling like she was on some great adventure. And little Christina squished between them, all neat and prim in a pretty dress with silk flowers on the bodice, those big brown eyes watching everything, that beautiful red hair of hers in a long, thick plait, all the way down her back. So pale. Skin like alabaster. Tiny, tiny little thing. Right then Jim nicknamed her 'Tiddler', she was such a slip of a thing. Mind, I don't want to go giving the impression she was a frail child. Far from it. Not in character, not if you knew her. She had this way about her, of watching. She wasn't like most little girls, she'd often sit all quiet and neat, like she was just here to watch the world. Oh, yes, she was a beautiful little thing, a little dolly. I dunno, I can't go describing it better but Miss Minnie from the post office said she must've been kissed by the angels when she was born and I reckon that might've been true. I used to tease her, little Christina, and tell her they must've forgotten to give her the wings. Oh, dear. Where's my hanky? Dear me. Never mind, eh?

Mr Mansfield was quite well to do, you know. When he died there was a picture of him in the local paper and lots of writing and the world and his wife apparently turned out for his funeral, according to Claudia. All we knew at the time when the girls was coming was what my sister Mary had told us and she wasn't much at describing folk. We knew he had a big house and that, and a building company, so I'd imagined this grand businessman, all big talk and fat cigars. But he was a small man, bit quiet. Very dapper. His boots was so shiny you'd have seen your face in them. Claudia said he had always been a stickler for clean shoes so I was always careful to polish up the girls' shoes before he came visiting most Sundays. His hair was cut really short around his ears, thick and black and shaved all neat like a sergeant major. I suppose he was handsome, yes but handsome is as handsome does in my book. No, I shouldn't speak ill of the dead .....

Oh, well …. I saw it in him right from the start. I could tell, here was a man with a temper. You wouldn't have wanted to fall foul of 'im. Shouldn't say that really. But it's true.

Oh, I won't deny he looked after me and Jim. Fixed things in the bakery when we had any bother, even sent a man down to mend the roof in that dreadful winter of forty-three when you couldn't find help like that for love nor money. Jim took quite a shine to him if I'm honest. He did used to go on about him to folk. Like he was a bit of a hero. Tch! Jim's head got turned from time to time, he could be such a silly.

So Christina was a tidy little thing like her daddy. Neat and quiet. Never made a mess, always tidied up her books and her toys, folded her clothes neatly on the chair in their room. Her big sister, though, ooh, now she was a one. A right tomboy for starters, always rushing about and so untidy, Lord, Christina and me, we was *forever* tidying up after that Claudia, picking up her coat, finding lost shoes, school books, clothes. Wouldn't believe it now, makes me smile she's got so fiddly and fussy, what with her coffee mornings and her diets and her matching handbags and her bloomin' chiffon scarves and whatnot. Her little country cottage with roses round the door. But I tell you, that Claudia was a right pickle as a little girl and a right handful to boot sometimes and bossy was not the word for it. Now she hasn't lost that, has she.

Truth to tell, Claudia was always getting into scraps with the boys in the village, coming home with some tall story and her hair a mess and her uniform in a right state.

Sometimes I'd walk up to meet the bus and I'd see her clambering off, with her school blouse all askew, shoelaces undone, jabbing the boys with her elbows to get through, laughing and larking about. She'd be pulling her little sister behind, yanking her after her one day and then completely forgetting her the next. That little girl would have to walk home all by herself if her sister hadn't bothered to see her onto the bus. I don't know.

It all came out in the wash because after the first few weeks they were at that school together, there was some to do with the boys on the bus, some kerfuffle, I never did get to the bottom of it. I don't know that Claudia wasn't involved, it wouldn't have surprised me. Up to her tricks with the boys, I don't wonder. 'Cos all of a sudden, Christina just wouldn't go to school. Poor little girl, it was like she were frightened out of her wits. And we couldn't force her, we weren't going to *drag* her there, the little mite. She made such a carry on that in the end Mr Mansfield came down and arranged it so she could take lessons up at the convent school, just up the road. Christina was much younger than the other girls, it was a secondary school, the others were all teenagers, but she seemed to like it. And they did lots of other things there that Christina especially liked doing, drawing and painting and learning about nature. The nuns looked after her. They knew she was a special little girl. She cried when she left that school to go back to London. I can remember her, like a limpet, clinging to Sister Clare's skirts. She loved those quiet nuns. Dear me. Never mind, eh?

Funny thing, she never really made any friends, though

the nuns said she got on well with the others. She'd hardly pass the time of day with the other little girls when she saw them in the shop or after church. She'd just nod and walk on by with her head slightly bowed, hoping not to have to chat with them - bit like when you shake hands with the vicar after Sunday service. She had one friend, a very smart girl, quite a young lady … oh, what was her name? Never mind. I don't know but that Claudia made up for it. Now *she* had friends by the score, forever charging in and out the house with them, and changing her affections like the wind. But Christina, no, she was never like that. She wasn't an unfriendly little girl, it wasn't that other little girls didn't like her. Just that she was sort of – oh, I don't know - all sort of contained in herself. Even when she was a grown-up lady, there were only one or two she'd say were her real friends. And that girl from the convent school, she was one of them. Lived in a big posh house in London. I only went to London once, that was enough for me.

When we knew Christina liked the painting and drawing and that, I went and bought her some of those little wax crayons in a little box and I got a bundle of sugar paper from Miss Minnie at the post office. It was dark grey because it was meant for the blackout but the bright colours showed up all right, the yellow and orange and the red. She'd sit for hours out there, under that old pear tree, her back against the trunk, with her bits and pieces around her. She could really draw, you know, it wasn't all just silly childish drawings, though she did lots of those of course. But she could draw trees and animals, sometimes real ones –

the old cat we had or Amos that old bugger of a goat, she liked drawing him. Not that he was still enough for long. Proper drawings, getting them just right. Or sometimes she'd make up a picture. Sometimes she'd do a picture for her Daddy for when he came down on Sundays.

Oh, yes, she did her little pictures for me and for Will, like all kids do. Pictures with the sun too big and the grass a strip of green at the bottom of the page. We treasured them for years. I kept them in a tin with my mementos of the little girls - you know, bits they'd left behind, a little sock, a bracelet Christina made for me plaited out of knitting wool, a postcard from their mummy left behind. Bits and bobs Christina left when she came to stay with her own little baby all them years later. All the little things you keep because you think they have some special magic and if you throw them away you throw away all that happiness. 'Cause you think you'll forget. Thing is, after Jim died I lost track of things a bit. I expect it's somewhere. It had a horsey on the front. Little Christina, she said she'd have a horse one day and do you know, she had lots when she was a grown up married lady. She loved her horses.

It don't matter. I have my own memories of Christina, all locked up in here, in my heart, don't need reminding. Sometimes I see her clear as day, sitting in the garden under the pear tree. Oh, yes, she's there all right. I know that bossy Claudia kept telling folk I'm just a silly old woman with a good imagination. That's why I said I didn't want her to come here no more. There are some things Claudia don't know nothing about. Christina's out there from time to time, right under that tree. I see her. We wave to each other. I know what I know and I see what I see.

CHRISTINA

I'm so cold. But the light is better. The pictures are becoming clearer. I know I cannot stop this. It's too late. An image. A memory. I am whimpering. Fear, hot and bitter in my throat. There are brambles scratching my legs, something in my hair. Leaves and burrs. My father is talking to me in his sing-song, lullaby voice, almost crooning. His hands are in my hair now, gently tugging at the mess. I feel sick. I remember, I remember that voice. I am in the woods across from the home meadow in Flint Cross. Everything is running backwards. But why am I back here again? I remember, oh God I remember this.

I have Father's watch. I can feel its weight on my wrist and the heavy buckle. He made a hole in the strap with his penknife. The face of the watch is as wide as my arm but with the improvised shortening of the strap, it no longer slips round. And he's made it tight, so tight the back of the metal pushes into my wrist bones. Its weight makes my wrist limp and it has bruised the back of my hand. But I like it hurting, I want it to hurt so I don't forget, so I can be ready the next time.

Is this the bus? That hateful journey home from that school at Boar's Head. Claudia is joining in a noisy game, throwing the boys' caps up onto the luggage rack. It's her favourite game because it's with the boys and because it's rough and she likes to show her strength. There's a faint smell of dried sweat and plimsolls and grass. It's a Friday, after the boys' games afternoon at the grammar school. A couple of them wear dirty cricket flannels, with green stains at the knee. Some of the boys are chewing stolen tobacco and they are launching thick brown spittle into the girls' hair. One boy grabs onto Claudia. She's half laughing, half shouting; I can see the moment when doubt pierces her playfulness. I can see the fear smacking in. I know this boy, he looks much older, Claudia has talked about him, she says he plays for the school cricket team. She likes him. He has dark red scuff marks on the bulging front of his flannels. He sees that I see. He pulls Claudia to him, yanking her round by her hair, so her body is pulled hard against him. She avoids catching my eye and now her laughter becomes fake. The boy says something to me in a hiss and Claudia shouts at me and I am taking off Father's watch, fumbling with the buckle, handing it to the boy, who snatches it from me with his free hand. I look at him, stare straight into the eyes and I have a strange sensation that my eyes are swallowing him.

Is this now or then? He has blue eyes and a misshapen pupil
in the left one, as if someone had punctured a tadpole and
its black innards have oozed from its body. I can feel that
he's a little afraid of himself, I can see it in the nervous
glance over his shoulder, feel it in the sticky grab of his
fingers, in the hasty push of my sister, the false, over-
nonchalant, spider-slump in his seat. But *I'm* not afraid. Not
of him. There are things I am much, much more afraid of.

Oh, Emmy. Here's Emmy and me after Sunday service.
Bright, brittle sunlight after the coloured shadows through
the stained-glass windows of the church. Footsteps on
gravel, the crocodile of girls from St Clare's, the girls who
board at the school. We stop and spend a minute with the
vicar. He has eyebrows so dark it looks as if he has smeared
them on with his finger with black boot polish. I think of
Father's shiny shoes. I watch the vicar's cassock billowing
in the wind and I imagine him being lifted away on a sudden
gust of air, imagine him riding on soft summer thermals,
bobbing high above the tiny church. There's an
unaccustomed giggle, feathery-ticklish in my throat and
Emmy, looking down at me, giving me a conspiratorial
smile. She has laughter in her eyes, all sparkly. I look up
and raise my left hand to shield my eyes from the sun,
wondering if the vicar could fly high enough to bump right
into God. And I remember the watch because it is not there
and suddenly I know there is no God, because I pray and
pray but nothing ever changes.

Feet on gravel. Boots. Father's boots, shiny black. I feel
his kiss on my cheek, his public kiss, accompanied by that

"umwa" sound that always accompanies insincere, slightly embarrassed kisses. Like adults give one another at Christmas. One for Claudia, who proffers a spotty cheek. I can hear her busy chatter. Her voice is too loud, too clumsy in this melting summer afternoon.

Now Father's voice, too quiet, too soft. And too close to my neck. I want to cover my ears but he has my wrists in his fisted right hand, scrunching the bones together, dragging me through the bright green bracken, the sticky, succulent bracts smacking back at me. There is the talcum powdery, buttery smell of cow parsley and then a sudden hit of wild garlic. Now sandalwood and old cigar-ash breath and the salty graze of half day stubble by my ear. And pain, and pain and the undersides of branches, high above and a streak of sunset, hot and red, like a scream.

CLAUDIA

It was strange going back to London when the war ended. Parts of it had changed so much you could stand on a street corner that had been as familiar as the back of your hand and not know if you were in Plumstead or Peterborough. We hardly saw Dad during those last years of the forties, after the war ended. He got overloaded with work sorting out bomb damage and the business grew so much he was always on a building site or at a meeting. It's terrible that it's all gone, that there's nothing left of Mansfield Ltd but those old plans that I rescued when they sold the offices, and boxes of photographs of Dad on building plots, standing there with his fob watch and hat, looking like Winston Churchill.

I can remember Dad being with us down at the coast after the war. We used to spend whole summers there, right by the sea, in a bungalow he built for us. Fred once told me that Dad had really built it as a place to go for naughty weekends. That's typical of Frederick. I don't like to think that's true. Oh, well, he *was* a very handsome man so I'm sure there were many who were willing enough. Anyway, affairs were different in those days, all men had affairs. So even if he did have them, they wouldn't have meant anything. Things were different then, really and truly.

The bungalow was a funny little place, quite basic, whitewashed walls and some wormy old bits of furniture they'd brought from the cellar at Hunter's Lodge. It did have an inside loo but it was always full of spiders. We usually went in July and August with another family, business friends of Dad's, so there'd be quite a crowd of children. All us kids, we used to pretend we were gypsies. I have so many lovely memories of barefoot children, lots of shouting, sandy shoes in a heap by the back door and piles of shells in the sink.

Dad added a proper bathroom one summer. It had one of those huge cylindrical geysers that frightened the life out of us as children. It was always spitting brown gunge. I remember being dunked in the bath, Fred, Christina and me, after we'd run across the mud flats for a dare, but actually the bath was mainly out of bounds for us. It was for the adults really and truly. We didn't mind. Most of the time us kids had to get washed in the kitchen sink, bent up with our knees to our chests, freezing in the draught that came under the back door. All the parents used to go on about the lousy English summers and drink more whisky than they were accustomed to. I can see us doing the same thing, twenty years later, except we used to stand under each other's carports, having rained-on barbecue sausages. No whisky, though. Not at my house. A few bottles of brought beer maybe.

There was a garage at the end of the garden at that bungalow, built into the patchy woodland that bordered the garden. Dad built it first while he and Mum slept in a caravan that first summer – we children had old, mildewy tents. Dad hacked down lots of trees to make room for it. This garage could no more have housed a car than the ghosts I teased Christina about. It was absolutely choc-a-bloc with all those things that were hard to come by then - because of the rationing, of course - this was the overflow of all the stuff my Dad collected, the things that he didn't have room for in the yard or at Hunter's Lodge. There were all sorts of things in there, from cans of paint and bits of timber to yards of fabric; and shoes, all *sorts* of shoes. Even things like chocolates – those big glass jars of sweets and tins and tins of Quality Street. Sometimes we'd sneak in there to steal some sweets and find a whole cheese, wrapped in hotel tea towels or boxes and boxes of buttons.

Once we found a great leg of meat, oh my goodness! I can remember we made it a dare, to touch this revolting, stinking haunch of animal. Oh, dear, but we didn't think anything of it when a bit of it was served up for the Sunday roast. Really and truly he was *very* sharp, our dad, he was always doing some deal or the other so we didn't have to go without.

When I finally went back there to the bungalow, after

Dad died, when Christina's lawyers deigned to give me permission, all that was in that garage was a broken deckchair and the Hayter, a great monster of a lawnmower, all rusted up with a wad of dried grass clippings wedged under the blades. Christina's lawyer said she had 'disposed of the contents'. I think she must've had someone build a big bonfire of it all. There was a huge round area of the lawn that was just black and burnt. Terrible waste, terrible thing to do. Wicked.

That old Hayter lawnmower. It was always hauled out just before we left, at the end of the summer. It was a real performance, the final cutting of the grass, the grown-ups' ritual to signal the end of all the frivolity of the holiday. The kids would be sent down the lane with every pot and pan to pick blackberries for Aunt Margaret's jam-making back in London. The grown-ups would be standing around offering advice. Dad would be there for that last weekend, looking so strange to us on holiday, in an old shirt and trousers. He looked worn out, faded somehow, when he wasn't in a suit. And Mum would be there in her customary seaside outfit of an old shirt of dad's and a ancient tweedy skirt, standing there with her trug full of weeds, fanning her face with her gardening gloves. She always wore gloves to garden in, so her hands stayed really soft and white. She always had this bracelet of tanned wrist between the glove and the sleeve of the blouse she wore. What a funny thing to remember. You know, it was the only time I really saw mother being *active*. It was as if she took her own holiday from her immaculate, ladylike London self. She never did the garden at Hunter's

Lodge in London, Dad had someone do it although he liked the greenhouse, that was Dad's territory. But Mum always liked to do a bit of gardening at the bungalow.

I can see Dad, sitting on the grass beside her while she's weeding, talking, with his skinny white legs poking out of his rolled-up trousers like two sticks of spaghetti. And us kids, flopping on the periphery like vagrant children, with wellingtons on, but just wearing our knickers besides, or running between the garden, the canal and the beach, with our hands and mouths stained with blackberry juice.

The canal was fun. It ran the length of the lane and when we first arrived, in early July, it would still be deep enough to swim in. By high summer the water would be thick and green and smelly, clogged with weeds. Of course, we weren't meant to swim in it at any time of the year, but on rough and windy days it was a better place than the sea. We never got caught.

Well, except once. I was trying to teach Christina how to dive there, easier than high tide at the beach. She insisted on keeping her wellington boots on. I told her not to. Silly girl. I knew she wasn't a very strong swimmer. I kept telling her. Of course, once she was in, the wellies all filled with water and she started to go under. I remember watching her flounder, her arms flailing about, waving at me, shouting my name. I could hear the lawnmower in the distance and then there was Dad, running down the lane in his huge workboots, swearing like I'd never heard in my life. I think Freddie must have gone to get him. Dad kicked off his boots and leaped into all this green gunge at the water's edge.

When he pulled Christina out, he had to blow into her mouth to make her breathe. He kept calling her his princess. "Come on Princess, don't die on me now Princess". And he kept kissing her, all over, her face, her arms, her neck. It was terrible. Shocking. Afterwards, when she came round and everything, he didn't say a word to me. He just looked at me, holding her in his arms, just staring at me like he was bewitched or something. All these years and I still remember that look, his lips all thin and white with anger. I used to wonder what would've happened if he hadn't come. I couldn't have done anything, I couldn't swim at all. In fact, I've only just learnt to swim. At an over-sixties class in our local pool. I like to keep active and now I've got a grandchild, I want to be able to keep up with her on holidays. Of course, it's all the more important now, what with Christina and so on. I mean, really and truly, everyone should know how to swim.

HARRIET

My mother scrambled my brain. I used to imagine this huge whisk, splattering bits of my mind across the backs of my eyes. I kept on and on, having these wonderful fantasies about being a good daughter but all that did was set me up to be even more angry with her. And disappointed with myself. I can see that now. All that therapy they keep shoving down my throat, I suppose. But I hated what I turned into when I was with my mother. And I hated my mother for doing it to me. I would become this awful slobbering, gibbering, whining, fat child, my head full of hot, splattered rage.

The memory of it, of that feeling, it still suffocates me. Stops me in my tracks.

Was it really all my fault? Was it really just *my* response, just something she provoked in *me?* I can't believe it. I think some of it had to be her. She has to take some blame somehow. Someone has to take the blame other than me.

Example. She wanted shoes so I said let's go shopping. Idiot. We went to this huge store. She had said she wanted some sporty-type walking shoes to walk the dogs in so she didn't have to wear Wellingtons. So I took her to this place in town. There were dozens of different types of shoes. Some for tennis, some for running. Boots for walking, for climbing. She must have tried every type and every sodding pair at least twice. She sat on one of those benches in her black wool suit, cool as a cucumber, with that sweet, smiley, oh-so-sparkly look on her face while I and two sales assistants fannied about with boxes.

I hated the way she was acting. And it was an act. I hated the way she raised her hands, all trembling, to push back a stray hair from her face, tucking it neatly behind her pearled ears, into her immaculate, immaculately-cut, sleek hair. She was always putting it on, this old age trembling stuff. I hated all that pretend stiffness as she bent each time to try another shoe. I hated it because I wanted so badly to fight with her but I suppose there had to be a part of me was frightened that all the stiffness, the fragility, was real and that she might die in a few years and I might just regret hating her so much right at that minute. That it would haunt me forever. That the bitch would haunt me like that even after she died. I hated myself that day for not being ruthless. Oh and I hated myself for not being well-dressed, for not being beautiful and slim and all sleek like her. And I hated it that she could still be beautiful. That even as an older woman she could still have all that power over me. Me, a woman in my own right. Yeah, right. I was never able to be anything but Christina Hopwood's daughter.

In the store, seeing she struggled, I got down on my hands and knees and tried to help her, but she hissed at me to get up and batted me away with her hand, said that I was making her look undignified. I was near tears but she wouldn't have noticed.

That reminds me of something. God, I bet the counsellor will get a kick out of this one. Ha fucking ha.

When my grandmother was dying in the hospital she asked my mother if she would massage her feet because she sometimes couldn't feel them any more. Mother just ignored her, continued flicking through a magazine. "Oh, mother! I am not going to do that for you and you know I am not." She didn't shout, she just spoke clearly and firmly and that was that. I can remember going home later and crying about it. How much she wanted to hurt my poor, old, ill Grandma. The next time I went to the hospital to visit Grandma I was by myself and I took some peppermint foot oil. The soles of my grandmother's feet were all dry and scaly and her toenails had grown like horn. She had really long toes and the long nails made them look like the feet of an animal. It was pretty horrid really. Horrid but shit sad, you know? I thought of all the places her feet had walked. All the years her old, scaly feet had carried her. After she died one of the nurses gave the bottle of oil back to me. She had wrapped it up in tissues, but it had leaked. I thought of Grandma's life leaking out of her, out through the soles of her tired, old, scaly feet.

My mother had the same thin feet as Grandma, with those very long toes. When I was little I used to watch her paint her toenails. Always blood red. Often her fingernails too. When all of her friends were painting their nails coral or pastel shades in the seventies, my mother painted hers a deep, crimson red. She'd sit on the edge of the bed in her slip with one foot on the floor, the other on a white wicker stool, doing her nails. My father would be at the other end of the house having an early evening drink by himself. The smell of his cigars would waft along the corridor to mingle with mother's perfume and the eye-watering smack of acetone. She never stopped painting her nails red, you know. Only she had her lackey paint them for her when she got feeble.

My mother told me a story once, about the history of painted nails. There was this king, she said, King Massa, who liked his concubines to claw his back when he made love to them so their nails would be covered with his blood. She said, that's how and why women started painting their nails. What a thing to tell a child. It gave me nightmares. I dreamt of my mother, lying naked beneath my father in this sweaty, frantic coupling and she was tearing the flesh from his back in strips, like enormous slices of bloody bacon. I can remember running to their room, my feet hot and sticky, slapping on the parquet. When I got there the door was locked and I could hear my mother behind it crying and crying. Or perhaps that was just part of the nightmare. I don't know. It's all been one long bloody nightmare.

Two of the toes on mother's left foot were bent, they had been broken when she was a child but I never knew the story. That's one of the ways they identified her. I suppose they were bent from years of fashionable, ill-fitting shoes. What price vanity. She always had a corn on her little toe. When she was older she sometimes wore a special pad on it. When I used her bathroom I would always find packets of them in the cabinet, hidden behind the tubes of face cream and jars of little face oil ampoules that looked like huge sperm. Makes me laugh to think of that. Not many things associated with my mother make me laugh.

My mother had very thin heels. If she had told me that once, she'd said it a bloody thousand times. She used to have her shoes made for her because of this. When she and my father had plenty of money. She always had a problem keeping ready-made shoes on. She told me this again in the store, over and over as if I hadn't heard it a hundred times before. "These won't do, Harriet, I've got such thin heels" she said.

I often used to wish she didn't have such thick skin. I wish just one thing I had said in all those years could have got through to her. But I could have tannoyed a thick bile of invective at her and she would never have caught a whisper. She never heard anything I said, the years and years of words just dropped before her face, never reaching her ears. She was always turned away from me. It was a clever trick and she never stopped using it.

Finally, in the store, I asked "If you do want trainers, Mum, do they have to be white?" which she *does* choose to hear. She put her hand on my arm in that benevolent, falsely patient actressy way of hers and said, "Is colour the thing now? I can't keep up any more, we only ever wore white for tennis." And she laughs in a very *performed* way so that I can't miss what she *really* says underneath the damning rhetoric.

I remember getting up off the floor and turning away from her; so many times I used to wish I had the courage to just walk right away. To just leave her there. But I had tried that before and knew it didn't work. I knew I could never upstage her, however dramatic I tried to be.

Oh, because my mother was queen of dramatic exits. Her best was right outside the Sydney Opera House. Great venue for it. But I should have known she only took me on holiday with her to Australia so she could get her own back. I don't remember what started the row we were having. Actually, I only remember me shouting and mother turning on her heel and walking away. It's a familiar enough scene, seeing her walk away, her back turned to me, no glancing back. I was so pissed off. I went inside the Opera House and joined the backstage tour because it took two hours and I thought that would be enough time to let her stew in the hotel room. But when I finally got back to the hotel she'd gone. She'd packed and checked out. Of course I should have just left her to it. But I wouldn't. And she knew it.

I found her in the British Airways First Class lounge at Sydney airport, wearing that wan, vulnerable look of hers - another of the masks she could put on - behind her huge, dark, Jackie Onassis sunglasses. She was being fussed over by this gorgeous guy in a suit, he was getting her drinks from the complimentary bar. She had kicked her shoes off and had tucked her legs up beside her on the sofa like a girl. My first thought was that this guy was a member of the fancy staff they had in those lounges, but as I got nearer I thought that maybe he was some dodgy conman who had spotted that enormous diamond solitaire she never took off. This bloke with his smart, handmade suit and his gold signet ring. That it would bloody well serve her right. But he wasn't. He owned a company that built racing cars. His briefcase was Vuitton and she had her fucking shoes dangling from it by their heels. He had been completely floored by my mother's charm. It's laughable. I think I might have almost admired my mother that day. Now I'd just walk past and grab the bloke's wallet, the idiot.

We bought some trainers. In that store. After hours of fiddling about. I was practically apoplectic by the end of it. I remember going home and downing a scotch. Or three. And then in the dark, alcohol-fogged early hours I woke up in tears, hung over as hell, hating myself for being a bitch. Because I hadn't been able to even *pretend* to be kind. And I'd pushed her into buying shoes she didn't really like and that she'd curse me for it later. I often used to think like that, in the middle of the night. All that guilt. The counsellor won't have it, but I know full well that my mother's prime motive for any of these outings was simply to give me another load of shit to carry around. Every fucking time. And it always worked.

Oh, yeah, I rang her the next morning and she said she'd had second thoughts about the training shoes and asked me if I would like them. I suggested she just try them out for a while. But she gave them to Jemima, her 'assistant'. Yeah, right. Her adoring skivvy, more like. She often gave Jemima things, unwanted shoes and outfits and handbags. Jemima, the paragon of a parasite. Whenever I used to visit, Jemima would go scuttling off like some sleek little beetle in her secondhand Dior or whatever. She knew I could always see right through her.

You know what? I used to spend hours dressing before I visited my bloody mother. Once we had a lunch date and I went and borrowed an outfit from Lizzie Lawson-Owen. She's the daughter of one of my mother's old friends. We saw each other from time to time. We'd known each other as kids. Of course, this was before Lizzie got all snooty on me. After she got married she didn't want to know me, the double-barrelled bitch. Anyway, she lent me this Yves St Laurent outfit. It was canary yellow and fitted perfectly. And all my mother had to say was that it was naughty for me to go and scrounge clothes from her friends' children when she was perfectly willing to buy them for me. 'Perfectly willing'. Makes me sound like a charity case. Like she felt obliged to make a reluctant charitable donation towards me.

I can see now that I could have looked like a model out of Vogue, but she'd never have complimented me. She'd still have found something to have a go at me about. She would still have been snide. It's taken me all this time to see that whatever I did, whatever I had done, I would never have lived up to her expectations of me. I don't think my mother had any idea what I really looked like, inside or out. She only ever perceived what I was *not*. My mother saw me as indistinctly as she heard every one of my tears that dropped, fizzing impotently, at her thin feet.

HANDS

Eleanor is waiting while the receptionist crushes the phone in the folds of flesh between chin and shoulder. On the other side of the counter, Eleanor waits with a rehearsed line and a false lift to her face because she is finding it hard to smile. She thinks the receptionist looks like the caricature of a matron. Like a nurse from an old Carry On film. Willard would draw her well. Her chest is one smooth rolling breast, like a bolster. Eleanor watches her as she puts down the phone and looks up at the computer screen to her left, studiously ignoring the line of people in front of her. She has some grey coming through at the crown. Eleanor breathes deeply. She knows it is unlikely there was a mistake but now she wishes she hadn't come back in here for confirmation. She could have gone somewhere else anonymously, privately. Somewhere where there isn't a room full of sick people with watery eyes. Somewhere where there aren't any children crying and clinging to their mums. Eleanor waits.

When I was sixteen Mum and Dad took me to Sicily. It was amazing to be travelling abroad, we just weren't the sort of family that did that ever. It was such a big deal, the whole thing. Buying suitcases and 'holiday clothes'. We went the whole hog. We were in awe of it all, from the airport and the flight to the funny little hotel in Taormina with its rickety lift that took you down the side of the hill to the little swimming pool. We each of us loved every single minute of that holiday.

There was a car to meet us at the airport at Palermo. It had ripped plastic seats that snagged my mother's tights. She laughed. The driver kept the radio on all the way up the mountain. They kept playing Abba songs, one after the other. Waterloo, Knowing Me, Knowing You. The driver would sing the refrains in accented English. We squashed up to one another, trying to hold in our laughter as we wound up and up to Taormina. I remember thinking afterwards that no pop music would fit that cut-glass landscape. It should have been opera, the heady rise and fall of an aria from the rolling breast of a crinolined diva.

Finally the receptionist looks up at Eleanor. She smiles, tilting her head to one side. It's a girlish action that doesn't seem right, but the smile is surprisingly genuine. The lines around her eyes and mouth show that she is someone who often smiles.

We walked miles there. Dad often had to rest. We didn't

know about his heart problem then. One day Mum and I were by ourselves, just ambling along the Corso Umberto and we saw a little path; it took us to the very top of the hill above the town. It was a long climb. The sun touched my pale shoulders with hot vanilla kisses. I'd left my sunglasses back in the hotel room so Mum gave me hers; they were heavy and slid down my nose, so she tucked a squash of tissue around the bridge of the lenses. She said if we put a knotted hanky on my head, I'd be the perfect English tourist. We laughed.

"Do you have an appointment, dear?"

Eleanor finds she cannot speak now. She pushes a card across the countertop.

"Oh, a test result. Just a mo, dear."

She watches the receptionist shift her bulk off the chair. She sees she has snagged her tights. She thinks, please don't call me 'dear'. If you call me dear again I will cry.

There were steps further up that wound up the hill in shallow ledges. We could see the ruins of a chapel high above us, its gnarled black cross like an old, puckered wound in the smooth stretch of clear blue sky. Mum was slowing a little now. She took my hand. Her palm was hot and dry. She said: Do you remember the squeezing game, walking to catch the bus to school? As if I'd forget, I said. For every squeeze mum gave my hand, I'd have to squeeze back as quickly as I could. Squeeze, squeeze. Squeeze-squeeze back. In the winter Mum always used to wear enormous sheepskin mittens and when I was little, I imagined that it would feel like that to have my hand squeezed by a piece of a cloud.

Mum paused on the hill, to catch her breath. It was hot

and we wished for some water to quench our thirst. She said she didn't need her cloud mittens here. How had she known I was thinking that very same thing?

The receptionist returns. She settles herself back in her seat, pushes her glasses up her nose so she can read the notes in front of her.

When we finally reached the chapel we saw it still had walls but no roof. Inside there was a heavy-set woman kneeling in the dust, praying. Her black dress had a sweat stain on the back, shaped like a dagger. Spread out on the ground in front of her was a fringed black shawl and on it a china pot with tiny wild flowers crushed into it. And two photographs, of a man and a small child. She was rocking gently on her heels, backwards and forwards, backwards and forwards, in time with the papery whisper of her prayers. Her hands were small and very white and in them she worked a rosary of scarlet beads. I could hear the beads, click-clack, click-clack, like a child's abacus. Counting out the hours of a life. And I thought I heard a child crying, but it could have been the wind.

"Well, now. Let's see. Ooh, congratulations, it's positive! You're my second lady today, how exciting... Oh, gosh, it's a bit of a shock, is it, dear? Me and my big mouth."

The receptionist reaches out a small, plump white hand and squeezes the back of Eleanor's as it rests on the countertop. With her free hand, Eleanor feels for her house keys in her pocket and presses them hard into her palm, drawing specks of blood like tiny scarlet beads. She feels a thump in her chest, like a blow, as the kindness of the touch hits her heart. Her eyes are hot and full and she knows that if she blinks the tears will come out and if that happens she will really cry and she doesn't want to cry, not here. Wait, wait.

"I need to make another appointment with the doctor, please."

The words are like pips under her tongue and her lips feel thick. The receptionist pats her hand, then withdraws her own, quickly. Looks hard at Eleanor. "Right, dear. Let's fit you in with the locum. Four tomorrow all right?" and the receptionist leans forward to whisper, half conspiratorial, half apologetic, "I know you saw Dr Barratt but he's a rather strict Catholic, dear. Bit old fashioned." She coughs. "Right. Let's see." She quickly drops her eyes to the appointment book, shutting herself off, disguising her complicity. Eleanor bites her lip. Her throat hurts so much from trying not to cry.

I felt my mother so close to me then, at the top of that Sicilian hill, almost like we were inside each other's skins. I looked at her. The rims of her eyes were red. She looked back at me and blinked and when she did two fat tears dropped, one onto her cheek, the other into the dust at my feet. And then I felt her hand gently squeezing mine and a soft, soft crush of fingers. Squeeze, squeeze. Squeeze-squeeze back.

Eleanor pushes hard through the doors as she leaves. The afternoon has turned out bright after a morning of mist and she fumbles in her bag for sunglasses. She starts to walk, very fast, almost marching, down the road. She is whispering to herself, saying "It's all right, it's all right, it's all right" like a chant, like a prayer, like a pacer for a march.

And breathing in through her nose and out through her mouth and in through her nose and out through her mouth. But turning the corner, she breaks into a run and in the release and stretch of her body, she cannot hold back her voice: "No, no, no!"

Inside her little house, the house she grew up in, the house she inherited from her parents, Patrick and Joan, it is only here she will let go, feel herself sliding down the wall, knees buckling, her body crumpling as if in supplication. Her hands will push against her eyes as if she can push the tears back in, as if she can push the truth back in. She will kneel on the floor of the hall, the unswept dust and grit from shoes, a little curl of shaved wood she brought in from the studio on her sock, these will press into her knees and her palms. Up the stairs, one, two, on her hands and knees, her back arching like a vomiting dog. She will cry loudly at first and wail and beat her hands on the pillow of her bed until her head is tight with tears and snot and she can hardly breathe and as if her insides, her heart, her soul could come up through her throat. In a bit she will call Willard. Willard, her father's old friend, the man who's known her since she was a baby. Perhaps Willard will come and see her, in his old rumbling car.

And later, after tea and tender words, and hugs and reassurance, he will help her back into her bed and she won't bother to undress and she won't even take off her shoes. And Willard will tuck her in and say 'nightie-night, Ellie' And she will look up at the ceiling, seeing the dots in the stippled paint, and think they look like stars.

She knows that she will not be able to stop the fear from seeping round the edges of the room, seeping, creeping, oozing like blood through the cracks and she will feel the regret, thick and grainy in her throat. And finally she will press her hands tight together like a widow, like a crow-black widow. Squeeze, squeeze. Squeeze, squeeze back. And then she will know what to do.

CHRISTINA

Where's this? Oh, it's Hawksfield. It looks so strange. Surely there was a row of houses here? But all I can see is rubble. Oh. That's my father over there, he's inspecting war damage. He's got brick dust all over his suit. I can taste the dust in my mouth. There are voices, shouts all around me but there's only father and me standing here. Wait. There are definitely other people here even if I can't see them. And children. There's a baby crying. Its cries are all muffled.

Everything is muffled, soft. It's snowing outside. This is Father's store of things that are hard to get. It could be at Hunter's Lodge, or maybe by the sea. No, the windows are made of coloured glass. It's a picture of a saint. It makes my father laugh. I know where this is. I know what happens here. I look up at the image of the saint and I think I must be being punished. I can see the outlines of Claudia and two friends go past the windows, in silhouette. Father's palm over my mouth as they pass by. It has grit in the skin from the dirty floor.

It's raining. I'm running down the hill to school. There's a dead cat in the gutter, all crumpled up - at first I thought it was just brown paper someone had thrown away. It lies in a pool of watery blood. I stop to look more closely. Its fur is ginger and white and in the rain it looks like satin. It has green eyes like marbles. Eyes that see nothing, dead green eyes like my sister's. We do drawing at school that day. I am drawing the cat. The art teacher thinks the cat is asleep on a red rug. I tell her it's meant to be blood. She tells me not to be so silly.

There he is, there's Freddie, getting off the train at the coast. He's come to join us for the summer holidays. He's going off to do his National Service at the beginning of September. He seems so grown up. Claudia's jumping up and down for a hug but Fred only kisses me, he just pats Claudia on the head. Now he shakes our father's hand. He doesn't look at him when he does this, he just stares at the ground. We're getting into the car and Freddie pushes in between me and Father on the bench seat. I usually sit squashed up to Father. Freddie puts his arm around me and says, "Your big brother'll look after you" and he's looking at our father when he says it. He isn't looking at me. I'm not sure if this soft, warm feeling in my chest is fear or if it's relief. Everything is in strange overly-bright colours, like an old-fashioned cartoon strip. Kapow! Baaam!

Some of Claudia's friends are here for tea. Am I already

back in London? They're all sitting around in her bedroom looking at magazines. Claudia has her own room now. My bedroom is at the other end of the house. I don't like it there, I can't sleep, there are too many voices and hands and shadows and the fireplace is damp and it's cold. Mother's room is next to Claudia's, where it's warm and safe. Claudia sometimes takes things from Mother's dressing table to show her friends. She says she's just borrowing them, but I've heard our Mother talking to her about it and her voice has had that tight, red sound that means she's angry. She gets angry with Claudia but she doesn't notice me even though I am as good as good can be.

I'm sitting on the stairs in a stream of sunlight from the landing window. I'm listening to girls' chatter through the closed door of Claudia's room. There's new carpet on the stairs now, it's royal blue. I think how well the colour goes with the yellow of my dress. Aunt Margaret helped me make this dress. She took me to Liberty's on the Greenline bus so I could choose the fabric for myself. I had to guide her on and off the bus. Her white stick went tap, tap on the pavement.

I kneel down and drape the folds of my skirt over the blue. I like the way the colours go, it makes me think of a famous painting but I can't remember which. There is a shadow. I see my father's shiny boots on the step above me. I look up but he doesn't say my name in that funny sing-song way I think he's going to, that way that I know just what he means. It's because Freddie is standing at the bottom of the stairs, looking up at him and his eyes are so dark and so threatening they are almost black.

There's Claudia again. She's all dressed up to go dancing. Father says she looks like a prostitute with all that makeup on. Mother's walking down the front steps with her, smiling. I am watching from the library window and I'm kneeling on father's swivel chair. My knees are stuck to the hard green leather. There's often a man waiting for Claudia at the bottom of the steps. Mother shakes his hand and looks up at the house. Mother sometimes asks the young men who come to court Claudia to come in. She gives them drinks and they get a bit drunk and start to flirt with her. She and Claudia think it's very funny. I think it's cruel.

I jump. Father is behind me. He kisses the top of my head and reaches for my hand on the window sill. He prises my fingers from the wood, one by one. My knuckles are white. Sandalwood and cigars. I'm afraid, but I know if I'm quiet it'll all go away. I think I see Freddie's dark eyes looking back in the mirror over the mantel. Or perhaps they're mine and I am blind. Some of the buttons have come off my pretty yellow dress. Where are the buttons? I can't find them.

This is my life-drawing class, I go after school. I am tired trudging back up the hill to the bus stop but I don't want Father to drive me. I want to do this all for myself. I love the bus ride to Knightsbridge. I sit on the top deck and feel the sway of the bus as it rounds Hyde Park Corner. I imagine the bus leaning into the curve, grinning wickedly at the cars as it bears down on them, red and angry, nudging the cars' silver, shiny bumpers.

CLAUDIA

When we came back to London Mum was keen for me to go to St Paul's, but really and truly I wasn't that clever. Dad knew I wasn't academic enough. So I went to Oakwood until I left school a year later. It was quite a good school, girls only. It was just across the road from the boys' grammar and we shared the playing fields, so there was quite a bit of opportunity for flirting with the boys. The teachers were very strict though, so you had to be careful. And even though clothes were still rationed you were expected to have a proper uniform and to wear a hat - round felt in winter, straw boater in summer. It was a smart uniform, gold and navy and I loved it. I have a suspicion that dad kitted out most of the girls at school from stocks of things he'd picked up around and about. I think he quite enjoyed the wheeling and dealing; he always said he liked to keep his fingers in lots of pies. Even though he was a proper businessman, he wouldn't ever turn down opportunities if they came to him and everyone did it, you know, there wasn't really anything bad about it, he helped lots of people.

He'd built this really funny sort of summer house-cum-warehouse during the war, on half of the old vegetable gardens at Hunters Hill, to keep his stores in. It looked a bit like a chapel because he'd used some old stained glass windows that had survived the bombing of a church somewhere. It really tickled him, I think, using old church bits to build a store for what Christina and Freddie called his black market stuff. They were both quite spiteful about Dad at that stage. Christina had seemed to forget all of a sudden that not only had Dad put the fancy clothes on her back, but that he was the one paying for all her drawing lessons and private tuition.

Hunter's Lodge and its grounds had survived the war intact. At first we only used the few rooms Mother and Dad and Freddie had been living in for the war and most of the house remained shut up. It was quite luxurious though, after the little cottage at Flint Cross. It was a bit cold, so Christina and I slept in front of the fire in the library for some of that first winter. I know there was a particularly bad winter not long after the war, so I suppose it was then. It wasn't long, though, before Mother opened up the rest of the house and things started being done up. I remember Mother had some curtains made for the drawing room that properly fitted the tall windows. They were blue velvet and had braided sashes that held them back. Christina loved the blue velvet fabric and said she and Aunt Margaret could have made some fabulous evening gowns out of them. Really and truly, she was ever so silly at times.

Things I saw every day started to feel really sumptuous and rich. Dad was doing really well, his building firm was getting pretty successful, we had quite a bit more money. There was still rationing but I remember that instead of having to wear my school summer dresses on Sundays - or, worse, something Aunt Margaret had made out of mother's ancient trousseau - we started having new clothes and shoes. I started a collection of handbags, I remember! And there'd be lots of people coming and going in the house, all these handsome men in flying jackets and ladies in suits with nipped in waists and long flowing skirts that fell below the knee. It was called the New Look. I remember the girls I was at secretarial college with going on about the New Look and me dashing home to change out of my prim, horrid pleated skirt.

I was always the more stylish one. Mother always made sure I had the latest fashions to wear. I was quite a popular girl at the college. I had a lot of girlfriends and they were always coming home with me to tea or at the weekend. We'd sit in my room, looking at magazines and plucking our eyebrows and drawing them back in, higher up, with dark brown pencil filched from a padded box on my Mother's dressing table. We couldn't wait to grow up and be married, really and truly.

Oh, I left school when I was sixteen – I had got my School Certificate - and went to Pitman's Training College. Dad thought a good commercial training would be useful and he said I could work for him until I found some nice young man to marry. Quite a few of my classmates from school had come to Pitman's with me. I remember how exciting everything seemed to us, like everything was there for our amusement, like it was all one big party. The spirit of the times, in a way.

Christina went to the Girls' Grammar School. I don't think she was any brighter than me, it was just that she was more interested, she liked her school work. I suppose by that time, I was always too preoccupied with other things. I wasn't worrying about school work, I was worrying more about boys.

Christina wasn't like me, she didn't have many friends. Well, she had one or two who'd come with her if she came home to get something but more often she was *out* somewhere either with them or on her own. She liked to go to galleries. And museums. Perhaps that's why I never noticed her so much, she just wasn't around. And I suppose you'd say she was more the bookish type, really and truly; when she was at home she was always in her room at the other end of the house with her books. You know, it's a wonder that she ended up with all those fancy, important friends. To know her then you'd have thought she'd have ended up like Aunt Margaret, a batty, brittle old spinster. But then Dad paid for her to take some drawing classes, about the time I started working for him. Dad used to say that's when Christina came into her own, when she blossomed. It was certainly when she seemed at her happiest. Or as happy as Christina could be.

Really and truly, the classes Christina started doing

were more the finishing-school type drawing lessons than serious technical classes. Quite a few girls from the Grammar School - and from some quite well to do families - used to take them, along with deportment and that sort of nonsense. Then shortly before Joseph and I got married she started doing some sort of fashion and design course with this Frenchman who was quite senior at the Royal College of Art. He and his wife came round to the house once. They were both rather odd, a bit creepy, really and truly. His wife was much younger than him, very thin, she looked ill to be honest. There was some story about them living in Paris through the occupation. He'd been quite important, worked with some famous fashion designers in the 1930s. You'd not have thought it to look at either of them, her dressed like a child and he like some old boot-maker or something. Oh, you know, Pinocchio's father... Gepetto! Yes, that's it, that's who he used to remind me of.

I suppose it was still fairly go ahead then for a young girl to be learning about fashion. Modelling was becoming quite a fashionable, popular thing for girls to do before they got married but not so much being a fashion *artist*. I could have done that of course, before I married. Modelling. But I never dared. Dad wouldn't have approved of modelling. But he obviously approved of Christina and her fashion artist craze. All those classes and tutors and things must've cost him a pretty penny.

To be honest, I really don't know all the details of what Christina was up to then. It was all Dad's province really and Mother and I were always so busy - there were so many new things happening, and so many lovely handsome men home on leave from their National Service. I used to spend hours getting ready to go out. It became quite a game with Mother, deciding what outfit I should wear, how I should wear my hair. She was more like another girl friend really, my Mother. I used to wear rather a lot of makeup and it took a while to put on. Eyes were the thing. Really and truly, Christina had the eyes for that era. Audrey Hepburn's eyes, big almond-shaped conker-brown eyes. I have Mother's greeny-grey eyes. Green eyes aren't usually quite as striking. So I used lots of eye makeup. Like I said, Dad hated seeing me "dollied up", but Mother would tell him to stop being so square.

I loved to dance and I had lots of dancing partners. If any of them upset me, Mother would always remind me I was far too good for them and that I had broken a dozen hearts for every time someone crinkled mine. She was always encouraging me to have my friends round and she liked meeting the handsome young men. Everyone liked Mother, she was so young and fun. She always treated us like grown-ups, even offering us cocktails. I suppose that was really quite racy at the time too!

And then I met Joseph. He had just started a job at the BBC. We met through a group I used to go to see plays with. I hadn't really got to know him in the group, there was actually another chap who rather took my fancy but one day I bumped into Joseph outside Liberty's. It must've been my day off because I'd been working for Dad for quite a few years then and he was strict about time-keeping so I'd never have gone up town for lunch on a work day.

Joe. He was tall and dark and kind. And such a gentleman. Yes, the playwright. You've heard of him? I see. Well of course he wasn't well-known then. I stuck by him in those early days. Supported him. Or Dad supported both of us, really and truly.

We got married at St Luke's, the church next door to our old primary school. I had quite a conservative dress for me, with lace right up to the neck. Aunt Margaret and Christina made it up from a bought pattern and Christina did the final fittings. I remember it like it was yesterday, Christina sitting with all this cream satin around her, stitching on the buttons. I had orange blossom in my bouquet. It was a really hot August day. Dad gave Joseph and me a little detached house for a wedding present. It was a lovely little house, I was happy there. I was happy being a young wife. Happier still when I became pregnant.

I suppose Christina had boyfriends, though I don't remember her mentioning them. If I had asked her she'd have said she was far too busy pursuing what she liked to call her *fashion career*. That's how she liked to put it. She certainly did appear to be very busy. She even had a sort of artist's studio which she shared with Sophie Dexter, one of the girls she'd been at life-drawing classes with when she was still at school. Yes, she's Lady Lawson now of course. It was the top floor of her family home in Thurloe Square. Christina pretty much lived there most of the time, really and truly.

Yes, I would say that's where Christina started doing some of her funny paintings. *Peculiar* things – dark and gloomy. Little boats bobbing about in the sea with lots of dark, stormy clouds. She was still doing the fashion thing as well, but it was the paintings that created a bit of a rumpus in the end. The whole thing was peculiar, really and truly. Even that Sophie Dexter was rather an oddity. Still is, of course. Mother used to say it was all that inbred blue blood. It was funny because Sophie had actually gone to that same convent in Flint Cross - you know, where Christina went when she refused to come to school with me. Or whatever the reason was, I told you already I can't remember what that was all about. Sophie Dexter was a couple of years older than Christina of course. I think they knew *of* each other but they weren't friends then. Funny, those coincidences.

It was through *her*, Sophie Dexter – high and mighty Lady Lawson, whatever you want to call her - that Christina got to know all those 'arty' people. Fashion designers, artists, writers, people like that. And she even made some of them some outfits - just a few. They were the sort of people who were so posh they still had their clothes made for them when we were buying the new 'off the peg'. Aunt Margaret used to help her. Christina would make her own outfits too, for functions. I remember Dad taking her to a Rotary dinner in one of her creations; it was dark brown satin – the colour of coffee beans - with a tight bodice above an enormous skirt in layers and layers of taffeta and net. It had a little cape, matching brown velvet, with two satin roses that hid a clasp that did up at the neck. She'd actually copied that one, from a Hardy Amies design. I suppose it was quite clever really. There's no denying that Christina was a good seamstress. Joseph was always telling her she could make a name for herself in the fashion world.

She used to visit us from time to time, especially around the time Sarah was born. It was a surprise to find she liked the baby. Joseph was always very attentive when she came round - offering her drinks, inviting her to stay for something to eat. He was always telling her how talented she was. They'd sit for ages and chat about costume design and the history of fashion, although I'm sure he never had a clue what she was going on about half the time. Now I see things differently, it seems so obvious that Joseph would have wanted to be friends with her. He wanted to be part of the group of friends she had. I didn't know then that Joseph always got what he wanted. So really and truly, he was just like Christina.

Look, I'm not denying that Christina was good at what she did, she was. But she was good at the other side of it, too. She was very charming and she was very ambitious. Really and truly you would have to say she was rather calculating about some of the friendships she cultivated. I mean, being friendly with the right people, that sort of thing. She even got some of her fashion drawings published in some of the fashion magazines; in those days, there were specialist artists who drew sketches of the latest designs and ideas. Christina got the job through a friend of the Dexters who was a big magazine publisher. Not that that's all bad, of course, I don't suppose they would have used her drawings if they *weren't* good. But she did seem to have a talent, too, for making people do what she wanted them to – and, oh yes, she did love all the fuss and attention and of course it went to her head. Well, she'd never been short of Dad's and Freddie's attention growing up. So perhaps she thought it her due.

She had this exhibition of some of the drawings she'd done for the designers and a few of her peculiar paintings. People called Benson, friends of the Dexters, they owned an art gallery on Cork Street. The Benson husband and wife were famous for their involvement in lots of arty things. They used to have grand country house parties too. His picture was often in magazines, the huntin', shootin', fishin' type of magazines. Some of the things Joseph and I heard about the couple were probably a bit far-fetched but I don't suppose they were entirely innocent. Really and truly, Christina herself was far too calculating and manipulative to be entirely innocent herself, I'm quite sure of it.

When Dad died it was the Bensons who completely took over Christina's life. Looking back now, I can see that Jack Benson was probably a substitute, a substitute father. Anyway, it was Jack Benson who hired that expensive legal firm for her, the one who later cheated us out of most of Dad's estate.

Of course that was when Christina disappeared from our lives. What with all the bad feeling it wasn't surprising but it was *her* choice, I didn't do or say anything. She chose to cut herself off completely from all of us, using the lawyer as her contact over Dad's will and all the shenanigans over his estate. She didn't come to Dad's funeral, you know. I never forgave her for that. After all, family is family, she should have been there. It wouldn't have mattered what was going on between solicitors, she could have had the decency to be there.

Joseph found out from someone in those arty circles she moved in that she'd been living that whole spring and summer with the Bensons in their house in Sussex. It was near Arundel. I only found that out because my solicitor told me where it was. Even then, I had to pressure my solicitor to get the information. The whole situation was ridiculous. It was Christina, not me who turned it all into a ridiculous, hurtful drama. Just what my sister loved best. Just what she wanted to achieve, I've no doubt. You can't blame me for thinking that if that was the way she wanted to play it, then I'd give her as good as she gave me. Believe me, I had reason to be angry. And, besides, in the middle of the legal battle I got pregnant again. Sarah was only a tot and what with the business of Dad's estate - and my marriage falling apart at the seams - well, I had enough to be getting on with, without some dramatic nonsense from my younger sister.

And then I lost the baby. At five months. I really hated my sister then.

So there was no communication between us, not over the will, not what would happen to Mother once Hunters Lodge was sold, nothing. That was it. That's why we lost touch then. As far as I was concerned, for those three years, Christina ceased to exist.

Yes, we did know about her marriage, but only because Joseph saw a picture of her in a magazine. About a year after Dad had died, in *Country Life,* or one of those society-type magazines. I don't remember. I don't really care, really and truly. There was a picture of Christina with an older man, sitting at a dinner table. And underneath the caption said 'Sir Edward Hopwood and Miss Christina Mansfield, celebrating their engagement at a private dinner in Taormina, Sicily'. I remember the caption exactly. And I remember wondering what could possibly have made her want to marry such an *old* man. I mean, it couldn't have been his money, she had enough of her own. So it must have been his title. Christina always was a secret snob.

CHRISTINA

Here is Claudia. She's working for Father now. She thinks she's so important, but she's only a secretary. She likes to talk business with him. She says "we" this and "we" that. She wears suits to the office, with tight skirts that show her fat behind. Really she just wants to get married. That's all she and her friends hope for.

This is Monsieur Beaumont. He is my special art teacher. He teaches part-time at the Fashion School at the Royal College and he gives me and my new friend Sophie private lessons. These are his rooms behind the V&A, right around the corner from Sophie's parents' house. He always wears that same style of suit with wide revers and big trousers, like the fashions twenty years ago. He has a soft French accent and sometimes he gets his sentences confused. His voice is always full of tears. He has a cough.

On some evenings Monsieur Beaumont is too sick to be at the college. Sophie and I go to his home instead. It's a basement and it smells of mould. That's Helene, his wife, in that corner, sitting in a high-backed chair. She likes to sit with us. She's so thin, she looks like a ghost. She is always anxious. She fidgets and distracts Monsieur Beaumont with her fluttering. When she speaks to him she puts her hand up in front of her lips as if to hold her voice in check, as if the words might burst from her. The noise of footsteps from the street above frightens her. I know that fear. I know how it feels, waiting for someone to come and get you.

Sometimes Madame Beaumont babbles about grey mice. Monsieur tells me she means the Germans, in Paris, in the war. I don't know if that's true, but I feel her fear, cold and damp and rusty-tasting. Monsieur and Madame have a little boy called Louis. I hear him coughing in the next room. I see his face pressed against the glass of the window when I leave after my lesson. He is dying. But they know that too.

This is me in the garden at Hunter's Lodge. With Aunt Margaret. She's coaxed me out into the sunlight. She says the sun will bleach it all away, sunlight and lemon juice, she says, that's what you use to get rid of a dirty stain. She has brought me here because it's my special place, here behind the trees. When I sit here, sketching, I hear nothing but the sound of our breathing. This peace is precious because I'm finding it harder and harder to shut the voices out. When I am drawing or painting, that's when they can't come in. Everyone says how hard I work but they don't know the reason why I cannot allow myself to stop.

Claudia's wedding. I made her dress with Aunt
Margaret's help. It is cream satin and has tiny buttons down
the back. She's pregnant, but none of the others knows yet.
Not even Joseph and Claudia. I know only because I've
heard the sound of the baby's heart in my head right from
the start.

I'm in a pew with my mother. There's a sweet, sickly
smell of orange blossom and cheap scent as the bridesmaids
swish past. They look very hot in their full-skirted dresses.
I'm glad Claudia didn't ask me to be one. Joe's voice sounds
small and tight as he says his vows. He is so in love with my
sister but he's also just a little frightened.

Oh, look, that's Sophie again. Sophie Dexter. Pretty,
isn't she? We pass on the stairs at the RCA as we go to our
extra lessons, avoiding each other's eyes, as if we are
engaged in something very special and secret in M.
Beaumont's dusty rooms. Now a tentative smile, an
exchange of pleasantries. Sophie's hand on my arm, her
fingernails are painted pearly pink, and I think, how can
your hands be so clean? My fingernails always have pencil
lead or paint or wax under them. And then sometimes I
have dirt and skin and hair under my nails because I am
clinging so tightly to the surface of the world.

Here's Sophie and me at Fortnum's. She's half hidden
behind a mountain of sugar-powdery cakes, breathlessly
chattering between gulps of tea and forkfuls of pale
confectioner's custard. She tells me she has just come back
from America. I think she's so glamorous and brave. Her
blue eyes dance with laughter. I'm watching her, desperate

that her brightness will rub off on me. But I feel so shut in. I am grey, everything around me is grey, except for Sophie, my beloved friend. I can hear her laughing, softly and far off. I wish I was that fearless. Sophie, how often I wished that I were you. All my life. How I have loved you, worshipped you, all my life.

Where's this? Here is our studio in your parents' house. Darling Sophie, can you hear me? Sophie, are you there? Are you here? We work on the top floor. Look out of the window. You can just see the statue of the V&A above the trees. I can feel that the summer is here. There's a heavy scent of lilac from the gardens in the square. I've got one of your father's old shirts on. One of your maids has laundered it for me and it has that scorched, matt-white smell of starch and hot ironing. You are wearing men's overalls with a collarless wool shirt. You look like a character from a D H Lawrence novel. We are so *à la mode, risqué, n'est-ce pas?*

There is so much laughter in this room, it makes the walls curve. You are making a bust of Churchill. I tell you it reminds me of my father and you look at me. Do I tell? I want to scream but all I can hear is a roaring sound in my head, like my mind has fused and now you, my beloved Sophie, close to me and the sharp metallic smell of wet clay and the soft push of warm skin and the scent of sweet lilac coming in through the window.

Oh my goodness. What is this feeling? Rushing, rushing, it's all rushing ahead. This is a dinner at the Dexters'. Willard, Sophie's much older brother, is there. He's drinking too much, Sophie's mother keeps frowning at Sophie and subtly shaking her head, as if she should stop him. I try to distract him. He's makes me smile. Mr Dexter tells Sophie to take Willard outside for some air. We hear them arguing as they walk through the drawing room. I'm shy now because the rest of the table is made up of people my parents' age and I'm unsure of myself.

The man opposite me sees my awkwardness. He strikes up a conversation. He's very nice. His name is Jack Benson and he tells me he publishes a magazine. He says his wife has a gallery on Cork Street. What's this? I can feel myself falling, tumbling. I am laughing. This is laughter.

I am reading a letter from Freddie, I'm standing waiting for the bus, outside the V&A. He's in Paris, working for an airline. He says he won't be coming home for Christmas this year because of work. He signs off saying '*Look after yourself, Chrissie'* and I know what he means. I don't give Father the chance to be alone with me.

This is Claudia's house. I come here quite often because I don't want to go home. Claudia is softer at the edges now, I don't see her sharpness so much. Motherhood really does seem to suit her. She even laughs when we talk about all the makeup she used to wear. She's getting very fat and she wears coral coloured lipstick now, just on her lips instead of drawing them in bigger, with garish vermilion. Her voice is softer, as if the words are coral coloured; they ease out of her gently, instead of roaring in a red and angry splash as they always did when she was a girl.

A child. This is Sarah. She is a year old and she laughs a lot. Joe and I play with her while Claudia takes a rest upstairs. When Sarah's been put down for the night and is properly asleep, the three of us have dinner, and afterwards I tell them about doing some drawings for the fashion pages of *Harper's*. I have been invited to sit in with the designers in their studios to do this. Joe is so sweet. He is so very happy for me. We talk late into the night. Claudia has long since fallen asleep on the sofa, curled up like a big fat purring cat.

I think I loved my sister then.

This is the gallery in Cork Street. It's a private view of some of my fashion sketches and some of my new paintings. People say the paintings are very avant-garde. They say I have 'a diverse talent'. Really they don't like my paintings. Really I'm just confused and angry when I make them. Some of them are about my fear. Sometimes I can put the voices in my head down on the canvas. Sophie helps me.

Look. Yes, that's me. I know, I look so grown up. I'm wearing Aunt Margaret's mink coat. It almost touches the floor. I feel very sophisticated in it. Mother and I argued over who would wear it. I need the heavy coat because underneath I'm wearing a sleeveless silk dress. It's dark green and the bodice is fitted to my waist. It has a bell-shaped skirt and the net under it catches on my stockings. I feel a heaviness about my throat because I'm wearing Daphne Benson's emerald necklace, huge stones mounted in thick gold.

Daphne and Jack are there, by the door, waiting for me. They shake hands with my father, all smiling and talking. Even my mother is here, glamorous in black velvet, her red hair in a tight chignon, secured by a pearl-tipped pin. All these people, all these yards of silk and satin and velvet and row upon row of pearls and paste, all those high foreheads and high-minded people, here for me. But there is silence. No voices. Nothing. I see their lips move but I cannot hear. Why are there no voices here? I'm trying to hear. Wait! Someone is talking somewhere. Only they are whispering very, very quietly. Hello? Who are you?

This is Father and me returning late from his Rotary dinner. Why wouldn't Mother go with him? I begged her to go, I even made her this dress, Aunt Margaret helped me make the silk roses for the clasp of the cape. I can see my father's hands tight around my wrists. But I feel nothing, I feel nothing. That voice, that whisper, it has told me how I can step out of this, taught me how to step outside the me of me. I listen to the whisper and I am not here and nothing can touch me and there is nothing but the whisper keeping me company.

Voices. Oh, my, I can hear this one now, quite clearly. Jack. His voice is always so distinct. He's telling me he loves me more than life itself and I tell him I think that sounds silly. He says that he'll do anything. I'm in Jack and Daphne Benson's London house but it is just Jack here. I feel so sick, waves of nausea sliding up my throat. I'm standing at the huge windows of the master bedroom that overlooks Green Park. I have a sheet wrapped tightly round me. It's white linen, starched to be smooth as paper and it's got butterflies embroidered on the edges. Jack is behind me, his arms around my waist. He's trembling slightly as he speaks. He smells of sandalwood and old cigars. He smells like my father. Oh, god, oh god, oh god.

Daphne? She's so very tall and thin, so glamorous. I'm learning to be glamorous from Daphne. The papers say she looks like Princess Margaret and she's almost as scandalous. She's standing directly in front of me, telling me something. I'm looking deep into her eyes. Her shiny red lips move and I know what she's saying even though I don't hear the words. I can see them stretching across the ether. Daphne is holding me to her. I can smell her face powder. Chanel No.5. I don't know if this is laughing or crying. I'm telling her a secret but at first she doesn't understand. There's a feeling of something soaking away. I feel faint.

Daphne is kissing the top of my head. I can't hear it but I can feel my voice in my throat and now Daphne kisses my lips, as if to silence me, as if to stop me speaking. I'm looking up at her and she's telling me that I don't have to be afraid anymore, he can't hurt me anymore. Her eyes are pools of clear, still, blue light and all around me I see the tangled steel of a car and punctured flesh and the smell of scorched hair. And the gut-splitting sound of metal ripping and oh my god, oh my god, the sound of a man. I don't want to see this, please, please. I can hear a man screaming. It is my father. He is in pain and he is dying and I don't know whether I am laughing or crying or screaming.

CHRISTOPHER

Christina Mansfield was the torment of my adolescence. She had that incredible sex appeal that people attribute to great cinematic heroines. Though, darling, she was more Audrey Hepburn than Monroe. That gentle, quiet vulnerability. She had the Hepburn eyes, almond shaped, chestnut-brown, flecked with gold. Stunning. And this long, sleek auburn hair against very pale skin. Incredible bone structure, dear. Don't I sound so superficial, just describing her in pictures. That's the trouble with spending a lifetime watching film, people flickering on a screen; you assimilate information on the basis of a million tiny dots of light. They're not real. But then I sometimes wonder if we aren't all characters in some huge projection, wandering on and off the screen with this audience of higher beings rolling in the aisles, laughing ....

Chrissie was a friend of my wonderfully scandalous,

hedonistic parents. Actually, she hated being called that, Chrissie. And, my dear, she was actually - if I am to be frank with you - she was more than just a friend of theirs. Remember darling, in those days, nobody ever mentioned that kind of thing. Never. Oh, it went on, of course it did. But no one was as overt about their sexuality as they are now, homo or hetero. Poor darlings, Mummy and Pater were still living in the shadow of all that turgid Victorian reticence. Such hypocrites, bodice-bound ladies and lovely stiff chaps. I'm awful aren't I? But seriously, darling, this was the late 1950s; most people were more interested in home appliances and celebrating the end of rationing than in any sexual practice - or *mal*practice. Am I being too frank? One doesn't like to embarrass, darling.

So, there we are and where are we? Christina was a close chum to the Parents but she was also one of the Mater's projects, her protégées. Mummy-darling owned a gallery on Cork Street at that time. A bit of fun for her and a potential investment for the pater. Didn't matter though, the investment malarkey. Mummy was actually rather rich, richer than the Pater. And she liked to be a bit of a patron of the arts, darling. She got the idea of bringing on young artists. She was very generous, helped lots of up and coming young people, including Chrissie. Artists, designers, architects, right across the board. Her intentions were good, genuine enough. But I don't think I'd be being entirely honest were I to tell you she had the gallery purely for aesthetic gratification. Oh, there was a bit of vanity there, darling. Mummy wanted to be *seen* to patronise the arts.

And she did love her glamorous parties, so having this Cork Street gallery, well, she was able to combine both things, do you see? Does that sound a bit bitchy about Mummy? Hmmn? It's not meant to. It's honestly just the way it was. I think it's all rather wonderful, actually. I just love it darling that I had such larger-than-life folks and that they had this rather *naughty* reputation. I mean, really darling, right up my street!

Oh, Pater met Christina through the Dexters. The families all knew each other, mixed in all the same circles, it was – well, still is - all very close-knit. Sophie Dexter – beautiful girl, darling but ...well ... she was always a bit of a – now what's that hilarious expression? Oh, yes! A bit of a 'chunky monkey'. Love it, darling. Anyway, feet firmly on the ground, that one. Bit butch if the truth be told. Still is, but don't say I said it. She's Lady Lawson now. Hilarious. She's just like something out of P G Wodehouse, darling, an utter delight! All tweeds and Country Life and Labradors. Just divine. Wears brogues and strides about the estate. Oh, dear, I mustn't laugh. She's lovely, darling. The *most* wonderful anachronism. Big voice but a big heart, though. Protects her own. You know what's so extra wonderful? She just doesn't give a fat rat's arse what anyone thinks. How liberating is that? Darling, if more of us lived like that, the world would be much less of a divine comedy, don't you think?

Sorry, off on one again, what *am* I like? Right. Now. Let's see. Sophie Dexter shared a tutor with Christina Mansfield. When they were doing the fashionistas thing at the RCA. Funny little Frenchman. What *was* his name? He took some classes for the fashion department there. He'd apparently worked with the top designers in Paris in the thirties. There was a rumour that during the Occupation, he and some of the other designers made deals with the Nazis. Now the Nazis were *seriously* vain, weren't they, so there was a ring of truth about it. But this chappie, he wasn't the only one who did it. We all know that particular household name who was definitely up to no good. And I bet there were a few more of them who weren't above a little exploitation of the Nazi vanity, the Nazi wealth. Wasn't old whatsisname a spy? Delicious. Anyway, can't say this little old fellow exactly looked the type. Hang on, maybe he did something in the Resistance. I'm sure Mummy once told me something about it. Or maybe it was Christina herself. I don't think Christina would have made it up. She was one of those people you had this impulse to bare your all to. Some people just have that effect, I think, you long to tell them your deepest, darkest secrets. What is it about a personality, hmm? Perhaps you just recognise a bit of yourself in them, a bit of your own fragility. Listen to *me*, who am I to say, eh?

Oh, I remember! He had a wife this tutor fellow. That's right. She was a young couture model before the war. They came to London as soon as the war was over. With just the clothes on their backs, I dare say. Goodness, of course! They came down here! Yes, yes. Here, to Deal. Oh, my dear, it's all coming back to me.... she looked awfully young, like a schoolgirl – the wife, I mean. Not quite right. Talked to herself. She was very beautiful though. They had a child. He died. Terribly sad. Goodness, fancy remembering that.

Anyway, Christina and old Sophs met through this little Frenchman and then they became great chums. Inseparable for a while, hardly ever apart. They made a sort of studio at the top of the Dexter's London house. They still own it, it's one of those big old Edwardian houses in South Ken. Of course, some folk thought it very odd behaviour for young women. I know girls nowadays do it all the time but in the fifties, well, frankly it was a bit odd, you know. Different. Different days, darling. For a woman to say she was an artist. And then to actually have a studio and all that malarkey. I remember my male chums thinking it was a terrible shame those two beauties hiding themselves away like that. And of course there was talk. About the two girls. Oh, you know how people talk. Darling, I am *the* worst to ask about that sort of thing!

So anyway, the Pater. Well, he and Christina met at one of the Dexters' awfully grand soirees. Or was it a dinner? Anyway. It was at something at the Dexters'. The old Pater got in touch with some of his chums and she did some sketches for a group of designers. And they got published in … oh, *Vogue* or something. *Harper's*. I don't know... Pater had financial interests in a few magazines of that type at the time. These designers, you see, they were all in the news. They dubbed them 'the top twelve' and they were the crème de la crème of the fashion world. So then Mummy-darling said she'd give Christina a little show at the gallery, of the original fashion sketches and also of some paintings she was doing then. The funny paintings caused a bit of a stir. They *were* strange. Lots of black horizons and little grey figures with red shadows coming out of the darkness. Dark, sinister seascapes with little, teeny, weeny boats bobbing in the distance. Very peculiar at the time. Nowadays they'd be quite the thing, I'm sure. But it was all rather alarming then. You will guess that my naughty parents just loved inviting such a fuss. It was a chance to show off. By that stage I shouldn't have thought anyone was surprised at anything my parents did, but there we are. Anyway, the upshot for Christina was that she started to move in all those arty circles of the time. We'd call them bright young things now. There were painters and poets and academics. People at the Beeb. Of course there wasn't the celebrity malarkey there is these days - heavens, no - but Chrissie had her photo and a little profile in *Vogue*. And bits and pieces about her and her crowd in some of those Society pages. You know the type of thing. I think she was even in a picture in *Horse & Hound* with darling Sophie! Hilarious!

Listen, here I am telling you all about the dear girl as if it's gospel but I didn't meet the poor darling myself until well after the show in Cork Street. Not until she came to live here. A bit later on, some months after the show and all that. Dear Pater, he made her a studio out of the old granary. We can show you later, it's a super-duper little place. Perhaps you'd like to take old Paterpoo for his little afternoon perambulation through the gardens? If you go down to the right, past the veggie plot, you will find the granary. Actually, darling you might take a look at it for me.

Would you mind? I've got a chap coming to see it next week, interested in using it. He's a puppeteer or something like that. No, perhaps he just makes them. Puppets. Oh, I don't know. They've been renting in Hastings but it's all being sold. Dear Pater and I, we still like to flirt a bit with the arts. And don't tell – shhhh - but if he's pretty perhaps I'll let him have it for free. If I can get away with it under the accountant's big nose. Pater won't mind. He's a poppet.

Pater? He's quite remarkable for his age, the old fellow. He had a stroke last summer, I'm afraid, so he's a bit slow. I have someone come in to help him every day now. I just can't do the nursey stuff, darling. God, I'm not the type for all that bum-wiping malarkey, not likely! Oh, I love the dear old chap but really, I'm not doing that. Ugh.

Where was I, darling? Oh, yes! But the thing is, by the time I *did* meet Christina, the sweet thing, she'd been a bit the talk of the dinner table for quite another reason. Oh, her family had this little building business. Good, solid little firm. Anyway. Her father had been killed in a car accident and it transpired he had left Christina everything. It's a dear story, y'know. Chrissie's old man had started out as a bricklayer and – as the saying goes – he'd made good. Of course, we all thought how Christina, this arty little thing, this *vision* came to be born of a bricklayer! Any road up, his building firm was by then quite a thriving concern. Now we're not talking McAlpine, darling. Not that sort of thing but Christina's pater had apparently done lots of work after the war, rebuilding houses, building new. If you go to bits of south London you can find the houses he built, a few streets of them. Oh, there was a bit of gossip going about - that there'd been some very *unsavoury* business practice, something a bit underhand. That he was a bit of a drinker and that was how he ended up crashing his car. That he was really a bit of a rogue. Oh, that makes me giggle, sorry. 'Rogue', it's such a lovely, warm word. We don't have 'rogues' these days, do we? The world doesn't have a place for the term. Nor for 'rogues' really. Sad. We might all be that bit more liberal but we're so hard on each other. Cripes, darling, hark at *me*! Sorry and all that.

Anyway, it did the rounds. The gossip, how Mansfield was a bit of a thug, bit of a Mafioso. Frightful rumpus. There was even talk that the car accident he died in wasn't so much an accident. That is was all based on rather filthy lucre, darling, his whole little empire. Empirette. Like I say, not big business. Anyway, it was an easier time to cover things up, hide things. There was gossip but the unsavoury detail, well, any detail, just got brushed under the carpet. It just took a word or two from someone and that was the end of the story and nothing more was said or heard. And darling, there were bigger stories on the horizon than the silly old Mansfields, remember – oh, the Suez Crisis, all that shenanigans but there was Marilyn Munroe and Grace Kelly, this was movie star time too don't forget! I don't think even Mummy and Pater could have trumped those two, goodness, no. Though they had a jolly good go!

Anyway. Turned out Chrissie's Pater had left it all - the business, the property he owned, even the family home – he'd left it all to Christina. I don't know quite how much it was all worth I'm afraid, darling. I don't think there was all *that* much to inherit. But there was a sister – I think there might even have been a brother, but he wasn't part of it – and this sister wasn't at all happy about it. But you know what they say, darling, don't you. The love of money and all that. All that glisters. But it's also true that money makes the world go round. Ha, ha, ha. Sorry. 'And it pays for hookers and drugs!', ha ha ha! Oh, dear, sorry, read that in a loo in LA, darling..... ha ha ha!

But Christina, you want to know about her, sorry darling, getting carried away. What was she like? Well. The day I first met her .... well, I was home from school for a weekend, an exeat. Love the Latin names, all that public school tradition, it still goes on. Frightful, those poor darling boys. So there I was, languishing in that ghastly adolescent sexual torpor a boy has to go through. God, darling, yes, I was yet another etiolated public school boy, emotionally foetal, sexually explosive and totally powerless. My *dear,* why does no one prepare you for that adolescent agony, all that throbbing, sticky confusion? Well, imagine when the Mater arrives with this *vision*, this pale, willowy thing who wafts up to me and my friends in the garden, in a wave of mother's Chanel No.5 and then kisses me, right on the lips. *proper* kiss, darling, not your peck on the cheek. Heaven help me, I was sixteen and I thought something would break! And not just my heart, darling, not just my heart. Dear heaven. I was in turmoil. Not all of it delightful either, darling. You see, I think I knew chaps were more my cup of tea - you know - even then, but lovely Christina would pop up in my dreams every so often to torment me. All my chums adored her of course. I had lots of chums visiting on weekends at the beginning of that summer and I don't think they came to visit me – much to my own disappointment - it was to see *her*.

So it was just as well Paterpops despatched me to France for the summer hols because I think I'd have gone insane - or done something simply *unforgivable* - if I'd had to stay in such close proximity to this creature, to this real-life walking, talking fantasy. Of course, he'd guessed at my lovely crush on Christina so it was more than my needing to brush up on the old froggy French. Dear heaven, I was so full of myself at the time you know, we had a frightful row about it, Pater and I. I told him he was just jealous of me and all my friends, of our youth, our energy. That's why he was sending me off. I think we both said some horrid things. No, I *know* we said some horrid things. That's why I haven't forgotten. Maybe that's why we're here, Pater and I, keeping each other company.

Anyway, darling, by the time I got back to Blighty for the autumn term our Christina had gone off to Italy with a chum of Paters, Edward Hopwood. I didn't put two and two together because he was older than her, old Hopwood, oh, by a good thirty-odd years. And then the next thing I knew, one Saturday I was having an idle flip through *Country Life* and there she was, staring up at me. She had got herself engaged to Edward Hopwood. That was it. My scrumptious threesome fantasies dashed in an instant. Did I say threesome? Well. I'm not going to pretend. Like they say 'it's bleedin' obvious innit?' But imagine, my nonchalant flip through a magazine and my dear heart burnt with such sulphurous self-pity – jealousy, self-pity, rage, the whole kit and caboodle – darling, I'm surprised I didn't spontaneously combust! To add insult to the injury, when I finally asked the Pater about it, he told me he'd made the introductions himself. He thought they would be suited. Very romantic, I'm sure. I was furious. Quite unreasonably, of course, but at that age, in matters of the heart – well, matters governed by testosterone - one is so irrational.

I remember travelling up to London to meet the Pater, in the most dreadful rage. The jolly old train got held up in Colchester - a mercy as it turned out and the only occasion when the inadequacies of public transport were in my favour. Pater simply credited my temper to the journey. It would have been too bad to have blurted out such passions. Ah, passion. What was so terrible to me, you see, was the difference in age. I couldn't bear to imagine it. The two of 'em. You know, rolling about in the throes of sexual ecstasy. When you're a hot-blooded eighteen-year-old the idea of *anyone* over forty having sex is the stuff of nightmares. Cradle-snatching. That's what we used to call it. What a horrid expression. Better, I suppose, than calling someone a frightful old perv though, don't you think?

It wasn't surprising the newly-weds went to live abroad. Went to live in the West Indies. Quite mad. But Hopwood's father had been one of those lovely crusty-brown colonials Mr Waugh had such fun with. Had he been Viceroy, or something? Don't remember. Lots of money and lots of influence. Old Hopwood senior had owned several newspapers, up north I think, Leeds or Liverpool or somewhere. *Edward* Hopwood had been a war correspondent at the end of the Great War, at the ripe old age of 18. That's how he knew my father, they met in the war. Went through both wars together, as a matter of fact. There was a story that Hopwood junior saved my father's life in the second one. They came down in a fighter plane, crashed dear, somewhere in Sussex, by the coast. Gunner was killed and hero Hopwood pulled my Father from the wreckage. Imagine, the Pater pulled from a burning plane. There *is* a memorial to an airman on a bit of heathland, somewhere down in East Sussex. In fact, it's not far from Heron's Gate, the Hopwood family pile. Paterpops once told me it was to commemorate that very crash. I'm not sure I believed him even then and I'm quite sure now it was only one of his own little fancies. You can ask him, if you like. He probably won't know what you're talking about, but you can try. I don't suppose we'll ever get to the bottom of that one now. Or to the bottom of my father's relationship with the handsome Edward Hopwood. Well, what do you *think* they were? Bosom buddies, darling, just doesn't cut it. Ooh, I am *so* naughty.

Anyway, Christina. Yes. So Hopwood had been left some land out in Never-Never Land and after Hopwood married his child bride, they went out to Trinidad. I think we were led to believe it was to manage the family properties but I doubt there was much to the rumour, or if there was, not much to the task itself, beyond sipping rum with a few well-chosen, well-heeled folk.

Yes, I could just see them doing that. Hopwood by all accounts was a bit of an eccentric. Did you know he spent thousands refurbishing the old racecourse in Port-of-Spain, built a whole training yard and everything? Since the only horses on the island were steady old nags used for police work, Hopwood had twenty thoroughbreds flown in from the States so he could have race meetings for his friends. Canny old fruit, it wasn't just the entertainment value he was planning on. No doubt money had a lot to do with it, the disposing of it, yes, but the making of it, too. In lovely large piles. But there have always been hints that the horse thing practically wiped them out. The way I heard they lived it wouldn't have surprised me if they'd got through quite a few noughts' worth of the family inheritance. But it's rather distasteful, really, isn't it, to talk about that sort of thing. Here we go again. Filthy lucre. Ha-ha! I remember now. "Teachinge thinges which they ought not, because of filthy lucre." Oooh, get *me*! Public school boy memory, don't you know!

Nope. No. Not for a minute do I imagine Hopwood loved our poor, sweet Chrissiekins when he married her. The conventions of those sort of marriages rarely inclined to love on the chap's part. But I can tell you without a shadow of a doubt, my darling, that he grew to love her, in his own, quiet way. They were positively doting later in life, quite the lovey-dovey couple.

Well. But, look. Here's the thing, darling. The sad thing about it all, if you must know, is that no one ever loved Christina Mansfield like my old Pater did. Still does. There, I've said it. But what could he have done about it? He could never have left the Mater, it would have cost him too much, financially and socially. And, darling, it just wasn't *done*, not by our sort of people, not in those days. Oh, *of course* they had an affair, Pater and Chrissie. Now that *was* done, no one batted an eyelid. And of course the Mater loved her too and there was all that malarkey, so nobody got hurt and nobody made a fuss, darling, didn't matter one jot.

So I think it went like this: the Pater did a generous, honourable, ridiculous thing - he gave the woman he loved to the man who had saved his life. You see, perhaps there was a deal between them, some sort of pact, perhaps they struck some sort of bargain, does it matter, darling? For all Pater's sweet, darling heart why would I ask? After all these years – I'm not going to pry. There are too many bones in too many closets to go ferretting about in. This house fairly rattles with them. But there you are. Now you know about as much as I do.

C'mon. Let's go and get the Pater up and about. He'll just love meeting you, darling, what a treat for the old chap! Haven't you got lovely hair? Hope you don't mind my saying. Do you come from a family of redheads or was it just a rogue gene? There's that old rogue again, haha! C'mon, let's go and get our old rogue up. I told you he's not been the same since the stroke, didn't I? It's why we came back to Blighty, darling. Much better care – much cheaper! – than we had for him in LA. Here we go, darling, this way.

CHRISTINA

That's Jack's son. His name is Christopher. He's handsome like his father. He's talking to some school friends he's brought down for the weekend, but he knows I'm watching them. We're in the garden of the house at Nore Hill. Christopher is trying to make me join them in the rose garden. He's beckoning me. He's got such a beautiful smile. I'm smiling too but I don't really mean it. My jaw aches from the pretence. I shake my head. No. I'm walking away now but I'm wishing I'd had the chance to speak to him, alone, there's something I've been wanting to tell him before he goes to France. I want to tell him I am carrying his father's child. I want to tell him because he's kind and sweet and I know he's a lost soul and I think that one day it might help him feel a little less lost in the world. I kissed him full on the lips, right in front of his friends. I shouldn't have done that. I just wanted to give him something.

Ah, my lovely studio, the old granary. It's cool here. There I am, in that smock, standing at the easel. I'm feeling sick, my legs ache from standing. I'm six months pregnant and it's unusually hot. Perspiration runs down my back. Jack's coming, making his way down through the orchard. He smiles and raises a hand to wave. He's got his briefcase with him, it's sleek black leather with heavy gold catches. In it are papers for me to sign and a bottle of Krug. We call it our medicine. He hands me a single, scarlet rose. I hear a gentle 'woof!' as the champagne cork pops.

Oh, God the pain. I'm in pain. It hurts so much I want to scream but I can't get enough breath in my lungs. Am I back in the cottage in Flint Cross? No, I can see people walking in Green Park, people stretched on the grass in hired deck chairs. A shilling an hour. And butterflies in the park, butterflies on the linen. Emmy Reed is here, my Emmy is here, I can hear her talking to Jack. Butterflies on Emmy's apron. My arms are above me, reaching for the cold brass of the bedhead and my hands drip with sweat and Emmy's wiping my forehead with a cool cloth. She's smiling down at me, her huge bust with her butterfly apron taut across it. I can smell rosewater and blood. Pictures fading in pain and tears. I can feel Jack's hand, his fingers locked in mine, one solid grasp, like our hands are moulded from one piece. And a moment when I feel the weight of the child on my chest and see my eyes in hers. She has my red hair.

Shhhhh. Baby, baby, baby. They are letting me keep you
for the night. I had to plead with Jack. You're there, see? In
that cot beside the bed. I need you close so I can memorise
the sound of your breathing, the sound of your cry; so I can
draw in my mind the shape of you, so I can soak in the
colour of your eyes and the way you blink. So I can make a
memory of you, before they take you away. I believe that if
I wish it enough, I will be able to leave a gentle imprint on
your mind, as soft as a kiss blown from a palm. I am sitting
here and you are there in the cot that Daphne has lent me.
I pick up another button from a pile in my lap. I am sewing
them onto an old envelope. They are antique buttons, some
are fine, smooth ivory. Some are brass, from military
uniforms. Helene Beaumont gave them to me. She said, sew
on a button for every wish for your child. I snip the thread
with a pair of tiny gold scissors. I pick up another button.
There are so many things I want to give you.

When I fall asleep I dream I'm walking on a beach and
I'm holding a child's hand and we're laughing at the feeling
of the sand between our toes. I can feel the laughter in my
chest but there are no sounds. Just silence.

All these people, moving all around me, Jack and Daphne
and Emmy, smiling tight, anxious smiles but they are just
faces, silent and without bodies, coming in and out, in and
out. And all the time, there are other people in the shadows,
black and white and grey people I don't know. There are
people here I know I don't want to meet and they are reaching
out their arms for me. For you. Baby, baby, baby.

Jasmine! I can smell jasmine, my favourite scent. It is seeping into my pores, filling my mind with its smoothness. See below me, a landscape so beautiful I think that if I blink, it may disappear. It's so still here, where I'm standing but I can see there is a breeze in the valley. It leaves misty brushstrokes on the trees. I look down at my feet, bare on the cool tiles, white and black in the centre, like a chessboard. I'm in the hall of the Dexter's Italian home. Tuscany. So beautiful. I see myself as if I'm in an oil painting. Everything is rich and warm. I feel safe here. Things are real again, things have their insides back. It is early autumn, the air has that pulling, faded ochre touch. The afternoon sun is still strong enough to warm my face. It's so still. I am spying on them. Two male backs on the terrace. This is a fine vantage point. It's Jack and another man I haven't seen before. He's an old friend of Jack's, oh, he's very handsome. Very tall. I hope he's staying for dinner. I'm trying to hear what they're saying but the faint breeze carries their voices away across the vines. I have this sense that something is shifting; land, earth, tectonic plates. My world, my life is shifting. And now I am being lifted up on other people's breath. Lifted up and taken away from me. From you. From here.

Breathing. Trying not to as I creep down this corridor. Into this room, here, where the light comes under the door, white on the cold marble tiles. He sits up in the bed, a pillow at his back against the heavy carved wood. He smokes a cigarette, holding it oddly in a damaged hand. There is a bottle of red wine on the dresser, two glasses, one half full. The liquid looks black in this half-light, and thick, like molasses. I hope he won't ask me to drink it. It would turn to tar in my throat. I'm standing by the bed and now he reaches for my wrist. I can feel my knees shake. He smiles. He says I mustn't be afraid. But he is trembling too. I can hear his heart, a deep resonant beat beneath the hiss of his hand through my hair. There's the faint sour smell of the wine on his breath and now the peppery scent of Wrights' coal tar soap. Familiar and frightening and yet somehow safe. His hand is brushing my back. There is a thick ridge on the palm and he shows me, a deep welt of a scar, his four fingers twisted into a claw. He tells me how it happened. He tells me he rescued Jack. Like he's telling me a fairy tale. His voice has that distinctive rise and fall, an adult voice explaining something to a child. And now something else is said, something that makes his heart beat very fast. But I'm no longer listening to the words, just their soothing cadence. I like this man. He tells me he will cherish me for all the days of my life. He will look after me. Jack has sent him to rescue me.

It's time. Time to believe. Edward, it took years but I finally learned to believe in breathing because of you and now if I take another in-breath I will die.

Rome. The heat of the evening gives the sounds of the traffic a curve so they are muffled like when it snows. We are sitting on the Spanish Steps. Edward has arranged for some champagne to be brought out here. There are some men with guitars and they sing sentimental ballads. One of them is singing "*Que sera, sera*". The stilted English makes us laugh. Edward and I drink a toast. *Que sera, sera* darling. Our glasses ting-ting as they touch.

This is the Trevi Fountain, see the winged horses strutting in the water. They are alive, I am sure they are alive. Their muscles ripple, I can feel their hot breath. I am holding onto their manes, galloping wildly. Is this happiness, is this what it is? Galloping firestone horses over a thousand acres of memory. Their flaming hooves will cauterize the pain.

My feet are in soft pumps. They are made from such soft leather, like chamois, and tight so they can't slip off my thin heels. Where is this room? Sophie is next to me, there's a strange texture to the light around us. It's our studio, now a makeshift dressing room. I can feel the slip of the bare boards beneath my feet. My gown is made of silk with a long train behind, very traditional. Sophie is doing all the buttons up for me. She says it would have been easier if I were wearing gingham. This is what Brigitte Bardot has just got married in. She is trying to make me laugh. Sophie knows that I have made a plan, struck a deal, to protect myself.

I never thought I'd be so nervous. How much I need Jack to tell me that this really is all right. This was his idea, I know it was. How much I need to feel the pressure of his hand around mine. But there are just minutes before the ceremony, before I marry Sir Edward Hopwood. There is a silence in this space, as if the world is coming to a stop. I feel I am suspended. I am afraid. I want to cry but I can't, even in this safe place where the late summer breeze carries the lilac to me again. I feel as if my heart shall burst here. Jack is coming now, I know his footfall on the stairs. It's a long climb. Now his face close to mine, his hand on my cheek is cold. And his voice, I can always hear Jack's voice above the clamour of the light and the lilac saying *I've come to give my pretty girl away.* My lungs are full of tears. My heart will surely stop beating now. This is dying, isn't it? Is this dying? Am I dying?

PLUMS

They walk down the brick path through ancient rose beds, the old man and the young woman with dark ginger hair and conker-brown eyes that seem strangely familiar to him. The sweet, heavy crush of all these roses seems to cling to her face, kissing her cheeks with their velvet scent. She has never smelt roses like this. Jack Benson walks haltingly in front of her, leaning heavily on a cane. Eleanor can see moisture on the back of his neck where his crumpled panama meets the faint, white hairline. She has this impulse to touch him, as if she might reach something of her own reality through the texture of his pale skin. This man who is her father by blood and who loved her birth mother but gave her away to another man. Just as Christina Mansfield had given *her* away. So what is love if it can do this, how can she ever again believe in love?

Peter is the man I have always believed I loved. But now I am so full of hate for him, hate and despair. Because last night I was a fool. I went to see him. I set myself up. I deserved it. He opened the door, smiling. The familiar smell of wood smoke from the huge black stove and the knots in the panelled walls and the squeak of the wheels of the huge leather chair where he always makes me sit. Oh, God, I have always been his fool. I saw the fridge full of weekend food in neat delicatessen parcels, overripe brie on the breadboard, creamy white on the stained wood slab. A gold box of Belgian chocolates. The bottle of thick red wine on the floor by his chair. I couldn't tell him then.

And later, in the shower, the plastic curtain with a map of the world on it in vibrant pink and green. How could I have been such a fool, such a deluded fool. I'm not some teenager, not even some young, naïve woman. Though of course I had been at the very beginning. Behind the door are notches with names beside them in felt-tip pen. They are the heights of all the women Peter has slept with. Every time I've seen them I have forced this stupid smile, pretending it didn't matter, pretending it was funny and I was so, so chilled about it. I can't believe I have lived like this. I can't believe I have been so deluded. How could I tell him then?

And then being together in the tiny bed, tucked up under the eaves of that ancient, crumbling house he never renovated, as if we were curled into the crook of a huge, comforting arm, listening to the trains in the valley, rumbling like distant herds. And his touch and the press of his mouth on mine. But it was all different. His breath tasted of cigarettes and wine. How hadn't I seen it all? How could I have been so stupid? Surely that's not love?

I still haven't got rid of the taste of his lips. I couldn't get rid of it all the way along the ribbon of road home, up the lane, bumping over the level crossing, weaving through country roads, and when I had to stop to throw up, in the cruel ammonia light of the motorway cafe, with the clatter of cutlery and the cries of fractious, over-tired children, still I couldn't get rid of him. The bastard. And I really believed I had loved him! Even the sounds of those words in my head make me feel such shame. Fool, fool, fool!

Eleanor walks faster, stepping herself out of her reverie, and hears the old man's breath catching in waterlogged pockets, bubbling in small gasps. The path is uneven and he stumbles. She jumps forward and takes his elbow. He looks at her from under the crisp brim of straw and holds her anxious eyes in his rheumy gaze. She feels the tension, tight in her chest, senses a split second beat in the air between them. A connection. He is making a decision.

"You could do me a great favour if... " he says, and she is frightened because she knows there are other lives crushing up behind them, rushing ahead of them in this perfumed garden. But in this moment, beneath this unfolding of her life, beneath the tap of the old man's cane and the shuffle of his feet on the path through the roses, in this second, she senses the tiniest, tiny movement, as if this moment in her reality has been punctured and a spark of someone else's life is flashing through. There is a flutter deep in her stomach. Fear, perhaps, or excitement, the sensations are so similar. Lives fluttering. So much is here. But the old man has decided one thing and not the other.

"...if you could help me to the seat. It's that way. Help yourself to the plums. These trees always have a good crop. The granary is over there.'

He waves her away when he is comfortably seated. Weak evening sun filters through the leaves above him, making him half shadow, half real. She can feel his eyes again, now on her back as she stretches to reach the fruit. There is a pin-pricking catch in her thoughts, like static on an offshore communication link. She is in a tiny boat, bobbing in dark emotional seas. She ducks under the low branches of a plum tree. There is the slip of damp grass under her feet, the sweet, sickly smell of rotting fruit and the incessant drone of tired, drunken wasps.

The granary door sticks at the bottom. She puts her left shoulder against it, bending her arm into her chest. The door releases to her weight and as it does the plum she held in her fist bursts against the front of her shirt. Its flesh leaves a yellow and purple smudge, like a bruise, right above her heart. The juice goes through to her skin, sticky and warm.

She is expecting dusty shadows in this place and is not prepared for a clear, white light. She has a strange sensation of being enfolded as if she is shrugging into herself, her real self, like snuggling into the soft, familiar folds of a favourite, ancient coat. In the sensitised afternoon air, the roughly plastered walls reveal their bumps and shadows. She thinks it's as if the plaster has been embossed with all the words that have been spoken in this place.

But one word is louder; it hums in her chest, rolls up from her throat, pushes her lips together.

"Mummy?"

And she hears the tapping of the old man's stick and hears him step through the door behind her and just as she turns, she fancies she sees him standing tall and straight and his hair is thick and dark. He is stretching a hand towards her and in it he holds a scarlet rose.

HARRIET

We had this row after my father's funeral, my mother and I. She was doing her drama queen bit, the weeping widow. She'd invited all her fancy arty-farty rich friends, people who had hardly known him. It should have been just a few close friends. She had this really sentimental funeral service in the scruffy village church. When I was thirteen or so they'd made me join the church choir there. The choirmaster had disgusting breath and he used to spit when he shouted. I hate that church. As if that wasn't enough, my mother decided to have a huge dinner party after the wake, a dinner party for *her* friends; she said she wanted to celebrate his life, that *he* would've wanted it, he would've enjoyed it. They all got really drunk, all these fat middle-aged men and women slobbering over each other, talking about the past. I think my father would have absolutely hated it. Sentimental shit.

Mother and her 'BFF', Sophie and her brother Willard, bloody odd name – the cartoon bloke, yes, Willard Dexter, the very same. You know him? Huh. Whatever. They ended up, the three of them, drunk as shit, walking across the fields to the Airman's grave. In the dark. It's a memorial to a fighter pilot from the Second World War. It's in a clearing in the woods above the village. When Mother got back to the house, she had mud all over her dress and on her hands, like she'd been digging. All her mascara had run, she looked like a witch. Her husband's funeral and she comes back late at night with mud in her hair, looking like a lunatic. And I thought, here we go again. Another one of her spirals into make believe madness.

The fact is that my mother couldn't bear to be out of the limelight for a second, that's what it was really all about. That party. And she couldn't have the manners to behave properly even then. It was so undignified. I'm still angry. Even now. So anyway, we had this huge row. It was in the kitchen. It ended with her having one of her screaming fits. The screaming heebee jeebies. When she had one of these she would threaten me with anything she could grab. A book, a plate of food. A knife. She never actually assaulted me, she would just pin me in a corner, shouting at me, so close I could see the spit on her teeth. Willard Dexter, he was the one who came in and pulled my mother away. He said he'd take her over to his sister's place for the night. My Mother and Sophie Lawson as good as lived in each other's houses anyway. They were inseparable. Butch old cow. Up to her ears in horseshit and Labradors. So they all went off in her old shit heap of a Land Rover. Took our dogs. *My* dogs. Bloody bastards.

Later, yes, I did feel a bit bad about it. I even thought I should make amends, I really did. So I rang the Lawsons', but that bitch Sophie wouldn't let me speak to my own mother. But guess this, guess who came to the phone to talk to me? Go on, guess! My cousin Sarah. I should have guessed she'd been in on the act. My cousin Sarah always thought my mother was some sort of fucking saint. Jesus. So she'd gone up to the Lawson place, too. Bloody witches' coven.

So I was in the house by myself. And I was pretty pissed off they'd taken *my* dogs. I see now that it was simply to spite me. Ben and Sam had been a present from my father for my fourteenth birthday and if there was any comfort to be had at all in that house, it could have come from my little terrier boys. And it was more than that, of course it was. Mother knew I was nervous in the house without the dogs. It'd always been a creepy house. She was always laughing about my nervousness, always asking me if I could hear the voices. She knew she could get her own back by leaving me there on my own. Oh, yeah, she *knew* I would be scared.

I couldn't sleep, I didn't *want* to sleep, so I just wandered round the place. I don't know, I think I was looking for bits of me, bits of my childhood to stick together to make a happy memory, bits of my father. I wanted to find something I could keep by me, keep close to me. Something that smelled of my father. I was looking in his wardrobe when I found a box of photographs. They were photos of Trinidad. I was born there, on that unfashionable island. Sounds glamorous, it wasn't. Den of corruption and real life voodoo shit you would not believe. Well, these pictures were stuffed into lots of envelopes. There was the house, wooden, two storeys, with servants quarters tacked on to one side. And a picture of them, seven servants, one for every imaginable domestic task. And a separate photograph of a tall black woman in a lime green shift dress, smiling directly at the camera. Gloria, the housekeeper. I can still remember Gloria's green 'best' dress, the coarseness of the fabric against my face. Even now. She cared about me, Gloria did, she tried. She really tried to protect me. But by then my mother had worn her out, she had nothing left. Like everyone who has had the misfortune to live in my mother's orbit.

And I remembered the heat and the feel of the burnt grass. The time there'd been an invasion of bugs on the lawn and hundreds of crisp brown beetles came up from the baked earth and lay siege for two days. And the bushfires, we were always having bushfires, high up on the hill above the house; we'd smell smoke and hear a distant, tinny crackling. And earthquakes. We always knew a tremor or a quake was coming because every dog on the island would go wild, barking and howling, chasing their tails and then it would start, the ground would start to shake.

There was a picture of Singh, the driver, in a pale green nylon shirt. He always had big circles of sweat under his arms and he does in the picture, big dark shadows. I could remember there was a time when every morning Singh had to climb out and drag a mad boy off the car, away from the passenger window where I was sitting, when we were just leaving for Singh to take me to school. And Gloria standing in the middle of the yard, shouting at him, holding a bowl of bread and milk she kept wanting to give to the boy. I remembered the boy's palms on the glass, pale cocoa colour and the gurgling sound he made. There were bubbles at the corners of his mouth. After a few days he disappeared. I never knew what happened to him.

There was a picture of my mother in her sewing room, making me a dress. On her sewing table were tiny red silk roses which she was about to stitch onto the bodice. You couldn't tell from the picture but she'd been crying. I'd been behind the door, watching her, watching the tears dripping off her chin onto the fabric. I hadn't wanted her tears on my dress, I was very cross. My mother spoiling something of mine yet again.

And then I found this photograph of me. As a baby. It had been torn in half and someone had Sellotaped it back together. The Sellotape had gone all dry and crackly. I thought it looked like burnt skin. And whoever had stuck it back together hadn't bothered to join it properly. Across my middle was this ragged white tear, and one of my hands was missing. I just knew my mother had been the one to tear the photograph.

I needed air, space. I went out to the stables. It was one of those really still nights, and so quiet, as if the world has stopped. Mother still had a couple of horses then, although they were really pets. I'm scared of horses. I don't think my mother ever forgave me for that. They were called Doughty and Peg. Peg was short for Pegasus. Doughty was a chestnut, Peg was grey. They were offspring of some of my father's riding horses and he'd brought them back for my mother, from the West Indies. Mad. Can you imagine what that cost? Father hadn't ridden for some years but sometimes my mother used to ride them. And then when they got older, more often she would walk them down the hill to the beach, so they could dance about in the sea. Bloody dangerous or what. She said the sea was good for their old legs. My father used to sit on the terrace back up at the house, and watch her, far below, leading the two horses into the water. She used to nag me to go with her, on and on, about how the sea air would be good for me, about positive ions and all that crap. She was always saying how wonderful it was in the wind and the sea spray, how the horses were angels and we should dance with the angels. Jesus. Fucking mad.

Those bloody horses. When I was small, we'd trek half way across the country every other Sunday to see them in some type of quarantine place they had to go when they came over from Trinidad. Can you imagine what all that cost? I was always bored out of my mind, I dreaded the motorway jams and my mother's displays of sentiment and my father being so solicitous towards her.

So there I was, we had buried my father, my mother had fucked off with her dykey, doggy mate and the weird brother and the stupid horses were stamping about in their stables. It must've been about four in the morning, maybe a bit later, it was just getting light. I unbolted the stable doors and let them out of the yard. They went down the lane. They were so stupid. They kept stopping to eat. I thought if a car goes past I shall pretend they've escaped and I'm trying to catch them. I couldn't make too much noise in case I woke anyone in the farm cottages. But once they were past the yards I let rip and screamed at them, "Ya, ya!" like a drunken cowboy, "Ya, ya!" And they went crazy, galloping wildly, their feet slithering on the tarmac. It was so exciting, I felt as if I could run and run forever, my feet slapping on the road, their hooves, the clatter, the thrum, the beat. I could run, run, run. I can remember that hot horse smell, the scrape of their hooves as they scrabbled to keep their footing.

It could hear it was high tide, I could hear the crash of the waves. The wind had got up. It felt like I'd stepped into another world, with the roaring of the waves and the wind. I know I was out of control. I knew it then. I could feel my heart, it was almost bursting out of my chest. I imagined I was this great power, that I could control the turn of the sea and the wind. I thought I could make the horses come back to me. I called them. I called their names. But my voice got whipped from my mouth by the wind. Just for a minute, I saw them hesitate and I thought they might stop, but they were going too fast. It was too dark to see clearly. I could just make out their shapes as they leapt into the air.

I ran back to the house and locked the front and back doors. I thought I could lock out all the wickedness of what I'd done. Oh I knew what I had done was bad. But part of me was really excited. I had changed something. I had *done* something. I poured myself some brandy. But the smell reminded me of my father, of sitting with my father, late at night, with that *woman* my mother, lying there in a darkened room. I wasn't ever allowed to make any noise. We all had to be silent for my mother. And then I thought, but it isn't mother I am hurting, it's my father. And I was absolutely terrified, terrified that he'd appear before me, some terrible, sunken, dead apparition, but his eyes still there, straight from the coffin, red eyes, like in a bad photo, staring at me in rage.

I kept drinking. I fell into a drunken sleep. And that's when I had my disabled dream the counsellor always obsesses about. That was the first time. That's what I always call it now. A recurring dream that I am unable to move. I had it most nights for about a year after my father died. It was one of those dreams where you know you're asleep and all you have to do is wake up but you can't. Then you dream, yes, at last, that you really are awake but you can't move. So you're not awake but you think you are and you're paralysed and you can't breathe. Even when I recognised the dream over and over again, I still dreamt it in the same way. Only the frustration and desperation of not waking up got more complex. More real. I'd think I *had* woken up and that I was locked in this stupor state. That's what I mean by disabled, why I called it my disabled dream. Because in the dream, I can't move my limbs, or lift my head, or swivel my eyes, like I'm paralysed. And because I can't open my eyes up properly, or move them, I see things through little slits of light and I'm trying to open my eyelids, stretching my face, like the Munch painting The Scream, and I'm always saying 'if only I could just make myself wake up' and then I think I have. But I haven't and there's the paralysed feeling, still there.

God.

Well, this night, in the dream, I was reaching out for my mother's hand and I could see my wrist, without a hand, stretching in front of me and it was like my flesh was encased in a thick, black shadow. I was the shadow of me, with an outline but no contours or colour, just this thick, black, somehow *meshed,* shape. And I was calling in this small, child's voice, "Mummy, help me, mummy!"

The thing is that the dream sort of isn't over when I wake up. I mean, always following this dream I'd feel really strange, like the experience of it went beyond, further into my *consciousness.* When I finally wake- finally, for real - it takes me a long time to come round, to feel normal. I'm in this weird, semi-conscious state where my mind feels shell-shocked, numbed. And I am really shaky, trying to wrestle away this odd drowsiness, like I'm drugged up. Only this particular night, when I woke up and lay there, in that terrible inertia, I saw people dancing. I still believe I saw them. People dancing in the room, clear as anything - fat men in dinner jackets, skinny women in flowing dresses, and two children circling around and around. Girls, with ribbons in their hair, twirling round and round, together. And I think one of the children was me. And I heard laughter. I *know* all these things were real. It was that I was in a different reality. *They* were real. I was just the shadow, looking on. I was the unreal one.

I went into the kitchen to make coffee. I stood waiting

for the kettle to boil, stuffing biscuits in my mouth because somehow putting food in my body made me feel less hollow, more real. Because everything was starting to feel like it was a moment behind itself in time, a shadow of itself, and I had this sensation that I was just outside myself, just a few inches, a few seconds to one side. Like everything took that much longer - the sound waves to reach me, the heat of the kettle, the light to go through my eyes to my mind. I remember being frightened then and I went crazy turning on all the lights, the television, the radio by the kettle, all the time stuffing myself with biscuit after biscuit, leftovers from the dinner, swilling down half-finished glasses of wine, like I was trying to stuff something down, like I was trying to fill myself up to make me solid. Real.

HORSES

Mummy, Mummy, Mummy .....

Sometimes she hears the voice calling, just before she wakes up. She doesn't know this voice. Perhaps it's her own. Sometimes when she hears the voice she sees an image of the world like a child's globe, and there's a figure jumping from country to country, calling. It starts faintly, the voice, distant, slightly echoing but it gets closer and closer until it is a shout, loud enough to thrust her awake.

A particular memory keeps jabbing at me, like a finger, poking, poking. I was with Daddy, on the beach, in the wind. The day I saw the woman with the horses. A woman and two horses, dancing in the waves. I saw she'd left her sandals too close to the water so I let go of my father's hand and ran down onto the wet sand and moved the shoes and then I stood there watching them dance and dance, the horses and the lady.

The horses, one chestnut, one a dapple grey like a storybook horse. They were prancing around the little thin lady with the wind in their manes and I thought they were so happy, I thought I could hear them laughing, laughing, the horses and the lady both. And I could hear their breathing and the blood rushing in their dancing legs, smell the salty air in their nostrils. I could feel their colours, copper and clouds and the heat of their blood. And there was this peaty smell of lathering fur. Everything was twirling around and around, like a wonderful carousel. I saw the lady looking at me and she smiled and her hand reached towards me and I saw her eyes, huge, dark chestnut-coloured eyes, with flashes almost gold, staring and staring and she was smiling and laughing and she looked so happy and she was saying something but the words were whipped away by the wind.

And then she and the horses were walking up the beach and everything was suddenly quiet, everything, like the earth was standing still but wobbly, like when you have been spinning round and round. And suddenly it was very late and it was getting dark. And I could hear Daddy's voice, urgently calling, the sound scuffing the chilling, late summer air and I turned round to see him standing stiff and stick-like at the top of the beach and I thought, please don't take me away from here, Daddy, please don't take me away. He was standing there just waiting and I was standing there just breathing, like I was just the air of my breath. And then he walked towards me and lifted me high up, high above his head. And when I looked back at the beach there was no one there, no one, just the sea and the beach and the glowering sky.

I miss my mum and dad. Patrick and Joan. Mummy and Daddy. So I was their adopted child, but they were still my mummy and daddy. I miss the smell of them, lilac talc and the lemony soap my father used. I miss that heady bubble of life, that warm, sweet feeling in my chest, the feeling that life is rich and thick and safe. Even now, aware of who they really were, of what they really were. So who was that woman in the wind, dancing with the horses? I thought I sort of knew her then and now perhaps I sort of do.

I once asked my dad – my Daddy Patrick - where I came from and he told me I was a gift from the angels. Now I want to believe him. But how can I raise my face to the sky to look for the angels, if what I am about to do will rip my soul from my skin? I shall be floating, lost on the wind, a lost feather, a shadow that belongs to no one, to nothing.

"Mummy-Mummy-Mummy-Mummy..." The sound of the little girl's voice next door stretches itself across the soft light of late afternoon.

Eleanor wakes up. Under the apple tree, in the softening evening light, her old ginger cat sprawls at her feet. He twitches slightly in his sleep. She likes to think he dreams of a summer kittenhood, fields of corn and poppies where fieldmice scuttle through spines of wheat and whiskered barley. She raises her face to the autumn sun, opens her eyes and surveys the little garden she has known all her life. Her childhood swing is long gone but the ancient little shed is still there. She suspects it's really only the great thick stems of the clematis holding it up now. Eleanor thinks how Joan planted the clematis when Patrick died. It had been his shed, it was still full of cracked clay pots in tall stacks and old brittle seed trays. But much as she and Joan had tried, they'd never really been the gardeners of the family. They had let the clematis take its course and it had grown like Topsy. It had taken the view of the shed away from them and it seemed fitting. She remembers that it is called Clematis Montana. There is only one flowerbed now, just down one side of the little garden and in it Eleanor just about manages to tame the shrubs. After the long, hot summer and the dry September it's all looking a bit tired and dusty.

"Mummy, Mummy, Mummy, Mummy!" The child's voice next door is anxious now, rings out more strongly, and Eleanor listens for the tone of the mother's response. Sometimes the mother appears at an upstairs window, her voice like a sniper's bullet. But today, the response is mellow and comes – with a wisp of cigarette smoke - from behind the tall fencing at the end of the garden, near where she sits. Eleanor looks down at the sleeping cat, slightly ashamed, as if she has been caught eavesdropping.

She crunches her toes in the too long grass, still damp from last night's rain. Her mind is whisked by thoughts of motherhood, by her fear. She knows she could feel the joy here but still she will not. This is not a celebration of life.

And who am I to make this choice, who am I, here, with my toes in the grass, here in the soft, buttery autumn sun, single and lonely and pregnant and wishing I wasn't? And everything tired and dusty, nothing holding its colour, with the stink of the neighbour's cigarette smoke over the fence, circling in the breeze. And I keep thinking of the old man with the cane walking me through the rose garden and that voice, "Mummy, Mummy" in that place. And knowing what I now know about my own mother, my birth mother, how do I ignore this whisper? No, no, no, I will not let my mind play these games; already I have begun to disassociate myself from this growing thing, seeing tubing and the flash of metal and a nurse in a cap who says I have a pretty name, who is counting me out, counting you out.

CHRISTINA

Cascade. The house in the valley where we lived in Trinidad. I can hear the cicadas chirruping on the steamy night air. I love their bristle-call, their rhythmic whistle on these hot humid nights. Edward is next to me on the verandah. He holds my hand. When he kisses me I can taste the whisky on his breath. The dusty, warm scent of horse clings to his flannel shirt. These moments are so rich. There is so much love here, it slides between us like a curling cat, arching its back in joy. I never thought this could happen. How did this happen? Someone like me, to be alive in this safe place so full of light.

A cocktail party, one of many. Clinking, ice-filled glasses that make the palms unnaturally cold in handshakes. Expensive perfume blots out the delicate milky scent of jasmine. Edward whispers something in my ear and I can hear the smile in his voice. We're shaking hands with another couple, he florid in the early evening heat, she, young, too plump, bound too tight, like a pupa, in stiff satin. We play the wooing game with them, knowing they have money to invest. They have no dress sense. Edward is so charming to the gauche, plump woman. Her name is Dorothy.

And the hired staff with slightly stained, off-white gloves, moving stiffly, almost robotic in their movements. Their long-limbed bodies are awkward in starched white jackets that so harshly contrast their beautiful dark skin. They look like photograph negatives. Edward whispers to me. We brush shoulders and laugh quietly without showing it beneath our fitted smiles.

The master bedroom. Everything so white. The linen embroidered with tiny blue flowers, reminding me of forget-me-nots in the rockery at Hunter's Lodge. But it's so long ago. Edward coming out of the steam of the shower, his body slackening with age. His skin is rough against my pale, thin thighs. I catch sight of myself in the mirror opposite, my eyes dark and wide, chestnut brown, flecked with gold. Eyes that see so much, too much. My eyes can only just hold back my soul. I feel the pull towards Edward. He is whispering into my hair. He says I smell of love. I am looking up into his face. I say love smells like candlelight and it can burn. I am expecting him to smile but he doesn't. I think this coiled feeling must be fear. I close my eyes. I am afraid of the dark. I am afraid of the darkness that is coming back into my mind. I am falling. Please, please, don't let me fall. Into the abyss. Why is it so dark?

This is my birthday. It must be very early because it's so quiet. Edward has already left for the horses and the yard. At the end of the bed is a long box wrapped in brown paper with thick string round it, like a caricature of a parcel. It's heavy, pulling the bedcovers tight over my feet. I untie the string, pull away the paper. A wooden box. There are two small gold hooks. I unhook them and lift the lid and inside I find neat rows of tubes, acrylic paints, with their labels all turned the right way up with the manufacturer's name *Liquitex* and the little squares showing their colour. Colour upon colour, cerulean blue, green earth, geranium lake, hooker's green, viridian. And I know what my beloved husband is trying to do. But he doesn't understand. I can't allow that part of me breathe this warm air. I have to let it all die. It was all right, it was dying, that connection. It's only just alive and it's rotting away and I don't want to bring it back to life, don't you see?

The races in the savannah, at the track we have made here. Too hot an afternoon for the horses. The black stable boys run across the scorched grass with buckets of water. The track is just sand, almost white in the too-bright light. Edward is talking to some of the new owners. There's the plump, gauche woman again, this time in a pale green suit; it's a man-made fabric and it reminds me of the inside of cucumbers. Dorothy. Her skin has caught the sun and turned it an almond brown. Her husband approaches me and asks me whether I would consider painting her portrait. He says he and Edward have spoken. I am hurt because now I know the gift of the paints was not a private gesture. I have been discussed. And I'm frightened because soon they will see that it's not all right. They will begin to notice that I am fading. I look and see Edward touching the woman's tanned arm. The air between them is very, very still. Is it me? Is it all of me that's not all right again or is there something going on?

This is the yard. Later, because there are three sides to the block. When we first built it there was only an L-shape. Different coloured heads poking out over the doors. We're here in the middle of the night because two of the mares are due to foal.

That's the yard manager I can hear, his voice somehow wrongly pitched, too high and sharp for such a solid, muscular body. His name is Joshua. He's very young for this job, he works hard because Edward is his hero. Footsteps, a commotion, now the faint scent of ammonia, wet straw and the smell of wet horse.

Edward is talking with his back to me and Joshua smiles at me over Edward's shoulder, his teeth white as bleached bone. Edward turns to me and leads me to the foaling box and says this is my other birthday present. He says, can I think of a name? I am reaching out to the soft velvet nose of the foal. His hair is all matted and sticky about his face. He's a little colt foal one of two born this week. I can feel my eyes filling, such a strange sensation to cry. When I am the living dead, I don't feel anything. Everything around me is spinning like a top, all the colours blurred and streaked. But this little foal, he is there, standing shakily, bright and alive. For me. I will call him 'Pegasus' and on his back I will fly above this madness.

I'm in the kitchen at Cascade. I wish Edward would come home. It's mid-morning and I hear the rhythmic swish of the houseboy's brush on the tiles. There are orange rinds hanging from a piece of cord suspended over the work top. They are beginning to dry, the edges are wrinkling. Gloria uses fruit peel to make tea. I wish Edward would come home.

Here is Gloria again. She is the housekeeper. She's so beautiful. Gloria is my friend. See how very black she is. She's very strong. Dear Gloria, with all those raggedy children she wanted to save. Always there with some bread or some 7-Up when they came up the hill. I wish Edward would come home.

I'm so tired, I keep feeling so tired. Me and Edward. We're in the garden, at the end, away from the house. It's night. There's a tray with two bottles of wine and some sandwiches. The bread is grit in my mouth. The mosquito-coils, set in the grass a few feet away, twirl their acrid smoke. We used to like to eat supper here, with our backs against the trees. Tonight we drink more than usual. But I want the wine to soothe me. It makes me feel free. It makes me free.

Edward whispers. But these are not tissue-paper whispers, gently rustling. These whispers hiss and weave. He smiles too early in the sentence so I know something isn't quite right here. He isn't quite telling me the truth. Grandmother, what big teeth you have.

I get up to run but he grabs the top of my arm. The grip hurts. He pulls me round so my face is close to his. I can see the words are so angry they don't fit his lips properly. He is speaking in a voice that is not his but it is one that I recognise. He tells me we will make a deal. He says I must stop hiding but I can't, I can't. There are tiny flecks of spit in the corners of his mouth. There are tiny flecks of broken dreams, silver and flaking, at the corners of my mind. But you said you loved me, you said you would keep me safe. Jack made a deal with you, so you would keep me safe.

Gloria's laughter echoes down the long, dark corridors, high-pitched, giggly, child-like. She carries cool, freshly laundered bed linen. Stark white against her smooth black arms. She is making up our bed today because I am sick. Pregnant and sick. I keep bleeding so they've told me to stay in bed. When the doctor calls me a 'new mother' I want to laugh. At least, I think it's laughter. Everything is jumbled up, all my insides are jumbled up. There are flecks and slivers, sharp shards that are cutting up my heart.

I am lying beneath the air-conditioning unit. It is the only one we have in the house. Gloria is making up the bed. She bends and straightens, bends and straightens as she tucks in the corners of the sheets. She comes to me and stoops, picks me up. She smells sweet and faintly of oranges. She lifts me easily in her smooth, strong arms. She shakes her head and says "Too t'in, Miss Christina, too t'in for da baby." All I can do is cry, I can't seem to stop.

Night. I'm thirsty. Can't drink the water in the bathroom. There are voices in the sitting room. A woman's voice, familiar but not one that fits in here. Shapes in the darkness, growing out of the shadows. Whispers and soft laughter and the smell of sweet alcohol. No one drinks sweet alcohol here. Somebody's moaning. I think it's me. Edward leaping up, running towards me, he's naked and there's this hot pain and the floor meets my face and it's all sticky. A woman's arms lifting my shoulders, pulling me up, holding me tight to her. The nylon of her slip is full of static. She rocks me slowly from side to side. She holds me so tight I can hardly breathe. She's wearing too much musky scent, cheap scent always has too much musk. Dorothy. Of course.

Edward is here. I know he is, I can't breathe when he's here, the air becomes too thick wth the things in my head. He's sitting on the edge of the bed. I can feel his anxiety, like a rasp on my skin. I am pretending to be asleep. He is moaning softly, like he's chanting. Sorry, sorry, sorry, like he's praying, begging me, over and over and over. He's telling me to hold onto something. Life? Why? What for? I thought you were the one I could trust. His hand squeezes mine but I am too shut down now to respond.

Edward, again, on a step ladder, look, painting navy sky and yellow stars and a moon in soft grey, on the ceiling above our bed. A child's picture, bold colours, Van Gogh yellow and blucs. Evcrything around me is slightly out of my reach. He has unpacked all the tubes of paints and they are everywhere, there are blobs of sticky colour smeared on the wooden floor and drips of blue and gold like jewels. And red. Like drops of blood.

I can't stay here. Please let me go. The sun is reflecting off the water now. The light is hurting my eyes. Please.

CLAUDIA

It was quite a shock, all of us turning up one Sunday to find Christina at the Reeds' cottage. And with a blotchy, angry baby on her shoulder, about three months old. "This is our daughter, Harriet." That was the first thing she said. Well, shouted, above the racket. I remember thinking what an ugly baby, if only she'd stop screwing her face up and howling she might look better. I remember Christina handing the child to Joseph and him carrying her outside, into the garden, Sarah clucking behind him like an anxious chick. Emmeline Reed pottering out behind them with some crusts for the birds. And then Christina coming over to me and touching my cheek with the back of her hand. Such an odd gesture, I'll never forget it. Like you touch a child to see if she has a temperature. I remember her fingers were freezing cold. I didn't know what to say. Really and truly, I didn't know *what* to think.

We went into the scullery to make tea, busied ourselves with the clatter of cake tins and plates and cutting the crusts off and finding teacups and matching up saucers. I can't remember what we talked about. I was bursting with all those years of pent-up fury, I wanted to shout at her, ask what she thought she had been up to, extract some explanation, I don't know. But she just smiled and talked as if nothing had ever come between us, as if nothing had happened, as if we'd seen each other just the week before. I remember asking her about Harriet and her telling me it had been a difficult pregnancy and changing the subject. She talked about the horses they kept, how she and Edward rode their horses out at dawn, every day; how the sun would burn at seven in the morning. Her arms were hard and muscled. She looked strong and sleek, like a gazelle. She was beautiful. I felt totally inadequate, fat and frumpy. I'd put on weight when I'd had Sarah and I had never lost it. Well, thank you. It took a lot of hard work to get into shape like I am now, of course. Still does. I can't afford to touch anything remotely delicious, I just pile the weight on. Christina of course was one of those people who never seemed to put on an ounce, who could eat anything and still be as thin as a stick. Harriet's just like her mother was but she still thinks she's too fat. Poor Harriet, she always had such a low opinion of herself. She was such an *attractive* thing before all that stuff, before it all went wrong. It's dreadful, really and truly. Dreadful but not sadly not surprising.

Sarah says she remembers meeting her aunt Christina

that Sunday afternoon. She likes to say that Christina was the first adult to talk to her as an adult would, not silly child-speak, as she puts it. She was three, so I suppose she might remember bits. But I expect it's all got a bit embellished over time. I remember her saying something funny, like kids do; 'is that thin brown lady a princess, mummy?' Christina a princess? I practically choked on my tea. For more than one reason. Yes, that's what Dad had called her, that's right.

Anyway, that's how we met up again, at the Reed's. Then we started writing to one another. Like normal sisters. I'd write once a month or so, it became a Sunday evening task, when Sarah was in bed. I never wrote anything other than everyday news, so, no, they weren't intimate letters. Well, why should they have been, we'd never really been close. Maybe I *was* still a bit angry. Well, she'd dropped us all, hadn't she and then waltzed back in, expecting us to behave like family. Once I found out about her mood swings, it seemed to make a bit more sense but all this guff about depression – such a lot of twaddle. Christina was just spoilt, always had been. So when things didn't go her way she sulked. That's all. And all this stuff they talk about nowadays. Anxiety, depression, no self-esteem. Rubbish! Really and truly, people should just pull their socks up. I had to. No-one was going to do it for *me*.

And so anyway, yes, we wrote to each other. I would write about the additions we were making to the house, Joseph's job with the BBC, how Sarah was getting on at nursery school. We scrimped and saved to make sure Sarah had a private education. There wasn't a good school near where we were living then. I didn't write anything to Christina about our marriage or Joseph's bloody-mindedness. I didn't want her to know. Well, why would I? It would only have made her feel even more superior.

She always wrote her letters back in green ink, addressing the envelope to all of us. All this wild loopy green handwriting, almost impossible to read. Sarah loved those letters, she used to get so excited. Really and truly, they were more than a bit eccentric, over the top; children respond to that, don't they? She'd write about all sorts. Pages and pages about another foal being born, ramblings about life's magic or something; or about dancing all night at Carnival with all these black men with talcum powder on them playing the steel drums and the people fainting under the weight of their huge costumes.

Sometimes she would get onto a subject - something really odd - and write pages and pages. One *whole* letter was about the colours of the sky when the bushfires broke out. I remember at the time asking Joseph if he thought Christina was all right, out there in that dried up, uncivilised place, but he didn't think there was anything strange about the letters; he said they just showed Christina's passion for life. I had to laugh. My ex-husband has always had a pompous streak. Of course, I thought at the time that maybe it was all a bit far-fetched, not quite as rosy as she was making out. I thought something was up. Didn't realize she was billy-bonkers.

It was Joseph's idea that I take a holiday out there, a

visit to my sister. Of course it was an excuse for us to be apart, me and Joseph, because by then it must've been pretty obvious to everyone that our marriage was a shambles. He never believed I'd actually do it of course, he said it as a challenge. Go out there and see your sister. He was always doing that, suggesting I do things - go back to work, go on a diet - knowing that I wouldn't and that it would make me feel worse about myself. He's very good at psychological games. Well, I showed him all right. I drew out some savings, booked the flights through a travel agent place in the high street, did it all by myself and I just... took off.

It was a hell of a shock, arriving in Port-of-Spain. I just don't know how people live in a place like that. I don't expect it's changed much even now, has it? First of all there's the humidity - just terrible, it's like walking through hot wax. And there was a smell everywhere of rotting fruit and sewage. The way Christina had described it, you'd have thought it was paradise. I was just grateful I hadn't brought little Sarah. It was no place for a child. Filthy.

They sent a driver to meet me at the airport in an old beaten up Ford Zephyr. He had the most appalling body odour and great patches of sweat on his shirt. We drove through the centre of Port-of-Spain. I couldn't believe that this was the capital of the island. I mean, there were chickens running in the streets and half-naked children outside shacks, sucking on great sticks of sugarcane.

I suppose it wasn't so bad once you were out of the town. The house Christina and Edward lived in was the old colonial type, made of wood, with shutters and a raised verandah, really quite grand. It was in a valley with these huge hills of scrub rising up behind it. I remember there were hibiscus flowers all around the front of the house, very pretty. And jasmine growing by the French doors. They had a gardener of course, to do all that. And several other house staff to look after them too. I'll give Christina and Edward their due, though, they treated them all very well. One maid, Gloria, she was more like a friend to Christina. They were very close. In fact, I don't know what spiteful things Christina had told her about me, but it was obvious Gloria was wary. She was positively chilly towards me the whole of the time I was there. Honestly, what a cheek. And not an appropriate relationship in those days if you ask me, the lady of the house and someone her husband employed.

Edward and Christina were leading such a wild social life at the time. They were always with their racing cronies, at the stables, playing tennis or having drinks at the Hibiscus Club. Really and truly, there wasn't an evening went by without some get-together. And most lunchtimes the wives would meet up at the swimming pool at the King's Park Hotel. They had their children picked up from school by drivers and delivered there mid-afternoon. What a life. Christina was, quite simply, spoilt rotten. Really just more of the same. Indulged. Dad had indulged her all her life and now there was Edward Hopwood with his pots of money, handing everything to her on a plate.

They were obviously a popular couple amongst the other ex-pats. Actually, even though it was quite a glamorous set they were in, Christina and Edward were without doubt the most glamorous of the lot. Which would have been all right but they knew it, too. They were quite superior. Especially with me. Edward could be very cutting about other people, they all thought his humour was very droll but little did they know he'd be making comments about each of them behind their backs. I never heard Christina comment, but she could give some looks and she was just as two-faced. I know she took a real dislike to one particular couple, some Americans, but she was so charming to their faces - to the point of it being a joke, a farce. Of course I didn't realise at first it was the *wife* Christina disliked so much. Once or twice I saw Edward shoot Christina a warning look. Of course, that was the first sign that things weren't perfect between them. That and the fact that they both drank like fishes. And then there was the problem with Harriet. She was almost three and she didn't speak. She didn't *squeak*, much less all that yelling she had done as a baby. Really and truly, it was all a bit peculiar.

Oh, Harriet wasn't withdrawn in any *other* way. She played with the other ex-pat children quite happily and they happily accepted her the way she was - children do, don't they, they just accept things, just get on regardless. I've noticed it with my granddaughter if ever we meet a funny child, one that's a bit – you know – not quite right. Oh, I know I'm not meant to say it but we used to use the word 'spastic'. It was just the way my generation put it then.

Oh and believe me, Harriet was a positively charming, angelic child but without even making a murmur. She inherited her mother's lovely thick red hair and those same big brown eyes but she had her father's skin tone, so she tanned very easily. She looked almost Spanish. She was quite a little star at the swimming pool, jumping off the top diving board with her daddy and swimming underwater like a little fish. But she didn't speak. Nope. Not a peep.

Well, yes, they must've been a *bit* worried about it though to this day nobody ever said anything. Really and truly, they may not have been like ordinary parents but Edward brought Harriet to England a few times to see a specialist, to make sure it wasn't a physical thing. I remember Christina getting quite hysterical about that, about Edward wanting to take a trip to England without her. All sorts of things were said, it was quite a row. But as I said to Edward at the time, Christina had always been in the habit of making her own little dramas, of getting things out of proportion. I don't know why she imagined he wasn't capable of looking after the child, it was patently obvious that he was quite besotted, that he just adored his little girl. I tried to talk to Christina, I asked her about it, about what was wrong with Harriet, why she didn't want Edward taking her to England. But, like I said, we'd never been that close. But I did try. In my own way. She was still my sister, after all. And like I always say, family is family, whatever happens. My daughter Sarah says blood *isn't* thicker than water. Well she's quite wrong, of course. She knows it upsets me when she says that.

I was there for two weeks. Sometimes Christina came back from those early rides out with Edward and she'd look just terrible and I would know she'd been crying. But she'd put on this bright smile and ask me how I'd slept and start organising breakfast and then she'd seem fine, getting on with it, being bright and jolly, so I just let things be. Let sleeping dogs lie and all of that.

It was there, while I was with them in Trinidad, that Edward had told me all about Christina's so-called psychiatric problems. Such a fuss. Well, yes, often Christina seemed a little tense and she'd be upset but other times she'd be the life and soul of the party. Edward said her unpredictability was a clue. Oh, I don't know. Look, I have to be honest. It's like I said, really and truly there's too much fuss about this too much of the time. People are *indulged*. They're given all these ideas and all those pills and something to latch on to and it just makes them worse. Frankly, anyone can pull themselves together. Look what I did. Left by my husband, having to be a single, working mother. I didn't moan and take to my bed and wear widows' weeds and get the world and his wife running around after *me*.

You know who I felt most sorry for? Poor Edward. He didn't say so, people like that never do, but he must have been pretty much at the end of his tether. All those tears and dramatics. He told me sometimes she'd lie in bed for days at a time, refuse to get up. The awful thing was that while I was a bit shocked to hear all this, like I told Edward at the time, I wasn't - in all honesty - that surprised. Well, I told him he shouldn't let her get away with it, he shouldn't let her drag him down with her. That she'd always been a nuisance. Dad would have put him straight about her if he'd still been alive. Dad would've given her a jolly good talking to, told her to be a better wife and mother.

Shortly before I left, Edward decided he would send her to this sort of convalescent home, he said it was a mission or something, on the other side of the island, where people could go for rest cures. That American couple, they'd heard about it. That's right. That would fit, wouldn't it. Americans have always been keen on that sort of thing, retreats and so on, haven't they. Before all that alternative, hippy-dippy psychiatry stuff became fashionable this side of the pond, that is. God help us.

I flew back home a couple of days before Edward was due to take Christina there, to this rest cure place. When I got back and finally had the chance to tell Joseph about my trip and all the fuss and nonsense with Christina, he went absolutely mad. He was furious. He said I should've brought Christina home, that I should have protected her from Edward, that they could do anything to her. He rang Edward a number of times, I heard him shouting down the phone. Honestly, how did he dare? He knew absolutely nothing about it, he knew nothing about Christina. He had no right to make such a fuss, to make all that drama over it. But then drama is my ex-husband's speciality, isn't it. I expect the story to turn up one of these days, in one of his silly little television plays. Really and truly, I'm surprised it hasn't already. If and when it does, I shall sue him for every penny he has.

SARAH

Yes I do. I remember meeting Aunt Christina for the very first time. My mother says I couldn't possibly, I was too small, but I can recall the whole scene, all the little details.

We were visiting Emmy - Emmeline Reed - in Sussex. Emmy and her husband were the people my mother and Aunt Christina had stayed with during the war. We used to go and visit them, once a month, for Sunday tea. I still go, every few weeks. Emmy Reed is a dear, sweet thing; she still lives in that same little cottage they lived in during the war. She has an agency nurse who lives in and looks after her and helps keep the cottage neat. I potter in the garden. Make up some pots in spring and autumn. My daughter Katherine loves it there. Emmy Reed tells us stories about the people who used to live in the village. She's got an amazing memory for detail. And there's my mother telling everyone she's losing it. Honestly! Emmeline Reed is as bright as a button.

I'm sorry, where was I? Oh, yes, the first time I met my aunt. We were just getting out the car when Mum suddenly gasped and put her hand up to her mouth. I remember Dad looking at her, then turning round and making one of his funny faces at me. He does it with my daughter still, it's hilarious. Sort of raises his eyebrows and puckers his lips. He calls it 'my scandalized schoolmarm face'. He used to do that when he and Mum first split up. I'd say something like "but Mummy says I shouldn't something or other" and he'd put on his scandalized schoolmarm face. It used to make me really laugh. He can be so funny, our dad, when he wants to be, he's really not as serious as you might imagine. He writes all these sad, family dramas but really he's a lovely cuddly old bear with a great sense of humour. I like to think I've got his cuddly, funny side. He and Mum are so different. Mum is so very stiff upper lip. Nothing is allowed to be complicated with her, everything has to be straightforward. Black and white. Buck up and get on. I can't figure out whether she actually feels things and is just very strong and brilliant at shutting it away, or whether things just don't get to her and she's really is simply a sort of 2-D person. Dad says Mum can *feel* things, she just can't empathise, isn't able to put herself in anyone else's shoes. Dad always argues that people like that have no curiosity, they're intellectually and emotionally too lazy; they don't climb any mountains so they never know how it feels to stand on the top of the world. I'm sure he's right and there have been times in my own life when I think I would have been better off happily grubbing about in the lowlands like my 2-D mother.

No. Mum wouldn't understand one iota if Aunt Christina really did end her own life. She just wouldn't accept the whole idea. I don't know what it feels like to want to do that but part of me understands. If it's true, then I would want to forgive my aunt. And to do that I think the more I can understand it, the whole self-destruction thing, the more I will be able honestly to forgive her. I miss her. And it's ironic because the thing I miss most is Aunt Christina's *love* of life. Of the world. Of the natural world. Her sense of fun. Her energy. I regret her loss, not just for me but for my own daughter. She could have learnt so much.

My mother said to me the other night that there's nothing to understand and that forgiveness doesn't come into it. That if Aunt Christine really did mean to drown herself then it was just a selfish, stupid thing to do. Yeah. That's right, mum.

This is what I remember about the first time I saw my aunt. A tall, thin lady standing by the kitchen window in Emmy Reed's scullery, all dressed in white. She had this baby on her shoulder - my cousin, Harriet — and it was bawling its socks off. Dad went up to her and took the baby away from her, put it over his shoulder, took my hand with his free one and off we went outside. This screaming, clamouring baby, I can see her face over my Dad's shoulder. It's really funny. Funny and poignant and sad.

We went into the garden. It had just stopped raining and everything had that earthy smell, you know? It's as clear as anything to me, this memory. Dad was bouncing baby Harriet and going 'shh shh shh' and he called over to me and said "That's your Aunt. She's your Mummy's sister." I couldn't believe such a beautiful lady could be my mum's sister. She wasn't a bit like my mum.

When Dad took me and Harriet back inside Aunt Christina bent down to me and put out this firm, brown hand for a handshake. She had this incredibly long plait of dark red hair. As she leaned forward it fell over her shoulder, like a length of thick shiny rope. Like Rapunzel. And the hem of her white dress brushed my feet. I remember the rustle of it and this swish of cool air that was full of a scent like crushed rose petals. And then I said - I've never been allowed to forget this - I said "Are you a princess?" and Mum spluttered a sort of false laugh, a bit too loud and coughed and spilt her tea and Aunt Christina just smiled and looked at me with these enormous brown eyes and nodded. I was mesmerised. I could see myself right there, in her eyes, a tiny little speck with a huge head. Like I was looking into a mirror at a fairground.

Aunt Christina and Uncle Edward lived in Trinidad then. They lived there for about ten or eleven years I think. Harriet was born there. And though it appeared to be coincidence that Aunt Christina was at Flint Cross when we visited that day it wasn't - Dad told me later that he and Aunt Christina had planned it. Aunt Christina had come back to England for a visit *because* she'd wanted to see Mum – to see her sister again. Which means that she must have cared, that it did matter to her that she had lost touch with her sister, in spite of my mother being so horrid about her. Saying it had been all Aunt Christina's doing that they fell out and lost touch when Granddad Mansfield died.

But it *was* the only time Aunt Christina came to England in the whole of the time they lived abroad. Uncle Edward used to come to England quite a lot, with Harriet. Dad and I sometimes met up with them in London. I can remember one time when Harriet was about four or five; I was skiving from school. I had just started at Ashford - a boarding school - and I absolutely hated it. So I got my Dad to make up some excuse to get me out for a few days. My parents had just got divorced then so the headmistress was really anxious to be seen to be compassionate. And probably my Dad being a bit of a playwright and working for the BBC and everything, that probably helped.

That's what we did, we went to see a play. Well, a musical actually. Dad had brought along an outrageous casting lady who was about to cast one of his television plays, so we went to the theatre to watch this actor who had all of three lines. Uncle Edward met us there with Harriet and a glossy American woman called Dorothy. I remember Dad telling me not to say anything to Mum about 'Uncle Edward's friend'. I've often wondered about it because when, a few years later, I saw them together for the first time, Aunt Christina and Uncle Edward, they were so loving towards one another, so soppy, I mean, it was almost *embarrassing*. Mum says there's a lot I don't know and I'm sure that's so but I *do* know that by the time I started spending school holidays with them at Heron's Gate, Uncle

Edward and Aunt Christina were absolutely devoted to each other. So the suggestion that Uncle Edward was a womanizer – the way mum would have it – well, it's just silly.

I think it's important to say that, because my cousin Harriet is always saying that her parents lived - and I quote - "a disgusting lovey dovey lie". That's just so mean and it's typical of Harriet. It makes me very angry. I don't see how anyone could doubt how much my aunt and uncle meant to one another.

Lizzie Lawson and I were talking about it with her mum, Sophie, just last night. Sophie and Aunt Christina were close friends for years. Lizzie reckons that Harriet always said that because she was jealous and she had a father fixation. Lizzie is a bit over the top with her amateur psychology, I know, but it did get me thinking. I think most daughters have father fixations to some extent. Perhaps sometimes the relationship can be a bit skewed. Look at my own mum and my grandfather, for instance. Mum has always made out he was this hero, a sort of saint, but Emmy Reed once told me he was a cruel, manipulative man who never thought twice about the consequences of his actions. Emmy said he terrified Aunt Christina when she was a girl. Terrorized, not terrified. She said terrorized. I remember because it's not the sort of word Emmy Reed would usually use.

If you think about it, perhaps there's some peculiar genetic balancing out, an odd little link. I mean, Aunt Christina being so scared of her own father, 'terrorized' by him and then her own daughter adoring *her* father. Perhaps there's some weighing up, like Harriet needed to make up for some sort of imbalance in the universe, make it up on behalf of her mother. That sounds silly, doesn't it. My mother's always saying I have wacky ideas. My Dad's a bit kinder – he says we're just so desperate to understand life sometimes, we think up all sorts of things. We make up all these psychological puzzles that are really nothing but splinters of information that we shape into some theory with gossip and speculation and a sort of blind faith. Well these ideas comfort me. Some people still rely on God, don't they. In a way I think they're lucky – imagine believing that you are loved whatever you do, whatever happens to you.

LIES

I am afraid. This fear bubbles up in my chest and drip-drips from a puncture this truth is making. The blood runs too fast, too thick. Sometimes I think I hear it roaring in my head, a blood-rushing roar.

She sits in a small room above the clamour of a Monday morning street. The air is stale and thick. A photocopied sign tells visitors not to open the windows. There's an insulated jug of hot water. A jar of cheap instant coffee. With chicory. A bowl of lumpy sugar with sticky coffee granules mixed in because there's only one spoon. An opened carton of milk explains the slightly rancid air.

Opposite her, sitting tight in themselves, a mother and daughter also wait. The girl has been crying. Her face is red and puffy. The mother sits very upright; trying to look composed, she sits rigid, looks distant. Disgust and disappointment are there, in the clench of her jaw. Eleanor feels desperate for the girl. She wants to find the courage to step across the dusty carpet and wrap her arms about her.

Fear. It drags through this place, blistering our veins. So much fear here, here in this room. Fear like unripe persimmons, drying the mouth, catching in the throat.

Eleanor so wishes she hadn't gone to see Peter, that she hadn't told him. She knew the moment she stepped out the car that her timing was all wrong. He was surprised to see her and there was an air of expectancy about the house that clearly wasn't meant for her. He asked her to be brief since he was expecting one of his other girlfriends to arrive. Terrible timing. He's the sort of man who constantly tells you he will be straight with you, knowing his honesty rips out hearts. And what does honesty really mean to him? It means he can just say what he wants and because he's prefaced it this way, it just absolves him of any guilt. He doesn't even have to *participate* in his own truth. But Eleanor had always known she was just one of his collection. His harem. Another pencil mark with a name behind the bathroom door. She had known, in her heart of hearts, that she was just another of those women who sometimes like to think that *she* would be 'the one', the one he would finally fall in love with. Peter has that gift, of making each of these tired, hungry, lonely women he screws and screws *with* feel special. His mother gave him this gift, wrapped up in a sticky gauze. With love and kisses and lies. But no shame.

Eleanor lied. She said:

Peter. Look. I'm just going to come out right with it, tell you something.

And she did, told him something. With her voice and her hands. But she lied with her eyes and her heart. She lied to him, but to have told him how she really felt would have given him more scope for mockery. He mocks emotion. Fabricates a mock-up of a relationship. Mockingbird, imitating calls. Love to him is nothing but a burlesque. Painted faces and bodies and too-red lips. Manipulation. Sex. Power. And underneath it all a kind of hatred. For women.

- What did you think would happen, Eleanor? Did you think we would end up getting married and having brats and living happily ever after? Is that what you thought? For starters, I've been married, I've got a mad ex-wife who is a total pain in the arse. And, listen, love, there is no happily ever after. It's time you outgrew fairy tales, Eleanor. Nobody's going to rescue you, nobody's going to come galloping across the seas on a fucking white horse.

- Don't mock me, you bastard!

She had shouted at him, for the first and the last time, spitting the words across the room, spitting her anger, her rage. She *had* hoped for all those things, *had* day-dreamed. This was bad enough but that he had *witnessed* her dreaming all along, that was worse. The very worst thing. He had been laughing at her, playing her. But of course, he is the accomplice in each of his women's dreams. Dancing by candlelight. Soft strains of a violin. He needs romance like they do. He needs the myth so he can play the Prince himself for a while. *He* needs the fairy tale too. Touché, Peter, I get it. Sleeping Beauty and the Prince. She is a beauty while she's sleeping. Is she still beautiful when she wakes up?

- So you didn't do this deliberately then?

- *What* did you say?

- Get pregnant. Up the duff. Bun in the fucking oven. Last chance saloon for you at your age, right? You scheming bitch.

- No, Peter. I didn't do this *deliberately*. And by the fucking way, *we* did it. The two of us.

Somehow she was still standing there, in the kitchen, shaking. She told herself she would keep calm, keep her voice low, not wanting to let her anger go again. The modulation even and precise. One more flicker of anger and she knew she would crack. Her anger would burst out of her chest and she was frightened what she might do.

When I was little I had a terrible rage, so terrible that I used to frighten myself. I'd been out for a walk with Daddy. This was a special occasion because I had new wellington boots. They came from Woolworth's. When Dad had brought them home they had been knotted together with a piece of string that went through tiny little holes in the back of each boot. He teased me, pretending that was how they were meant to be worn. With the string still attached.

We went up to the woods at Guestling, to go kicking through the leaves. In some places the leaves were deep enough to come over my knees. It was a game we often played, a game I loved. A game he loved. "Isn't that a wonderful sound?" he'd say, as we kicked and swished and kicked and swished. And on the way home he picked up a sycamore seed and held it high above me and when he let it go it swirled and swirled and swirled. I thought it was some special magic that only he could do.

When we got home I found I couldn't get my new boots off. Mum had made me wear so many socks and my feet had got so hot, the boots had become really tight. My dad laughed and sat me on the stairs but I didn't want his help, I wanted to do it myself and I started shouting and kicking and screaming "Go away, go away!" and he tried to grab my feet but I was flailing madly saying "I hate you, I hate you!". I can still remember the feeling of that childhood rage, the heat and roar of it.

Something, just at that minute, something in his face caught my heart. I knew I had hurt him. But I was so angry I couldn't stop. I kicked and kicked and as I kicked again I caught him on the jaw. We just stared at each other, with this fire burning my skin, the tears on my cheek seared in sticky streaks. Him, Patrick, my Daddy, holding his jaw. And then he had walked away. And suddenly I thought he might never come back. And I was so desperate that he didn't walk away.

Peter had told her that if she needed money she could have it. He'd paid for that sort of thing before. Cruel words that bit deep into her flesh. She could feel her face burn. And *then* she let go. She let go of her anger, her disappointment, her frustration at finding herself stuck, stuck here in a life she had never envisioned. She stood, knocking over the mugs, the bloody silver teapot his mother had given him, his homemade apple pie baked in a big metal tray. And she had screamed at him "I hate you! I fucking hate you!" And he had *smiled*. A nasty, condescending, mocking smile. And he had walked away from her, through the hall. He had opened the front door. Held it open. *Get out, Eleanor. Go on. Go. Just fuck off. You knew what you were getting into. Fuck off out of my life.*

A door opens to her left. A young woman with a clipboard smiles broadly at the three women in the waiting room. Two women, one hardly more than a girl. The woman with the clipboard has very long front teeth. They must have once been buck teeth, tamed by a childhood brace. She looks down at the sheet of paper in front of her, still smiling, as if her features are stuck in that one position.

When we made faces the teachers used to tell us that if the wind blew, our faces would stay that way forever. And that nice girls didn't raise their voices. And that kissing boys could get you into trouble. What sort of trouble, Miss Starns? Tell us, tell us.

"Let's see... I am looking for Eleanor?"

She stands and follows the woman through a door into a smaller room. A desk with a chair behind it and two chairs in front. The windows are too high and make the room like a cell. The woman indicates one of two chairs but instead of going round to the other side of the desk, she sits in the chair next to Eleanor's. Eleanor thinks it's absurd that she is old enough to be this young woman's mother.

"I'm Charlotte. I'm a counsellor for the advisory centre. I'm here to listen."

Charlotte is uncomfortably close. Eleanor thinks she

looks too plain for her name. A Charlotte should have long wild hair, acres of it, tumbling down her back, a pale face with thick, voluptuous lips. Charlotte Bronte. Kathy. Heathcliffe. Eleanor hopes Charlotte is a good listener. That what she does is actually more of a vocation to her than a job. She probably goes on courses. Eleanor hopes so, not for herself but for that young girl in the waiting room. She hopes they have taught Charlotte how to deal with mothers.

Eleanor realises that there's something slightly downtrodden about Charlotte, something slightly sad, seedy almost. But then this whole thing is seedy. Charlotte keeps smiling and talking but Eleanor doesn't hear her. To Eleanor, Charlotte is just here to adhere to an obligation to the law. Just as well she doesn't need any counselling, isn't it, she thinks, just as well she is so certain that this is what she wants to do. But that poor young girl in the waiting room, she doesn't know what's hit her. It is a shame that her mother will make the decision for her daughter purely on the basis of how difficult it would be with the neighbours, her friends, her husband's business colleagues, if her young daughter had an illegitimate child.

EMMELINE

Here. This is for you. I found it. Take it home with you. I don't want Claudia ever getting her hands on it. Is the tea made?

I didn't get the chance to know the girls' mum. She came down here just the once to see them. I don't think she and Mr Mansfield were the closest of couples, that's only what I've guessed, mind. I never saw him and her together, Mr & Mrs Mansfield. She got the train down here when she came that one time. He didn't bring her. Whereas he came down in his big black car, on his own, most Sundays and surely every fortnight.

She was a good-looking woman, so far as I can remember. Soft spoken, quite timid. Beautifully dressed. She wore a big fur coat, made out of hundreds of tiny pelts. I remember Jim talking about it later, wondering how many animals you'd have to skin to make a coat that long. It had these big full sleeves. It weighed a lot. I tried to hang it over the banister but it slid off, so Jim took it upstairs and put it on our bed.

Claudia had the afternoon off school because her mother was visiting. She was a different child with her mother there, behaved like a little girl, young like. She curled herself up at her mother's feet, resting her head on her knees. I think Mrs Mansfield felt a bit awkward. I don't think she was a natural with the little ones, if you know what I mean.

Christina had permission from the convent to come home early too but she didn't come. So after tea Jim took Mrs Mansfield and Claudia up the lane to meet her at the usual time. I watched them walking back down. It was almost time for Mrs Mansfield to leave to get her train. I can remember her reaching down to give Christina a kiss and the child twisting away and running off. Mrs Mansfield shouted at her and then she coughed and turned away, started talking to Claudia. She knew I'd heard her. I won't be saying what it was she said but it wasn't very ladylike. I thought it wasn't nice to shout at the child, never mind using words like that with a little girl. Not nice at all.

We got to know Mr Mansfield well enough. He'd turn up, come rain or shine. He said he liked the countryside. He'd always have a chat with Jim when he arrived, just the two of them, in the office. Like I said, couple of times he sent someone down to do some repairs for us. When we were really hard up he sent someone down here to look at the books with Jim. All Jim ever said was he was helping us out and I didn't need to know the details. I didn't know Jim had sold him the property, I only found that out when Jim died. It belongs to Christina. It's her that lets me live here. Pays for me to have a nurse. Pays for everything. Always. I bet old bossy knickers Claudia would like to get her hands on my little cottage. Well she can't, not while I'm still here. And I'm not going anywhere for a while yet. Never mind what she wants, eh? Little Christina will look after me.

Mr Mansfield took the girls for walks when he visited, across the meadows, to the village and back. Often as not, Claudia would come back early, by herself; she was never one for exercise, Claudia. She was always keen to make the tea, she'd make piles of sandwiches, cutting off the crusts and eating them, picking at the edge of the cakes. She wouldn't do it now, would she? Worries about her waistline. Y'know her daughter Sarah, she does the selfsame thing, stands there with her back to me, picking at the cakes as she puts them on the plate, thinking I can't see. Sarah makes her own cakes. She told me that Christina taught her to bake. That's nice, isn't it. That Claudia never made a cake in her life, I bet. Always brought those revolting sickly shop cakes. Reckon she thought she could sweeten me up, eh?

Claudia, Claudia. Nosey woman, she turned into. Wanting to know about some things but she don't want to know about others. Well, she couldn't have it both ways. I used to tease her. Pretend I was gone soft. I'd say, 'Here, Claudia, there are soldiers for tea. They're home from the war." She thought I was losing my marbles. I told Sarah, that's what I used to do. Oh, how we laughed. Sarah, now she's not a chip off the block that one. Nothing like her bossy mother. Much softer, more thoughtful. More like her father. Now he's a nice man, Mr Joseph. I always liked him.

I like Sarah visiting with her little one. She's a good girl, Sarah. Shame about that husband of hers. She's such a sweet thing, she didn't deserve that bad luck, bless her heart.

I won't have her mother here now. Told you that, didn't I? Won't have that Claudia in the house.

She knew. I don't know much but she should've been there looking after her little sister. Looking out for her. Claudia was always a coward underneath. That's why she was always such a bully. Kids that are bullies are always cowards underneath.

Poor little Christina, coming back across those fields with her face all red and her hair all a mess. Mr Mansfield laughing, saying they'd been playing tag. Tag! I ask you. I used to get the old copper out and give her a bath. Lots of hot water. Sometimes I managed to get some bath salts from Miss Minnie. They made the water smell nice. She used to have dirt right up under her fingernails. She never said a word. Just looked at me with those big brown eyes. Poor little bugger, frightened out of her wits. Jim told me I was making it up but he knew I wasn't, he knew all right. "Stop your nonsense, Em", he'd say, "stop your bloody nonsense!" He wouldn't let me say anything because if I had we'd have lost everything, see - the bakery, our livelihood. We'd 've lost the roof over our heads. Only I didn't know it then.

I see her sometimes. As a little girl. Christina, yes. In the garden. I do. I'm surprised you haven't seen her yet. You should be able to see her. She knows you're here. She knows.

You look just like her. It's all right, love. Come here. Come here and give me a hug. Shh, shh, never mind eh, never mind. She knows. She knows you're here with me.

HARRIET

I don't know what they diagnosed it as. A nervous breakdown probably. They called them that then, didn't they. They were almost fashionable. Her nineteenth nervous breakdown. For all I know, the Stones wrote that song about my bloody mother. Wouldn't surprise me.

When I was a child – when she was mad - before I went to bed my father would always make me go up to say goodnight to her. I'd go into their bedroom and not be able to see anything at first because all the blinds were drawn. They kept it really cold with the air conditioning unit blaring away. It would always be freezing in their bedroom. I hated the dark and the cold, air-conditioned air. Sometimes my father would sit with my mother in that freezing, dark, dead room for days on end. I had forgotten how frightened I used to be when they were like this, I don't know how he stood it. There'd be this faint smell of rotting oranges from the disgusting tea Gloria made from saved rinds she dried on a wire in the kitchen. The cold, stale air. And my mother. A tiny figure in the huge, white bed. Wrapped up like a corpse in a winding sheet. Half alive. I remember wondering if she didn't get up, would she shrivel up too, like the orange peel? Would her skin go all brown and tight and start to smell? I know I wished often she would just go. I don't know where I meant, just go away somewhere. Anywhere. I just hated the hold she had over our lives without making any effort to participate in them. She held all the power playing this victim thing. Most of all I hated it that my father could still love her. How *could* he?

For ages my father kept telling people she was homesick. Then that she had migraines. And then this Indian bloke, a doctor, started coming to the house late at night. And one morning I got up and my mother wasn't there. The bed had been stripped and all the windows were wide open. There was a light film of dust on all the furniture. I thought she'd died. And, yes. I was relieved. How could I not have been? Living that way had been torture for all of us.

But they'd taken her to this play called Mount St Bernadette. It was an old monastery sort of place. Not monastery. Nunnery? Mission? I don't know, what's the difference. I don't remember it really. I only went there once, to visit her with my father. The nuns only let *him* see her in the end, I had to wait outside. Oh, right. Nuns, so nunnery then. Who cares.

I wore the dress, the one there's the photograph of her making, the one she with the red silk roses and matching sash. Gloria had finished sewing the hem so I could wear it to show her. But they wouldn't let me in to see her so she never got to see it. I don't think my mother ever saw me in that dress. Served her right. One of the nuns took me into the garden. She showed me how I could suck nectar from the insides of hibiscus flowers. You pull out the stamen and at the bottom is this blob of nectar. That's how I remember it anyway.

Afterwards my father took me to the King's Park Hotel for dinner. We sat at a huge round table and I was given a cushion from the cocktail lounge so my chin didn't rest on the table. Father smoked all the time, Benson and Hedges cigarettes. We had a French waiter. He said I was very well-behaved. He said English children were much better behaved than French children. He kept bringing all this food, flourishing it grandly, on huge, silver platters. I think my father thought it would be a treat but I was just overwhelmed. And all the food was much too rich for me. It still makes me sad to think of it. I've seen men in just the same position, on their own with their children in hotel restaurants, usually at Christmas time, thinking it's a nice grown-up treat for their daughters when really it's just awkward and sad. I sat there, desperate that I grow up faster. I wanted to be eighteen, and tall and thin. I wanted to wear beautiful grown-up dresses like my mother did. I didn't want to be his fat, seven-year-old daughter in a homemade dress, listening to him telling me about how he'd proposed to my mother on the Spanish Steps in Rome.

They had got married after my grandfather died. I never knew my grandfather, he was killed in a car accident. But Claudia, my aunt, always talked – well, talks, still does - about my maternal grandfather in glowing terms. Claudia and I used to talk about the family a lot, when I was younger. My mother never spoke of her parents and I wanted to fill in the whole picture. She's all right, Aunt Claudia. She doesn't hate me, like the rest of them. Because she knows who I really am, what I'm really about; she sees me as a person in my own right, beneath all the shit of being my mother's daughter. The others, they just want to blame someone. I'm their scapegoat.

Gloria was against my mother going to St Bernadette's. There was this disgusting episode when she begged my father to bring her home. She was literally crying at his feet, moaning and pulling at his legs. God knows what she imagined a bunch of bloody nuns could do to my mother up there. But she must have thought something to have been so upset about it. Or maybe my mother had just beguiled her like she had a habit of doing. It was usually women who fell prey to my mother, especially ones with torrid pasts. Yeah, dig the irony. Doesn't get on with her own fucking daughter but helps all these bloody 'wimmin' friends of her. Sophie high-and-mighty Dexter-Lawson-oh-so-posh was one of them. God knows what she and my mother were about when they were young. There are stories.

Yeah, Jemima, she was one of them. I told you about her, did I? Yeah, when I said about the sodding shoes. She was a sort of housekeeper-companion for my mother. A 'paid companion' – how pompous can you get? Well, Jemima, she was the last one wasn't she, the last of Mother's bewitchings. Another poor little damaged bird that needed saving. What crap. Another weak-willed person with nothing in their own life, who could be relied on to develop a crush on my oh-so-glamorous mother.

Okay. Trinidad. So my mother had become very unpredictable by the time she went away to the nuns. She would have these phases where she would get up and wander about the house like she was in a trance. Like she was sleep-walking. And then the next day she'd be perfectly normal, wanting to play with me in the garden, wanting to read me stories. Then the next, wailing like some bloody banshee. It was awful. I just never knew what she'd be like. Can you imagine what that's like for a child?

Aunt Claudia came out for a holiday but she just missed one of my mother's mad phases. She only stayed for a fortnight. Poor Aunt Claudia, she absolutely hated it. Hated the heat, hated the ex-pat wives, hated all the socializing and absolutely detested all the parties my parents gave. She was really fat then and I don't think that helped. And there we were with faintly Trinidadian accents and she with her South East London twang. No, she doesn't have it now. But she used to be right gor-blimey.

Anyway, Aunt Claudia's visit really brought mother up short, made her behave herself for a bit. That's how I know it wasn't genuine, see? It was all this evil game my mother played. But Aunt Claudia must've guessed what had been going on. Mother had been very good at deceiving me and my dad and all the servants. She deceived us all the time. She even pretended to care about *me*, did this big number about how I was her precious daughter, blah blah blah. But only because Aunt Claudia was there.

The thing Aunt Claudia couldn't get – still doesn't - was how bad it had been for me. I was a *child*, for god's sake! I had no stability, a lunatic mother, a father on the edge because of her and surrounded by all these ex-pat women, in and out of each other's husbands' beds, the husbands shagging the living daylights out of anything that moves. Of course it was like that, you can't be that naïve. It was the bloody sixties.

For all that I want to admire Claudia's down-to-earth attitude to these things, I wish she could have understood how frightening it was for me then. She still thinks my not talking was just a little fad.

I didn't speak at all as a little girl. They told you that? Oh. Well, it's simple; I thought if I locked myself up tight I would be safe. I had to put something between me and the world. Me and other people. Between me and my mother. But what happened? Nothing. My mother had everybody's attention, everybody crooning over her. Nobody was given the chance to see that I was terrified, petrified by my mother's madness. Stunned into silence by it.

There was one good thing that came out of all the shit that went on then - my mother being up at that nuthouse nunnery place. My father and I got close. We had to. *I* had to. I was a small child. I needed him and I needed routine. We had this ritual every night where I would wait on the verandah for him to come home from the yard. First I would hear the rumble of his huge old car. It took eleven minutes for the car to wind down the hill into the valley. I used to time it. Counting the seconds. Six hundred and sixty seconds.

When he'd poured himself a drink we would sit together on the back verandah and watch the sun go down. And he'd tell me what had happened at the yard that day or at the racetrack if it had been a race day. I'd curl up under his arm. He always smelt of sweet hay and sawdust. He would find flakes of maize in his pockets and give them to me. They were like hard cornflakes, more chewy. I was happy. I began to trust being happy.

People would come for supper, friends of my parents or business associates of my father's. Sometimes one of the wives would come to cook for us when it was Gloria's night off. When my mother first went to Mount St Bernadette we got lots of the other wives, especially the British ones, offering to help out. Some of them were definitely on the make. I might've been a child but I could tell the difference between a solicitous touch on the arm and a *soliciting* clutch of the hand. A chair positioned just a bit too close or angled for intimacy. Dorothy was my favourite of the wives. She was American and made me things my mother would have hated, big fat steaks with candied yams, peanut butter and jam sandwiches, banana Nesquik, as often as I liked. And she always brought ice-cream from the American supermarket. She made great breakfasts. French toast and pancakes with syrup. My father loved her breakfasts.

Well of course things went on. My father was the most handsome man on the island. And there were a lot of very bored women. And like I said, it was the swinging sixties when swinging meant shagging, right? Well, it's a classic, isn't it, don't be thick. The mad invalid wife and the tall, dark, handsome – rich - husband. But y'know what? I am quite sure my mother knew exactly what was going on. I'm positive she had every intention of creating all this high drama while she was hiding in her fancy nuthouse. Because then she could be seen to burst out into the limelight again, dashing everyone's hopes. Like one of Uncle Joseph's plays. No, not that. A fucking French farce.

BUTTONS

Eleanor looks closer. On the front is a Constable picture. *Flatford Mill*. A small child with bare feet sitting on a draught horse in the shade of some trees. Bits of the picture are repeated on the sides, in ovals, little cameos. The gold decoration is chipped. Some of the images have faded almost completely away. "Reeds Bakery" in small, etched, copperplate lettering, in the top right-hand corner of the lid. The corners are slightly bent and rusted. When she opens the tin there is a smell of wax and stale cake. Madeira perhaps, or a light Victoria sponge with a layer of cream and strawberry jam. Or mince pies at Christmas, with pastry so short they fall apart in your hands. Eleanor imagines sticky children's hands held out like tiny starfish. And a grown-up spitting onto a hanky that has a lipstick blot on it, and dabbing icing sugar from the edges of children's sugary smiles.

A tin of sweet, sticky things. She thinks of the old lady, Emmy Reed, in her tumbledown cottage, seeing shadows in the garden. Here, Eleanor. Won't you have some cake? Here, have a slice of life. Well, just a tiny piece, it's very rich. Eleanor smiles again and stretches her legs out in front of her, the tin on her lap held tight between her palms. What sweet nourishment for a hungry heart.

An envelope, so soft from handling, it feels like chamois. It has buttons sewn on part of it, in neat rows according to size and shade. A tidy task. There is an address on the envelope. Sophie Dexter in c/o Georges Beaumont, RCA, Kensington. The 'K' of Kensington is out of line, below the 'e'. No stamp. Inside the envelope is a crescent of hair. A bit creepy. It's very thick, an orange gold. If she held it to her own, it would be a perfect match.

A cork from a bottle of champagne, with a sixpence stuck in the end. For luck. Krug. She wiggles the coin but it is stuck fast.

A photograph of a man beside an old car. He wears a hat. Big black boots. His top button is undone, the tie askew. She holds the photograph up to the light. The suit looks a little tatty. She can't see the man's eyes. The shadow from his hat obscures the top of his face. The chain of a fob watch looped on the front of his waistcoat.

A pressed rose, faded with age, between two pieces of white card. As she picks it up she sees it has left an imprint, like a blood-brown stain. A pair of tiny gold scissors underneath, with curved points.

A pen and ink sketch on a piece on cream vellum. It's

folded irregularly as if it were once screwed up. The ink in the creases has almost gone, leaving the image looking cracked, like crazed china. In the foreground a tree, meadows behind, a path disappearing into a copse on the horizon; and what seems to be three shadowy figures either going into or coming out of the wood.

A postcard. A reproduction. *Lot and his Daughters. Unanimously ascribed to Bonifazio.* Written on the back in black ink, 'Voluptas or virtus?'. Nothing else. No address or postage. She turns it over to look at the image. One woman holds a mirror. What's the symbolism? Not virtue. Intellect or wisdom, she thinks. And prudence? The other pours wine for her father. She remembers some bible story Tom's boyfriend Martin had told her, what *was* that?

Two angels came to Sodom.

Of course. The story of Lot. Genesis. The destruction of Sodom. Lot's wife. Lot's *daughters*. She doesn't understand, why is this postcard in here? Eleanor never paid enough attention in her RE class. Nobody did. The RE teacher had been blind. The teacher had spent a whole term reading the whole of Genesis out loud. Most of the girls spent the time trying to get the guide dog's attention. Throwing bits of paper at it to make it at least move. But Eleanor had been fascinated by the teacher's fingers, skating along the rows of Braille. She had been wondering how words looked in a blind person's head. Not rows of letters but what? And did they have colours? Could blind people *have* synesthesia?

Eleanor has a modern bible somewhere. God knows where it came from, haha. In full colour. There are smiling faces on the front, all the different nationalities of the world. Very hip language. But the print is very small. Here it is.

The elder daughter said to her sister, "Let's make our father drunk so that we can sleep with him" and that night they gave him wine to drink.

"Oh my God, oh my God."

She closes her eyes tight against her thoughts. It's nearly dawn. She gets up slowly to pull back the curtains. The sun is just coming up and as she stands there, it rises above the horizon. So bright.

CHRISTINA

There is a gap here. I don't understand why I can't see the pictures. I am sinking. It's cold. I want air but… the air is heavy and cold.

I can feel Harriet on my shoulder, as a baby. Even this small she fights so hard, her fists pound on my chest as if she can't bear for me to hold her. I love you, Harriet. You don't know what you mean to me. Please don't cry, please don't cry. I wish I could explain to you. One day, my darling child, one day.

A tiny, hot, makeshift airport. I love to travel, that feeling of suspended animation. Suspended above the earth. Suspended in time. Everything delights me. Oh, we are hovering above London. The orderliness of that view. The pilot has a clipped British accent. Descending, descending. Everything so rich and green. I didn't know how desperate

I was to see patchwork fields green and thick, waxy hedgerows. And the softness of the hills' folds. Cherry blossom! My throat aches. I want to cry with gratitude for all of this. I thought I would never see this again.

Flint Cross. Emmy at the door. We are hugging. She wears a floral dress from the '40s. Nothing has changed. For a moment I can be a child again, safe in her arms. I feel my heart, finally stirring in my chest, unfurling, opening. When Emmy hugs me her spirit slips under my skin, like a film of protection. I need this.

The nights are so quiet. I feel my body, my mind, my whole being stretching out again, uncoiling. I think, I wish I could capture this coolness, this peace, take it and give it to my baby girl. My Harriet. But she was born into a burnt and brittle landscape where the sun is too hot and the mosquitoes whine and the women moan. Where I am charred beyond recognition. I fear my marriage is nothing but cinders; love has blistered in the heat and my fragile heart has split its skin because it is so parched. Scorched. I pretend I don't hear the murmurings, late at night. Edward thinks I am all right now. He thinks Harriet makes it all right. He doesn't see that I have to protect her from me.

Still Harriet cries. Why? What do you need from me? I would give you anything but I have nothing. Why do you fight, wrestling with me as if I were pinning you down? You are like a butterfly writhing on a pin. Perhaps you know, perhaps you see the black black tar of my soul. But, my baby, your crying pulls the stitches that I thought would hold my heart in one piece. Don't you see, I am only trying to protect you? I want to love you so much but I think if I love you I will suffocate you. I will destroy you. My baby baby girl.

Noise. Voices. Children clamouring. A large woman in a too-tight dress. Oh - my sister Claudia. So fat now! There is something undone about her, something unravelling and desperate. I can almost touch it. Her image is unclear at the edges. Joe, her husband, dear, soft Joe, holding the hand of a toddler, little Sarah, their first child. What a terrible haircut. Why do mothers cut their small children's hair into that ugly pudding basin shape, like children from an institution? They think children have no pride. Perhaps it is spite. I wouldn't put it past Claudia. Her little girl is very pretty and Claudia wouldn't like that.

Claudia? Her face wavers before me. I touch her cheek to make sure she's really here. There is some shift here, some slip in the reality. And shadows of people I don't recognize. Shouting and anger and I can see shadow hands picking at my sister and I can hear the slap of their palm slicks as figures tumble between us, tumbling and rolling, like lunatics in undone straitjackets, their sleeves and leather straps flapping. I need to talk to Claudia but I know that the words won't make it through the snagging, vicious thicket of anger and guilt and the years and years of ignoring that stretch between us. And the shadows, dancing madly around us, pointing at me. I was the one. Claudia got away and I was the one.

Chatter, chatter, chatter. Claudia chatters as she unwraps cakes. She picks the crumbs from the gaudy packing. Peck, peck, like a nervous bird. Peck, peck, crumbs and words. My hands move in front of me. My lips form words but I am only half here. I am one of the tumbling lunatics, wrapped up in a jacket so my arms can't move.

Sarah whispers to her mother, I hear her ask 'Mummy, Mummy, is she a princess?' Claudia slaps the child on the arm, 'Don't be so silly, Sarah, honestly!' I turn to the little girl and I tell her, "Gosh, no, thank goodness. I would hate to be a princess. They have to do all sorts of horrid things - sleep on a mattress with a pea underneath. Kiss frogs. Yuk!" I am kneeling in front of her as I speak. She puts her hands on my shoulders. I see myself in her bright blue eyes, eyes just like her daddy Joseph. Oh, she has a beautiful, warm soul, this child. She will find it a little hard out there.

I am no princess. I am Rapunzel, banished to the woods while the witch lures up my prince. See her fetch the scissors that cut the braid. Tiny golden scissors. In my lap there are wet snakes of orange-gold hair and writhing coils of lies.

Shhh. Listen. Late at night. Emmy and I are sitting in the scullery. On the table is my old crayon tin. The one with the Constable picture on it. I loved it when I was little, I loved the big, strong horse. I imagined myself to be the barefoot child, sitting atop his sturdy back. Here a postcard from my mother, a biblical scene, I've seen the real thing in a gallery. And the envelope with buttons on. I had forgotten my buttons. Look, look. Little Harriet is curled up to Emmy's chest, snuffling softly in her sleep, finally subdued. Quiet. Still. Soft. But somewhere, far off, I can hear a child chattering. Emmy hears it too. She looks at me. We nod. We smile. We know.

Trinidad. It's the rainy season. Grey, heavy clouds. Heavy clouds that don't descend in one big breath of grey, oh, no, they spread as shadowy tendrils, feathery. Bird-wings stretching inside my chest. Or a web, sticking and light but suffocating me, growing like a cancer up into my mind. The air in my lungs is stale. I am in a vacuum. Everything outside of me is still. I sleep. Curled up on Edward's lap. It is too much effort to blink, too much to breathe. I am trapped in myself. I have no more energy. I am stuck. I cannot crawl outside my mind. The rain is too noisy. Please be quiet, please be quiet. Harriet be quiet! Don't you understand that breathing is too much effort? I wish it wasn't this way, my baby girl. I am so sorry. I am so sorry.

Wait. I can hear the windows rattle. The tiles beneath my feet are cracking. Above my head the light bulb dances on its wires. All the stars are falling. Gloria, my beloved Gloria, is grabbing my hand. She is shouting because the house is roaring. Our house in Trinidad. And Edward is not here. I call for him, Edward, Edward! We are running, running, Gloria and I, down the corridor to the kitchen. Where is Harriet, where's my baby? Singh has brought her. He has wrapped her in an old blanket from his own bed. He hands her to me. She looks like she is sleeping. The lashes on her cheeks look as if they are painted on. China doll. She is so still while everything around us is crumbling.

Stop! What is this? Everything is slowing down. What

is this? The house is quiet. I sit in Gloria's chair. Rocking, rocking. We are safe but still I see the people digging in the rubble. A woman is looking for her baby. I feel the flesh on her hands as she is scrabbling in the dirt. Listen. Someone is singing. It's a lullaby. No, perhaps a requiem. No one is here but Harriet and me, but someone is singing. They are very close, I can feel their breath on my neck. Are they singing for me? Harriet is quiet at last. I hope she is still breathing. I wouldn't want her to stop breathing. I would give her my very last breath.

STARS

"I don't know what to do. I don't know what to do for the best."

Willard walks down the steps in front of Eleanor. She imagines the words being shuffled in his head. She feels a strange calm. Nothing can surprise her any more. Numb. She is grateful for that. She is grateful for so much. She is grateful that she has Willard who is always there, who has always been there, the figure in the photographs and the real person, connecting a million dots to make her world. Willard is here and he will help her join up the dots and the dots will plug the holes in her heart. She hopes.

She catches him up and they walk down into the chill, into the cloisters of the cathedral. They join a group of tourists with bored eyes and mouths. It is cold today but colder down here, underneath the spires whose tips pierce the heavy, rain-filled clouds. Above Willard and Eleanor, a group of choristers practise a psalm. Their voices echo in the hollows.

For the best. Why did I say that? It's for the best. Why do I keep saying these stupid things? This scenario surely needs more that such common-place remarks. Such platitudes. Gratitude, platitude, latitude. How much latitude do I have here, how much of this picture will be restored and how much comes from me? And this tiny dot, just here, that has to be joined up, that will not be rubbed out. And I thought I had the courage to paint what I wanted to paint. To be what I wanted to be. Single. No dependants. Sole occupancy. All these years I have been designing my own life, sketching, painting pretty pictures. And now as I hold the brush, the paint drops off the bristles. It drips onto my skin and it burns like hot wax.

She drops coins into the box and takes a card and a candle. She is not remotely religious, but somehow this solemn observance feels right to her. Willard comes to stand beside her. He smells faintly of mothballs. She smiles up at him. He puts his hand over hers, guiding the wick of her new, smooth candle to the flickering flame. She sees the cuff of his coat is frayed. As their candle catches alight the original flame snuffs out. Smoky coils disappear into the darkness. A light for a light. A life for a life. She tries to read the words on the card she is holding but her eyes are full of tears. She hears Willard reciting the words, his voice a low resonant hum beneath the itchy scuffle of tourists. A blob of wax drips onto her shoe.

Why did Peter have to ring? What is he doing in Montana? Of course, he was checking up on me. The moment I heard his voice I could feel his fingers on my heart, closing around it tight, stopping the valves. I stood there, in the dark, biting my tongue, biting my tongue so hard it ought to have bled. I should have known he would go on being cruel. I should have known he would check up on me because he is a coward. I could hear his spite in the muscle-tight, jaw-tight words. All the way across the miles.

Willard's arm is around her shoulders, leading her away. She leans into him, anxious for warmth, anxious for comfort. She wishes Joan were here, she wishes she could ask her advice. Joan always knew what to do for the best.

My mum Joan taught me to believe I could do anything, be anything. And as I got older - and started to learn that sometimes we don't always manage what we set out to achieve - she taught me how to laugh at myself, how to take the tumbles laughing so I didn't break any limbs, so my pride and my courage remained intact. She taught me how to fall, to tuck and roll, tumble and fall and then get up again. Dust myself off, dust off my pride.

When I was thirteen I wanted so desperately to play Juliet in the school production. For weeks I practised my audition piece and every afternoon my mum would take the time to sit and watch me rehearse, with my tattered, dog-eared copy of the play on her lap. And in spite of my relentless renditions she never ceased to be stirred by the piece. "O happy dagger!" and her hand would go to her mouth. "This is thy sheath; there rust, and let me die" and I would see her eyes moisten and the flush of her cheeks. She would smile and get up from her chair to stand, clapping and clapping. And then my Dad would come home and she'd say "Patrick, I think we've an actress in our midst, you know, quite a little superstar in the making" and I'd feel so proud and clever and puffed up, like my chest would burst.

But I didn't get the part. Laura Maddox did, a dumpy blonde fourth former, with breasts. It must've been the boobs that did it, she couldn't act her way out of a paper bag. I was devastated. And furious at Mum because she had made me believe I was good enough, had made me believe I might be a star. I felt I had been set up and betrayed. I remember sulking for days, not speaking to my mother. What I really wanted was a row, a real shouting match with mum, but she wouldn't be drawn. She just carried on as usual, letting me huff and puff until I had quite huffed and puffed myself out.

Then one Saturday afternoon they came and found me, Mum and Dad. I was sprawled, still sulking, on my bed in my room. Mum had been in the kitchen making a cake. She was wearing her customary old black plimsolls, the kind with the stretchy elastic bit across the front, and they were speckled with flour. My Dad had this old curtain as a cape. Mum had two skeins of wool pinned above each ear to resemble long hair. They were giggling like children. Then they started acting out the balcony scene from Romeo and Juliet, leaping about my bedroom, on the bed and off, Dad tripping over his curtain cape, mum holding her wool hair in place. And I laughed. We laughed. We laughed until our sides ached. I loved them for that. I love them for all of that.

And then mum said we all deserved a good cup of tea. Tea was medicine in our house. We trooped downstairs to the kitchen and there on the table was a plate of pale yellow biscuits, shaped like stars and on every one was my name, in tiny, pink, sugar-icing letters.

"Eleanor?"

They are sitting in the car outside her house, Eleanor and Willard. She didn't notice the journey. She feels suspended somehow, as if she is stuck between two time zones. She doesn't know which to pick. The memories are so comforting, so sweet. She suddenly craves sweet tea.

Like the tea those plump ladies used to bring you after you'd given blood. Sickly sweet tea and a digestive biscuit. They used to take your blood at the local school hall, but now they have a hard white mobile unit that comes every six months. They offer you orange squash. There aren't any plump ladies. There are hard white nurses who are rough with the needles and who test you for Aids. There aren't any biscuits. Everything is so hard and efficient now, where has all the softness gone?

"Are you sure you don't want me to see you into the house, check everything's all right?"

Willard is as gentlemanly as always. Her Guardian Angel. When her mother first died, Willard came round each night to check the house, room by room. She'd felt childish about it. But tonight she must be by herself. She has so much to think about. So much to process. It isn't just the decisions she has to make that will shape her future but those other people made that shaped her past. So much regret. So much loss. So much to regret and to lose.

And anyway, Will, the bogeyman's already got me. And I'm getting to know most of the skeletons in my cupboards. And all I will find under my bed are biscuit crumbs. And stardust that has lost its light. And bits of my name, trodden in the dirt.

"Nightie-night, Will. Thank you for taking me out. I needed to get out."

She is out of the car before he can give her another hug. She is floundering in her grief and one more drop would have her drown.

CHRISTINA

Night. My room. Here. A brass bed, very narrow. A crucifix above the bedhead. A table with a cracked saucer for night candles. The nuns have cool hands and voices. When I speak I catch them looking at each other. They know. Outside the window there are scarlet hibiscus flowers, full and voluptuous. Voluptus, virtus. I can hear one of the nuns talking to Harriet. Harriet won't answer because she will not speak. Her voice is trapped. Somewhere inside her. Somewhere inside me. And it is all my fault. I have broken my baby girl. I have made her too scared of the world.

Edward looks very handsome this afternoon. He is being a little rough because he is anxious. Is it guilt that makes him behave like this? Lies won't fit in this room where the air is smooth and still. He is chatting to me about Dorothy and about how she isn't leaving her husband. I feel the breath pushed out of me. Edward is saying how she will be going back to America. He holds my hand. Does he need forgiveness? Are the voices I've heard the ones who tell the truth? You see, Edward, I know that there is your truth, my truth and then there's the truth. You ask for my forgiveness that she took your attention. This is the other side of Edward, the other side of the fire. Where it is light and the flames cauterize my soul. I cannot live without Edward. He tells me that he cannot live without me. There is only a solution, resolution. Nothing life-changing after all.

I stare at the crucifix above the bed and see, as if superimposed, the image of a saint, the saint I used to see in the stained-glass windows of my father's warehouse at home at Hunter's Lodge. The robes he wears are black and red. Soul sorcerer. Conjuring up my past, pulling out my fetid soul. Is it me who is screaming? Is that me?

Loose ends flailing. Some years here, ticking round and round, unravelled like loose film on a spool. And people are talking, very fast. Tongues wagging, shaggy dog tails and tales. Laughter? I haven't forgotten how laughter feels in the throat. Years are spinning, flip-flipping, teeth and smiles and laughter.

Here's Edward. Driving my father's old Lagonda, careering round the drive in front of Sophie's country house. Harriet is holding my hand. Harriet's laughter. She says, Mr Toad, Mr Toad, poot, poot! I love her beautiful voice. I can see Sophie in the background, her face red with laughter. And little Lizzie, Sophie's darling daughter, sitting on her uncle Willard's lap, tugging at his thatch of beard.

Lizzie calls him 'Uncle Wol', after the owl. Because she's been reading *When We Are Six*. She likes to call me Kanga. She knows it makes us laugh. We say she'll make a great comic actress.

Sophie and me again. This is in the kitchen of her parents' old house in Thurloe Square. Edward and I are renting it from them until we can move into Heron's Gate, his home in the country. The house is full of children. We're making spaghetti Bolognese, a huge pot of it. Sophie starts to sing, play acting opera. She's singing in Italian, it sounds so beautiful. But now I realise the words are names of dishes and Italian foods. She sings, her chest heaving, *insalata mista, pomodori parmigiano, un po di mozzarella*, waving her arms and leaping about the room. I can feel myself sliding down the wall, laughing. She grabs my hand, she says, do you remember, do you remember?

We're running, like children, up the stairs, half climbing, hands and feet, like children do, our palms slapping the stairs. I am short of breath. I don't know if I am laughing still or simply out of breath. We've come up to our old studio, at the very top of the house. I've been too afraid to come up here in case I hear the voices again. Sophie knows this. But there is nothing here except sunlight. I look down at my feet. The floorboards are bare and very dusty. Balls of dust, like owl pellets. Look, here is a button. A tiny silk-covered button. I bend to pick it up. Sophie watches. She says, I never got your letter, the one you said you were sending me, from Jack and Daphne's. What did it say? What was it that you said you had to tell me?

Stop.

Here's the orchard behind our beautiful house, Edward's and mine. We moved here in the spring, finally. It took a year for the builders to make it habitable. Edward's father had let it go to rack and ruin. I planted that may tree. Oh, the anemones in the copse! My heart is bursting so see this, I love the spring. I love this house, every bird and every tree and every brave daffodil and every stone and every clod of earth.

See the horses there, in the shade at the edge of the copse, in the front paddock. See them dozing, nose to tail. The days seem so fat and rich here.

Summer now. The horses' tails switch and twitch and their heads occasionally bob away a fly. There is something about English summers, like full-blown roses, sumptuous and smiling. The horses are Doughty and Pegasus. Doughty's the chestnut. This is before the accident. Oh, how I love my horses. Peg was the gift from Edward, my birthday surprise, my birthday foal.

I'm in the garden. Mr Noble is the gardener. Hear the click click click of the shears. He cuts the beech hedge twice a year and always by hand. It runs round the whole of the lower lawns. In the spring he wears a panama hat and in the winter an old flying helmet, the flaps tied down, under his chin in a neat bow. His hands are twisted with arthritis. They remind me of ginger roots. He drinks his tea in the greenhouse. He says it's warmest in there. I give him three biscuits, two plain, one chocolate. I've seen him dunking the plain ones in his tea. He saves the chocolate one until last and when he eats it he closes his eyes.

See, I'm working on part of the terrace with the children, Sarah and Lizzie and Harriet, we are making a mosaic. Harriet doesn't want to be here, she always wants to be somewhere else, she's never still. Her energy is like a messy charcoal scribble. From up here you can see the sea. The black and white tiles I am using for the mosaic come from the Dexter's old house in Tuscany. I remember their cool kiss on my feet when I was a young woman. Black and white tiles, like chess. I remember watching Jack and Edward on the terrace of that old, Italian house, all those years ago and if I look hard enough I know could see them again. But I don't need to. They were playing games with my life, picking up the pieces and stitching them together. Saving some, discarding others. And Jack pawning my heart for a life. Because Edward had saved Jack's life. Life. Love. Lives and lovers. An eye for an eye and a truth for a lie.

The pattern I make in the mosaic is a heron. Its eye is where I have got to, it's meant to be like a whirlpool. It draws the eye deeper and deeper. It feels good to kneel in the dirt. I kneel before forces bigger than me. Some I love. There is nature, trees and birds and the feel of the sea over my bare feet and the sound of the horses wickering to me. And then there is my mind. I have pills to stop my mind's eye going deeper and deeper. The pills give me courage. Courage and trust. Sophie says I have to learn to trust, I have to be brave enough to trust. She comes to see me every day. When she speaks to me, everything I feel is smoothed out and cool, like ceramic. And still. Like the space I was in at St Bernadette's only this is home and I am safe. Or am I?

I am waiting for something. I'm waiting for some news.

That's Harriet, at the window. She is sixteen. She is staring down at me and her father. She refuses to come out of her room. She lives in the house like a ghost. She refuses to eat. I know she is hiding alcohol in her room, I can smell it. I wave up at her. She just stares. Glassy-eyed. Magpie eyes. She has been caught stealing again. Jewellery from a shop in Knightsbridge. The police brought her home. When Edward asked her about it she laughed. Magpie child. Cuckoo in the nest. She is waiting. She was always waiting for her moment.

I can hear Edward's footsteps on the gravel. Feet on gravel. The dogs raise their heads. Edward comes to me and takes my hand to help me up. He is shaking his head. I see my shadow stretching on the side of the house like it is coming away from my feet, like I am breaking away from me. We walk up the garden. Mr Noble snips at the hedge. The sound is so close to my face, snip, snip, snip, I feel the blades so close to my neck. People are talking, whispering. No one hears, why can't they hear the voices?

Shhh! Edward's voice. It's so clear. He sounds so like Jack used to sound. He reaches for me, wrapping me in his arms. Like that first time. Saving me from myself. His hand is on my hair, stroking my hair. He says, perhaps it is for the best, my darling, for the best, after all these years. She died in an accident. I don't believe him because if she's no longer in this world then where is she? I don't find anything of her in the shadows. The shadow children who come to dance in the garden at night are all strangers. She would not be a stranger to me. I would know if she had died. Edward, you didn't have to lie.

My hands are shaking. So much deceit, staining the sky. Is it safe to tell him that the sky is falling in? Henny Penny, Henny Penny. Nothing is safe. If I let the sky fall in there will be nothing between me and the sun. Already my Pegasus's wings are melting.

Harriet. I know this is Harriet's scene. A sound like a shotgun. Glass breaking. Edward shouts. Run, run, run. There is blood on the white window frame. Up the old back stairs. Wooden stairs with splinters. I feel the splinters in my feet. I trip on my skirt and feel it tearing apart at the waist. Harriet tears me apart. Edward is hammering on the door. He is an old man. Why do I see this now? Did I see it then? Did I see it as I pushed him out of the way, as I thrust my shoulder against the old wood, again and again and again, until the lock on Harriet's door has split the wood of the doorframe? The pain in my shoulder is excruciating.

HARRIET

I hated school. All the schools. In Trinidad I went to a broken-down local school first. It was in a rickety old wooden building and the rooms smelt of pee. We were taught reading and writing by a fat Spanish woman. She wore huge stiff black dresses. They were all shiny and rustled when she moved. Above her desk she had a picture of Queen Victoria. The resemblance wasn't lost on us. We were terrified of her. She used to hit the boys' knuckles with the edge of a ruler. The room she took her lessons in was high up, a garret. You had to climb these rotting wooden steps. In the rainy season they had a slimy film. We had to climb up on our hands and knees. This teacher hated me because I wouldn't recite the words she held up. She seemed to consider it a personal insult that I refused to speak.

Then they sent me to an American school. I started to

speak then. All such a fuss to start with and then no-one took any notice. Lots of squeaky-clean boys with grown up haircuts and drip-dry shorts. I got behind in maths, so I had extra lessons after school. With an American boy called Danny. Mrs Borde was the maths teacher. She had a mobile classroom, at the far end of the playground. She was the black version of Cruella Deville. She was tall, made taller by straightened sticky hair, glued up into a bouffant style. Incredibly thin, like a stick insect. She would make us write down the combinations of numbers that made ten. If we hesitated she twisted our ears. I remember the pain. She said if we told our mummies about it she'd break our fingers. She made Danny's ears bleed. Danny used to cry. I saved the biscuits from my lunch box and shared them with Danny after the lesson. They were animal shapes with hard pink icing. We would nibble all the icing off first. I remember the feeling, sitting there on a bench, eating biscuit after biscuit. Sometimes I'd be there for hours because my mother would have forgotten to tell Singh to pick me up. The school was scary when no one was there. Danny used to say that this was what it would be like if the world had ended. He said his Daddy thought there was going to be a nuclear war. His father worked for the American government. Danny was eight years old and he liked to talk about death. He used to say 'How would we know if we were dead? What if we were dead and we didn't know?'

I was eleven when we came back from Trinidad. I didn't go to school until almost a year later. They sent me to a boarding school. The girls spoke with such uppercrust accents and guffawed like boys. They teased me about my voice. They said I spoke like a darkie. Angela was my only friend. She had protruding eyes and sticky out ears and very messy blonde hair. She looked like a troll. Angela always sounded as if she had a cold because she was deaf, so she sort of talked through her nose. I think she could hear a little, I don't know. She wore crescent-shaped hearing aids behind both ears. She spoke very loudly in a sort of roar, her words sort of over-rounded, in a thick stream, without consonants. When we went out to church on Sundays, whoever you walked with you had to sit next to in the pew. I was always stuck with Angela and Angela liked to sing. She always joined in the hymns. I don't know why they let her. They should have stopped her. Everybody would stare and the teachers who had come with us would look straight ahead, with their spinster lips all tight. Spitting out the words of the hymn like they were spitting out some disgusting, bitter food. I never sang. I can't sing. Angela always sang. The other girls always laughed.

At school there were six girls to a dormitory. They were ordinary rooms but we still called them dorms. They had that rotting smell, like dead lizards, like the smell I could remember from underneath the stilts of the houses in Trinidad. My father called it The Smell of the Great Unwashed. Sweaty plimsolls and sheets that were rarely laundered, just turned, top to bottom and over, every week. The smell was overlaid with Roger & Gallet soap that some of the girls got sent by their silly mothers.

The girl in the bed next to me was called Rosalind.

Rosalind was very religious and she hated to be dirty. She took cleanliness being next to godliness literally. She had nosebleeds, so she got her bedclothes washed every couple of days, instead of just once a month like the rest of us. Rosalind always smelt of starch and lavender. Her mother had her clothes laundered outside the school and her laundry was collected and delivered every Wednesday by a man in a dark green van. The clean things fascinated us. They would come back all starched and folded in a canvas laundry sack, with a little damask bag of lavender at the bottom.

Rosalind came home with me for a weekend once. She hated it. She said the house smelt of dogs and horses and my father smelt of whisky. She told my father over supper that alcohol was the blood of the devil. He thought this was hilarious. He started laughing his huge laugh and he leapt up from the chair, started chasing us across the room. Rosalind was terrified. She screeched like a stuck pig. He caught me and tickled me. I loved being tickled by my father.

Angela came home with me once, too. My mother had one of her Mad Hatter's Tea parties on the Sunday. That's what my father called them. He pretended to enjoy them, joined in, indulging my mother always. They invited all these people, some of them they hardly knew. Let them come to our house and stuff themselves stupid with sandwiches and cake. My mother and Sophie Lawson would stay up most of the night making cakes. They were always drunk. I would hear them screeching with laughter in the scullery. The cakes always sagged in the middle and sometimes they forgot to put in an ingredient, like the sugar. Everybody thought it was so funny. The grown-ups drank gin and whisky or fancy cocktails and we children had lurid orange squash.

Mother always put on music, very loud in the dining room so you could hear it in the gardens. My mother and father made cocktails and carried them out on a silver tray to the gardens. People danced. My mother asked Angela if she would like to dance. She knew she couldn't hear the music properly. They twirled round and round, completely out of time with the music. They were waving their arms and legs around, laughing. Everybody was clapping and smiling. Angela's laugh sounded like an elephant trumpeting. Or a lunatic screaming. It was just awful.

My mother always had to have a project. She liked to make things. She said crazy things about creativity being the life force. Jesus. Once she painted up an old bicycle for me. Did I tell you? I wanted to do the Cycling Proficiency Test at school in the summer. The school provided bicycles if you didn't have one to bring from home but they were really disgusting, the sort of bikes small children have, painted pink with white tyres and ribbons on the handlebars. I finally persuaded her that I needed a bicycle of my own. So she gave me this ancient boy's bicycle that they had found in the old stables. She had painted it herself. You could tell. The paint was thin in some places and in others had formed sticky globules, like wax. She'd painted it pillarbox red like a postman's bike. I didn't want to take it back to school with me but my father insisted, said my mother would be heartbroken if I didn't. When the girls at school saw it of course they took the piss out of me. They called me Postie. I wrote to my mother to tell her just what I thought of her stupid bike. My father wrote back saying how much my letter had upset her. Good. So she knew what it felt like.

I left boarding school when I was fifteen. I wasn't expelled, they just thought it would be better if I was living at home. So I went to the local grammar school instead. There were some really wild girls there, they were great fun. We got ourselves quite a reputation. We were the gang that smoked behind the bike sheds and stole make up from Woolworth's. And skived on games afternoons to go down the town to try on everything in Top Shop.

The gang was led by a girl called Jill. You had to watch Jill. You might be her firm friend one day and her worst enemy the next. Jill had a fat sidekick called Georgina who was very butch. They called her George. If you fell foul of Jill, George would be sent to intimidate you. Often you hadn't a clue what you might have done. I was only in the gang because I lived in a big house with horses and dogs. Jill and the other girls liked that. And I could get money and take them up to London. Jill and I went to Knightsbridge a couple of times. Harvey Nicks for lunch. That's funny. We'd go there to nick stuff. It was great. Jill had a crush on my father – no, all the girls had crushes on him, the girls and their mothers. Some of the girls thought my mother had been a model. I told them she was once a mad artist but never a model.

There was a teacher at that school called Mrs Stewart. Bitch. Sometimes I *still* think of the things I'd like to say to her. I imagine writing to the school to find out if she's still there. I imagine the letter and everything. But I expect she's long dead. I hope so. She used to wear long skirts in bright colours, with great wide belts round her waist. And tailored blouses. With neat little jackets in bobbly wools. She ran the drama group. She chose really obscure plays that nobody understood. Sophocles, or social statement plays by her theatrical friends, which the parents complained about.

She also took psychology classes. Once she made me stand up in one of her psychology lessons, in front of everybody. She told the rest of the class that I was an example of a personality being distorted by self-pity. She told them all about me not speaking when I was little, why I spoke the way I did now. She knew everything. My mother must have told her, the cow. She said I would ruin my life if I didn't stop feeling sorry for myself. She said I had to let my aggression out, not hold it in against myself. Afterwards she took me into the stationery room. We sat on some boxes. She put her arm round me. She had chalk dust on her sweater. She smelt of Joy, the perfume my grandmother used. I was crying and I didn't have a tissue. My nose dripped on my skirt. I had this pain in my chest and a funny taste in my mouth.

When I left school, Mrs Stewart gave me a book of hers.

It's called "Traps of the Mind". I still have it. Her name is in the front of it, in her big, swirly handwriting. Underneath there is a red ink blot that looks like a bloodstain. The page where she wrote an inscription to me has been torn out. I tore it out.

SAND

Eleanor stops the swing and helps the child off the seat. She is reluctantly minding her neighbour's child while her mother – she of the sniper's bullet voice – does an unexpected lunchtime shift in the pub. The child whines because she has sand in her shoes. Eleanor takes each shoe off and tips it upside down and watches the sand sift out. Enough to fill the bowl of a tiny hourglass. The sands of time. Eleanor shakes her head at the silly phrase. She feels lightheaded, delirious perhaps. The child, sitting back on the cracked, plastic swing seat looks down at her, her face one big frown.

All that time. All the way from the beginning through the middle. To this end. What was it that kept me going back? What had I been doing? And now this stupid postcard.

Eleanor puts the child's shoes back on and lifts her off the swing. She takes hold of the child's right hand with her left, and stuffs her own right hand deep into the pocket of her coat. And there is the postcard from Peter. Just two lines.

'Don't do anything until I get back.'

The child has stopped. Her feet are planted firmly and squarely in the grass. Eleanor hadn't bargained on this.

"I don't want to go any further."

"Well, if we go just a *bit* further we'll get to the magic beach. Have you ever been to the magic beach?"

The child shrugs inside her little blue cagoule but she smiles and of course makes no attempt to resist Eleanor's tug on her hand. Eleanor has planned to walk along the beach where she used to walk with her father. She has this notion that the magic will still be there. She could do with some magic. She could do with a spell that would whisk her through the next twenty-four hours without touching the sides. Without touching her insides.

'Meet me at the airport. Terminal 4. 10.15. November 5th.' And that's all it says. Remember, remember the fifth of November, gunpowder, treason, and plot. Treason.

The wind is getting up. It whips her hair across her face. Red hair, thick and shining. Would her child have ginger hair? Her child. Eleanor can smell the sea. It is drizzling slightly now and the grass beneath her feet is slippery and treacherous.

Words and definitions. For Peter there are only words, words in random patterns that never make a picture. He is just a mess of words, a jumble of definitions. Idle scribble on a page. Treason and treachery, tied in a knot, the loose ends flailing about my face. Mad words, bad words.

Eleanor can hear the sea, the push and pull of the waves over the shells. For a moment there is a break in the clouds and the sliver of sand ahead of her sparkles. Eleanor looks down from the high sea wall. Stretching out before her are cement blocks, each about three feet square, put there when *she* was a child, to keep the sea back. An artificial dam. They are covered in green, slimy seaweed that looks like coarse hair. She looks at her feet at the edge of the sea wall. Next to her, the child crouches down to look at something.

"Horses."

Her mittened fingers are tracing the shape of a hoof print. It must've been made when the cement was still very soft. The impression is very clear. She runs forward, finds another print, just at the lip of the wall. Eleanor looks down to the blocks, stretching onto the sand, and back at the hoofprints on the wall. Imagination. No horse could get down here safely. He would have to have wings. Pegasus, lifting himself high into the wind.

"Lift me, lift me!"

The child stretches up her arms. Eleanor climbs down first and then lifts her down and they start to walk along the length of the wall, on the step between it and the cement blocks, until they reach the gap that leads to the biscuit bite of beach. There is a little group, a woman and three children huddled together by the breakwaters. The woman is leaning in the breakwater shielding something and as she gets closer, Eleanor sees she is trying to light sparklers.

Remember, remember the fifth of November. His plane will have landed by now. He'll be coming through the gate looking for me. He won't even consider that I may not have come. I wonder how long he will wait? He'll have me tannoyed. My name shall be indecipherable, a distorted hiss above the airport hum.

A hiss. Several of the sparklers suddenly light up. The woman hands one to the taller child who runs off twirling the wand of white light in a smear of wind and sand and mist, laughing and shrieking. The woman calls out to the child as she hands out the other sparklers and then they are all running, the children and the woman, laughing, calling their names as they wave their sizzling lights in the wind.

My father used to bring home sparklers on bonfire night. He taught me to write my name with a sparkler. He and mum would say: a star should have her name in lights. I could never do it fast enough to see the whole word, even when I had learnt joined up writing and could do it really fast. But I still tried, every year. I can do it now.

I can still see my father, waving from the kitchen window of my own tiny house, the house I live in now. I can feel the itch of my scarf, see my breath in the damp November air. And my mother beside him putting a blanket around his too thin shoulders, wrapping her arms around his frail body.

Eleanor huddles into her coat. She takes a breath. She thinks, if she were going to name a child, what name would it be? All this time she thinks of a girl child, but what about a boy?

But this is silly. *Sentimental.* There isn't going to be a

child to call anything. She's just conjuring up silly images. Projecting them onto this beach. Confusing her past with her future. Her own childhood with her future and her future cannot hold the image of a child, it is just a trick of the light. A miasma, a *trompe d'oeil*.

She looks back at the sea wall and sees a figure standing there and for a minute, because she wants to hide from her reality and because her emotions and her imagination are out of control, she thinks it is her father she can see. But this is a different time and Patrick Ashfield isn't alive and the woman with the sea horses is not there, just a stranger with a huddle of children, lighting sparklers in the wind. And the figure on the sea wall is the child's mother, waiting to take her little girl away. So now it is time and all the sand has slipped through the hourglass of a child's life and the top of it is empty. Now is the time.

I have to do this or I will run out of time.

CLAUDIA

I had divorced my husband by the time Christina and Edward came back to live in England. *I* divorced *him,* you understand. It wasn't common, you know, that way round. It wasn't even a decade since the Married Woman's Property Act and divorce was still looked on as shameful, really and truly.

My husband and I were separated for the statutory five years before we divorced. He said he wouldn't let me off the hook that easily - those were the very words he used. Of course he was still a relatively unknown playwright then so naturally he didn't want to be on his financial uppers and while we weren't exactly living the luxurious kind of life Christina and Edward had, splitting up the family home was going to cost us both a pretty penny. We'd bought a bigger house by that stage, a little bit further out but not quite in the country. There was no mortgage on it because I'd decided to put the bit of money we finally got from Christina - from the fortune she had inherited from Dad – into the property. So my ex-husband knew that in spite of the law I'd fight for my share and he might end up with the thinner end of the wedge when it came to a sale. I don't think he relished the prospect of having to move into some poky flat in Islington with a mortgage round his neck. So don't think he held out on me for a divorce because he *cared* or because he wanted to keep the family together. That's just rot. As it turned out, of course, his career had begun to take off by the time things got sorted out between us so he never had to suffer any hardships, did he?

When they first moved back to England, Edward and Christina rented a house from Sophie Lawson. The same place they'd had that peculiar studio together when they'd been young women, when Christina switched from doing fashion sketching to her bonkers painting phase. Sophie Lawson had inherited the house. I have to tell you that the Christina who came back to England in 1971 was an entirely different person from the one I'd seen on that godforsaken island. Lively, outgoing, there simply wasn't a hint of that pathetic self-pitying little woman she'd been then. I was suspicious, of course. Looking back, I realise she would have been on very strong drugs. Well, you don't go from slashing your wrists one day - in her sixth month of pregnancy, just in case no one's had the courage to tell you that - to being the life and soul of the party without some very strong drugs, do you?

Edward was very different too. Frankly, he seemed a little frosty towards me. But he was probably just being careful because of Christina. I think he was desperate not to provoke her in any way. I didn't want to say this earlier but the fact was that Edward and I had got quite close when I was out there. There were a couple of evenings when things got a little precarious. *You* know - being in the eye of a storm together, let's say, these things can bring people together in odd ways. I can remember watching him bending to put on some music and this incredible urge to touch him, to feel the skin at the back of his neck. It was the first time in ages I'd felt the remotest physical attraction for a man. But really, I'm making too much out of this. It isn't really worth mentioning except someone's bound to tell you he and I didn't get on. And you ought to know that it was the fact that we had got on so *well* that maybe made him realise afterwards, now they were living back here in the UK, that he needed to play it down. Be unfriendly even. That's what it was about. Really and truly, he had liked me a little too much of course. Do you see?

They'd only been back in England a matter of days when Christina called to invite me up to London. I thought it was quite something to be asked, actually. Christina sounded so bright on the phone, so keen to see me, so I thought that maybe, at last, we'd get to know one another as adults, married women with children, a nice sisterly relationship. Rather than just through the years of letters and that frightful visit I'd so foolishly made. I took Sarah with me – she would have been coming up thirteen. Sarah is two years older than Harriet. When we arrived I have to say I was rather disappointed to find there was a houseful of people. Sophie Lawson was there with *her* four children - four of them but then they could afford them couldn't they? So what with Sarah and Harriet – who, oh my goodness, who had turned into this *total* chatterbox - it was pandemonium. And there were two other women, people Christina and Sophie Lawson had known years ago; those sort of 'terribly terribly' women, so *frightfully* smart and *frightfully* witty. I felt about two inches tall. Of course I knew they would have no idea about the commercial world, *they* would never have worked a day in their lives and I'd worked for my father from the age of sixteen. They didn't have children with them because their children were at boarding school. One of them was awfully horsey. Her daughter went to the school Princess Anne went to, that horsey place. Benenden, is it?

I remember Christina hadn't even unpacked; there were trunks and boxes everywhere. We went into the square for a picnic because there was no furniture to speak of, not a table or a chair in the house. Sophie Lawson and Christina had made this huge pot of spaghetti - quite unsuitable for a picnic - and we ate it from whatever dishes they had found, with torn-off bits of bread. I think I even had a bit to drink, which I would never normally do. Edward was there – the only man – and he gave the children rides around the square in his old Lagonda - it was just like the one Dad had had during the war. I remember saying to Christina that if he had had shorter hair Edward would be the spitting image. She and Sophie Lawson thought this was very funny and they started howling with laughter. I don't know. It was just a passing thought. I was just trying to join in the conversation a bit, they were so wrapped up in themselves. They hardly involved me in the conversation at all. Really and truly they were quite bitchy... but of course I could hold my own, they didn't used to call me 'The Duchess' at work for nothing.

So they lived in that house in Thurloe Square for nearly a year before they moved to Sussex, to Heron's Gate. It's a rambling old country house - Edward had inherited it years before. It had been left nearly derelict, Christina told me, so that's why they stayed in London that first year. When they eventually moved into Heron's Gate, there were only a few finished rooms, the kitchen and scullery and a huge dining room that they camped out in, like gypsies. They seemed to think it was some hilarious adventure, Edward and Christina. Honestly, they were just like overgrown children. I wonder if they may have been going through a period of being a bit short of money? You'd have to wonder where it all went. Champagne and horses perhaps? I once made the mistake of asking Sophie Lawson whether that was the case. It was just a polite enquiry, but she simply ignored the question and started talking to me about something quite other. It was such a put-down. Those upper class country ladies can be so rude. Sophie Lawson was always very good at putting me down.

You know, Christina and I did actually spend quite a bit of time together then. I like to think that was the real Christina, my real sister. Of course she was probably on all those drugs, but she was so much easier to be with, even quite good company when I had her to myself. I like to think that underneath it all and in spite of the nonsense over Father's will, she realized how important family really was. She even started introducing me to some of Edward's friends, because she said I needed something to boost my self-esteem. I was absolutely fine of course, I didn't need anything of the sort, silly American psycho-whatnot talk, but it was thoughtful of her. Yes, she was into all that stuff, what do they call it, 'psychobabble'. I've told you already what I think of all that stuff. I think there is absolutely no point in delving into your childhood. For goodness sake, all that navel-gazing is such a waste of time. But, no, I mustn't say that because really and truly I think her ideas about helping me were meant to be a kindness. She was most insistent, too, that I spend that first summer with them at Heron's Gate, but I'm afraid the thought of sleeping in all that mess with builders wandering in and out wasn't one I relished. Besides, with the various other house guests of Edward's and a gaggle of Lawson children, I don't think she would have had much time for me. I think she knew I wouldn't accept. Oh, don't get me wrong, it was kind of her but … well, you know. We make offers, don't we, you know… we don't *seriously* think they will be taken up, it's just a gesture, isn't it?

Sarah stayed there that summer, though. I think Harriet felt a bit like me, it was all a bit too disorganised - we're both very tidy people - but Sarah loved it. She's never been a tidy person, dreadful as a child and hardly any better now she's a mother herself.

In fact, I have to say I didn't really see much of my daughter at all through her teenage years. Heron's Gate was more her home than her own. It always was really, right up until she married. My daughter was widowed at twenty-eight, you know. He had acute lymphoblastic leukemia which is very rare, especially in adults. We'd had no idea. One day he seemed fine, the next he was in hospital, the next thing we knew he had died of an infection while in surgery trying to sort out a problem with his digestive system. Sarah was an absolute fool not to sue the doctors. She still could but she won't. Really and truly my daughter doesn't know what's good for her.

Heron's Gate, yes. Well, Sarah always liked animals so she loved it there. She used to nag and nag at me to let her have a dog, from about the age of four. Of course I couldn't let her have one because she they're so messy. Well, to be frank, I'm not really a pet person myself, dogs or cats. All that hair and having to clear up messes. Horrid. So, yes, Sarah loved it at Christina and Edward's, where there were dogs and cats and horses and great hissing geese wandering about everywhere. Her own home probably seemed very dull and unexciting after a wild month or two in the Hopwood household. Boring and middleclass, she once said to me. Cheeky little madam. Anyway, as it turned out, I rather inherited Harriet, so really and truly it was just an exchange, wasn't it?

Poor Harriet, she was such a lost soul. I like to think she found a bit of a refuge with me for a while. Some comfort. She said she preferred my neat little house, after Heron's Gate and its draughty rooms and not enough hot water for a decent bath. I suppose I was flattered. And she liked coming here to see her grandma, who was living with me by then. Mother was very fond of Harriet. I think she felt a bit sorry for her too. She was always saying, "How's Harriet? Have you heard from Harriet? How's she getting on?"

She came back again for a few weeks just after her marriage broke down. Oh, no-one knew Harriet was even getting married. She just turned up on my doorstep one day and introduced this man as her husband. His name was Peter. He was very charming, that public schoolboy charm; good looking of course but Harriet was a very good-looking woman, she had our family genes. Sadly, the years of alcohol and goodness knows have taken their toll on her looks now. You wouldn't recognise her. He was a journalist, travelled a lot which was all very glamorous no doubt. They were quite besotted with one another, couldn't leave each other alone. It turned out he was a frightful ladies' man, couldn't give up chasing other women. Really and truly, Harriet was on a hiding to nothing from the start. As far as I know, they were only together for six months. Maximum.

Poor Harriet, she didn't have much luck. I really did try with my neice, you know. But of course in the end, it was her own mother she had to have it out with, not me. I don't think genes have anything to do with the behaviour side of things. You read about these problem children, don't you, such bad luck if you get a problem child. Much worse if you have a problem mother, of course. No, really and truly, Harriet didn't have much luck.

TRAINS

Eleanor takes the train and spends the night with Fiona, a girlfriend she'd known at university. So as to be nearer the address for the op. A tube ride away. Ha ha. They eat a takeaway Chinese, straight from the foil trays, and drink a bottle of rough Rioja that Eleanor bought in the shop on the corner. The shop didn't have any wine above £3.99 and most of it was Zinfandel. One bottle of dusty Blue Nun. When Eleanor and Fiona were at uni together this was the sort of corner shop that still sold sherbet dips and flying saucers in pastel colours; chocolate animals and marshmallow shrimps in vibrant pinks. You could pick them out with your fingers then and put them in a small white paper bag which by the end of the day would be soft and floppy with creases. But now it sells tired groceries and cheap wine and bent, sentimental greetings cards and piled up bargain toilet rolls.

A small selection of ready meals (faggots in gravy; chicken korma with pilau rice). Some tins of soup. Cheap, generic, non-branded. Processed cheese with an alarmingly futuristic sell-by date. Rows of magazines, the celebrity gossip kind.

Fiona is kind. And gentle. She is watching Eleanor closely for the crack she thought she would need to plaster. Fiona has always been great in a crisis. She is honest and good and deft at applying emotional bandages, good at threading needles to mend hearts with. Good at putting darts in hearts to keep their shape. Good at plastering fractures. But Eleanor won't fracture, although there is a hairline crack, deep down. Fiona picks it up in the febrile tremor of her friend's voice, and there, beneath the brittle laughter over embellished reminiscences of spotty boyfriends and Ms Dalgarno's migraine fury about someone leaving orange peel in the bin in fourth form French. And throughout all those hysterical, wide-eyed, finger-pointing whatever-happened-tos. "That tart Clare, did you know she's married to a stunt man? Or is it a porn star? He drives around in a Rolls Royce with a crate of champagne in the boot and an envelope of hashish in the glove compartment. She's got false boobs now. No! You're kidding!"

Eleanor sleeps on a sofa bed. The mattress smells of Chinese food and cheap perfume. The wine is making her stomach clench.

What's happened to me? Eleanor Joan Ashfield. Born: London. Marital Status: None. Dependants: Nearly none. Occupation: Children's book illustrator. Hobbies: digger up of bones, skeleton rattler.

Names and faces slide in front of her eyes, some of the images are upside-down or just fragments, shuffled together haphazardly, a collage of lives and letters. An alphabetical life.

E is for Eleanor. And Edward. F is for father. And Frederick. H is for Harriet. And Heron's Gate. I is for an island a long way away. An I for an eye which doesn't want to see. Or an I for an I who will not be born. And J is for Joan, who was my mum. My proper mum. But C is for Christina. My real mum too but not my proper mum. K is for kisses and L is for lies. And M is for mummy. And N is for No and O is for Oh... And P is for Peter the bastard traitor in oh, so many ways... how funny am I, hahaha.

The room lurches. She imagines herself in the belly of a huge animal. She can hear the thud of a heartbeat that isn't her own. She can smell blood, feel the stretch of flesh around her as if she herself is pushing again skin, kneading it, trying to find a way out. The air in the room is tight, cocooning her, swaddling her. She finds herself with a sheet and a blanket caught up beneath her and feels trapped.

Okay, okay. Open my eyes. The people who were my parents. Who were they? They were Joan and Patrick. Stop, stop. Jack and Christina are my blood, my bone, my chromosomes. Joan and Patrick were my parents, my parents, my parents.

Eleanor puts her palms over her eyes. She knows that if she closes her eyes the room will spin but she doesn't want to see keep seeing the pictures of these people she can never meet. She feels her eyelashes crushed against the palms of her hands.

My parents… Joan and Patrick… mum and dad… had a huge bed with a cherrywood headboard. The wood was smooth and warm. Mum would polish it with special wax in a flat gold tin. On Sunday mornings I would crawl into bed with them. It was the only morning my parents stayed in bed, they were early risers really but they liked to read in bed, propped up with extra pillows. Only on a Sunday morning; heavy, pale blue blankets tucked up under their arms and around their middles like people you see in bed in storybooks. My dad always read biographies, of great leaders, film stars, or less famous but not lesser men - travellers or doctors. Perhaps he was looking for clues, clues on how to live his life. My mum only ever read fiction, light novels where the clues were clearer and the lives were always tidy and safely tucked up.

I would be between them, upside down, with my feet on the wood, making steamy little footprints. I liked to pretend I was a wild animal running through a dark wood, and these were my tracks. My tread would be so light, like breath. I imagined landscapes in the swirls of the wood, dunes and hills and woods and rivers. And cherry trees laden with pink blossom that snowed onto the grass, carpeting the way before me. Mum was always shushing me, "Shhh, sweetheart", she would say, and pat my legs, playfully, gently, without looking up from her book.

Eleanor thinks she hears a bell ringing. A warning bell. Or the bell at the level crossing near Peter's house. It's far away. She doesn't see the warning lights are flashing.

On Sunday afternoons my Dad used to spend hours in the spare room, where he had a fabulous railway layout. It was hinged to the wall and folded down over the single guest bed and could be folded back up flat, against the wall if ever the room was in use. The railway landscape was perfect in every detail. The hills were made from polystyrene and crumpled up newspaper, painted different shades of green. The clumps of bushes were made from bits of pulled-about pan scourers. I had donated two Friesian cows from my toy farm set. They were not the right scale but my father had understood the sincerity and sacrifice of the gift and put them on a hill to graze all the same, giant cows grazing in the sun. The track was just one loop but kinked in the middle like a kidney bean, with the station in the centre of the curve. A road - made from grey sandpaper cut into lengths and painted with white lines - crossed the track as it reappeared from beneath a hill, and there was a perfect miniature level crossing. There was a pair of gates at the crossing, that could be opened and closed with tiny red levers. And a sign that said 'Do not stop on the tracks' in teeny writing. There was a little red car, made of metal, with people in it - a mother and father, and a child on the back seat with a dog. My Dad let me push the little car to the gates. I would wait for the train to go by and then open the gates for the car to go through. I used to wonder what would happen if the car stopped on the tracks, if the train hit the car. Would the car get flattened? Would the little dog escape? Would the little family inside get all squashed and broken? For years, that's what I pictured when people talked about divorce, breaking up.

Little people with their arms and legs all squished. I always thought of that when I drove over the crossing to Peter's house, in my old red car. Because he was married and his marriage was all broken apart.

There were other little toy people, waiting on the platform. Dad sent away for these little figures. He had a catalogue. The platform people were plastic and came in sets of four, a ready-made population. The details were perfect. There was a fat stationmaster in a peaked cap with a scrambled egg emblem on the front; a lady in a blue coat and hat, carrying a shopping bag. Out of the top of the bag poked some carrots with green tops, just like the carrots my mother would buy in the greengrocer's, that smelt of earth; a businessman with a bowler hat and umbrella, his briefcase at his feet, attached to his leg like an extra limb; and a boy waving. I used to move the boy about, pointing him away from the station so he could be waving at the giant cows. Waving a warning perhaps. I can see my Dad standing with the control for the trains in his hand. I can smell the hot smell from the transformer, hot metal, like the smell of caps in toy guns. I can see myself standing beside him, the track at eye level, imagining myself on the platform, waiting for a train to take me somewhere.

The sound of a bell is getting louder, more insistent. Stop the train, Eleanor, before it's too late. Pull the cord. Smash the glass and pull the cord. That's all you have to do.

Smash the glass. With a fist, wrapped in a blue blanket. Sky blue for a baby boy. Pink for a baby girl. Do not stop on the tracks. It's too late, it's too late, I can't stop. Everything is tearing apart, twisting metal, hot metal. Fire, fire. See how the hillsides are burning, see how the sky is turning scarlet with the heat. Save them, save them. Can you hear me? I am shouting, I am shouting but nobody can hear me! The fire is burning them all and I am stuck here, stopped on the tracks, with my mother and father who weren't what I thought they were, in the front of the car, waiting for the impact of the train. Waiting for my family to be broken. Waiting for the train.

"Eleanor?"

I was always waiting for the impact. Waiting for Peter at train stations, airline gates, waiting in beetle-black cabs, their comic diesel patter like a chant. Waiting for a postcard from some strange place, and when it came, stretching myself across the distance until my skin was so thin I could see through it to my soul. And there he always was again, raising a hand in recognition. Always smiling. But part of him shut off from me, tight, I could see the lie on his face like a stain on the skin, like a burn. It is that face he turned to me when I told him I was pregnant. That burnt face, with no hair. Lashless and blind. It was always there.

"Eleanor, come on, wake up."

Peter?

It is Fiona's voice, sharp in the nuzzling grey dawn light, sharp with urgency and toothpaste breath.

"It's half-past seven, Ellie. I've got to dash. I'll miss my bus. Give me a hug. You'll be all right. It'll all be all right. I'll phone you tonight. Bye, love, bye."

Eleanor blinks. For a minute her vision is shaky with her heartbeat, from the force of fighting in her dreams. She lies there, breathing hard, blinking the images away. She feels sweat running down her chest in rivulets. She waits for the things in the room to be still, for the shapes to grow solid and real out of the thick, grey light.

Eleanor is a good guest. She puts the sofa bed back into its daytime shape, plumps the cushions, folds the sheet and the duvet and the blanket neatly and leaves them in a tidy pile over a chair. She cleans the waxy ring from the bath when she has finished and hangs her towel smoothly over the towel rail. She clears away the abandoned supper things. She has the washing up water very hot, it scalds her hands. They are still red and damp when she leaves the flat. She slams the front door and walks to the tube station and goes down, down into the belly of the earth. She stands on the platform and waits. The train is coming, she can hear its animal rumble, and feels the huge gust of warm air as it flattens her coat to the curves of her body, before it rolls across the miles, gathering littered pictures and discarded words, gathering momentum until it curls high, high up into the wood of a roof where two wooden puppets are waiting. Watching.

SARAH

I used to go and stay with my aunt and uncle most school holidays. The first year I stayed, the house was still being rebuilt and we all had to make do. That was the best summer of all, that first one. Aunt Christina and Uncle Edward slept in the orangery and Harriet and I had a tent in the orchard. The tent leaked so when it rained, we slept in the scullery. There was a small portable black and white telly in the scullery. If one of Daddy's plays was on, we'd be allowed to watch. They let us watch all the rude bits, such as they were then. Censorship was much more strict in those days. I can still remember that awful embarrassed feeling, sitting there with the grown-ups, while there was *snogging* on the telly. Ugh. I think I had a bit of a crush on my uncle Edward then, and that certainly didn't help.

Isn't it funny, getting crushes? Some of the girls at school used to get crushes on the teachers. Or older girls, especially sixth-formers. Schoolgirl crushes. Harriet had a bit of a crush on one of her teachers once, an older woman who taught them drama and psychology, it caused a bit of a problem at the time - she'd hate me for telling you. Crushes all round, it seems. Uncle Edward was awfully crushworthy though. Even my mother found him attractive, although it was obviously never mutual. Mum fancied her chances with most men, she was a frightful flirt, but she wasn't Uncle Edward's type, God, no. Did I tell you how gorgeous looking he was? A real heartbreaker, even by then and he must've been getting on for seventy. He was very tall and incredibly fit. He had lovely crinkly eyes, they were pale blue, with a dark blue ring around them, really unusual. I used to think there was a hint of melancholy about them, some sort of hidden pain. What can I tell you? Perhaps I imagined it, perhaps I just wanted him to be my romantic hero. You know, something sad and dark in his past. Some intrigue. Very Gothic. Yeah, right. Very Mills & Boon, more like.

Everything was so topsy-turvy that first summer. I remember it as some great big colourful whirl, like a fairground or a circus. We were allowed to do anything we wanted really. After my school and mum and home being so, oh, I don't know, *tight, uptight,* it was all so liberating. Imagine it, for a child. Fantastic. We were allowed to be quite wild and naughty really. If she had known half of it, my mother would have been furious. If we didn't want to wash we didn't have to and I'm quite sure I wore the same shorts and shirt the whole summer. No one ever said anything. No one ever nagged.

There were always people dropping in and out, sometimes staying for the weekend. Aunt Christina would have these lavish teas, high teas, if there were visitors on Sunday afternoons. She and Aunt Sophie made all the food, everything. No, Sophie wasn't really my aunt, but I called her that. She was Aunt Christina's oldest, dearest friend, they were very close. She's lovely. Strong and kind and doesn't take any nonsense. She lives a wonderful country life, she still rides horses and has lots of dogs. She and her husband do loads of work for charity, they're amazing.

She and Aunt Christina loved cooking together, they'd spend hours and hours getting everything ready if there was going to be a gathering. Everyone would flop out on the grass, on horse blankets or in terrible old deck chairs with their bottoms poking out through the rotten canvas. Oh my goodness, I can't help laughing, just thinking about it! Oh and all this food …. plates piled high with sandwiches, egg and cress, salmon and cucumber, ham and mustard. And cakes with soggy middles, on chipped cake plates Aunt Christina had found in the attic. There was this enormous teapot, one of those ugly brown round ones. She said it came from my grandfather's building yard and it was the only decent thing she ever got from him. You could get about twenty cups out of it and it weighed a ton.

Some of the grown-ups would have cocktails or a Scotch-on-the-rocks or a G&T . Uncle Edward had this line, "T or G&T? What's it t'be?". You can imagine what it was like for me, after Mum's teas with her 'ladies', all horrid, old-fashioned doilies and antique cake stands, nasty paper napkins and dry little cakes from Sainsbury's that she pretended were homemade. And after the rigours of that hideous boarding school she sent me to for a while when she and Dad divorced - all you got for tea there was the left-over slices of toast from breakfast, the burnt bits they had scraped the blackened surface from.

Aunt Christina and Uncle Edward were really sociable, they loved having a house full and often there'd be hordes of children, running amok: the Lawsons - there were four of them – and children who belonged to business acquaintances of Uncle Edwards, or one or two of Harriet's rather odd little friends from school. My mum would have absolutely hated it! Perhaps it was because they were just big kids themselves in lots of ways. No, that's not right. It was because they could still somehow find that childlike joy in things, you know? Child*like*. Not child*ish*.

Uncle Edward was famous for his Cowboys and Indians games. He was the bane of the local pony club. Oh, dear, he was just such fun! He once went charging across the meadows on their lovely old horse, Doughty, right in the middle of one of the Pony Club's fancy rallies, galloping flat out, bareback, hollering like an Indian. Since they were his meadows and the Pony Club needed the field, they couldn't do much about it. Can you picture it? All these plump little girls scattered to the four winds, carted off on their Thelwell ponies, mothers in Huskies and scarves waving their shooting sticks in the air; instructors, hands on hips, speechless, mouths moving like fish. I can remember all of us laughing and laughing and Uncle Edward doubled-up with laughter, his face going all red. And Aunt Christina and Sophie bouncing across the meadow in the old Lagonda to apologise to everybody. Oh, god, such laughter, such love. Oh, I don't know whether to laugh or cry. Everything's been so difficult...

Aunt Christina was always *making* something, she always had some project on the go, she was incredibly industrious. I really admire that in people, don't you? Not like the rest of us, just crashing in front of the telly after work, demanding we be entertained. Entertain me *now*! Make me laugh *now*! Make me feel satisfied, make me feel good. And of course we never feel good, we're never satisfied.

Aunt Christina was satisfied simply by the process of a project. She said it was *making* something that was the point. She was always saying how mankind had forgotten that need. We don't make our houses, we don't make our clothes, we don't chop the wood to make the fires, we don't even have to make our meals any more, or the pots we put them in. We just unwrap our food and put it in a trick box to heat.

During the first summer she made this beautiful mosaic on the terrace at their house. The terrace itself overlooked the firehills and the sea. It was a mosaic of a heron - after Heron's Gate, the name of the house, you see - and its eye was like a spiral, a bit like one of those psychedelic patterns they used to say could hypnotise you. She made the whole mosaic with broken bits of tile that Aunt Sophie had saved from a place her parents once owned in Italy. They were handmade and they'd been in the hall of the house there, I think. Aunt Christina did the whole thing practically by herself, although she pretended we were helping. Who was there? Harriet and me, Lizzie Lawson and a friend of hers from school; Lizzie's uncle Willard. Oh, and Christopher Benson – yes, the film critic. Oh goodness, he was another ever so handsome man. He was the son of some old friend of Aunt Christina's. He was a real hoot, quite outrageous sometimes, but a great disappointment to us all in terms of crush-value because he was gay. Mind you, that didn't stop him flirting with Aunt Christina. He doted on her. He just adored her. Oh, I think everyone adored my Auntie Christina in their own way. It was her … oh, I don't know, her *spirit* maybe? Her energy? Her love of life?

Christopher Benson? He was an actor then, he didn't start out as a film critic, you know. Well, I think he did more commercials and that kind of thing, although I know Aunt Christina and Uncle Edward went to see him in some experimental theatre thing once. I remember him meeting my Dad and being a bit fawning and embarrassing. I think he had the idea he might wrangle a part in one of Dad's plays. Dad was very polite but I don't think he took him seriously. Dad said he had the wrong temperament for a serious actor. And he was right, wasn't he?

He went to live in Morocco for a while. Before he went to LA. I remember Aunt Christina being quite anxious about him. Well, there's something a bit sordid about gay Europeans in Morocco, something a bit Lawrence of Arabia.

I'm not sure what I mean. I expect I'm sounding just like my mum. Anyway, it's great that he's now quite a respected - and respectable - film and television critic. Not for the big newspapers, but he does a lot of the reviews for the glossy women's magazines. You know, *Good Housekeeping, Cosmopolitan*, that sort of thing. I expect all the lady editors adore him, he was always so sweet with us, camp as anything and huge fun. Some time ago he wrote a rather mean review of one of my Dad's plays that had been made into a film. It was all *petty* criticism and written in that really condescending style he sometimes uses. And there were one or two personal comments about my Dad's career, that he'd been given some lucky breaks, like he didn't deserve his success on the merits of his writing. Lizzie says it was just bitching, that Christopher's the stereotype of the bitchy, middle-aged gay who never forgets a slight. She says he really plays it up. I know Aunt Christina thought the things he said about Daddy were unnecessary and cruel. But by then she and Christopher had stopped seeing each other. They had a huge falling out. I know that she felt Christopher wasn't very helpful when Harriet... well, when there were problems. When things got a bit difficult.

Anyway, I was telling you about Uncle Edward. Yes, he was always mucking about, going off on some adventure, sometimes with us, sometimes with some of the people who were staying at Heron's Gate. He had amazing energy for an older man. I remember it was him who found that ancient bicycle we all painted up. He called it 'George', I don't know why. It was the Easter holidays. I remember it because we had an Easter egg hunt on Sunday. But that's another story. Gosh, I'm running away with myself.

Anyway, Uncle Edward found this old bicycle in amongst some unused furniture in the stables. It was one of those sit-up-and-beg type bikes, with a basket on the front. It was in a bit of a state, although it was all there. It was just rusty and the tyres needed replacing. When he first found it, he took Lizzie and me down to the beach on it, me on the handlebars and Lizzie on the saddle. Oh, it still makes me laugh to think about it. There was this boat ramp at the beach and we had races to see who could ride down it the fastest. You have to picture the scene, this old bicycle covered in rust with no brakes so you couldn't stop without jumping off and no inner tubes so you couldn't steer properly. So you'd go haring down the ramp, you see, and down onto the beach. You'd be charging down toward the sea, with the wind behind you, flat out, no brakes, nothing. And then you'd hit the wet sand and you'd be stopped dead. There'd be about three seconds while you were suspended there, upright, with your feet on the pedals trying to keep your balance and then you'd just go splat, into the wet sand. God, I remember laughing so much my stomach ached for a week. Oh, dear, we were *so* silly. Really, I know it loses something in the telling but it was so *funny*.

Well, yes, it was the same bicycle. Aunt Christina tidied 'George' up, got new tyres and a smart leather seat. George became one of Aunt Christina's projects, she thought she'd refurbish him for Harriet, as a surprise. You see, Harriet had been making all this fuss about her friends at school having bicycles and how much she wanted one. She was such a nag about it, she went on and on, one of those awful foot-stomping, plate-throwing sulks she sometimes went into. I'm amazed she didn't get a real telling off, especially as she was always having these silly fads about things - she'd wanted an easel and some painting stuff one holiday and when she got it she never used it; another time she said she had to have a whole new riding outfit and she got it, which was really silly because she hardly ever sat on a horse. She was really very spoilt. No one ever really told her off either. Although I did see Uncle Edward slap her on the back of the legs once for throwing a plate right at her mother. It hit Aunt Christina on the side of the head. She had to have ten stitches in her temple. I'd forgotten that till now.

Anyway, Aunt Sophie and I went into the town and got some metal paint and Uncle Edward bought new tyres and inner tubes and did all the mechanical bits, with a bit of help from Mr Noble, the old gardener, who was really handy at that sort of thing. When George was all fixed and they'd done the rust and the primer, the four of us - Aunt Christina, Aunt Sophie and Lizzie and I – the four of us spent ages painting him and polishing him up. He was black, white and pillar-box red. It was fantastic, a real transformation. We were so proud of ourselves.

Aunt Christina made a big thing about giving George the bicycle to Harriet. She put a huge white ribbon on it and locked it in the garages and gave Harriet the key, wrapped up to make a big square parcel, layers and layers of wrapping so she couldn't guess. It was so exciting. But

Harriet took one look at it and said it was stupid. She walked up to the bicycle, disgust on her spoilt face, and just pushed it over and it clattered to the ground. I felt awful for Aunt Christina. She was so hurt. We were all hurt. But that was Harriet. You never knew how she would react.

Funny. I remember all these things, can feel all those feelings so richly and vividly and yet I can hardly remember anything about school or university or when I first started work. Or even being married to my husband, Liam. We were married for two years, it was a good marriage. He was a good man. He had leukaemia. We had no idea, he'd just been feeling a bit tired so I persuaded him to go for some tests and the next day they called him at work to tell him to go to the hospital. He died within a week. Not the cancer primarily, he had a blockage and they tried to operate and he got an infection. Because of the leukaemia he had nothing to fight it with. Awful. We could have taken the hospital to task, my mother wanted me to, but Liam had always railed against the way society was becoming increasingly litigious, it was one of his pet hates, so it wouldn't have been right. Katherine was eighteen months. It was a very difficult time. Aunt Christina was amazing. So was my dad, he can be quite aloof but he really stepped up to the plate when Liam died.

Yes, Harriet was married for a short time - even less time than me but hers ended in a divorce. It was crazy. Peter was twelve years older than her and a complete womaniser. He's a writer of sorts, written a couple of travel books and articles about holiday destinations off the beaten track, that sort of thing. So he always had plenty of opportunity to sleep around. I think Harriet believed she'd be the one to stop him in his tracks, the one who would make a faithful husband out of him but of course she was wrong. Aunt Christina didn't like Peter, clearly she sensed something about him. It was a bit difficult for a while. Of course she was always polite, I don't think she could be any other way. But she held back from him. And you can imagine how hard he tried to impress her. Silly man. He wasn't used to a woman not responding to him, his public school charm, his wit, his... *sex*. Oh, it's water under the bridge. Or over the bridge. Or both probably. I don't think she ever tried to talk Harriet out of marrying him or anything, she wasn't like that. Perhaps she should have. I don't know. Thank goodness they never had any children, it's hard for children with a single parent however it happens.

Sometimes I look over my life and see it as blocks of time all joined up in strands, do you know what I mean? A chunk of childhood, a chunk of boarding school, a few chunks of university, all in different colours, but the same *shaped* blocks. Shorter or longer strands depending on the length of time. And all the bits where Aunt Christina and Uncle Edward featured have lovely, colourful little splodges. And the ones without them are just a sort of dreary, pale grey. Like a dull sky. I think the best years of my life were with Aunt Christina and Uncle Edward.

I used to be so excited about life – everything - when I was staying at Heron's Gate. It was as if each new day was just waiting there for me, all this sunshine and magic.

My aunt tried so hard to help me grow. Oh, in so many ways. I mean, simple things she taught me. My mother never had the patience to teach me anything; if she tried, she'd just get cross that I was making a child's hash of it and snatch away whatever I was trying to do. Aunt Christina had such patience and she didn't care how wrong things might go and how long it would take. There were fun, practical things - how to plant a row of runner beans and set up the canes; how to iron a shirt; how to watch the sticky buds on the chestnut trees as they unfurled in the warmth and light of spring. How to lead a horse properly and turn it away from you if you were turning him around. How to poultice a hoof. How to make profiteroles, a quick salmon mousse. How to chit potatoes (Uncle Edward used to tease her about her 'chitting her spuds'). How, when you find a tired bumblebee on the lawn, you give it English honey on a matchstick – English honey only, mind, nothing foreign – and it will perk right up. And she taught me to sit still and watch – a mistle thrush digging for a worm; a buzzard being chased by two crows; how the sheets flap and curl on the washing line, the shapes they make. She taught me to be in the moment. To really breathe. I think that has to be the most important thing. There are so many things she taught me, showed me. But the best was that: how to be still, solid, at peace with myself even when everything around me is raging in a terrible, heart-wrenching, gut-twisting storm. She saved me from drowning in my grief when Liam died.

I'm making her sound so serious and weird, aren't I? And that's not right because one of the best gifts she gave me was teaching me to laugh, to have a sense of fun, a sense of the ridiculous, a sense of humour about *me*. About life. So if she could hear me now, she'd be laughing.

I want to be able to laugh again. I want to believe that the winter will end, that the chestnut trees will sprout their sticky buds and then their coloured candles. That summer *will* come round again. I want to believe in *life* again. But it's hard when your mentors have gone. When the people who believed in *you* have gone. That was the best thing she did for me. She believed. In me.

JOSEPH

Be careful what you hear when you listen. Be attentive. Bear in mind, there is always a hidden agenda with my former wife, Claudia. Nothing she says is without a malicious turn, nothing is said nor done without some selfish motive. Not one thing. Poor Sarah, ever in search of a more honourable side to her mother, she believes there's more to it. Some deeper significance to it all, something Claudia has to conquer. This is what my sweet, gentle daughter believes. What do *I* think? I think it's all about money. Claudia has a cash register lodged in her brain. Yes. I like that. A cash register. She's always ringing up the value and emotionally short-changing the people she shouldn't be charging in the first place. You can see the pound signs in her eyes. Claudia hated it that Christina married a wealthy man. A toff.

You can imagine how annoyed she was that she divorced me before I became well-known. That must still smart. What she doesn't realise is that if I'd stayed married to her, I'd have just gone under. Well, that's a bit strong. I'd have probably drunk a lot more, so who knows how that might have panned out.

It's a shame Sophie won't talk to you. Sophie Dexter. Yes, Lawson as she is now. She was after all Christina's closest friend. Sophie herself has no illusions – delusions - about Christina, but she still loved her. *She* was her real sister, in spirit. I don't doubt that's why my former wife hates the Lawson clan so much, it brings her inadequacies into sharp relief. Claudia is always saying family is important but it's all nonsense, she's a total fraud. Claudia would have sold her grandmother for the price of a new outfit. So don't go believing it if she does any of that filial whining crap.

Christina got quite wrapped up in the whole Dexter family when she was about seventeen. You can see why. There were very close-knit, a very loving family. Sophie had three brothers - I met one of them just recently, he used to make documentaries, very highly rated in factual programming in its day. The youngest one was a satirical cartoonist of sorts, and the one in the middle, he lives in Italy, I think. Very clever, all of them. Christina might have dated one of them for a while, but I don't remember. I think it was really the whole family she was trying to establish a relationship with, get her bearings with. Christina was looking for surrogates, of course, for somewhere to fit in, to find her place. I don't think the psychology is difficult to work out, is it? But who am I to theorize? Sometimes I'm suspicious of my daughter Sarah's inquiring generation, the need to explain every human experience, extrapolate every memory, every *nuance* of memory and experience. It is good for some things to be aired but others may be better buried because they are too ugly to face and once faced, make no difference at all, they just distort the present. For instance, Sarah believes she could have helped her aunt, *saved* her, by helping her face her demons, exorcise her ghosts. I think it might have been dangerous and certainly not helpful were any one of us to have glimpsed a shadow of some of the things Christina feared. It is my belief that Christina Hopwood did the very best she could and if she chose to end her life, we must respect that. If indeed that *is* what happened. Yes, that's what the coroner recorded but ... I don't know. I really don't know.

So. Yes, Christina was regarded as a talented young artist. But she never believed it herself, never thought she was good enough. She was greatly hindered by her self-doubt. And she found the attention a bit bewildering. People have been saying she wasted her talent. But why should a talent necessarily be exploited? Does an aptitude for something necessarily mean it will be good for you to exploit it? Christina found the process of painting very uncomfortable. We all have this romantic notion that the process of making art somehow releases your spirit and that's a good thing. Or connects you to some cosmic greatness. But why should it be, why should flailing about inside your subconscious necessarily expurgate your soul? Christina was frightened of it, of herself. She found it hard to reconcile her need to paint with some sort of fear of it. I think confronting your internal darkness is the hardest thing about creativity, because it can go either way. You can reach the greatest heights, or you might die of the heat, climbing up that mountain. Or end up down in the abyss. I get it.

Christina was only twenty-one when she had the show on Cork Street. Remember, a young woman being an artist then was fairly unusual, less so in the States but here she was one of just a handful of female artists. She got quite a lot of attention in the press, such as press attention was then. It was also a very glamorous crowd she was moving in. Rather overwhelming for her, perhaps. Jack and Daphne Benson were her patrons, her backers if you like. Jack Benson was in publishing, very wealthy. Daphne had inherited her father's fortune from... God, I don't know, something South African, diamonds maybe. Anyway, she was wealthy in her own right. They met Christina through the Dexters. Jack commissioned her to do some fashion sketches for one of his magazines and it went on from there. The show they put on for Christina was of these sketches and some new watercolours. She had done some huge, fabulous landscapes, very dramatic, lots of black and red. Nowadays they'd be really admired but I think at that time they were seen as all very peculiar. "Very peculiar", yes, that's the way it would have been put. That's the way my former wife Claudia would definitely have put it. Quite different from the work she painted in the last few years, all those soft beach scenes, sunsets on the water, lots of yellow and blue, children playing on the sand. Sarah has tried to track down some of those early pieces but she hasn't had any luck. I must put my mind to it. It would be nice for her to have a piece of her aunt's work.

By the way, Claudia didn't go to the exhibition. On the day of the show, Claudia had some sort of bug. Of course she did. Bugged about her sister being successful. I went by myself, met some interesting people. Claudia would have hated not being the centre of attention.

So. What else are you unsure about? Well, yes, there *was* a rumour among some journalists at the time that Christina and Jack Benson were lovers. But because of Benson's publishing might, nothing was ever written about it.

Well I don't see what difference it makes now. Yes. Christina told me after Edward died that she and Jack had a brief affair around that time. But it shouldn't be a surprise that Christina found him attractive. He was a powerful man. He protected her from her sister and the possible speculation in the press over her father's death. He hired the best lawyers for her. And she needed them. Although it was a car accident that killed George Mansfield, there was a long inquest; the car had burst into flames and burnt at such a rate the attending fire crew thought it should be looked into. It all seemed simple enough though, that he'd been driving home after a long board meeting, he was tired, then crunch - one of those accidents you hear about, only a few miles from home and something ignited the fuel tank – a freak accident, incredibly unlucky.

The whole thing beyond the inquest was all Claudia's
doing. She insisted on experts of every kind putting in their
tuppence worth. It was a real mess because of her. The
verdict by the coroner, finally, was death by misadventure,
but the rumours had by then gone out that he had been
blind drunk. I suppose it was a big deal also because George
Mansfield was this rags-to-riches local hero, a bit of a pillar
of the community, Rotary member, mason, all that jazz. And
everybody would've felt as if they'd been had, if the myth
had been destroyed. Claudia still only acknowledges the
mythical view of it all. She will still insist - as she insisted
then - that her father 'never touched liquor'. She uses those
very words, sounding like some character from a Eugene
O'Neill play. She always believed somebody had been out to
get her father. She was obsessed with it. Probably still
obsessed with it now. Underneath her new, slimmed-down,
respectable, sweet grandmother image, that's an enormous
venomous hydra trying to get out.

So. Well, Jack Benson was obviously *Christina's* hero of
course. Until Edward carried her off. They were close friends,
Benson and Hopwood. Some old story – I have no idea if it's
true – about one of them saving the other's life. He's still
alive, Jack Benson, did you know? He must be hitting the
century by now. I think the family moved back here from LA.
I'm pretty sure. They lived in Los Angeles for a long time,
went there in the early seventies. Jack was into television
then. Headed up A&E, the Arts and Entertainment channel.
Yes, Christopher Benson, the film-critic, he's the son.
Christopher and Christina were friends, yes. Quite close

friends for a long time. He used to stay at the house quite regularly if he was this side of the pond, when she and Edward lived at Heron's Gate. But *Jack* Benson, he didn't feature in her life by then. For all there may have once been between Jack Benson and Christina, I don't think she ever once set eyes on him again after she married Edward. But Christina and *Christopher* fell out over his – Christopher's - drug use. She wouldn't let anyone use drugs in the house and he knew that very well. He'd managed to keep it hidden for a long time. At that time he was doing a lot of cocaine. They never reconciled. I wonder how Christopher feels about that now he's a sober addict? He could be spiteful. I'd like to think that spiteful people *are* capable of remorse. But Christopher and Claudia? Maybe not.

But that wasn't what you were asking me, was it? Quite honestly, there isn't much more I can tell you. Yup, after Claudia and I married, Christina came round to visit us quite a lot. She was a sweet auntie to baby Sarah. Well, she always was. She was always a good aunt to my daughter. They were very close. More so after my son-in-law died. Heartbreak.

What more can I tell you? Christina was sweet and funny and sensitive. Self-effacing. A bit too easily led sometimes perhaps, a bit naïve. She could be shy, but she could also be the life and soul of the party, she got a lot more confident after she and Edward were married. Yes, withdrawn sometimes. But not seriously, just quiet. And like any creative person, she needed her space, she was sometimes a bit obsessive about projects she was working

on. Could be sharp, very serious. Very moral. She had a
formidable intellect but didn't often show it. But she could
also play the fool, she and Edward brought that out in each
other - huge sense of the ridiculous.

I can give you facts if you want. Okay.

When Christina married Edward Hopwood they went to
live in the West Indies - oh, you know that. It was the best
thing they could have done, given the crap over Mansfield's
will. And bits of gossip here and there. You've probably
realized gossip wasn't like it was then. It was much more...
parochial. Contained. But still, it could be cruel if you were
sensitive.

I saw Christina once during the time they were living in
the West Indies and that was at Emmeline Reed's, the old
lady she and Claudia had been sent to for a little while
during the war. The meeting was planned, it wasn't the
accident Claudia always believed it was. Christina wrote to
me saying she would be coming over with Edward and her
new baby, Harriet and that she would be staying with
Emmeline Reed at Flint Cross on a specific weekend; she
asked if I thought Claudia would agree to see her there.
Well, I wasn't sure, so I told Christina that I would get
Claudia there and what would be would be. They'd not
spoken since the death of their father. So, yes, I engineered
the whole thing and Claudia had no idea. The upshot was
that while I wouldn't say Claudia was exactly warm towards
her sister, it was a start at re-establishing a relationship
between them. I think Claudia was intrigued by the fact
that the baby was there, Harriet. That her sister had had a

child. She'd always said that Christina was far too selfish to be a mother. The irony. But Claudia is one of those women who doesn't really like other women, doesn't think much of female company. She certainly doesn't rate a woman *at all* unless she has been a mother. Some women are so damning of their own sex. It's an interesting dichotomy with Claudia. Apparently dislikes other women but thinks rather highly of herself. She must be very torn, deep in there. Or not really think of herself as a woman at all, that might be it. Like I said, I think that's why she's such a perfectionist, why she is so obsessed with orderliness and things being 'just so'. She's keeping the lid on that multi-headed writhing beast she has in her psyche.

After that meeting at Flint Cross, Christina went back to the West Indies and she and Claudia started corresponding with each other. And when Edward telephoned me to tell me that Christina was unwell, I thought it might work if Claudia were to take a holiday and stay with them for a few weeks. I had made a bit of money and I thought it was the least I could do for my wife after all the support she had given me. But I hadn't quite got the measure of her obsessiveness and her compulsion with cleanliness, her intolerance of *any* remote discomfort. Plus, I didn't know then quite how deep was the thread of her jealousy.

God, how Claudia hated the tropics. So there was all the fuss about *that* and from the dismissive and spiteful way she spoke of Christina and Edward's lifestyle, she was probably quite overawed by it all. And at the same time it exacerbated her jealousy. And as for cementing the relationship with her sister, Claudia clearly decided that here was a good opportunity for her to put the boot in by meddling in her sister's marriage. There you are again, an example of her spite. More knife-twisting. Not only did she start telling Christina that Edward was having affairs left, right and centre – which I can say without hesitation he was *not*, he is simply not the type, not even in those days .... Friendships with women but he was a friendly man. Oh, but Claudia didn't stop here, she came home with the ridiculous story that Edward's behaviour with *her* had been inappropriate. I'm sorry, you have to laugh. Silly cow.

I wish I had been as sure of it then as I am now – as sure of the extent of Claudia's duplicity, of her ability to be so very manipulative. Edward would never have responded to Claudia. She was never his type, much too blousy. And besides, the real point is the one thing that was never in doubt - then or now - that Edward Hopwood adored Christina. They adored each other. Naturally the relationship changed over the years. I mean, she was twenty-two and he was nearly fifty when they married so probably there was a bit of the Svengali about it then, but over time, they became .... I hate the expression but I have to say it – a unit. Joined at the hip. Welded. Fused.

But we were all younger and with Claudia coming back to the UK saying Edward was having affairs all over the island and that he had had Christina committed, I didn't know the sort of man Edward Hopwood was. And while I could probably quite safely ignore the first, the second was quite another matter. No, you must remember, I didn't know Edward then.

The picture Claudia painted when she got back from Trinidad was that Christina was completely unhinged and that Edward had given up on her and sent her packing to an asylum. The fact is, Claudia was wallowing in it, loved the drama, she wanted her sister to be insane and to have been abandoned by her glamorous, wealthy husband. She liked the vicarious attention she got. And the sympathy she got for herself. Playing the victim/sympathy card is Claudia's MO. I can just hear her: 'Of course, my sister is *completely* mad. No, *really* mad. In an asylum. Her poor husband, lovely man...' I can almost hear her saying it.

It's sad. That I didn't know anything about how hard Christina really found life. Just life. Just living and breathing. I didn't know, none of us did. And in those days, mental health didn't have the prominence it does now. It was shameful. ECT was still used widely, without question, for god's sake. People still used terms like 'looney bin' and 'asylum'. And drugs were crude and the side effects were appalling. Things were so different then medically as well as socially. Serotonin and dopamine weren't the buzzwords they became.

Edward I got to know eventually in fits and starts. I met him in person for the first time when he brought Harriet to London to see a specialist in Harley Street. Harriet didn't speak until she was ... oh, about seven may be? I'm not really sure how hold she was. At that early stage, though, when she was little more than a toddler, they were still uncertain as whether it was physiological or psychological. He actually rang me at my office at the Beeb, said he was

due to go back to Trinidad the following week but that he
was spending a weekend at a hotel on the coast. I was
writing a Play for Today at the time, set in a seaside resort,
so it was perfect. I suggested we meet at his hotel. He said
he had a couple of things he wanted to bring me up to date
on. And I had a few items on my agenda too. Things weren't
going well my end - Claudia and I were separated, in the
throes of drawing up divorce papers, plus I had our daughter
Sarah staying with me, she was unhappy at school and
needed some space from it and from her mother. I probably
had a casting director on my back as well, I usually did then.
They were like vultures. Probably still are. I'm glad I'm well
out of it.

Yes, I saw Harriet. Edward had sent her off to play in the
gardens with another little girl, the daughter of one of the
staff who worked at the hotel. I met up with Edward in the
hotel foyer and we went out into the gardens to find her. I
saw her playing with the other child. Edward called her over
and we shook hands. It was very sweet. She sort of curtsied.
Didn't smile though. Her little friend said they were watching
the butterflies. She was a little chatterbox. Bit older than
Harriet. The perfect companion for a silent little girl.

I had a bit of a go at the poor bloke again, about
Christina. Poor sod. What was he thinking putting her 'in a
looney bin'. Yes. I would have used that very word myself.
Truth is, with hindsight, I just wanted a rant about
something, what with Claudia being such a sow. He just let
me let off steam. He didn't get angry, he didn't even get
warm under the collar. When I had finished, when I asked

- like the pompous little twit I was then - what his explanation could possibly be, he turned his chair to face me, looked me straight in the eye and told me that he loved his wife; that he had done and would do everything in his power to care for her and to protect her. To protect her from herself. That he had been desperate to save her from herself; that St Bernadette's had been the ideal place. I wasn't stupid. I knew what he meant. It clicked. He didn't need to say she had been trying to take her own life.

You have to picture it to get it right. You have to bear in mind this was a man I did not know, my senior in years and in status - a wealthy, powerful man. His physical presence alone was quite startling. Formidable. No, wrong word. Charismatic. Powerful and wholesome. Terrible words. I embarrass myself. Something to do with strength and truth. Yes, very good looking. White-grey hair. Yes, 'statesmanlike', just as you say. A man like this saying these things. Saying them *then*. Oh, it would work in a sappy film now, of course it would, but things were different then. And so. I understood. I accepted that there wasn't anything else he could have done. He did the best thing he could for her. He thought he was saving her life.

Years later Edward apologised for that afternoon. For being short with me, for embarrassing me by showing his feelings. As you realise, I hadn't been embarrassed, I'd been humbled. And besides, he had nothing to apologise for. But by then I'd spent enough time with them – with him and Christina – to know how he cared for her. How he loved her in spite of her own self. But the fact that he felt he should apologise was typical of Edward. He was such a gentleman. A gentle man. Noble. Kind. Fair. Oh, yes, he could also be *terribly* funny. Like Christina. They could really play the fool, muck about, really make you laugh.

I'm grateful that I had the opportunity to get to know him properly over time. I have my daughter, Sarah, to thank for that. And I'm especially grateful for all the time she spent with the Hopwoods at Heron's Gate which meant I was often there to drop off and pick up, which – with the Hopwoods – was never done without being invited in for a drink, a meal, given the time to talk. To be enfolded in the warm embrace that life in their messy, eccentric, laughter-fuelled house offered.

You know I never heard Edward Hopwood say a bad word about any thing nor anyone. He just took it all on the chin and dealt with it. Even the constant crap and carping from Harriet – and God, did she put him through the mill – he just dealt with it; no drama, no hysterics. Well, only Harriet's own. Harriet is a deeply troubled woman. You must know that by now.

I like to think that Christina having Sarah around helped her too, that it was reciprocal. No, Sarah didn't usurp Harriet. That's an interesting take on it. Whoever suggested that? The two cousins were great friends for a while. But Harriet... well, Harriet is another story. She's her own story. Though you have to question what is real, what *she* thinks is real. Years of drugs and alcohol, on top of a .... Let's say, 'disordered' turn of mind, none of it helped her keep any sort of equilibrium.

So, yes. That's right - much to her mother's chagrin from about the age of twelve Sarah spent the best part of every holiday with Edward and Christina. And to all intents and purposes Heron's Gate became her home in her late teens and right through university, right up until she and Liam were married. She'd be the first to admit she considered it more her home than my flat or her mother's place. And then when Liam died - complications with leukaemia, he was only thirty-one - Sarah spent that first, sad Christmas with them. Katherine, my granddaughter, was only eighteen months old. It was a terrible time. Christina and Edward were such a help. And even when Christina was going underground in a depressive episode - even when Harriet was practising for her role in hell (and they often coincided as events, yes) – even then Edward remained his usual, warm and hospitable self towards all of us.

Dear Sarah, she's always had a good, open heart, my daughter. Honest and open. Not at all like her mother. Perhaps being so much with her uncle and aunt rubbed off on her – nurture not nature. But you'll need to talk to Sarah about that. I'm sorry, I have to go, I have an appointment the other side of London. It has been ….. well … odd, curious …. talking to you. I hope I have helped you with your research. What did you say you were studying again?

CHRISTINA

Back, back, take me back, I don't want to go this way. My hands are numb with the cold, I'm cold from the inside out. None of these later pictures has me in them, just my shadow because Edward isn't in them with me. Please, please I want to go back to before Edward dies.

Sarah is here. Such a good girl. She holds my hand in the darkness. Her hands are always clean. But I can smell the earth on them inspite of her scrubbing. She's been digging in the garden, trying to clear the weeds, but everything is too knotted in the roots. She mustn't dig up the past. It won't help. Not me, not Harriet. It won't.

My darling Edward. I'm so, so sorry.

Gosh, there you are, playing croquet on the lawn with Sarah and Harriet. And that's Christopher Benson. Snake in the grass. The grass of the croquet lawn is so green and smooth, it looks like velvet. Like the dress I wore all those years ago on that incredible night on Cork Street. Green as Daphne's emeralds.

I know she has just died. Daphne, Christopher's mother. In Los Angeles. She should be here, is she here? Will she tell them our secrets? Do they tell your secrets here? Or do they already know all that we did, all the things that happened? Daphne? I know what you did for me - my father's death - what you and Jack did. I know. But why did you tell Edward that lie, that my baby girl had died? I can smell Daphne's perfume, so why can't I see her?

I don't want to see my father. I will not see my father here. I have no breath. There is nothing of me left to give to him.

Claudia's here. She's come to check us out because Sarah wants to spend the summer here. It is such a hot day. Claudia is zipped up tight in a middle-aged dress, buttoned up in her middle-age. I am holding on to her arm but she is miles away from me, buttoned up in her self-righteousness. Oh, we can't have that, forgetting your buttons, do up your buttons. Right up tight under your chin. Keep it buttoned up. Or else. Or else what, Claudia? What would you reveal? You, who knew all along. Who let him and then let him move on to me. How do you hold it all in there?

But Claudia, I have forgiven you. I knew it was the only way to survive. Don't you remember? That story of Lot's daughters? I gave you a postcard but you chose not to see. You always chose to ignore the truth and how you locked it up all so tight. You think no-one remembers. I have forgiven but how could I ever forget?

Running, this is running, feet on sand and laughter and shouting children, running down a pebbly path and out onto the beach. Oh, the dearest children! But wait, who *are* they? Do I know these children? That looks like Sophie's brother Willard waiting on the sea wall. I think Sarah is here but she is not a child, not one of these. Is one of these children *hers*? I don't know. Time is all mixed up. I am running with the children, I can feel the roar of the wind. Let's blow the cobwebs away! Oh, but sometimes the whirl and shout of life, it is so strong it knocks the wind out of me. The wind, whipping our faces, see how my hair is coiling, am I Medusa? Am I being punished? I was once a Princess, locked up in secrets, held in secret places where it was dark and my face was always pushed down into the dirt and life was close to extinguished.

But they keep pulling me back, these images are keeping me awake, keeping me staring into that place with all those secrets I could hardly breathe for fear of my lungs filling with black tar and sand and stagnant water. I am falling down and round, down and round, in a spiral, slipping down and down into the dark at the bottom of the sea and there are no mermaids and nothing but watery silt in my mouth and blackness. Edward is at the edge of the place I am falling into, he stands on the lip of the abyss. He is holding my shoes in one hand and my soul in the other. My soul is dark and swirling. If I take one more breath in, my soul becomes the sea and the sea becomes my soul.

Shhh. Spirals in the eye of a bird. It's the heron. See him on the other side of the pond. His old twig legs. We're all getting old. There are weeds on the terrace and I don't have the energy to pull them because I'm slipping into the eye of the heron. I'm in a room that smells of anger and whisky and here is Harriet, slumped in an old leather chair in the corner. Harriet? I put my ear to her chest to see if she is breathing. Her breath is foul, whisky and cigarettes. My daughter. Lost in the world, lost to me. Both my daughters are lost, the one infront of me and the one I gave away.

Easter. The Easter egg hunt. I'm hiding chocolate eggs in the orchard, before the children are awake. Can you hear the birds, did someone teach them to sing this way? Sophie's over there, I can hear her, talking with Christopher. Are we all drunk? It's only ten o'clock in the morning. Or is it just me? Something is making me so woozy and forgetful and ….

Oops! I'm wearing my favourite thing; my old nightgown. It used to belong to Aunt Margaret. It is lawn cotton and it is rotting. I have just caught it on a rose bush and the skirt has a rip in it. Christopher calls out, he says "Is that Cinderella over there? Yoo-hoo, darling!" This stretch on my face is a smile I think. Did you know you can forget how a smile feels? And this other feeling, like someone playing a glockenspiel only it's on my ribs, this is laughing? Swirl and whirl. You can forget what these things feel like, do you know that? Edward says he wishes he could capture my laughter in a bottle and when I am deep in the abyss, he could feed it to me, sip by sip until the life of it would fill my heart so I would begin to rise, up and up, slowly, from that dark and cold and airless place. Only he doesn't know what really holds me down, what pulls me

down, filling my wellingtons with green slime and shame
and shame and shame.

Sip, sip. That's Christopher in the kitchen. He is stirring
a pot of soup, tasting it with a spoon. His cigarette ash is
about to drop in. He is always drunk now. I don't know what
to say to him, I don't know what to say to anyone. He is
starting to cry. I can feel his tears. Thick and sticky in his
throat. I can see them, they run down his face and drip into
the soup. Salty. He says 'sorry, sorry, sorry' over and over
again. He doesn't really know the consequence of what he
has done,what he has said. He was only acting with his
words, just acting in that way he has, all pretence. He can't
see that he has broken a tiny, cobweb's thread that was still
holding Harriet to me, the last tiny row of untidy stitches,
the last silken loop of our connection. He doesn't know the
damage he has done. He doesn't know that one day the drugs
he has just introduced her to are going to make her do
something that no one will be able to fix. Now. Here. Already
it's too late, already the path he set her on is coming to a
place where she will only ever be able to go round and round,
she will never be released from her guilt. From her prison.
One day everyone will know everything but it will be too late
for me. And much too late for Harriet. If this is dying, if this
is my death then I will be released. But Harriet? They will
lock up her soul and she will never find peace.

Harriet. The words between us spin like acrobats, all
this clutter of emotion. You would never let me hold on to
you, you would never let me hold you tight to me. When you
were young I used to pull you to me, hold you so tight

against my body, so you couldn't fight. Now you have even greater weapons than your hands and feet and spittle, weapons that Christopher has given you. And here you come with your anger, to smack the truth against my chin. See these smudges of pain, purple and scarlet on my face. There are nails raking underneath my skin and blood that will never clot.

This is Sarah. With me on the terrace again at Heron's Gate. Edward has gone with Joseph on location. They are shooting a film in Ireland. I'm sipping orange rind tea. Sarah makes it for me, from orange peel, just like Gloria used to. Sweet, gentle Sarah. The drugs Edward says will help me make me sleepy and hollow and I don't want to eat. Sophie is reminding me about the high teas we used to have here. I cannot hear her properly. I am in the cracks of the world, wedged in narrow passageways, hiding from him, from me. And all about there is smoke and heat and a bell ringing, long and slow, like a death knell and my father's hands reaching, clawing.

The house is sleeping. Can you hear the old pipes clang and wheeze? I love this house. Gentle ghosts live here, you can sometimes hear them singing. Lullabies to the children, the living ones and the lost ones. But there is some static tonight, there is not enough oxygen, they cannot breathe enough to tune into me. The little spirits know there is danger. Prickling skin, cold sweat.

That's Harriet I can hear. She is hammering on the door. 'Let me in! Mother! Sarah! Let me in you bitches!' Somebody open the door, for God's sake, open the door! Harriet? What have you done, my daughter, what have you done now?

Here is Harriet but she is sleeping now. Quiet at last. I gave her one of the pills. The room still smells of alcohol. And vomit and disinfectant. It's a beautiful afternoon outside. I am sad that she is missing it. But would she see it if she were conscious? Last night, when she was fighting us all, fighting poor Sarah with her fists, spitting in my face, kicking out at Edward and her stiletto stabbing heels, when she threw that plate at me that cut my head, she said nothing here was real, that it is all a sham, that she hates us all for the sham. Well, her hatred is real because I can see it, sticking to the walls, thick and black, like wet tar. But the sunlight that is filtering through the curtains, silver threads, that is real too. And this love I have for Harriet, pumping through my veins, scarlet, sore, tangled, that is real, that is real too. But she is in her own darkness and even if she wanted to open her eyes and she did... she wouldn't see the sunlight and the swirling dust motes. She wouldn't want to see my love, swirling gold and silver.

Silver threads, silver buttons. We are in the dining room. Edward and I and a man in a uniform with silver buttons. He is a policeman and he is here because Harriet is in trouble again. There is more to these nights when she comes home drunk. Edward is telling the policeman about it. There are things Edward has kept from me. He has to tell the police. We have to, even though it feels as if we are betraying her, betraying our daughter. Edward is finding it hard to speak, he is close to tears. Edward is an old man, this is not what his life should be like now. I want to protect him because he has always protected me but do I have enough left? Is there even enough air in this house now that Harriet is here? She is a raging fire that takes the oxygen, burning everything in her path.

Oh, no. Please, no. I don't want to watch this. Edward's last birthday. We are having a dinner party. I can smell the candle wax on the long dining room table. Our friends are here and there is so much goodwill, so much kindness in this room. The scent of newly-cut grass comes through the open terrace doors. Here is Joseph and there, Sophie. And dear Willard. And Lizzie, Sophie's daughter, with her husband Mark. And Sarah and her husband. Now that one won't be long here. I can see him, even as he sits right in front of me, I can see him fading away, see him turning to ashes. Poor Sarah, my poor child. You did not deserve this. With your trusting heart and your soft, soft soul. I wish I could change all that for you but I don't know how. Wait! Wait a minute. Who's that? That young woman between you? I know her... what's she saying? Damn it! The candles are flickering. Is that her? Is that you? Hello? Hello?

Damn it, Harriet! You always break a mood! We have not heard from her for two months this time. She is walking through the French windows. She is very drunk. She is wearing a cocktail dress, it has some staining down the front, red wine I think, some food. Her shoes have dried mud on them. She has bleached her lovely hair. It falls around her face in peroxide yellow rats' tails. She is so very thin. She is talking, but most of her words are too slurred to make sense. She always wants the same thing, she always wants money. I see Edward closing his eyes for a moment, taking a deep breath. Not again, Harriet, not again. I will not let you do this. I will not let you punish us.

Watch me standing up, watch me speaking quickly, asking politely, firmly, if dear Willard would give me a hand. Harriet is too drunk and stoned to fight, although she tries at first. She bites Willard on the back of the hand and draws blood. This makes her laugh. I grab my handbag, ask everyone to please excuse us. I tell them I am just going to pop Harriet upstairs. Oh, but I'm not doing that, not this time. Willard and I are walking out to the car, it is raining so hard, we are holding Harriet between us. She smells. She needs a wash. A good long soak. She smells of urine and whisky and sex. And this time I will not let her in. I will not. See how plaint she has become now she has what she wants, now she has disrupted our lives again. Now she has hurt me. Again. She leans forward between the front seats and hisses at me to give her money.

I am saying quietly, 'You drive, Willard. Take us up to the forest, by the airman's grave, that'll do.' Oh, yes, Harriet, you need to find out what it's like to feel abandoned and alone with no-one to rescue you. With dirt under your nails and your face in the mud. Left out in the rain.

HARRIET

When my mother was well again, well enough to be left in charge of the house in Trinidad, my father brought me back to England. He brought me back with him three times, each time in July. We always stayed in London for the first week and then on the coast, at a small hotel for the second, a short walk from the sea. Not round here. Somewhere.

We came because my father wanted me to see a psychiatrist in London. We went to this tall building in Harley Street. It echoed. The floors were wooden and there were Persian rugs and high-backed leather chairs with gold studs all around the edges. The man we saw specialised in treating children. He told my father there wasn't anything wrong with me. I just didn't want to speak. He said I would, when I was ready. He knew my silence was my security. He said it would happen one day, automatically. He didn't know

I was holding my breath so I could see the pulse in my eyes. Because I wanted to feel my heart beat so I could be sure I was really alive because no-one noticed me and I didn't know if this was living.

Once, after the appointment we went to the theatre. I remember that day so clearly; this whirlwind of glamour and excitement. Dorothy came with us, she met us at the theatre. Yes that one. She was living back in the States but I suppose she was in London for something. It seemed weird seeing her there, in London, on a damp Wednesday afternoon. Not in the sun, not in the heat. She looked ordinary. Drab even. She held my father's hand when the lights went down in the theatre.

That was the first time I ever went to a theatre. I can still remember walking into the auditorium that very first time. Gold and lots of crimson velvet. And the airless hush as the curtain rose. Oh, I don't remember what the play was, I can't remember everything for Christ's sake.

Dorothy came back with us to the hotel my father and I were staying in. I sat squashed up between her and Dad in the cab. She put me to bed. I remember her coming back into the room later to check I was asleep. I wasn't, so she sat on the edge of the bed and told me about her animals back home, she had a dog named Blue, she said it was named because of a song. Me and you and a dog named Blue. Her perfume was very strong. She was wearing two thin gold bangles. She took them off so I could look at them and she let me hold them in my hand. When I woke up the next morning Dorothy was gone but my father gave me an envelope. In it were those two bangles.

We left London then to stay at the funny hotel by the sea. I had the box then, with the bangles in it. But eventually I lost them. Or I may have sold them, I don't remember. I didn't see Dorothy ever again. I don't know what became of her.

I remember I cried a lot when we were in England because part of me wanted to go back to my mother in Trinidad but part of me didn't want to be near her. It was very confusing living with my mother. When she was normal she was fun but she could suddenly change and everything would go wrong. I don't know. I was a child for Christ's sake. Before we left England I would just lie on the bed in the hotel, crying and crying. There was a woman who worked in that hotel who always looked out for me. She had a daughter who was a couple of years older than me and this woman found me crying so she took me downstairs to play with her daughter. Her daughter was very pretty. She had red hair, like you. Like mine would be if I let it. I hate red hair. You obviously feel okay about it. I hate it. I've bleached mine since I was seventeen. Haven't you ever wanted to change it? Didn't you get called names at school? Each to their own.

We played in the gardens, this carrot top girl and me. There were bushes full of little butterflies. Some special bush. My mother would've known what it was. But I'd never seen so many different types of butterfly. There were dozens of them. We sat on the grass together, that other girl and me. The wet grass left green smudges on my skirt. Looking back now, it's like it's all in slow motion. The whole thing.

Wow. I am there and I can see the movement of the butterflies' wings. Wow, I can almost believe I'm really there again. It must be the drugs they're giving me in here. I was really missing my mother. God. I wanted to take the butterflies back to my mother because I thought they would make her better. That girl, she had said something about butterflies being happiness, something like that. Christ.

I don't want to do any more of this. Enough. That's enough. What do you want from me anyway? There's nothing to find in here, just rubbish, rotting rubbish. Just shit. Stinking shit. All this digging. For what? All this digging for words and worms and lips and lies and kisses that turn to hisses in the wet black grass. Don't make me angry. I haven't done the anger management class yet, so you had better watch it. You with your bloody orange hair.

Once I put my fists through a window because I was angry. Look. I've got scars, see? Jesus, I was angry *that* day I can tell you. I've told them here all about it. I told them I didn't mean to do it. But I did. I was sixteen. I can remember it exactly. Standing at my bedroom window at Heron's Gate, looking down into the garden. I could see my mother and father. They were standing on the terrace, facing each other, and my father was talking. I opened the small top window to see if I could hear but I only heard the low hum of his voice. I couldn't make out the words. I tried to make out the shape of his lips. I remember the gardener was cutting the beech hedge that wound round the lawn. Click click click, I could hear the click click click of his shears and the click click click of their tongues.

And then my mother started blubbing about something. Always bloody blubbing. Then she's sort of crumpling, all pathetic and my father put his arms around her. She folds into him. She was wearing one of her big black linen smocks and when he hugged her to him it was like she was this big black crumpled bird. All squashed. A squashed blackbird. I could hear her crying. It just felt like my head was full of her crying... and her moaning and lots of shadows and black crows flapping in my head, so I started banging on the window, banging, banging with my fists. I felt the glass give. That slow motion thing again. Pieces of glass like diamonds. And a tinkling sound. Like water, it was like water in a fountain. No pain or anything. My father's face, my mother's face. Looking up. Then the feel of hot blood down my arms. Blood is much warmer than you think, you know. It's quite a pleasant feeling.

They couldn't get in because I'd locked the door. I could hear them shouting. They were banging on the door. More shouting and then a crashing sound. It was my mother who pushed the door in. The wood splintered at the lock. I remember bits of white paint flying off, flecking the carpet. Like snow. And a smell of splintered wood and blood. Blood smells like rusty iron. I didn't mean to do it. I kept telling them. But I did.

They called an ambulance. The ambulance man put me in a wheelchair. I couldn't look up at him. I was worried that they would all think I'd tried to slash my wrists. I didn't want them thinking I'd tried to slash my wrists, that was the sort of thing my bloody mother would do, not me. I think

I said that to the ambulance man. It had been an accident. The ambulance man wore heavy boots that were very shiny and black. When he jumped out the back of the ambulance I saw he was wearing odd socks, one grey, one black. I thought, perhaps he gets dressed in the dark, so he doesn't wake his wife.

The floor of an ambulance has rubber circles on it. My mother was kneeling on the floor. She was stroking my hair. Tucking it behind my ear.

It wasn't so bad. I had stitches, twenty-one of them. I was unconscious when they did it. When I woke up the doctor was there. He made a joke about maybe taking me out for a drink when my age matched the number of my stitches. And he winked like a dirty old man only he was young, not old at all except he looked very tired of life. He sat on the edge of the bed. He had a moustache. He said I was lucky. He lifted my good hand and squeezed it in a sort of handshake. The backs of his hands were very hairy. He said my mother was just next door. He told me that she'd damaged her shoulder when she broke into my room to get to me. He said what a lucky girl I was to have such a lovely Mum. I was lucky she got to me so quickly. I just cried.

They made me see some psychiatrist woman before I left the hospital. I had to go down to some shitty old hut for the appointment; they had these ancient wooden huts for the psychiatric unit, out the back of the main building of the hospital. It was dirty and falling down, like I imagined an abandoned prison camp might be. I was meant to go back as an out-patient but I didn't. I couldn't believe I'd got away with the drug thing I'd been into with that pervy Christopher Benson bloke and I wasn't about to give them another opportunity to find out.

I remember going home and the dogs jumping up at me and my father calling to them to get down. And lying on the top landing of the house with them, the three of us looking out at the front drive and the beech hedge just turning green in spots. Me and the two dogs. They were quite old then. I think I was waiting for something to happen. We were all waiting for something to happen. I felt I was in this bubble. It was hard to breathe. Something had to happen to burst the bubble so I could breathe. I wanted to move about in my life again but I was stuck somehow. I could feel myself getting smaller and smaller and deeper and deeper inside myself. I was terrified I was becoming my bloody lunatic mother.

CRUSTS

Leafy suburbs, just on the edge of the main town. Big houses with neat front gardens and gravel driveways. This doesn't seem the right sort of place. Suburbs and subterfuge.

Number twenty-two. There are two terracotta tubs by the front door. Little purple-faced violas clustered amongst a variegated vine. There are two cigarette butts in the left tub, one has a red lipstick smudge.

Eleanor pushes through the door. A hallway with smart, tubular furniture, a glass-topped table, a hexagonal mirror with a design on it, lillies and hummingbirds. There is a small sign that says 'reception' on a high wooden, semi-circular counter, like a hotel. And a woman with a neat, blonde bob standing behind it. She smiles; her teeth are perfectly straight and very white. Eleanor thinks this could be the reception for a dentist. Or a plastic surgeon.

Everything so clean and perfect and neat and smiling. The woman is professional and welcoming and friendly all at the same time and Eleanor wonders how much of it is her natural demeanour and how much of it corporate training.

Eleanor has a wad of notes in an envelope. The cash machine only had tens available. She thinks it is right that this whole thing makes her feel seedy, dirty, cheap. One hundred and fifty pounds in used notes. She hands the thick envelope to the woman, who takes it, smiling, and discreetly counts. But the notes Eleanor got from the machine are too crisp and clean, they stick together, so the woman opens her drawer and gets out a little pink, rubber thimble which she places on her thumb better to grip the edges.

The King was in his counting house, counting out his money.

When she speaks to Eleanor, the woman looks right into her eyes; she must've been told to do that, Eleanor thinks. All part of her training for the job. The woman's hair is so smooth and neat and thick, it tucks behind her ears, a perfect shiny curtain. Eleanor wonders what it looks like first thing in the morning. Does it take her hours to get it like that? She remembers reading once about a famous magazine editor – with a bob just like that - who had her hairdresser come at five every morning to do her hair. Or maybe it's a wig, made from the tresses of some Norwegian woman who now sports a short, masculine crop.

"Now you haven't had any breakfast have you? Nothing after midnight, I hope."

Concentrate. Stop letting my mind wander.

Eleanor shakes her head. Her mouth is dry with that stale toothpaste taste. She is dying for a cup of tea, a slice of toast with a dab of honey.

The queen was in the parlour, eating bread and honey.

"That's great. Shirley will show you to the lounge. Is there someone with you or coming to meet you after the procedure?"

Eleanor shakes her head and swallows hard, takes a deep breath, forces a smile. Really she'd just like to let the tears roll, to let herself dissolve. We are made up of what percentage water? If she starts to cry she thinks she will end up just a puddle on the floor with a face on top.

Shirley is a very petite Asian woman in a pale blue zip-up overall with pockets on the front, like dinner ladies wore at school when Eleanor was a kid. She will have been very beautiful when she was young. But her skin has that sallow, drained look that the English climate often gives to Asian women. She looks faded. Or perhaps her luck just ran out; the colours faded to shiny white and surgical blue. And now she works here.

She guides Eleanor by the elbow to a small sitting room. There is a strong perfume in the room. She sees another vase of lilies on a corner table. The scent is overpowering. A horizontally slatted blind is pulled across and the words "Fire Exit" glow green above it.

"You okay?" Shirley puts hand on Eleanor's forearm, looks back towards reception as she does so. "If you like, you sit in garden, it is nice. Fresh air for you. There, garden through there, fire exit. See? No alarm, is okay. I come later and find you, okay?"

Eleanor shrugs her overnight bag, the things she had at Fiona's, higher up her shoulder and steps out into the little urban garden and finds a rustic bench to sit on. Goes through her things. Toothbrush, underwear, pyjamas. Her favourite flannel pyjamas. She'd bought them in the men's department years ago, for a camping trip with Fiona. They have a paisley pattern on them. She hadn't thought how paisley looks like tears. They have a drawstring waist. She had sewn up the flies. Her mother would have laughed. Joan would have laughed. Toothbrush, underwear, book to read, pyjamas and here's what she's looking for - a packet of sanitary towels that they tell you to bring. She'd felt embarrassed buying sanitary towels, as if the woman behind the counter would think her naive and unsophisticated. The book is Iris Murdoch. *The Sea, The Sea*. It's an old copy of Willard's. There is a teacup ring on the front cover. Glancing over the fence, she sees a normal, family garden next door. A smart, substantial whirligig washing line, thick towels and heavy sheets, pairs of socks sharing a peg each pair. An odd, lone sock – child sized - with a peg to itself at the end of a row.

The maid was in the garden, hanging out the clothes.

The garden of the clinic itself is a surprise. The flowerbeds are newly turned, the earth rich and dark. A gravel path, bordered with a pretty clay edging, like a pie crust or a plaited loaf. A bird bath on an ornate stand. Someone has thrown some bits of bread out for the birds.

Rosebushes, neatly pruned, with name tags stuck into the ground. She bends to read the names. Pink Penelope. Victoriana. She can smell the earth. There is a worm, wriggling. A blackbird waits a few feet away.

Along came a blackbird and pecked off her nose.

When Joan, Mum, read that rhyme to me, we played another of our little games. She used to try to grab my nose and I would dive under the sheets. Floral sheets, sewn sides to middle when they wore out. My mum was always making do when I was small. Bleaching pillowcases in a bucket by the back door to get a stain out. Patching things, darning elbows and the heels of socks on a wooden darning mushroom. Sitting up at the kitchen table, unravelling an old sweater for the wool, while I did my homework. Humming to herself. My mum, Joan, sitting in my Dad's – Patrick's - plaid dressing gown, with the sleeves pushed up her arms. Humming. Brown arms, strong wrists. A tiny gold watch my father had given her. Freckles on her arms in the summer and a white patch where the watch went. I can see her in the summer, kneeling on the grass by the flowerbeds, with a cardboard box for the weeds. She loved her garden. See her smiling at a blackbird, waiting for worms. And my mother, humming to herself. Strong, capable hands, turning the earth.

Eleanor is kneeling on the grass now. A supplicant. Lost, praying to something, someone. The knees of her jeans are getting wet. The blackbird has hopped nearer. He is pecking in the earth, she can hear the snip, snip, snip of his beak. Snip, snip, snip at her heart.

She jumps. Shirley's hand tapping her on her shoulder.

"You get bad knees on wet grass. You come now?"

Eleanor follows Shirley back into the house. Thick, cream carpet on the stairs. A pale lavender-themed room with the blind pulled down. Three leather-look daybeds, royal blue thows with rich, satin edging; one daybed occupied by a sleeping mound turned on its side, the other by an older woman, reading a magazine. She looks up and smiles at Eleanor; a half smile, one side of the mouth, a resigned smile that says *but what else can we do, eh?*

Shirley shows her into a cubicle, tells her she can leave her things and her shoes here.

I am shaking. But I'm hot. I have to get this damned cardigan off. The buttons are hard to undo. And so stupid to wear jeans, why did I wear jeans, stupid.

"Ready?"

Along a landing. Music from a radio. Terry Wogan. Val Doonican, Engelbert Humperdinck. Music that would normally make her cringe, singers' names that usually make her laugh, but not today, walking along a hushed corridor. Her feet in disposable towelling slippers, the sort you get in a hotel or a beauty spa, perhaps, with a towelling robe. She wishes she had painted her toenails.

My head is empty. Nobody knows, tiddly-pom, how cold my toes, tiddly-pom, are growing.

A room with lights and frosted glass at the windows and a sort of dentist's chair, long and high, with a paper covering. A male nurse in a plastic cap, like a hotel giveaway shower cap, saying -

"So let's see... Eleanor. What a beautiful name. We okay doc, leaving that ring on?" He has a lilting accent, musical. Irish. .

"It was my... my mum's. Please don't take it off."

"No problem. Not a problem." He squeezes her hand.

Hold my hand, hold my hand. 'I just want to be sure of you' said Piglet to Winnie-the-Pooh. Winnie-the-Pooh and Christopher Robin. Jack Benson and Christopher.

"Just a little prickle and you'll feel lovely, lovely and relaxed. Think about walking on a beach, rolling waves, pebbles turning over and over, and the wind in your face, cool and fresh and the rush of the sea... " She sees the male nurse wears an earring. More faces. All smiling. "Here we go, then, five, four, three ......"

Counting me down. Counting you out. Moonlight and shadows and running, running down a corridor with thick cream carpet and paintings of flowers and black birds and everything is trembling. The world is trembling, breaking through its crust. Crumbling, tumbling, tissue paper thoughts. A-tissue! A-tissue! We all fall down. Light bulbs on wires, naked neon dancers, static sparks and I am in the eye of the storm, in the eye of a bird. And something is roaring and the houses are cracking at the seams, see them falling. Walls and roofs like numbered flaps, flopping like a film set, slapping on the sand and all the unlocked secrets of a life are tumbling into the sea, the sea. And something is dripping, dripping. Coloured tears, staining the front of my shirt. I'll never get that stain out. Dripping, dripping, I am going down, going down but there aren't any mermaids and they are not singing each to each. There is a blackbird flying high above, do you see? He is looking for a place to land but there is water everywhere and a car skidding and a train and then Eleanor is in the path of the train and a sign says 'No Stopping on the Tracks'. And a woman's voice saying 'Stop the train. Please stop the train.'

"Stop! Stop! Stop!"

SARAH

Stop, please stop right there. It's not that I haven't been honest with you. I'm not being selective in what I'm telling you, why would you think that? Really. It's just that the other stuff, the times when Aunt Christina was poorly, I just don't remember them so clearly. The *impression* I have of life at Heron's Gate, looking back across all those years, is honestly one of happiness. Like I said, sunlight and magic. And maybe I don't want to remember, maybe there's that too? Why would I? Would *you*?

Well, of course there were signs. Sometimes things weren't quite... Oh, I don't know. They weren't always quite as easy and happy. But it certainly wasn't all doom and gloom. I don't want you to think that, it's so important to me. It *was* so important to me, all that time with my uncle and aunt. Surely you can understand that? But, no, I don't want to give the wrong impression. I want to paint the right picture. Funny - paint the right picture. That's funny.

Okay. Certain scenes I remember. Sitting with uncle Edward in their bedroom. In the dark. Aunt Christina crying quietly under the covers. Whimpering. It was like whimpering. Aunt Sophie and I made her orange-peel tea. That was all she would drink. I never really liked oranges, but I ate them when I was there so there would be peel to make her orange tea. Oranges tend to give me stomach ache now. Silly how your body reacts to your mind, your emotions. Silly how we can't control it.

There was one Christmas, after Harriet had been in trouble... shoplifting was Harriet's particular thing at first...when she was about sixteen...

It snowed that Christmas. There were icicles hanging down outside the bedroom window and I broke off a piece of one and wrapped it in a towel to put on Aunt Christina's forehead. I remember her hair all stuck to her face. Her hair was still quite long then, she didn't have it all cut off until after Uncle Edward died. Beautiful, thick red hair. Like in a Botticelli painting. Is it Botticelli? Oh, dear, Aunt Christina would be furious that I can't remember that.

But sometimes she would smile at me and that brief, stiff smile was everything. It curled my heart. Just to know she was there again, somewhere there. Somewhere, somehow back with us, just a bit of her; and that we were back for *her*, just a bit of her reality. Afterwards, when she was better, she would tell me that smiling was impossible when she was in that place, in what she called her living hell. That to smile would have been as if to tear the skin of her face. Awful. But I understand that now. I don't think you can unless you have experienced depression yourself.

She would say she was somewhere else but nowhere when she was depressed, as if she were living in another plane. They say the perception of another plane means you're insane. Insane. It's such a silly word. In. Sane. Out of your mind. Funny expressions.

It was so sad - so poignant, cruel even - how someone who was so connected to nature, who was so full of life - somebody so loving, so beautiful, so inspired by the smallest things of life, by nature - how she could succumb to those depressive episodes. How she could be so fragile. Yes, it was confusing. It would have been confusing for a child. I don't think I found it confusing though. Well yes, you're right, she wasn't my mum. It was easier for me being one step away.

Aunt Sophie – not a real aunt, no, I mean Sophie Lawson - says Aunt Christina was always very sensitive, always had been. She says a touch could be a punch, a whisper a scream and love to her was heaven and hell both, side by side. And surely it *was* about extremes. Christina lived extremes; she never lived it in the middle, never a mediocre, middle ground. When she was up, bright, she used to say she was glad she wasn't ordinary, that she could connect to life, was so bound to life. And yet there she could also be, falling away, grabbing for but not reaching a flailing, loosened end.

She was always chatting away to her little terrier dogs. She would chat to a bumble bee! It's okay to giggle, it *is* silly.

But it was beautiful too. She would fish a ladybird out of a water trough. Spend ages trying to get a spider on a piece of paper so she could lift it out of the sink or the bath. If she saw a dead badger or hedgehog or squirrel in the road, she would be so distressed.

Yes, but I'm ashamed to admit it. I *was* a little frightened of my aunt when she was struggling with her depression. Everyone thinks I was this wonderful little nurse, but I wasn't. All the time I sat with her I wished and wished I could go outside. Get away from that dark room. My heart wasn't in it, my heart wasn't *there* for her. I wanted it to be but it wasn't. I wasn't very brave. I was just a teenager who thought playing nursemaid was fun until it got too .... weird, difficult. It's hateful saying that. Hateful. I'm so sorry.

I think my aunt was brave. I think it took courage to live with sensitivity like that, to be that sensitised to the world - to the pain of the world. Perhaps it was her courage that made her seem to shimmer with life when she was normal, when she was okay.

I definitely believe it takes a certain type of courage to die, to end your own life. I know that's not a popular or comfortable thing to say. My mother says it is the most selfish act one can ever perform. They always say people's minds are confused - "*not in their right mind*" - or that the drugs worked against them. Don't they? It's what my mother says - but I think that's because we can't bear the truth that somebody might choose to *face* their death. Confront death with their *life*. It's too frightening a concept for us. It's all too frightening. Do you see? That's why I say she had courage. I don't think suicide is cowardly. People say it's cowardly, don't they? But that's just old-fashioned and religious, isn't it? Life is precious, blah blah blah. Well it is if you can really live it. But life isn't a gift bestowed on us by some deity with a beard; life is *ours,* my life, your life, his life, her life. And we have a right to decide what to do with it. We should have the right to decide not to live it. And, yes, there is pain and hurt for those let behind but they have to understand the pain and hurt that that person lived with every moment of their lives. The *distress* of just living.

I wonder if Harriet feels *any* guilt. Does she? I mean, we know Aunt Christina tried to end her own life a few times before. And I think she *meant* to do it even if I don't want to believe that. It wasn't just trying to get attention like Harriet says.

No, I don't think that. I don't think it's that we weren't important enough for her. There was no betrayal. Like I said. If life is intolerable, then ....

Harriet doesn't have depression. Harriet has too much anger and fight. Harriet is essentially deranged. She is evil. I don't want to talk – to *think* about Harriet. None of us wants to think any more than we have to about Harriet and the things she does. Has done. That's why Lizzie Lawson and I won't see her any more. Yes. I do mean evil. Evil and deranged.

Aunt Christina never gave up on Harriet. I wish she had. Time after time Harriet would turn up drunk and foul and Aunt Christina just got on with it.

Yes, there was that one time when she and Willard Dexter drove her up to the heath and left her there. But that was only because Aunt Christina had wanted to protect uncle Edward. It was his birthday party. You have to remember he was an old man when all of this was happening, when Harriet was stealing, drinking, dealing in drugs. She used to turn up drunk or completely out of it on drugs, just pitch up at Heron's Gate. Sometimes late at night, hammering on the door. One of us would always let her in and Aunt Christina always tried to help her. Or other times we would find her asleep in the garden, under a bush or in a stable. Every time, Aunt Christina took her in again and nursed her. Over and over again. I know Sophie Lawson had a real go once, shouted at Aunt Christina, told her to let Harriet go to hell, but she wouldn't give up. She always said the same thing. 'She's my daughter, how can I? She's my daughter. I will *not* abandon her.' How did she stand it? If Aunt Sophie is right, how did such a soul, such a sensitive soul, stand such spite? So you see, she had courage to face that too, to keep on trying with Harriet. Until that one time. That one, single time when she – when we all – had had enough.

Oh, what Harriet did with the horses, that was terrible. There you are. Evil. It was evil. And the worst thing she could ever have done to her mother. She knew it, of course she knew it. Of course it wasn't an accident. Aunt Christina never said otherwise but I'm pretty sure she knew it wasn't. Of all the things that Harriet did, all the terrible trouble she got into, the drug dealing, the stealing... of *all* the things, the worst was letting the horses out like that. That night, right after Uncle Edward's funeral. No, no, no she wasn't just letting them out. It would be easier to think that but... she knew what could happen and part of her wanted it to happen. It would be consistent with the rest of her behaviour. She was out of control, with drugs, drink, something, of course she was. She wanted to hurt her mother. Because Pegasus – the oldest horse they had - had been a birthday present to her mother from her father. He'd been born in their own stables in Trinidad. What was so awful was that the poor old horse suffered. Christina had to ask the vet to destroy him. They had put large concrete blocks below the sea wall to stop sand erosion and there had been nowhere for him to land when he jumped. Harriet knew what would happen. I'm sorry if you don't like hearing that, but she *knew*.

Aunt Christina was never the same after that. A double grief. Losing her beloved husband and then her beloved horse. I stayed with her for quite a while after uncle's funeral. My Dad came down a few times too. Sometimes he'd come down to work, when he needed to hide from his agent. My mother wasn't ever invited. She and Dad had long divorced by then.

But, you know, there were still glimpses of the old Auntie Christina. Glimpses of happiness there at Heron's Gate, in spite of all that pain and sadness. After a while she had a few little dinner parties; and there were still children running about the place, Dexter grandchildren. "Rug Rats: The Next Generation" - that's what my Dad dubbed them.

A PRIVATE REASON

And she travelled a bit too, she even took Harriet on a trip
to Australia for Harriet's thirtieth birthday. To have
forgiven her for all of that and then take her away for a trip
around Australia, that took guts. And love. Don't you think?

They did seem to have a sort of truce for a while, when
Harriet stopped drinking. Temporarily. Sometimes Harriet
would be at the house already when I arrived with
Katherine but she didn't show her face much. Sometimes
she had a boyfriend with her. A different one every time.
There was even a husband once did you know? A sort of
travel journalist, called Peter but the marriage was short-
lived. I think he was a bit of a player. The usual good looking
charmer she often chose. Harriet was once very beautiful,
like her parents. Before all the drink and drugs and God
only knows what. Funny. I was always surprised by her
beauty then. It's as if I always had a sense that there was
evil inside, always thought it should have disfigured her.
What do I mean? It's as if one can't accept such evil lurks
inside someone with such a face. We want evil, cruel people
to *look* evil and cruel. We don't want to be misled.

Some people thought – my Dad among them – that Aunt
Christina should have moved out of Heron's Gate after
Uncle Edward died, but she would never have left. She loved
the house too much. In the end she hired Jemima. She's -
she *was* - a sort of housekeeper. I think that's what she was
actually employed as but she became a good friend to all of
us, almost part of the family really. It was really Jemima
who encouraged Aunt Christina to paint a bit again, did you
know? Those seascapes. They're stunning, aren't they? Dad

found them for me. He found them through a friend of a friend. I'm so glad that whoever it was finally agreed to sell them to me. I know, they're amazing aren't they? You can feel the wind on your face. I've been trying to track down some of the work she did when she was young. It would be very interesting to compare the pieces, wouldn't it? But not even Aunt Sophie has any.

The last time I saw my beloved auntie, we went for a walk on the beach. Me and Auntie, little Katherine. One of Jemima's many nephews was with us. It was one of those windy, dirty-brown November days, where the sea looks really grubby and the clouds weigh heavy. When you can't imagine that summer will ever come round again. It suited my mood. Well. It was the anniversary of Liam's death although I didn't say anything. Aunt Christina would have remembered, of course she would, she never forgot things like that. But she didn't say anything. She knew she didn't have to.

Aunt Christina had some sparklers hidden in her pocket for the children. They all ran down the beach together. Little Katherine trying to keep up. They had to huddle by a breakwater, in the lee of the wind, to light the sparklers. I stood on the sea wall. They were laughing and laughing, running. It started to rain and they came running back up the beach. Auntie Christina ran up to me and she held my face in her hands. She looked at me... oh, I'm sorry. Sorry. Just give me a minute...

She said "I hope somebody told my daughter that I loved her."

At the time I wished she wasn't talking about Harriet. Harriet didn't deserve her love.

What? I'm sorry?

You? What do you mean? What are you saying?

HARRIET

When I was little, I thought my mother was a witch. She said stupid things about magic and voices whispering on the wind. Voices. It really used to give me the creeps. And when I was old enough to understand that actually she was just bloody mad, even then it still frightened the hell out of me. Especially the voices bit, when she talked about hearing voices. Even later, when I knew it was just a sign of her going over the edge into one of her depressions, that it was just my mother being a nut job again. Even then it was still a bit scary.

You want to know what it was *really* like. Ha! I'll you what it was really like, I'll tell you. Don't you dare let Sarah and Joseph and all those idiots feed you that romantic, tortured-artist-with-a-wise-soul shit.

She would be wild with energy. She'd throw parties and

stay up all night talking and drinking and smoking. And dancing. All her gestures became extravagant, excessive. She would wave her arms about when she was talking. Like she was trying to catch the words as they came out of her mouth. Everything was always *exaggerated*, *extreme*, larger than life. She'd laugh at the slightest thing, cry at another. All this black eyeliner sliding down her face. And she'd dress really oddly. When she was being *normal*, ordinary, she wore normal clothes, just like any other mother. But when she was being mad she only wore black or white. One or the other. Completely. Do you understand? Com-bloody-pletely. I mean from her underwear to her shoes. It was embarrassing to be seen with her, dressed like that. People keep making out they're surprised to find out she was mad. I don't know why they have to pretend. It was bloody obvious. Even to the fucking gardener. Maybe everyone pretended not to notice for my father's sake. He was always very dignified. He used to say he didn't care what people thought. But I know it embarrassed him. He just never let it show. He always put on a brave face. He used to say, "She's just *unravelling* a little, your poor mum, that's all". That's *all*. He was very, very brave. It was shit. And he never said a bad word against her. A bloody saint, my father.

Once my father found her walking to the village in her nightie. She was carrying an old tin, full of buttons and bits of stuff, all sorts of rubbish. She wouldn't let it go. She always wore a particular nightdress when she was sick. It was Victorian, white of course - yellowed with age, falling apart. My mother would run about the garden in it. Through the orchard, into the paddock. There'd be grass stains on the front where she knelt by the rose beds. She was always doing that. Kneeling and digging in the dirt. Mad as a hatter. And the skirt was all ripped. She wouldn't let anyone mend it. Even her precious little helper, Sarah. My cousin Sarah. Conniving cow. When my father tried to take it off her, to be washed, she would scream at him. She would scream something about if he took her nightdress off she would disappear. Jesus! She would *beg* him to let her wear it. On her hands and knees at his feet, covered in mud, wailing, begging.

Most of the time, if she was missing from the house for any length of time - I mean when she was sick - my father would find her on the beach. She was always rambling about that being where the magic was. She would go there in the middle of the night and stand on the sea wall, just staring out to sea. Or sit in a rock pool, with her back against a breakwater, crying, with the tide coming in and her lap full of pebbles and bits of shell.

My father finally agreed to her being given drugs, but they had the same effect as they'd had in Trinidad. All those darkened rooms again. No shouting in the garden by her window. My mother just lying there, moaning, muttering unintelligible things, begging not to be left alone. Bloody Sarah the Samaritan, hanging around, always in and out with cups of tea my mother never drank and magazines she couldn't possibly have read. Her eyes couldn't even focus on my face, she didn't have a clue who anyone was.

It was hard to get my father to leave her when she was doped, but sometimes he'd have dinner with me. Later on, he'd come up to town. I had a flat. Oh, yeah, they bought me a flat in Clapham, but I sold it ages ago. I don't think they knew that. Who cares.

When my father came up we'd sit and talk, like we used to when I was a kid. Only we'd both be at the whisky bottle this time. We both drank too much. But drinking had always been a big thing in our house. For as long as I could remember. No one thought it wrong. Whisky was a way of giving it all a different - bronzed - hue. Now it's all given this great significance, that my father drank. Because my bloody *Grandfather* for godsakes' drank. But everyone drank then. It's nothing to do with my family that I'm labelled *'an alcoholic'*. Big deal. Bloody Twelve Steps. Things we can change and the grace to live with the shit we can't. Stuff that shit.

Oh, yes, of course my mother would play the role. Look after me if I turned up at Heron's Gate a bit the worse for wear. Oh, my mother she'd 'always come up trumps' if you want to believe her sycophants. Of course she would. It meant she could have her spotlight again. It meant she could get everyone's sympathy. That's what it was all about. When she used to do her nursemaid act. When I'd been on a bit of a bender. But, listen, it only happened twice. Maybe three times. Four or five. Oh, I don't know. Who's bloody counting. Not *all* the time, no way. Oh, I bet those vipers have told you I was always rolling up drunk. I wasn't *drunk*, I was hysterical perhaps, bloody angry, not always drunk.

Yeah, I can just hear them. Goody-two-shoes Sarah. Uncle Joseph, pretending he was on my side when he was really completely besotted by my mother, too. Completely under her spell too. My mother was mad. Plain and simple. Mad as a bloody hatter, dear. And so she drove *me* mad.

Auntie Claudia knew, her sister, my Aunt Claudia. And Sophie Lawson, too, only she's so *precious* she won't let on. Auntie Claudia's the only one who'll admit it. Everyone else wants you to believe my mother was this fascinating enigma, wonderfully glamorous, exotic, so full of passion, so *'creaaaytive'*. Fuck that. She was a manic depressive. It was hell living with her. Sod creativity and all that crap. Don't give me that. Tortured artist. Bollocks! Torture living with her. Let's get it straight, there was never *anything* glamorous about her madness. And now they seem to think there's something *noble* about her death. Death by drowning. Not waving but drowning. You know, the great tradition in suicidal artists. Yeah, well they drowned witches, didn't they? More like the great tradition of drowning witches. Serves her right, the witch.

She abandoned me. She *dumped* me. Her only child. Yeah, right. But, wait a minute, she'd had some practice, hadn't she? Abandoning *unwanted* things. Yeah, there are things I know. Secrets. They were the only weapon I had left in the end. Her bloody secrets - I could get her with those.

Once I threatened to tell them all. All her fancy friends, all the people she invited over and who thought she was oh-so-bloody-wonderful and oh-such-jolly-fun. I still think about what they would have done. But I didn't tell. Because of my father, for my father's sake. They say I'm a monster, don't they? But I never played that hand. I only threatened. And do you know what my mother did to me? I'll tell you. It was my father's birthday. February the fourteenth. I'd busted a gut to get there. I'd driven straight from London, three hours in shit traffic. My mother didn't even look at me when I walked into the room. She just asked me to leave. So, yeah, okay I'd had a few drinks but I was *not* drunk. I'd driven all that way down hadn't I? Hah!

You know what? When I wouldn't she go she got up and dragged me from the room by my hair. By my *hair*. That big bastard Willard, he helped her. Fat git. They stuffed me into Dad's old Beamer and they drove me to King's Standing. It's a clump of trees on a hill in the middle of nowhere. It was the middle of the night. Pissing with rain. I only had a cocktail dress on. They never said a word to me in the car. They drove right onto the heath, on the dirt, right up to the top. Stopped the car under the trees. I don't remember how they got me out. There's an old wooden seat. I remember sitting on it. And my mother, tipping her purse upside down and all these notes and loose change falling into my lap.

Now she's abandoned me for good. For ever and ever, amen. And everyone thinks it's my fault. This is her revenge, don't you see? She's got her revenge. I got mine. Hah! Good riddance.

I'm cold. Do you have a cigarette? Can't you get me some?

Do you hear how my voice echoes in here? *My* voice, over and over. Amen. Amen mother of mine.

JOSEPH

Sarah says Harriet is evil. Sarah sees Harriet as evil and Christina as good. Evil is a very emotive expression with all sorts of ambiguities. Well, what does it mean to you? Evil isn't really seen as a human characteristic, is it? It's *of the devil*. So if you say someone is "evil" it implies that it was *bestowed* upon them by some other force, some unknown power. *And* it conjures up all those nice and tidy "good' versus "evil" fantasies. But whatever we all felt for Edward and Christina, the truth is that Harriet was their daughter, flesh of their flesh and all that. What makes me uneasy about the good and evil scenario is that it's probably us, the parents who actually create their monster-children. From all our damaged bits. I don't know. What I *do* know is that it isn't as simple as good and evil, black and white. It's all just murky shadows and a rather tedious, dull grey most of the time.

So. Well, Harriet *was* trouble. Right from the beginning. That first time we all met up again, she was probably about six months old and even at that age she had a terrible rage. All fists and feet. And, boy, did she have a set of lungs when she was a baby. It seems extraordinary that she went completely silent. Perhaps she exhausted her vocal capabilities in that first year. No, it's not right to joke about it, really. Speech impediments, speech inhibitions, they have all sorts of serious psychological undercurrents, I'm told. The stammerer wishes to punish the person whom he is addressing, for instance. So silence, utter silence, is a very powerful form of punishment. It's a method of attack. Passive aggressive.

So. Harriet. And isn't it odd that a child who was silent for nine years could develop such a rapier tongue. And odd that she should have a name that starts with an aspirate. A breath.

Harriet's teenage attacks on her mother were formidable. She made up for her silence all right. Boy, she had a mouth. Still has. The face of an angel and the mouth of a fishwife. Poor Christina had the wrong sort of voice to retaliate. Too husky. And Edward? He couldn't confront her, verbally, at all. He affected an appropriately stern silence. Appropriate for his age, I mean. Like I said, you need to remember he was that generation. The generation who thought that family scandal belonged under the carpet, preferably nailed firmly down under the floorboards. In a big, heavy box. With a lock. That was why Christina's manic depression had been so well hidden. All those years it had been breaking his heart, he never let anyone really see. It would have been an act of betrayal and he couldn't bear to let Christina down. But I suppose in a way he let her down with Harriet. Harriet wanted to *destroy* her mother, wrest her power away from her and she thought Edward's silence meant he was on Harriet's side.

Harriet tried all sorts of different tactics. Retreat. Hiding in her room, refusing to eat or drink. She smashed her fists through the window once. Christina broke her collarbone trying to break the door down to get to her. Can you imagine that? And there was the time Harriet threw a plate at her mother and it caught her on the temple and she had to have stitches.

That 'squawking rages' tactic we witnessed began when Harriet started drinking. After Christopher Benson told Harriet about her mother and *his* father. All of that. Harriet was pretty disgusting then, turning up out of the blue, demanding her mother let her stay, demanding money. Demanding attention. And every time Christina gave her what she wanted. And when Harriet passed out with alcohol or drugs or whatever else she was doing to herself, Christina would be there. It was like some sort of atonement to her, nursing Harriet, like she was atoning for her daughter's sins. Always, always there.

Yes, except that one occasion. That wasn't long before Edward died. Christina had organised a small dinner party for his birthday. Harriet turned up, looking like she'd been sleeping in a ditch. Or doing something in a ditch. Probably that too. She started the old routine, shouting about her mother being a witch, throwing her shoes across the room. Edward put his head in his hands and I could see he was trying to cover up awful, shoulder-shuddering sobs. He completely broke down. The only time. This stalwart, stoical old man, suddenly sobbing. And Christina leapt up from the table, grabbed Harriet by the arm and dragged her out through the French windows. Christina could be mighty strong when she wanted to be. She called out, asking Willard Dexter to help get Harriet into Edward's car. Harriet bit him on the hand, can you imagine? God, it was a mess. They dragged her to the car and drove her up onto the heath, right up to a clump of trees. Apparently they left her there. With a pile of notes, twenties and tens, some change, and an old horse blanket from the boot of the car.

Why did Christina go back for more? Because she had this sense of duty as a mother? Yes, and because after Edward died, she said Harriet was all she had left of him. I don't think she ever stopped believing - hoping - that she and Harriet would one day be reconciled. She was wrong, wasn't she?

And now Harriet is abandoned again. For good. For good or evil. Left on a hill top fighting dragons with jewelled bellies, her mother's ghost silently circling overhead, looking for a place to land.

There is nothing more. When I agreed to talk to you I didn't envisage some sort of confessional.

I did - *we* did - all of us who loved her – we did all we could. Edward kept Christina's head above the water. Kept her secrets safe. And without him, she sank.

Yes. Yes. I hear what you're saying. I have thought of it too. And we're not the only ones, there were rumours. Harriet would have been capable of it.

Are you okay?

CHRISTINA

I'm tumbling. I won't let go. Not yet. This moment. Clutching these old images to me, words tight in my chest. Holding this water in my lungs in lieu of breath. Just a little longer.

Why are the dogs howling? Earthquake. That's a sign. The dogs always barked and howled before an earthquake. Every single dog on the island. But this is England. Apple trees and oast houses. I remember going to choose the puppies for Harriet. My present to Harriet on her birthday. Their ears are like velvet. Tails wig-wagging, no bigger than my little finger. Puppy dog tails. What are little girls made of? My little girl? My Harriet? Sugar and spice? Rats and snails. I never betrayed you Harriet, you were my daughter too. The other one was made of dust motes when the sun came through the window. Some people thought she was just a trick of the light. A faulty synapse. A smut of ash in my brain. She was real, but you were *there*.

Edward, Edward, where are you? In the village church. If you would all like to kneel. Kneeling on a cushion in my nightie, it was my dear Aunt Margaret's. Let us pray. Our father.

I have nothing to say. Nothing to say any more. No breath to push out the words. Edward, you were my breath. There is no air in here. Let me out into my garden with the butterflies. The roses are in full bloom. There is dew on the petals. And tears.

Don't cry, Harriet. If you cry like that we'll have to build an ark. And there will be nowhere for the blackbirds to land. I can see them, dots in the sky, like stars. Join up the stars to make a picture. My boots are full of water. I can touch the bottom. I can feel the sand beneath my feet. Somebody is humming. All these pretty pebbles. And pieces of broken glass, rubbed smooth by the sea. Stained glass, from the windows of a church. My father's voice. "Look up at the window, Chrissie, and the angels will come." Daddy, do the angels know our secret? There are hands pulling me down into the dark. Don't hurt me, don't hurt me.

Who's that humming? Ashes to ashes, dust to dust. A handful of sand, blowing away in the wind. They are digging a hole to bury my beautiful horse. My Pegasus, my precious winged spirit. Digging, digging, sand under my fingernails. I cannot hold on to the sand any more.

I can see the emerald eyes of humming birds. Their long curved beaks, tiny sabres, dipping into the hibiscus flowers.

I know you're there, Harriet, under my window, watching. I've seen the nuns showing you how to suck the nectar from the flowers. The nuns look like angels. I can talk to the angels. Can you keep a secret? Do you promise you won't tell?

Hear the music? There are people dancing on the beach, look, look, see them dancing on the beach. The little girls have flowers in their hair. Liam! Dear Sarah's Liam! There you are. Mr Reed! How wonderful to see you! Is that our Freddie, handsome Freddie in his uniform? Daphne, wearing her beautiful emeralds. Where's Edward, surely he's here? There's my father and mother. There, look, standing on the sea wall. They will not be dancing. They cannot hear the music. I can see Harriet. She is very very close, her face above me, waterlogged while I am wildy flailing.

Somebody is coming. Edward. My darling, I would know your footfall anywhere. It's a bit hard in this water, to get a purchase, the tide is turning. Your hand touching my cheek. I can hear your voice, very close, feel your breath above the rush of the wind. And you are saying *I've come to take my pretty girl away, I've come to take my pretty girl away.* Hold my hand, Edward, hold my hand.

ELEANOR

Boxes and newspapers and bubblewrap, piled in one corner. Coils of crumpled packing tape like shucked-off snake skins in another. There is hardly room to breathe in the small hall where wooden crates stand on their uppers, neatly stacked for collection. The phone is perched precariously on a bundle of rolled canvases. From up the stairs, the giggly chatter of a small child stirs the dusty quiet. Eleanor smiles. She has been crying, so it is a sticky, tight smile. She has been crying for Jack.

When I saw Jack Benson that last time – in the hospice – we both cried. It was when I told him that I had found the rose, in the tin that Emmeline Reed had given me. He was holding my hand. He couldn't speak, his face was lopsided from a series of strokes. But he heard me and he cried and I hope that he knew. I watched his face. Tears, hygienically drained away by plastic tubing.

What would he have said to me if he could have spoken right then, while Christopher was out of the room? He squeezed my hand. A faint, weak squeeze, but I felt it. Squeeze, squeeze. I said 'My mum Joan used to squeeze my hand like that.' He looked hard at me. I think he would have smiled. I smiled. And then the air came out of his body, just as they say it does, a sort of long huff. A machine bleeped. A nurse came in and closed his eyes and Christopher came in behind her and he said "Thanks for coming. It was kind of you." And I knew he didn't know it was me, I was me. I was just the woman who had put down a deposit on the rent for an old granary that was going to be my new studio. Who said she was researching an artist called Christina Mansfield.

She glances out of the window. It's a busy late lunchtime at the pub across the road. Zip is there, sitting up at the window, watching, waiting. He's quite grey around the muzzle. He's become quite a feature, the pub mascot. He sits in the window all day, in his own patch of sunlight. He moves only as the sun moves, to stay in its path. Nobody complains if they have to move for Zip to sit in the sun. He complains, though, he growls. She remembers poor Philip, even in that last summer, huddled up into his coat, huddling in the doorway, waiting for opening time. She still misses seeing him there, waiting, watching. She turns the rings on her right hand. A diamond solitaire that belonged to Christina and the wedding ring that belonged to Joan. Her mothers' rings.

"Hi, how's it going? Nearly done? Hey, you all right, smudger?"

It's Tom. He comes over to her and gives her a squeeze. Martin is with him, dressed in a checked suit, with a red wool scarf found his neck. Mr Toad. He raises a hand to her and smiles. She nods, blows her nose to try to disguise her sniffling. Smudger. She'll miss Tom. She remembers when he first started calling her that. When she first found out about her mother. Christina Mansfield Hopwood. So many tears on so many canvases. Smudger. It seems a long time ago.

It is fading. The pain. The petal stain in the book. The name in the sand. Obscured by tiny feet, jumping about in the shallows. Alice's little feet. We walked on the beach, Jack and Alice and I. Just the week before he went into the hospice. We rolled our trousers up and paddled. Jack let go of my arm. He said the saltwater was good for his legs. And Alice held both his hands and danced around him in the wind. They were laughing.

Footfalls in the loft above. Alice is shrieking with excitement. Willard's voice, low and resonant. They are playing dinosaurs, their favourite game. It makes the furniture in the studio shake. Eleanor often wonders if Willard will come crashing through the ceiling, like one of the cartoon monsters he draws for Alice.

Tom is sweeping up the last wood shavings. He says, "I hear the kids are upstairs then." Tom is still coming to terms with Willard's role as Alice's playmate. He never thought Willard had it in him, the sense of humour, the energy. Eleanor is too but Alice and Willard never think about it. Willard is her Uncle-Daddy-Will-Friend and Alice is his Favourite Little Girl. But they have agreed, she and Willard, they will tell her everything, when she is old enough to understand. Eleanor doesn't want her daughter seeing shadows that do not belong to her. She knows what she needs to do to give her daughter her place in the world.

"What will you do with that old bureau, Ellie, take it with you? Only, if you *don't* want it, Martin and I would love it, wouldn't we? We... well, we thought we'd like to restore it. It would look great in our new place in Devon."

"What a lovely idea. I'm sure it would come up beautifully with your love and attention. I've emptied it at last. Dad would have wanted it to have a good home."

Dad. Patrick Ashfield, my adoptive father. I thought I might find something, some of the tiny pieces of the jigsaw that are still missing from the sky. But I didn't. It really did contain nothing but old papers; letters to ink manufacturers, delivery notes. A small notebook with 'Tea Fund' on the front and inside, in someone's neat hand, a note of who'd donated what: 'Phil Hedley 2/6.' 'Mrs Woods - homemade cakes 5th Feb.' And at the back, in the same hand, a dozen lines from a poem by W H Auden that someone had obviously liked. A ream of headed notepaper. P & J Printers. P is for Patrick, J is for Joan. They were my Mum and Dad. Remembering Joan, standing on a Sicilian hill top, folding her hand around mine, folding her heart around mine to protect me. Patrick, standing on the sea wall, waiting. Knowing he could let me run down to the water's edge, knowing it was

dangerous in the shallows with the woman and the horses,
but knowing I would come back to him. Always. Because he
was my daddy, good and kind and he loved me.

Willard and Alice come clomping down the stairs. It is
time for a promised ice-cream with Sarah and her daughter
Katherine, they are meeting at three. They're still each
gingerly picking over the pieces - tall and small tales, torn
photographs, betrayals and broken hearts - that come down
from a man called George Mansfield, a man who the two
women are still a little fearful to have discovered was their
shared grandfather. They have plenty of time and enough
courage to sort out the good from the bad, the right from the
wrong. But right now it's time for a break from the packing
up of paints, the rolling up of half-finished drawings that
belong in a different life, a different light. She is keeping
some of her old work for Alice. One day she might find
something in them. She's going to store them all in the
studio in the Bensons' granary. It's Christopher Benson's
now, but he says she can have it for as long as she wants
now Tom is moving to Devon. Eleanor has drawn up a
contract, though, just in case.

The three of them walk out into the fading summer sun,
Eleanor, Alice and Willard. There is a haze on the horizon,
on the beach. The images the illustrator drew for the
storyteller are fading and fading until they are just pale
outlines, their centres white on white, like ghosts of horses
in fog. The photographs for reference are floating on the
surface on the water. Eleanor looks back. She just
remembered something.

"Oh, Tom, I nearly forgot about your puppets .... thank you for letting me keep them all this - "

But Tom is already on a stepladder, has already cut the thread that tied the little wooden figures to the rafter. The puppets are falling down, dancing through the sunlight, released, free, wildly waving.

Following new information, police have opened an investigation into the death of Christina Hopwood, 71, who drowned off the Sussex Coast in February 1992. The Coroner had originally recorded the death as suicide. A woman is helping police with their enquiries.

SUNDEKING

C. STEPHEN HICKS

First paperback edition 2023

ISBN: 979-8-9864844-0-2 (paperback)

ISBN: 979-8-9864844-1-9 (eBook)

Brought to you by Tomes of Kharazim

Printed by IngramSpark

Cover art by Alex Winemiller

Map made in Wonderdraft

To Jaycee, my wife, my best friend, and most importantly: my harshest critic.
And to you, as well as all those who believed in me.

May Death Find You Alive.

Leviathan Sea

To Sylvanus

Sildenfeld

Lake Saria

Sildenfeld Forest

To Tavkal

To Aeris

Seraphine Forest

Seraphine Mountains

Myxthold

Valen

Feldsbar

To Myrtfell

N
W   E
S

PART ONE

The age of man runs strong. Long gone are the dwarves and dragons, but so too, are the Angelus and Daemons.

The Angelus, powerful beings said to bring the will of the almighty Gods, and alongside their righteous blades, came justice for all the races.

The Daemons, horrid creatures of The Seven Hells. Their power shook the world during what became known as The Daemon War. Their evil nature paving the way for untold destructions.

The Dragons, mythical beasts that were more aloof and mysterious than any that have ever been known, and their legacy still holds many secrets.

These creatures were the titans of the Daemon War, and the age long past. Scholars call it the Age of Turmoil, or the Age of Chaos. I simply call it the time when man had no say in his own destiny. Perhaps man still has no true say over his destiny, but I like to think otherwise. In my personal line of work, I often pray to the Gods for guidance. I haven't received much back in my entire lifetime, but I believe that what we find in our own hearts is the true way to our destined path. We may deviate from time to time, but despite any doubts and any arguments, I truly believe

1

mankind, and all the other races, are always capable of finding their true path.

Perhaps this is why, in this sudden end to our era of peace, I still believe man to be destined for good. A good friend of mine, an elf, recently told me, "Peace was always a fragile thing." I am not sure if that was his grief talking, or his guilt.

Nevertheless, I will always remember the tale of those brave few that stood against the tides of evil and chaos.

-Valk Cornelo, High Cleric of Sildenfeld

1

VALEN

Fifteenth Day of Commemorant, Year 1126

Autumn brought crisp, cool air and a colorful sky. Liveliness of the town seemed more than tenfold as the leaves began to fall. The harvest was nigh, and thus came the festival with it, decorations being strewn on the walls and fences of every home and storefront. The buildings were of simple timber, or occasionally brick and mortar, modest accommodations of a lesser town of the Region it dwelt in. Valen was no village, nor could it boast itself a city, but instead sat comfortably in the middle. A welcome respite for travelers moving north or south on the coast of the Leviathan Sea for supplies between Myrefell and Sildenfeld. Their sister town of Feldsbar to the southwest was more a stop for directions, usually leading travelers to Valen for any kind of commerce. Couriers rarely stopped in Valen though, as it was more out of the way on straighter treks through the western Regions.

One such courier did call this place home however. As Valen prepared for the Harvest Festival, he made his way through the streets with a purpose, dressed in a simple tunic of auburn, brown trousers, and worn leather boots. His long brown hair was pulled back into a neatly folded tie, mainly to clear it from his light blue eyes. A determined expression curtaining a simple joy was painted over his sharp face. His clothing was loose fitting, but a musculature could be seen in his forearms and his upper shoulders. He had tanned skin and calloused fingers used to climbing and thick legs accustomed to walking great distances.

A pair of girls ran through the streets, decorations in the autumn colors trailing behind him. They made to dress him in some loose streamers, but he quickly weaved beside them, offering a smile and a wave instead. The girls giggled as he walked away, eyeing his physique and making lewd comments as they bounced away. He paid them no mind, instead marveling at the hustle and bustle of the town, merchants moving to and fro, bakers setting fresh pies in their windows, carts of wheat and other crops being hauled one place or another.

Led by the rhythmic clangs of hammer upon metal, he eventually found himself face to face with the entrance of the town blacksmith. Already, he could feel the intense heat of the interior bleeding out of the wide openings. A pit opened in his stomach at the thought of the raging fire that dwelt within. After steeling himself with a deep breath, he opened the door to the workshop.

Inside was a calmly lit area, lined with tools of all shapes and sizes, mostly farmers tools, kitchen cutlery or builder's tools, but one section did bear blades and spears meant for the defense of the town. On the opposite side was the flame of the forge, burning brightly as the sole light source besides the spare rays of overcast sunlight through the wide windows. The smith placed his cooled work back into the fire to heat once more, the sweat dripping down his bare muscular arms despite the cool air temperature that breezed through the room, one hand bearing a well-worn hammer, and the other pumping the bellows. His skin bore intricate crimson markings in a curving pattern, running from the tips of his fingers, all across his massive chest and back, further beneath his trousers, and coming back into view on his large feet, bare despite his work environment.

He turned slowly and regarded the young man with a smile that moved his thick grey beard and the crimson patterns continuing up his neck and face. "Greetin's Irvine!" he said. "What brings ye to me forge this fine day?"

Irvine smiled back courteously, always amused at the man's thick accent despite living in the Regions for the last two decades. "Greetings to you, Master Versal, I was just here to check if my uncle's sword was finished?"

The smith stood, measuring the young man for a moment. "Aye, I believe Erika is just about finished polishin' 'er up. Should be comin' by to check in any moment now."

"I see. Thank you then, I suppose I'll wait outside for her to be done." Irvin replied somewhat hurriedly, backing for the door.

"No need to wait out in the wind lad! She'll be out in no time-" the smith cut himself off as Irvine was already through the doorway. He let out a heavy sigh, wondering if the young man would ever move past his fears and come work with them, at least for a few days.

Irvine stood with his back to the shop wall, making sure the burly man wouldn't be able to see him through the windows, but also staying within range for Erika to deliver the sword. He took a deep breath, trying not to focus on the flames of the forge any longer, and instead focus on the continual preparations for the Harvest Festival. Closer to the center of town, temporary stands were being constructed for the tavern owners to sell cheap wooden flagons of ale, the farmers to sell fresh pressed stock for the younger folk, the bakers to sell small pastries, and the craftsmen to sell small toys and baubles.

The sight was comforting to Irvine. The presence of the stands meant an abundance of food and materials this season, an abundance of wealth. Prosperity of the town was a welcome sight, promising plenty of work for him in the future.

His admiration of the town's well-being was interrupted though, as he recoiled from a sudden blow to the side. He stumbled several steps over, clutching at his ribs. Looking up to find Erika standing in front of him, her cheeks puffed out in frustration. Her bright auburn hair was pulled back in a loose braid underneath a patterned leather bandanna, and her thick arms were bare behind her stained leather apron. Her emerald eyes flashed in an aggression towards the young man.

"Ye couldn't 'ave conversed with Papa fer more than a few measly moments, eh?" she shouted at him, drawing the attention of several passers-by.

"Erika, it's not like that!" Irvine hastily tried to explain, but Erika proved his efforts futile.

"My papa toiled away on this 'ere blade, all fer yer uncle, all in good graces. All 'e wanted in exchange was a little friendly conversatin' with 'is best friend's nephew!" she continued.

Irvine attempted to open his mouth to explain himself when she cut him off again.

"But no!" she began again, dragging out the last syllable. "Ye're too afraid o' the forge to spend two moments tellin' papa how ye've been fairin'. He worries over ye! Don'tcha know that, Irvine?"

Irvine could feel his face burning red, both from the frontal assault, and from the attention garnered by it. He cautiously glanced back up at his verbal assailant to see her face bright red from frustration. "I know that, Erika. I'm sorry." he said quietly, holding his hands towards her in surrender, hoping the audience would lose interest and move on from this ordeal.

She sighed. "I'm sorry too." she said considerably quieter, holding out the sheathed longsword Irvine was there to retrieve. "Here's yer uncle's blade."

Irvine reached out with both hands and respectfully claimed the weapon from her, while staying out of range of another jab. "Thank you for your work on it." he said with a low bow before turning away.

"Irvine. I'm glad ye're back." Erika called out to him. "Will I see ye at the festival later? Papa's lettin' me have the night out."

It was a coy question, as they had already agreed to attend this year's harvest festival together, and as if her father could keep her away from the celebration if he even wanted to.

Irvine looked back at her nearly smirking, the wind blowing her bright hair over her shoulder as she angled a hip to the side. Her face was almost concerned, her lips parted slightly as if she wanted to say more. Irvine's amused expression was wiped away at the sight of her.

He nodded, giving her a warm smile, which she matched before waving and bouncing back into her shop.

2
DAEMON

A low rumble shook the interior complex from somewhere deep underground. The cavern had been untouched for centuries, the only things running through it were the magma and water that made up the central circular design. A lone figure cautiously measured each step into the room, his face obscured by the shadow of his hood, and his features hidden by the darkness that clung to his clothing. Abandoned civilizations and tombs littered the continent from ages long past, and the business of delving into dungeons was a lucrative one. Even now, the man imagined the coin he would receive for this particular descent, the letter he had been given detailed a sum that he had never seen from a score of thieveries. All he had to do was interrupt the flow in this cavern, and the riches of a Tarkalan noble would simply fall into his lap.

After arriving in the center of the cavern, he observed the rounded grooves in the floor beneath his feet, half flowing with glowing hot magma, the other with dazzlingly blue water. He stroked his thin beard as he watched the flows. He knelt beside the water, and lightly dipped a finger into it, but quickly recoiled as the liquid scalded his flesh as if it were boiling, though it appeared cool as a spring. He retrieved the letter from his waistcoat, carefully reading the instructions over again, unclear yet direct; he was used to this kind of language though. It spoke specifically mentioning the magma and the water together, never in separate sentences, so he made his way to the junctions. On either end of the circle, the water and magma met, both rolling under themselves in an endless flow, though the length of the liquid was still and unmoving.

He peered at them for a good while and retrieved two metal slats from his pouch, both roughly the same width as the troughs and bearing an arcane sigil on one side. Carefully, he slid the first directly in between the glowing orange and calm blue, and with the piece in place, both liquids ceased their movement.

A more noticeable rumble sounded through the cavern, giving him pause briefly. When no traps sprung to life, he quickly set to work on the other, unsure of the enchantment's strength. After placing the second, a moment passed, as the circular trough became still, the room then rumbled again, even louder than the last.

The thief grinned now, knowing that he was that much closer to the gold he was promised for this job, and how simple the whole ordeal was. He watched as the flows that filled the circle waned, and eventually stopped, followed by a series of runes lighting on the floor around the circle, leading up to the walls and finally on the ceiling. He looked around at the spectacle in some degree of awe, until his eyes began to focus more, and he began to realize why the job offered so much, yet asked so little. His grin faded quickly, and he broke out in a sudden cold sweat, finally understanding that he would never see the reward because he was never meant to return from this endeavor.

Frantically looking around, he spotted the entrance where he had made his way in, picturing the long complex of tunnels he had to navigate to find this particular ruin. All he had to do was get deep enough into those tunnels to avoid whatever this chamber really contained, be it magical or otherwise. He watched as a column of sparks rose from the center of the circle, and made his decision to run. Dashing out with all the speed he could muster, determined to not find out what the sparks truly meant. He counted each footfall, trying to extend his stride as much as he could, until his right foot landed on the smooth stone, and he no longer could feel the pressure beneath it.

He fell with a thud on the suddenly heating stone floor, less than a foot from the exit of the chamber. Rolling over to look at his suddenly unfeeling extremity, he screamed aloud in horror. His boot was a pile of ash a short way behind him, along with whatever cloth of his trousers and his flesh. All that remained was scorched bone from just below his knee, the remaining muscle cauterized and dancing with low embers.

He could only let out gasping screams, as he looked upwards at his assailant. From within the circle a skeletal being had appeared, with flames flickering endlessly from within its bones, torso bound in jagged crimson armor. It floated above the ground with no visible legs, its skull bearing two arcing horns like a ram and a cloth that covered both eye sockets. Loose chains dangled from its wrists, freshly broken from their bindings that were now visible, anchored in the circle that held the enchantment. Its mouth of jagged teeth opened, as a piercing cackle erupted from the horrifying creature. Sparks and embers spewed between its jaws, with a stench of brimstone and sulfur permeating the chamber.

A high raspy voice emitted from the creature, though its jaw moved slowly. "You flee like a hare from a wolf. You knew nothing of what you were releasing it seems." The specter glided across the edge of the circle towards the thief, raising a bony hand, causing the man to cower under his own arms, no longer concerned with his catastrophic injury.

"The enchantment has been slowly weakening against my power for a long while, allowing me some influence in the outside world. However, it seems that gratitude is in order. You were able to completely halt my prison with the help of certain enchantments." the creature lightly tapped its hands together in mocking applause.

"Zyrxak, Elder Daemon of Wrath. A pleasure to make your acquaintance, human." The laughter was sickening. "Now, let us see about your payment."

† †

Irvine carefully closed the door of his home, trying his absolute hardest to make as little noise as possible. He slowly released the latch and turned after making sure the door was fully shut.

"Stealth was never your forte." his uncle said as he stepped down the final steps of the staircase, startling Irvine.

"Apologies uncle, I wasn't sure if you were asleep still or not." he said with a slight bow.

Feldran gave him a sharp strike to the shoulder as he did. "Stop that bowing boy, you're damn well old enough to command a little respect of yourself."

Irvine grimaced at the second attack of the day. "Of course, uncle, my apologies."

"And stop with the constant apologizing as well. Guilt looks good on no one. Own your actions and own your life." he lectured as he tightened the straps and buckles of his guard's armor, straightening the breastplate in the mirror.

"Yes uncle." he said, trying to straighten his back. "I retrieved your sword from Smithmaster Versal." he said, holding the sheathed weapon forward.

Feldran turned, a nearly unnoticeable smile spreading his bushy mustache. "Thank you, Irvine. Though I doubt my old friend did all the work, his age is catching up to him nearly as fast as mine is."

"Yes." Irvine began cautiously. "Erika provided the finishing polish I believe."

The elder unsheathed the first third of the blade, inspecting the work. "I'd say it looks better than the day Versal gave it to me. His daughter is turning out to be a talented craftsman in her own right." he said, eyeing Irvine's reaction carefully, picking out the slight hint of joy in the young man's demeanor. He sheathed the sword with a loud snap, bringing Irvine's attention sharply back to him. "Have you a partner for the dance?"

Irvine laughed nervously. "I, believe so?"

Feldran smiled more conspicuously this time. "If her dancing is as rhythmic as her forge work, then you might actually have to work to keep up."

Irvine smiled behind his reddening face. "Yes, uncle."

The older man gave his armor a few tugs with a sharp exhale. "Right then. Off with you. Enjoy the festival."

Irvine nodded, and moved back out the door, leaving the elder with his mirror and his thoughts.

† †

Zyrxak eerily floated to the crest of the ridge, looking upon the valley before him, burning lights shining from behind the cloth that covered his eye sockets. The sun was beginning to set, the sky alighting with the colors of delicious flames, halted only by the moons that hung in the early evening canopy. The specter exuded a column of black smoke, tinged with embers, that danced around his jagged and sharp teeth before dissipating in the air around him. Teral, as the thief introduced himself, carefully stepped up to his side, the severed portion of his leg now encased in an arcane flame that allowed him movement even better than his original extremity. He glanced down at his new 'gift' with some concern for his new standings in the world.

"I presume that is the settlement of Valen?" Zyrxak asked, his jaw exuding smoke with each word.

Teral nodded. "Seems so small from up here." he mused lightly, but with a nervous laugh.

"Indeed." the specter replied. "Although it seemed much farther away whilst I was still imprisoned, I was only able to cause minor accidents and illusions in my sorry state. However."

The thief pulled his hood back, awaiting the continuation of the specter's sentence, but found none, as he instead began drifting down the side of the ridge, patches of grass suddenly turning to ash around the fringes of his floating garb. A path of destruction lay before Teral, with no way of turning back.

3
Harvest Festival

The sun dipped beneath the horizon, the blazing sky beginning to fade with an increasing eastward breeze that sent a crisp chill through the town, courtesies of the near coastline. Irvine walked through the streets with his hands clasped behind his back as the lampposts were being lit around him, filling the street with a comfortable glow in the absence of daylight. The music of the festival had already started and he marveled at the energy of the children dashing through the streets playing games and dancing along. The general commotion was on a steady rise, as food and trinkets were being purchased and merriment was being had. He paused on the side of the street and took in the sight of the darkening sky behind the brightening festivities, and smiled, knowing that this moment was his to cherish now.

Though it was abruptly disrupted as a sudden pain erupted in his side. He buckled over gripping his ribs with his hands, looking up to find his assailant. He grimaced at the prospects of being hit three times in a day in his own hometown, but softened quickly at Erika's visage.

Her normally rough exterior was starkly replaced, her red hair neatly combed, with braids adorning the strands every so often. She wore a long, flowing, autumn colored dress with pretty floral designs down the skirt, ending at her calves. Irvine couldn't help but take pause at her, the dress accentuating the sway of her hips, her muscled arms complimenting the soft skin of her neckline, her face the only rough sight with her flustered expression. She adjusted the thin straps over her exposed collarbones slightly as she eyed him.

Irvine finally recovered from her sudden attack and beautiful appearance. "Why is it that your greeting is always a punch?" he asked while massaging his side.

"It's standard fer the Fjordlings." she stated in a matter-of-fact kind of way, her confident expression turning to mush at Irvine's smirk. Erika's father had fled the Fjordlands when she was just a baby, though she was proud of her heritage still.

"Right. Well, a friendly smile and slight bow is custom for the civilized folk of the Sildenfeld Region." Irvine replied with a curt bow.

Erika's face became even more flustered at the verbal jab. She began to strike out at him again, Irvine knew she would though, and was able to easily dodge the half-hearted blow, grabbing her hand and twirling around. Her eyes met his and they paused, her expression even more flustered than before. She leaned forward onto her own balance again, clearing her throat and rapping his chest lightly with her fist.

"Come on then, ye more civilized folk, let's not ruin the evenin' with arguing." she turned away, dragging him along by his hand.

Irvine smiled more, appreciating her special way of showing affection, even if it was a bit painful sometimes.

† †

Smithmaster Versal tugged lightly at the collar of his ill-fitting brown tunic. The massive brute of a man was unaccustomed to wearing the clothes of the southerners, his barrel shaped chest usually bare save for his leather apron that he wore while forging, or a thick overcoat during the colder months. He would never admit the effort it took to squeeze his head through this particular piece of clothing, though he was somewhat impressed at the craftsmanship of it, as it resisted any rips or tears in the process. He turned to regard the heavy footfalls of former Guard Captain Feldran, his freshly polished armor shining in the light of the festival.

"Good to see you, old friend." the elder guard said with a smile under his bushy mustache.

A smile widened Versal's broad face as well. "Even better to see ye Feldran. How is retirement suiting ye?"

"Terribly, I'm afraid." he replied with a slight grimace. "I find boredom to be the most challenging enemy I've engaged as of yet."

Versal let out a hearty chuckle. "I see, well perhaps it's time fer ye to seek out a hobby then?"

"I have attempted a few occupations. Literature comes only in half-hearted memoirs of my time on the watch or our previous travels, while painting often leads to grisly depictions of the valley around us. It is amazing how easy it is to overuse a color." he paused a moment, sighing at the memories of his failed attempts. "I do find some joy in writing letters to our comrade in Sildenfeld, though that is less of a hobby than simply keeping up with old contacts."

"And how is our elven friend?" Versal asked, taking a drink from his tankard.

"Quite well it seems. Politics have grasped him firmly and refuse to let go, though it appears he has quite the aptitude for it. Ah, and he has found a mate as well, or at least, mate-to-be."

Versal raised an eyebrow. "Someone actually gave the stuffy bastard the time o' day?" he asked with a grin, and causing Feldran to let out a laugh. "You remember that frail aash we met all those years ago? Sárif's offer to him was genuine after all. It seems he is stricter than him even, he finds the few flaws in his routine and brings them down over his head."

Versal took his turn to laugh now, ending in an appreciative smile for the update on old friends. Just then, he noticed a familiar flash of auburn, as his daughter suddenly dashed by, with Feldran's nephew in tow. Versal grunted slightly, gaining a glance from the retired guard.

"Approval or nay?" Feldran asked cautiously.

"Approval more 'an likely. Amusement, maybe?" the massive smith answered as he drank again.

"Well, I'm glad the boy has something here that he can look forward to seeing when he ventures back." Feldran said with a sigh.

"I think you underestimate 'im. 'E has an appreciation for this town rare 'round his age. Though I meself gave 'im a personable reminder o' 'is home." he explained, somewhat cryptically. "I do agree, and I me'self am glad that Erika has found a companion. I only wish 'is parents could'ave met 'em both as adults. Me wife too."

Feldran nudged him with his elbow, after noticing his friend's gaze droop to the floor. "She is very proud. You've raised a beautiful and fine woman all yourself friend."

Versal wiped the spare moisture from his eyes, and smiled, placing his meaty hand on Feldran's shoulder. "Doesn't get easier, even after twenty-two years. I'm sure yer sister is plenty proud o' yer work too."

† †

The evening became a strange trance for Irvine. Time seemed to slow to a crawl, all of the details around him popping out in immense clarity, and yet time also seemed to move blindingly fast, everything threatening to end in an instant. He looked around the festival, at all of the people having their own wonderful experiences, and back to Erika's face. Her expression was filled with joy, a slight blush to her cheeks likely from being winded from dashing around, he thought. His face felt hot as well, especially while watching her bounce around with the enthusiasm of a child.

Irvine had always appreciated his friendship with the smith's daughter. It was far from the first time he had imagined more possibilities with her, though a fear of her rejection did sprout in his mind. They made their way to the vendors of the festival, and while Erika was off buying drinks and food, Irvine did his best to silently move off from their meeting place. He eventually found the stand he was looking for, that of the local jeweler, Damion.

Irvine glanced around to make sure Erika was completely out of sight, and while he did not find her, a stone dropped his stomach a foot lower in his abdomen as he met eyes with her father briefly. He quickly ducked toward the stand in an effort to make himself unseen, greeting Damion and looking over his selection, lit in a gentle candlelight.

"Finally looking for something for Erika, Irvine?" the well-muscled jeweler asked. Damian was not a small man by any means, standing a full head taller than Irvine and boasting arms nearly the size of Versal. His neatly trimmed beard and hair showed his attention to detail though, a quality that reflected his occupation.

Irvine eyed the man curiously. "Yeah, I suppose I am. Don't tell anyone though?"

Damion smiled widely, a sight that unnerved many people upon their first meeting with him. He prided himself on his charisma though, despite some first impressions of him. "Irvine, my business deals in a certain amount of secrecy, no man wants his sugary sweet love to find out about any gifts they may have purchased for them. If Erika happens to stroll by, believe you me, I haven't seen you all night. What might you be-"

Damion's voice trailed off in Irvine's mind as he scanned the limited wares of the festival store: silver or gold rings, ruby earrings, and a handful of imitation circlets to make children feel like Sylvannan royalty. A slight green glint caught his eye, and there he found a pendant of emerald clasped in a spiraling silver. The color seemed the same as Erika's eyes, deep green and enchanting.

He pointed at it with a determination, and Damion smiled. "Ah yes, that is a beautiful piece, for a beautiful girl I might add."

Irvine stood slightly and gave the crowd another look over, Damion nodding with a slight chuckle. "I see, well considering the expediency of your work in the past, I'll give you an added discount."

Irvine quickly counted out his aurums for the jeweler and traded him for the small carrying case that held the necklace. He gave his thanks with a wave and dashed back to their meeting spot, stuffing the box in his pocket. He tried his best to regulate his breathing as mere moments after he came to a standstill, Erika came around a cluster of people clutching two wooden tankards of ale in one hand and a well cooked turkey leg in the other.

She met his gaze with a smile, followed by a raised eyebrow as she approached him. "Ye alright?" she asked, giving him one of the mugs and the leg, reaching a hand up to brush off his cheek.

"Yes, I'm just fine." he said with a smile, still breathing somewhat heavily from his rush.

"Ye seem flustered Irvine, an' it took me a moment to find ye."

This time Irvine raised an eyebrow, which was met with a giggle from Erika. "Did ye get lost? We were supposed to meet over there, ye silly duck." she explained, motioning to a clearing a few yards away, before grabbing the leg from him again.

Irvine paused, his brow furrowing as he puzzled over his excursion. His thoughts interrupted by the leg suddenly in his face. "No matter." Erika said with her mouth partially full, and curled into a smirk. "C'mon, the dance is startin' soon, and I don't need my partner passin' out from a lack o' energy."

Irvine took a small bite to appease her, but his stomach hadn't quite recovered from the sight of her father just yet. The two moved to the side, where a few barrels stood on end as make-shift tables. They set their tankards down on the tops and leaned back on them slightly to rest their feet for a while, trading the turkey for bites as they watched the crowd under the dancing light of the lampposts and candles. Irvine began to lose himself in thought, but was suddenly snapped back to reality as he felt Erika press against him slightly, resting her head on his shoulder. He could feel her hair blowing in the wind and tickling his neck, and the coolness of her arm against his.

Any worries that he had from the previous days, weeks or even year, just drifted away. He caught himself locked in that moment, watching her breast rise and fall gently as the neck of her dress moved in the breeze. He could smell the sweet scent of vanilla and jasmine that drifted off of her. He hardly noticed the bare turkey bone clutched in her hand, or the tankard of ale that settled beside him. All around him seemed to disappear and all he could see, feel, or hear, was her. He felt his face get hot again, and his heartbeat quicken, his stomach no longer weighed down by a stone, but instead guided by a swarm of dancing butterflies. Erika pulled away slightly, Irvine realizing that the moment only lasted a couple of seconds. He glanced down, noticing that Erika seemed distracted slightly, making him feel somewhat better in his own daydream.

He swallowed hard, and felt his voice escape him as he tried to speak. "Erika, I-" but was promptly interrupted by her suddenly perking up towards the crowd. She jumped up, and slapped his arm with the back of her hand, causing his thought to sputter out of existence.

"It's startin'!" she said with an excited grin. Her joy was infectious, and Irvine couldn't help but smile back. He turned to take another drink, nearly choking as he heard her start to run off. He looked back and just barely saw her disappear into the crowd. He smiled and shook his head. "Alright then."

† †

Teral's gaze was fixated on the smoldering trail in front of him, the ash that covered the ground was thick and trailed off with the early evening breeze. His eyes were wide at the sight, barely blinking as he took in the sight of the horrific creature.

The thief wondered what he had awakened. Nothing like this should exist in their age of peace.

He knew of the tales of Daemons that once roamed the realm a millennium before, but he never believed he would ever see anything like that. He considered his options, glancing down at his new leg made of eternal flame. He had stumbled about with it at first, caught off guard by the power that it gave to each step, though he imagined he could attain a greater running speed with it, and escape this madness before it carried him too far. Though he wondered if the specter could just as easily revoke the new power as he had given it. Perhaps it was best to ally himself with the creature that introduced itself to be one of the Daemons of legend. After all, nothing could possibly stand against this creature's raw power.

The choice suddenly illuminated itself before him. One, on the side of the brush untouched by its power, to run and possibly live a full life before this monster caught up to him.

The second on the path of destruction created by it, live as its servant, and attain power no man could hope to rival.

His thoughts were shattered, as he looked ahead, witnessing a cluster of embers stray from behind the specter in the wind, coming to rest on the tree line beside him, igniting it within seconds. The blaze illuminated Teral's face, and nudged his decision with the thought that there would be no way for him to escape this monster's path of destruction, and that he would much rather be behind it, than ahead. He quickened his pace to catch up with Zyrxak, the specter turning its head to regard him. Teral did all he could to ignore the sound of the blazing forest behind him.

† †

The crowd almost immediately began the dance as the musicians started to play the upbeat drumming tempo, accented with the fiddling violins. The dancers coupled together, and followed in wide circles around the plaza, each smaller circle within reversing the direction, forming an energetic group motion. Irvine stood on the outside of the mass of people as he strained to find the singular person that he was looking for.

Laughter echoed all around, as the sound of stomping feet nearly drowned out the music itself, making a percussive rhythm all its own. Irvine inhaled deeply, and bounced on his toes lightly, of course Erika wouldn't make it easy for him.

He spotted his opening and quickly dashed through, following the same process with the next line of people that traveled in the opposite direction, this time narrowly dodging two girls on their orbit through as they tried to grab him, giggling as they went. He caught his breath and decided it would be better to move along with the crowd, rather than just cut through them. He started skipping alongside the next line, increasing his pace just slightly and this time easily passing through. He jumped up in his skips a few times, looking over the next line and into the fifth and final circle of dancers and at last found what he was looking for. He moved along with the fourth line of dancers, watching for that flash of auburn hair again, and when he finally saw it, he took his chance and dashed through, halfway tackling the young woman.

Erika squealed with laughter as he twirled around with her, and took her into the center of the final circle.

After they stopped laughing, they settled in to their position and took up in the rhythm of the music, enjoying their time in the center for as long as they could, until they traded places with another couple and resumed their dance in the fifth circle. Irvine found that he couldn't take his eyes off of her again. She twirled around, stomping her shoes with the music, and looking up and the stringed lanterns above them, the light illuminating her feminine features. Her dress danced around her hips and legs, while her hair began to crowd over her smiling face. Erika had stopped laughing, but still continued in small bouts of quiet giggles, glancing back at Irvine every couple of steps. Irvine simply wished he could live in this moment forever, watching her emerald eyes as shadows played around her face.

4
Catastrophe

Versal watched with a warm smile as he saw his daughter dance around the outer circle with Irvine. Bittersweet feelings filled his heart, and thoughts of those lost had him looking to the stars and two moons that filled the sky. It was then that he saw a glimmer of what should not be, a flash of light from the east that lit the side of his face briefly. He turned, to see a raging wildfire, claiming the trees of the forest and spreading into the grassland. His eyes widened, and he shouted in a low guttural tone. "Fire!"

Feldran heard the familiar call of his Fjordling friend, and jumped onto a crate, looking over the sea of civilians and saw the approaching flame.

He extended a hand down to a guardsman. "Your glass!" he requested, the guard fumbling slightly in momentary panic.

"Now, guardsman!" Feldran demanded. He grabbed hold of the spy glass and extended it out towards the fires, scanning for a moment and finally seeing the cause of the horrible flame. He slowly lowered the glass and muttered to himself. "Gods help us."

Irvine and Erika came to a slow halt as the music died down, screams ensuing in the crowd after the shouts of 'fire' rang out. The two of them huddled close as the swarm of people rushed past them, panic gripping the festival in a matter of moments. Erika buried her head in his chest and gripped at his tunic as people flooded around them. Irvine grabbed Erika's hand a moment later.

"We need to find your father." he said firmly as he began wading through the crowds towards where he last saw him. She felt a nervousness clawing at her as he led her carefully through the plaza.

†⸸

Zyrxak paused, some distance still lay between him and the edge of the town. Teral paused beside him, sweat dabbling his brow.

"It appears they have noticed our approach." the creature exuded, glancing over its shoulder at the, now towering, flames of the forest.

"Clumsy me." he cackled.

Teral winced at the laugh, as it sounded similar to the shattering of a glass pane in its tone. "What shall we do then? They surely have a formidable guard force at a town of this size." he inquired.

"Paltry more like. Nevertheless, I do believe my current state would have issues obliterating them all. Let's call for some friends then." he said, lowering to the ground and placing his skeletal hands to the cinders below him. He began muttering words in a language Teral could not understand, the words and syllables making his chest hurt and his heart feel as if it would jump from his ribs. As the creature spoke, orange lines cracked out from beneath him, as if the ground itself would shatter into the bowels of a molten pit, he raised slowly, letting his fingers drag beneath his palms, invisible strings seemingly pulling down on them. A low rumble echoed around them and the ground shaking with it. Teral glanced around nervously, startling as jets of magma sputtered around them, a heavy scent of ash and sulfur permeated his nostrils. Eerie skeletal creatures began to climb from the ground. Each of the thralls howled to the sky as they tasted the air, their bones smoldering with embers and sparks flying off of their forms.

"Now then." Zyrxak said with an impossible smile. "Let us raise some chaos."

††

Feldran screamed to the guards that he no longer technically commanded after his official retirement. "Focus on evacuating the citizens! Creatures will be arriving shortly, do not engage them!"

He frantically searched the crowd and finally found Versal, he grasped the large man's shoulder and said in a grim tone. "It's a Daemon. From the flames, I'd wager it's a Wrath."

Versal inhaled sharply. "A Daemon? We 'adn't seen one in years, where'd it come from?"

"I do not know, old friend, but we need to get as many people out of here as we can, we have no way of knowing how long it has been since it awakened, and I am not confident that we can fight it. The flames around it are massive, I don't think this is anything like what we've faced before."

Versal nodded. "I'll start a barricade fer it to work through, likely won't last long at all, but it'll give us some breathin' room."

While Feldran prepared the guard forces, the smith gathered the strongest workers and craftsmen available and began overturning stands, rolling barrels and stacking crates to blockade the main street leading to the plaza. Goods and trinkets spilled into the roadway, making the terrain a bit more rough than just the cobbled stone. He couldn't help but think in the back of his mind how well this would work against an opposing force that wasn't backed by a Daemon, but he knew he hadn't the time dwell on it either. All he could do was his best, and that had to be enough.

One of the workers, a carpenter, climbed onto the barricade and peeked over, calling down a moment later over his shoulder. "It's got monsters ahead of it! Unarmed, but burning like Versal's forge!"

Versal nodded, the statement confirming Feldran's fears of a more powerful Wrath Daemon. "Right then, all o' ye get some weapons, shop's got racks full, along with the guard 'ouses. Ye heard Feldran though, no fightin' unless forced!"

He watched as the workers scattered to retrieve weapons, and clenched his fists. He hated fighting fire with fire, but it seems it had come to that. He slammed his palms together, echoing a loud crack, and focused the energy between his hands. His arms flushed with an orange flame, and his hands turned a dark color like ash.

† †

Feldran found Irvine and Erika as they broke out onto the side of the road. "Irvine! Over here!" he called. The two quickly made their way to him.

"What's happening?" Irvine asked.

Feldran drew a deep breath and placed his hand on the young man's shoulder. "Our worst fears, I'm afraid. A Daemon has awoken."

Irvine and Erika both stared at the elder guard with eyes wide. "How?" they asked almost simultaneously.

"The answer to that is not important currently, what is important is the job I need you to do Irvine. I need you to go as quick as you can to our ruling city, Sildenfeld. You've made the trek plenty of times before, this one is no different."

"Except that there's a Daemon attacking my hometown." Irvine retorted through gritted teeth.

"Do not fight with me over this boy! I need you to do as I say. Take Erika with you, we will evacuate the town as best we can and find a place of refuge, ideally making it to Sildenfeld ourselves."

Irvine sighed deeply, but felt Erika grip his hand tighter. "Irvine, he's right, we're needin' to go, now. I'll go grab my supplies right quick, and meet ye back here."

Irvine looked at her, then back to Feldran who gave him a solid nod and a pat on his shoulder. "It's time to go, nephew."

Irvine groaned in frustration, but started off towards his home.

Erika glanced back at Feldran, concern furrowing her brow.

"Take care of him, Erika." he said with a slight choke in his voice. She nodded, fighting back her own tears as she ran to her abode.

Versal jogged up beside Feldran with a heaving chest. "Barricade is set, and I left 'em some gifts once they start to come across." he said with a mischievous grin.

Feldran started to ask, but was interrupted by a cacophonous blast, shaking the stones beneath their feet. He simply nodded to the Smithmaster in understanding.

He turned away and raised his voice in a commanding tone. "Guards and militia! Take your posts! Civilians! Continue to evacuate to the west!"

All around, the guardsmen and militia members unsheathed their blades and nocked their arrows, readying themselves for the first sight of hostile entities, flinching at each blast that rang out from the other side of the town.

† †

Teral arrived back at Zyrxak's side, still amazed at his new ability and how quickly he was able to cover the ground between their stance and the edge of the town. "It appears someone has left some kind of explosives, each one looks like a spot of magma on the street, and as soon as one of your creatures gets close, they go up in a fiery blast." he informed.

"I see. Meaning they likely have an Ignis blood among them. This just got more complicated than expected." the creature said with annoyance.

"So how do we proceed?" Teral asked.

The creature emitted his routine cackle, Teral flinching less and less each time he heard it. "Simple my new lieutenant, we burn the damned place from the inside."

The specter began to float towards the town himself, covering the scorched earth that still sprouted the skeletal thralls. Teral started after him, quickly overtaking him with his firey leg, leaping onto the first rooftop, and peering into the town as another blast disintegrated one of Zyrxak's mindless minions.

† †

Irvine dashed through his house, retrieving his blade and leather armor, quickly grabbing more comfortable traveling clothes and boots. He didn't have the time to change or buckle his armor or sword on, so he stuffed everything into his traveling satchel, along with any small supplies he could find on short notice. He roughly shoved the front door open wide, and paused for a moment, glancing back at his home for the past seventeen years.

At least this time he could see it one last time before it began to burn.

He shook his head, forcing the memories away, before heading back into the street. He looked to the side and saw the towering column of flames coming from the east, his eyes widening as he came to the realization that he and Erika needed to go east for his short route to Sildenfeld. He suddenly regretted not apprenticing with Versal, and not facing his fears sooner. This would be a lot more difficult than he wanted to think about.

†╎

Feldran and Versal looked on as the horrifying skeletal creatures began to round the corner. The first few sprouted arrows and crossbow bolts, promptly falling backwards into piles of ash. More still stumbled through, albeit a few at each time.

Feldran let out a satisfied grunt. "Seems our archers have been doing well in their training. Thank the Gods that these creatures fall so easily."

Versal nodded. "Aye, though we'll see how they do closer up. And I'm not lookin' forward to the Daemon itself getting over 'ere."

The two of them looked back at the continuing evacuation effort, glad that nearly all the townsfolk were escaping on time. A few moments later, Irvine and Erika arrived, each toting a pack and their respective weapon. Versal approached Erika, embracing her in his usual bear hug and checking her warhammer and breastplate, much to her protest.

Feldran similarly embraced Irvine. "Be careful boy. Make your parents proud. Make all of us proud."

"Uncle, I don't want to leave all of you like this." he pleaded.

Feldran held his head in his hands. "I know Irvine. I'm afraid you have no choice this time, but someone needs to warn the council quickly, and you're the fastest courier we have."

"The only, courier we have." he corrected with a glare. "Problem is, the route is-"

His uncle cut him short. "I know that Sildenfeld is in the same direction as that fire, and I hate to send you careening into the same thing that took my sister and your father. Those scars take much longer to heal than the physical ones. However, we have no other choice available. You have to go that way, there is no other."

Irvine nodded, fighting back the frustration of the situation.

"You'll be surprised at how much of a help Erika will be here Irvine, work with her, and you'll both be fine. Now go." he ended, giving him a shove.

They winced at a whistling sound, growing ever closer until another blast echoed out, but this was not like the ones before, this one was closer and caused an outward force of heated air that scalded Feldran and Irvine. They looked to the side, witnessing the arrival of the Daemon as it rose into the air from the cratered ground where it landed. Around him were several guardsmen blackened into ash statues, completely still in the stances they held in life. Flames burst forth from the hanging lights above the plaza causing a rain of sparks and fire all around the creature, its thralls beginning to gather around it.

The creature looked around at the eerie statues that now surrounded it. "Ah, yes. One of my favorite parts, is the works of art that I seem to create just effortlessly." it cackled, reaching out with one clawed hand, and lightly raking one of the guard's faces, the ash statue crumbling to dust.

Feldran gritted his teeth, waving off Irvine behind him and calling out. "Versal! Time to go!"

The Smithmaster gave his daughter a pat on the head, nudging her towards Irvine, and stepped forward to stand beside Feldran. The creature's gaze drifted to the two, its fleshless face seeming to contort into a twisted smile, Feldran drew his sword, and Versal slammed his fists together.

As his knuckles collided, his flesh suddenly ran black as coal, orange lines cracking up his arms and lining his torso, an oppressive heat permeated the air around him as his tight-fitting dress shirt burst into flames and fell to ashes. His torso enveloped in the flames, his greyed hair and beard taking the shape of a roaring fire

The creature laughed again, staring directly at Versal's altered form. "So, you are the Ignis blood that has been causing my light headache."

Versal raked his forearms across each other, causing a rain of sparks. "A headache is the least o' yer problems now, Hellspawn!" he shouted, sprinting forward with Feldran following close behind.

Zyrxak leaned back slightly, Versal lowering into his sprint with his fists lighting into bright flames, and Feldran dashing on the opposite side, blade drawn. Versal landed his alight fist into the creature's side, punching through to its bare spine, Feldran slashing higher on the torso, and ripping through the Daemon's form. The two recovered from their initial strike and dodged past two fiery blasts from Zyrxak's hands, immediately rushing back in for their next strikes.

Irvine backed away slowly, stunned by the display before him. He had never seen his uncle truly fight another, nor Erika's father taking on this strange fiery form. The creature too, was horrifying, but there was something oddly familiar about it to him, especially that horned skull, something that he couldn't quite place, but knew was there.

Erika came up beside him, grabbing his arm and pulling him back. He glanced back towards her, seeing the tears welling in her eyes, and the determined expression behind them. He pointed towards the ongoing battle, trying to choke out words but failing.

Erika nodded in some understanding. "I'll explain about my father later, fer now, we have to go!" Irvine started to look back, but Erika snatched his jaw in her hand, forcing his gaze back to her. "Irvine! There is nothin' we can do, we have to go! Now!"

Irvine nodded as much as he could past her gripping hand, prompting her to release him. She started towards the edge of town, refusing to relinquish hold of his arm. Irvine followed as best he could, trying to keep his own grip on his pack and supplies.

"We need to get to the plateau we used to hike to." he informed her.

She nodded quickly as they began to round a corner, nearly running into one of the burning skeletons prowling the town. Erika jumped back slightly, gripping her warhammer with her right hand nearly to the end of the haft and swinging it wildly. An audible crack resounded as the metal met the creature's smoldering skull, a rain of sparks and embers following the thing's severed head and spine. Irvine stood back, impressed with her strength, but still glanced back at the battle behind them, this time at the wrong moment.

Versal and Feldran took turns slashing and smashing at the creature, its form starting to contort from the beating, the specter seemed to be on the defensive, only firing minor fire bolts at the assailants when distance granted it. Around their battle, the skeletal thralls continued their own assault, the guards successfully repelling them, but their numbers refused to dwindle.

Zyrxak looked around at the relative stalemate and let out a sigh, the tone sounding almost mocking. "I grow weary of this game. Let's get on with it."

As his adversaries made their next attack, the specter hovered low in a crouch, lunging out suddenly and with blinding speed, leaving a trail of blue flames in his wake. The field went silent as the blast knocked Versal, the guards and the creature's minions outwards indiscriminately.

The Daemon rose up several yards from where he started his charge, lifting Feldran off of the ground, his jagged claw protruding from the soldier's back. The newly polished blade fell from his grasp, clattering to the ground as he struggled against Zyrxak's blow. The monster lifted Feldran higher over his head, extending his arm fully, before closing his skeletal fist.

Feldran's form disintegrated in a flash of flame, and Zyrxak emitted a hideous cackle.

Irvine tried to scream in protest, but nothing came from his lungs. The tears that had welled in Erika's eyes now flowed freely. She knew the consequences of stalling here though. She shouldered her pack and gripped her hammer hard, grabbing Irvine's arm even tighter, and pulled with all her might in their original direction. Looking back one last time, she caught a glimpse of her father, slumped against a wall, returned to his normal form.

She forced her gaze away, determined to hold her faith in him and her conviction to escape this night.

Irvine went numb behind her, falling from his feet as his eyes unfocused, and he seemed to choke on his breaths.

Erika looked around them, just outside the town in one of the fields as a farmhouse exploded into a raging inferno. Crops all around them popped into flames one by one and permeated the area with smoke and ash. Erika wanted to scream, wanted to just curl on the ground and wait for everything to stop. Of course, she couldn't do that though.

She rested the head of her warhammer on the ground, and leaned the haft against her side, before slapping her palms on her cheeks.

"Come on, Irvine." she said, leaning down and hooking her arms under Irvine's. "Ye need to get up, ye silly duck!"

She lifted him with all her strength, surprised by his weight slightly, but still managing to get him on his feet.

"Ye need to follow me, alright?" she called, looking him straight in his blue eyes. They seemed dimmed though, making her stomach sink further. "Come on, love, work with me here."

Panic filled her, as she hesitantly looked around, knowing she would find no one to help her here.

She reached down, ripping the skirt of her dress up to her hip, then secured Irvine's pack on his shoulders as he stared back at the burning town. She grabbed him tightly by the wrist and took a breath.

"We need to go, Irvine, come on!"

With a grunt of effort, she dashed forward, heaving Irvine behind her. Finally, his feet caught up to him, and they both ran full out across the fields. Burning trees grew closer, and the ash grew thicker. Erika could handle this though.

She wiped a hand across her face, trying to wipe her tears away, but only managed to smear ash across her face even worse.

Looking back, she wanted to wipe Irvine's tears as well, to hold him to her breast and promise that everything would be alright.

She knew that she would only succeed in making things worse right now though if she tried.

5
FLIGHT OF FEAR

Zyrxak descended back to his low hover, as the blue flames around him started to fade back into their standard orange luster. Teral landed beside him some time later, regarding the destruction around them from the explosion he created. Zyrxak eventually rose after several minutes.

"Well then. It seems I'm weaker than I had originally believed. The Ignis blood dodged my attack, but I assume he was knocked unconscious." the specter's head turned with a snap towards where the Smithmaster had fallen, but ground his teeth together when he spotted the vacant spot.

"It seems your last blow allowed the remaining townsfolk and the mage to escape. None of your thralls remained to stop them." Teral stated plainly.

Zyrxak started to straighten his posture. "It also seems that you hadn't the gall to stop them yourself." he replied with a degree of annoyance.

"With all respect, the mage and the soldier were able to give you a decent fight, I didn't possess the confidence to try and attack them, for fear of the mage bursting to flame as he did before." Teral responded.

"I suppose that is a fair assessment." the Daemon growled, his skeletal fingers grinding together loudly. "No matter, I'll corner them farther into the valley while I feed here to regain my power. Were there any other escapees?"

"Actually, I believe I saw a couple more fleeing the town separate from the evacuation."

Zyrxak nodded his understanding. "Right then, get after them."

Teral looked to the specter "What? You want me to chase them?"

Zyrxak's form shuddered jarringly, before lashing out and gripping the thief's placeholder leg and lifting him upside down by it. "I gave you this leg!" he cursed harshly through gritted teeth. "It gives you significantly more capability than my thralls that I can easily summon at this time! Meaning you are my only option to send after the two messengers before they warn the entire damned continent of my presence!"

He curtly dropped the thief afterwards, Teral barely managing to adjust his fall so he didn't break his neck.

"Now use that gift of yours, and begone!"

Teral didn't wait for the specter to turn around before he was dashing away from the scene and over the first rooftops. Zyrxak raised his palm to the sky, opening a fiery hole in the ground. From it, rose a pedestal bearing a thick tome, the cover the hue of volcanic rock with burning lines cracking outwards from a crimson sigil burned into the center.

"Such a pain to pull a grimoire from the Hells, just for this." he muttered angrily.

The specter waved his hand to the side, the book flipping open in a flourish. He then began his incantations, and his full return to this world.

↑↑

Irvine and Erika found themselves resting briefly on the crest of the hill that neighbored their hometown. The fire had moved past this area, leaving dead trees interrupting the landscape like gravestones. Both of them wretched and coughed from the falling ash of the fires.

Irvine had regained some degree of alertness, though he still had no idea how they were able to make it through the center of the wildfire. The flames around them seemed to drift away, as if they were opening for them, like simple doors.

He looked toward Erika, her dress now significantly more ripped than just the skirt that she had done herself, and her features covered in ash. A scrape shone red on her ribs where a branch had slit through, and her legs looked as if they had been whipped by ashen lashes. Her hair was tangled, and almost seemed darkened from the desperate flight through the falling cinders. He had never seen her so unkempt, even after the roughest days of work. Her chest heaved from the constant running, and sweat drenched her skin more than the tears did. Irvine figured he likely looked similar. The two of them looked back to their home, watching the trail of flame leading up to the burning buildings.

They averted their eyes in a flinch, when a blinding flash of light shone from the center of Valen, followed by a low rumble resounding across the valley. When they were able to look again, they both stared in shock at the sight before them. The town now appeared to be the center of a volcanic eruption, fiery crags opening up, splitting buildings asunder and stretching across the once grassy landscape. Only a moment later, they had to catch themselves as a quake in the ground moved past them, the shockwave of the sudden destructive force. Erika swallowed, trying to rid herself of the nervous bubble in her throat.

Irvine scanned the valley. "I'm sure your father was able to make it out." he encouraged.

She shook her head. "We have no way o' knowin' that. Nothin' we can know fer sure, 'cept hope."

Irvine unconsciously moved closer to her, wrapping an arm around her shoulder. She reciprocated by resting her head on his chest. "Come on. We're needin' to get to Sildenfeld. Ye're the leadin' one from here out, Irvine. I've no bloody idea where we're goin'." she said heavily.

Irvine nodded, knowing that their journey hinged on his expertise now. "I know a small brook where we can wash off and change. It's not far."

Erika turned and started off ahead of him, Irvine following behind her, before something caught his eye. He tried to focus his gaze, but couldn't manage much past the ash and tears clouding his sight. Unfortunately, his spyglass was too far down in his satchel for him to grab either. All he could manage to make out was an orange light making its way across the fields, very quickly.

"A scout coming to find us?" he muttered to himself.

Erika called from behind him. "Irvine? Are ye comin'?"

"Yeah, sorry. I'm on my way." he replied, turning back to her and jogging to catch up.

† †

Just outside of the town, the refugees hunkered down on the other side of a short drop-off. Smithmaster Versal breathed deeply after checking around and getting a rough count of the survivors. He shook his head, realizing that only a little more than half of the populous now rested here. The Daemon's minions must have caught up to some of the evacuation efforts and overwhelmed them. He peered over the shelf, seeing the still burning town, and past that, the hill leading to the Mystholt Ravine, where his daughter and Irvine should be heading. He couldn't make out any moving shapes past the heat waves, but still held faith that the two of them were well on their way to Sildenfeld.

A guard approached the man, offering a blanket to cover his bare torso, the intricate crimson patterns across his flesh dark once more.

Versal held up his palm to decline. "This be a warm spring's eve where I hail from." he explained, smoothing his greying beard and hair with his other hand.

The guard nodded and replied. "What is the plan from here, Smithmaster?"

Versal raised an eyebrow. "Why're ye askin' me lad?"

The young man stumbled on his words a bit. "W-well. Captain Jaris is missing, and Captain Feldran has fallen, meaning we have no leadership among us. I've heard stories of you and Captain Feldran's adventures and thought-"

Versal placed a hand on the man's shoulder. "Which's makin' me no more qualified than yerself. Instead of waitin' fer another to step up, why don't ye take some charge."

"B-but, sir I-"

"No buts man. Neither Jaris nor Feldran could orchestrate all this on their own, all of us are goin' to need to step up some, and work together to survive this. What's yer name?"

The guard nodded with a deep breath. "Merrick, sir. In that case, I'll start putting together a meeting with the other guards to plot a course across the fields."

Versal nodded with a grin. "That'a'boy. I'll keep an eye on the town, just in case our friend'll be sendin' anyone out."

Merrick began to walk back towards the larger group, when the rumbling sound started in the ground below them. Versal peered over the ridge again and saw a bright light, increasing in intensity. He jumped back down below the ridge and called for everyone to keep their heads down, before slamming his palms together, the flesh of his hands up to his forearms turning black as ash. He then crushed both fists into the ground, causing a wave of fire to cascade above them. The explosive wave of flame crashed into it, splitting onto each side of Versal's defensive wall, the ground shaking like a world rocking earthquake. He recovered, catching his breath from the exertion. On either side of the grouping, the land lay scorched and burning, ravines suddenly opening up in the ground and spewing magma.

Versal turned to Merrick. "Might want to expedite that meetin'. I'm afraid we might have some company soon."

Merrick nodded, and jogged off faster. The Ignis blood smith fell to a knee though, coughing past his labored breaths.

"Bloody Hells." he muttered. "It's gettin' a bit hot, ain't it?"

† †

Teral paused at the top of the hill where Irvine and Erika had just been, glancing back at the crater of scorched earth that held the town in its center. He couldn't make out any details, but figured Zyrxak was beginning whatever rituals he needed to regain his full strength. He marveled at the distance he had traveled, and yet he stood here, barely winded at all. This new leg was truly amazing, though he resented the gift to a certain extent. He lowered himself down and sat back, a small cloud of ash scattering around him.

What's the issue of them getting a little further when I can move double their speed? he mused to himself.

He reached into his pocket, retrieving the paper he had been given to hire his services. He scanned it over several times, seeing no mention of it releasing a Daemon on the world. He cursed himself and his avarice, knowing that the only reason this entire situation happened was because of the astronomical reward.

He thought back to his days with the guild. Raven Mitrios, the current leader of their branch, always said, 'If it's a large reward for a simple task, the client has an ulterior motive you likely won't support.'

How foolish he was to ignore the mentor's warning. It was too late to regret the situation now though, all he could do was the next step, and handle things as they came. For now, he needed to track the couriers going into the Mystholt Ravine a short way away from him. He rested his face in his hands, remembering that he was never very proficient at tracking living beings. He laughed at the notion, figuring it would make his task more interesting at least. For now, he would rest as best he could, watching the world burn with anger and contempt.

† †

The Mystholt Ravine was a thick expanse of trees and foliage. It existed in a massive tear through the Seraph Mountain, but on a lower altitude than the nearby valleys. The snow falling from the mountain tops above caused a nearly endless mist that permeated the upper canopy of the trees. Early morning sunlight lit up the fog cloud and the ravine as a whole, illuminating the path for Irvine and Erika, where the two of them had been wandering almost blindly in the dark. They were bleary eyed in the early morning light, but trudged forward despite it.

Irvine couldn't shake the feeling that the thing from the town was pursuing them, making him more tense than he would be normally.

Erika seemed to be doing somewhat better, her eyes still slightly red from the tears and ash, and her body more or less covered in the detritus and dirt.

Irvine looked down at himself, realizing that he was in a similar situation. He chuckled slightly at that, looking up at the tree line above them. He usually enjoyed coming through here, though he would have much preferred to take Erika under better circumstances than these.

He looked back down, seeing her going in the wrong direction, calling out to her. "Erika, we need to go this way."

Erika turned back towards him, wiping her eyes with her knuckle, though she only succeeded in getting more grime in her eye, which she blinked furiously in response.

"I'm sorry, glad to see yer back with me though." she said with a half-hearted smile.

He returned the smile. "No reason to apologize. I should be sorry for being so useless on our way out."

"It's alright Irvine. Ye were in shock. Everyone handles that sorta thing differently. I think it's startin' to set in fer me now." she said, her gaze lowering to the ground.

Irvine stepped down the incline to stand next to her, holding his arms up slightly to offer an embrace, which she seemed to happily accept. She pressed her face into his neck despite the dirtiness, gripping his sides with her arms tightly.

Despite how rough she could be, she still felt so soft.

"I'm not going to pretend I'm good at these kinds of things." he started, looking back up at the trees. "But on the bright side, we're almost to the brook. There'll be clean water that we can wash up with, and we can get changed into more comfortable traveling clothes."

Erika choked out a laugh. "Aye, these shoes weren't so great for dancin' either."

Irvine glanced down and noticed she was barefoot, carrying her dress shoes in her hand, her feet dirtied and bruised from walking.

He nudged her slightly. "Why didn't you say anything?"

She waved him off. "I can handle a little barefoot walk. Just lead me to yer brook so I can soak 'em a bit."

"Let me know if I need to carry you." he said gently.

"Ye sure ye can lift me, delivery boy?" she shot back.

Irvine turned, walking backwards a few steps. "I'm hurt, truly. Branch there." he ended, pointing beneath her next stride.

She looked down, seeing the thin wood, then looking back to him and puffing out her cheeks, stomping her foot down on the branch out of spite, which was too fresh to snap so easily. Irvine chuckled at the display, then turned back around and continued on through the pass.

Erika watched him as he walked, remembering how he had felt when she lifted him outside the town.

"Yer stronger than ye look." she mused quietly.

6
The Mystholt

Irvine led the way through his familiar terrain, helping Erika down slopes and drop offs. He offered to carry some of her supplies, to which she responded with a scowl. He tried to think about her, specifically, and her stubborn personality as they went. Focusing on her made it easier to put the situation out of his mind for a time, briefly forgetting that they were on the path to warn a neighboring town of the destruction of Valen, and the emergence of a Daemon.

Any time she would walk ahead of him, he absentmindedly directed her on the correct path, but regarded her features consistently. He noticed every new scrape on her shoulder or leg, every new smear of soil on her nearly ruined dress or skin. It helped to check in on her, to make sure she wasn't pushing herself too hard.

He was used to traveling, but he worried about her. She and her father had moved to Valen when she was just an infant, and she had never ventured far from the town. He never met her mother, as she had fallen ill, and passed away shortly before they had come to the Regions. Irvine knew not what the illness was or came from, but it was never a conversation topic with her or her father. He remembered their time together as they grew up, and chuckled at the notion of him looking out for her well-being out here, when she was the one that defended him from the larger and stronger children in the town as they grew up.

He reminisced in poor spirits, of the early summer days of his childhood, when he was being regularly thrown against walls or onto the ground, being kicked and called things like 'firestarter' or 'flamemaker'.

She would appear not long after, crashing her fists into each of the kids who bullied him. It was a common image, her standing over him with heaving breaths and bloodied knuckles.

They were the reason he started with the Courier's Guild, but she was the reason he came back each time. He supposed that uncle Feldran was one reason he returned as well, but shook his head of that thought. As he walked forward, he suddenly ran into Erika, who stood dead still in the pathway.

She turned back slightly and slapped her hand onto his chest. Her hand was warm, but her expression was terrified.

"Irvine, what was that?" she asked with some measure of panic.

"What? Did you hear something?" he said, backing away slightly, and cursing himself for getting so lost in thought.

She nodded in reply, holding her finger up and waiting for the sound to repeat. Moments later, a low trilling sound echoed from their left side.

Irvine muttered another curse and held up his finger to his lips. "Don't move."

He crouched down and dug around slowly and carefully in the underbrush, finding a decent sized stone, then uprooted it from the soil. He stood again, scanning the foliage on their side for any movement, eventually seeing a large fern shudder. He tossed the stone hard to their left side but back in the area where they had come from. As the stone landed with a thick thud, the ground rumbled slightly as if a stampede of cerotae bulls were trampling through the foliage.

Moments later, the ground where the stone landed exploded into a shower of earth and gravel. A bear-sized, grey colored creature burst forth and into the air. A gaping mouth as large as its body opened and took in soil and rocks, before clamping down and landing with a crash.

Erika stared at the display wide eyed, before Irvine grabbed hold of her shoulder. "Watch your step but move quickly." he said with a deadly seriousness, as he started to pull her into the opposite direction of the massive animal.

The two started into a run, dodging beneath branches and leaping over fallen trees. Erika did her best to ignore the stinging pain from the ground below her. She had been careful with her steps before now, but having to run again was worsening the condition of her bare feet and she wasn't sure if she could go very much further.

Irvine dodged off to the side, Erika suppressing a yelp as he dragged her in front of him, and landing them into a small space at the base of one of the trees. The ground was moist under her dress, and she felt a branch start to stab into her side, but she was able to stop from making any noise when Irvine placed his finger over his lips again. She glanced around, then up at him. He crouched slightly above her, making for a sort of shield with his back. She held her breath, looking up at his muscular form as he tensed, scanning the area behind them.

Erika found a gravity in his expression. He was more serious than she had ever seen him. There was a fire in his eyes that intimidated and somewhat scared her. She could hear her heart pounding in her ears, and felt her lungs struggle to not violently let out the air she held in.

She never pondered too much on his travels across the Regions, and all the things he must have faced. She thought back to a time several years past when he had returned from one of his jobs one evening. She had gone to his uncle's home to see Irvine, though when she peeked into the window, she witnessed Feldran stitching a large gash in his back. She hadn't ever seen that much blood, even when her father or her sustained an injury in the forge. She had forced herself to forget that memory for a time, though always fearing for Irvine's well-being while he was away from Valen.

She returned to the moment at hand when Irvine's features softened again, and she let out her breath as easily as she could, though she couldn't pull her gaze away from him. He reached down, grabbing hold of her arms to help her back to her feet with a surprising strength that made her heart quicken again. Erika removed the twig from her side, and brushed off slightly, trying to regain her composure.

"What was that?" she asked with a concerned look.

"Jordhak." Irvine replied calmly. "Solitary creatures that burrow underground and hunt using the sound around them. They usually go after deer or goats, but they're not opposed to going after people. Good catch hearing its call."

"Are they common?" she continued, unable to hide the hint of fear.

"Not really, no. Honestly a little odd seeing one so active at this hour. They usually hunt after dark." he explained, with all calmness.

Erika wasn't sure if she was comfortable with how casually he spoke about these creatures. *Is this really so routine for him?* she wondered.

Irvine started off again. "It's not far now, we're almost at our rest spot."

Erika sighed, placing a hand to her chest and breathing deeply, feeling her chest expand with the air. She hoped they wouldn't experience any more complications on the way.

† †

Zyrxak chanted in a low tone, arcane light pulsing from beneath the pedestal that contained his summoned tome. Pages flipped wildly, and sparks flew off of the book as if a raging fire burned within its binding. All around him, the buildings crumbled apart from the sheer heat alone.

The fissures caused by the initial ritual widened, and new creatures clawed their way out from within them. Horrifying visages of Minor Daemons stalked the streets, Zyrxak hearing the occasional scream cut short as one of its underlings found a townsperson that failed to escape.

A stone dais was raised nearby in the town square, where the bodies were laid out one by one. The specter counted eleven so far, a paltry number to be sure, but they would have to suffice for now. Mortal souls held little power, but enough to supply the Daemon's energy to greater heights than what it had awakened with.

He had considered consuming the soul of the thief that had released him, but the use he had gained out of the skittish man proved more worth his time that the small amount of energy he would have obtained from him. Now the thief stood to prove his worth even more by stopping the pair that fled had to warn the world of the Daemon's coming.

Zyrxak exhaled, imagining the glory that awaited him when he gained enough power to lay siege to the neighboring towns and cities. How he longed to hear the screams of a bloody raid, the souls of the masses released, only to be devoured shortly after. He savored the taste of these souls brought to them, but hungered for a proper feast.

The Daemon's daydreaming was interrupted by the sound of a body slumping onto the dais with cracks of breaking bones. He glanced over, seeing the fresh corpse missing a leg and half its skull, and clacked his skeletal fingers together in twisted glee. It was a shame he could not claim the soul of the warrior that had given him such trouble when arriving here, that would have been worthwhile, but sacrifices needed to be made in such a dire situation. The specter had nearly been destroyed before he had the chance to have any real fun.

His burning eyes turned to the morning sky above him, while a stray thought of his old enemies wormed into his twisted mind.

He grunted audibly and absently gripped a nearby thrall's skull tightly, until a sickening pop gave him the satisfaction he needed to resume his dark task. He looked again to his tome awaiting him on the pedestal, turning it through the haunting depictions of his former allies. He hated even having to use a tome, but desperate times were upon him. Many would serve his terrible purpose well, but he considered a certain one of his own domain instead. A cruel Wrath Daemon that served him in the time before.

A twisted smile cracked across his skull. The thought of the havoc that one could wreak was delicious indeed.

† †

The brook echoed a gentle trickling sound, fresh water rolling down from the west, fed by a waterfall from the mountain. It rested in this deep pond for a while, before flowing eastwards and into an underground cavern.

Erika promptly sat on a boulder bordering the edge of the pond and immediately submerged her feet in the cool water, breathing a sigh of relief after the barefoot trek. Irvine smirked at her, glad they were finally able to make it to his usual resting place on this route. He walked to a raised stone shelf neighboring the brook and began unpacking his satchel, separating out his fresh traveling clothes and leather armor, along with his weapon.

He dipped a small washcloth in the water, and began wiping his face clean of the ash and soil that he had accrued over the journey so far. Walking back to the shelf, he carefully removed his tunic, doing his best to avoid any burns or scrapes that he might have. Erika, who had been watching his routine thus far, averted her gaze quickly when he started to disrobe.

"I suppose ye're normally out here alone?" she said

Irvine nodded his head. "In general, yes. Don't usually have any other companions besides a riding animal, only occasionally other couriers. Though horses aren't very helpful in the

Mystholt, and you can only get them in from the Valen side, opposite side is too steep. Even runner birds have a hard time up here."

Erika glanced back carefully, watching his naked torso as it moved, and seeing the glint of a small metal pendant hanging by a thin chain from his neck. Her curiosity was stifled when she laid eyes on the maze of scars that wound around him, some even worse than the wound across his back she had witnessed through his window all those years ago, which she was able to find with ease.

She felt her hands starting to shake, a feeling of guilt washing over her. She had always protected him when they were children, but she had done nothing to aid him during his numerous journeys, and had no idea of the things he must have faced on them. Irvine looked back at her as he finished washing his torso with the cloth, seeing her hands clenched and quivering.

He retrieved his overcoat and walked over to her, draping it over her shoulders. "It can be a little chilly this time of year."

She shook her head, chuckling slightly. "It's not the cold, Irvine. Thank ye though, fer the concern."

He stood, cocking his head slightly, seemingly not understanding her meaning. He strode back to his supplies, retrieving his new clothes. "What is it then? If you don't mind my asking."

"It's nothin' really." she lied, turning back and absently observing his muscled form. "Just different seeing ye in yer element. Ye're still that young boy I knew, in my head."

He raised his face to the sky as he dropped his trousers. Erika flinched from looking with a reddened face.

"I am still that same boy you knew." he began. "I've just grown a little."

Erika smirked at that statement, seeing just how much he had grown without her realizing. She glanced back again to watch his muscled back contort with his movements. He took a small cup and used it to pour water from the pond through his long, dark hair, washing it of the ash somewhat. Erika watched as the shimmering liquid ran down his skin, her cheeks reddening again when her gaze fell too low.

"Sure, the courier job had me all over the Regions, seeing different things and experiencing different cultures and civilizations, but deep down I always looked forward to coming home." he continued, buckling his belt.

"What about Valen kept ye comin' back?" Erika asked, no longer watching him, but instead staring at her reflection in the water.

"Can't really say for sure. Uncle Feldran was important to me of course, making sure he was well and everything. I suppose you-" Irvine's gaze snapped directly ahead, realizing what he was saying suddenly as he finished pulling his shirt over his head.

"What was that? I didn't hear." Erika asked, turning to him with a puzzled look.

Irvine quickly settled his feet into his comfortably worn boots. "Nothing. Just ranting. Why don't you go ahead and change, I'll go scout ahead and make sure nothing has changed since the last time I was here. Call when you're finished, or if anything happens, alright?"

Erika started to protest, wrenching her legs from the water with a splash, but Irvine was already several yards off, buckling his leather armor pieces together. She let out a sigh, stepping carefully over to the stone shelf and setting her pack on it next to Irvine's open satchel. She glanced down, lightly sliding his belongings to the side carefully. Her gaze focused a bit when she noticed a small box next to his festival clothing.

She turned in the direction where he had walked, confirming that he was out of sight, before picking up the container and opening it carefully, the pendant of emerald entwined in silver lay inside, untouched by the chaos of the previous night.

Her eyes widened and she quickly shut the box with a loud snap. The sudden noise caused her to fumble around in a panic, quickly stuffing it back inside Irvine's bag, accidentally spilling more of the contents out as she did.

She placed her head in her hands trying to calm her racing heart. She peeked through her fingers, assessing the damage she caused, until she noticed a small piece of parchment with a painting on it. She carefully turned it over, the somewhat damaged paper seeming to be very old and worn. She exhaled sharply, seeing through the damage of it that it was, very clearly, a portrait of her. It was nearly identical to the one that her father had hanging in their home. She was clad in a dark green dress, that supposedly complimented her eyes, her hands resting on her lap, and her mouth twisted into a rueful smirk. She suddenly regretted seeing that annoyed expression again.

When did he get this? she wondered, before coming back to her senses and trying to replace all the objects back into his bag. She always had a fondness for Irvine, and she hated to admit that she worried that he would leave one day and never come back, but she had her doubts that he had any similar feelings for her. She had focused so much on her time with him, and how happy it made her, that she never paused for a moment to wonder if he did the same. Though the portrait seemingly confirmed what she believed he had almost said before, and the stray thoughts of his possible feelings for her.

She carefully put the portrait and jewelry box back into his satchel, slowly draping the flap over it, and swallowed hard.

She leaned back on the stone, trying to breathe and lower her heart rate, searching around for any sign that Irvine had caught her snooping in his belongings, relived when she found none.

After she took several deep breaths, she carefully pulled the straps of her festival dress from her shoulders, allowing it to fall away from her body, and onto the soft moss below her feet. She retrieved the washcloth and cup Irvine had used before, and set to work scrubbing her flesh with the water from the brook, all while her heart continued to pound in her chest.

The cool water running through her hair, and the chill air across her naked skin did little to calm her though, as she continued to ponder on the nature of Irvine's relationship with her. She sat down on the mossy ground, putting her legs back into the crisp water, and enjoying the soothing feeling over her bruised feet and calves. She leaned forward, resting her elbow on her thigh, while her fingers picked and pinched at her lower lip, forgetting her nudity in the clearing.

Her heart refused to calm in her chest.

† †

Irvine carefully stepped through the brush of the Mystholt, brushing off his leather chest armor. The small gold emblem of the Courier's Guild, a rolled scroll over a compass rose, shimmered in the light. The brook wasn't quite the halfway point between the two sides of the verdant fissure, though there was not much travel time after that. All that lay before them after the cave at the end was the Seraphine range, and then the open field that led to Sildenfeld. Easy travel for him normally, but with Erika with him, he would have to add some time to his route.

Everything seemed untouched here, giving him some degree of happiness. He would be happier still that Erika would soon have a good pair of boots and he wouldn't have to worry about her slicing her heel on the sharp rocks common in the Seraphine mountains.

He saw no sign of other people in the area, only finding the tracks left by the various animals that called the Mystholt their home. He paused for a moment, listening intently to the forest around him. A faint rustle in the branches not far off caused him to duck instinctively, feeling a hard impact like fists on the hard leather that protected his upper back.

He drew his sword smoothly and looked up, spotting his assailant, a nocturne gryphon. A relative of the eagle headed gryphon, only these bore the likeness of an owl, its cat-like hindquarters having a grey spotted pattern. Its wide wings tucked in as it grabbed onto a high branch and flipped under it, coming to an eerie hanging position, turning to face its would-be prey.

Irvine noticed a slight twitch in the creature's normally still head, even more bizarre of a behavior than it simply being out in the daylight. He wondered if the beast was sick, or if the Daemon's emergence was causing this alien behavior in the creature.

The gryphon screeched, moving itself forward into a controlled fall, spreading its wings just above the forest floor. Irvine bounced on his toes lightly, counting the moments as the creature approached. The gryphon closed in quickly, he dodged to the right, spinning clockwise and bringing his sword out in a wide arc, slashing cleanly underneath the creature's wing.

It crashed to the ground, bringing the feathered wing closer to its body to shield the wound before rampaging towards him again on foot.

Irvine backed a step, tripping over a tree root, which allowed the beast to leap over him. It savagely raked its front talons at him, though gaining nothing but soil, its sight impaired in the bright daylight. Finally, one stray claw managed to drag across Irvine's left forearm.

He called out and hissed at the stinging rend in his flesh, dodging the blind strikes as best he could while he angled his sword tip to the gryphon's breast. He suddenly regretted favoring the longer blade in that instance, but managed to press the tip of the weapon into the feathers of the raving animal.

In a flash, he leaned upwards from his waist, plunging the sword through its chest cavity, grunting when the blade skipped off of a bone. He breathed somewhat easier as he hugged the ranting creature with his wounded arm, binding its front legs with his torso so it couldn't rake through him again. The wild swings and wing beats of the gryphon slowed, Irvine could feel the warm lifeblood spilling onto his chest, and the labored breathing of its lungs.

"Hopefully this frees you from your ailment." he said aloud to the dying creature. The weight of it collapsed onto him, its final breath exuding from its beak and its large eyes staring off into nothingness as a paleness filled them.

Irvine braced his injured arm on the ground below, and his right arm on the handle of his sword, pressing both to leverage the dead creature off of him. He groaned with the effort, finally able to roll the heavy corpse to its side, and slide his legs out from underneath it. He stared at the mist above him, feeling the moisture dropping down all across the area. After sliding his sword from the gryphon's breast, and inspecting that the tip didn't chip on whatever bone he had hit, he wiped his blade clean on a stained cloth from his pocket, before sheathing the weapon again. After taking another breath, he looked over at the dead gryphon, finding some amount of peacefulness in its lifeless eyes.

He sighed deeply, plucking a long white and brown feather from the wing, and holding it between his fingers. After the moment passed, he brought himself to his feet, separating his torn sleeve from the torn flesh with gritted teeth, and rolling the sleeve over the wound carefully. With one final look at the gryphon, he set back towards the brook.

⸱   ⸙ ⸙

Erika finished fastening her boots on under her grey skirt, and adjusted the straps of her metal half breastplate. She had to take a moment to fit it to herself better, wincing at the pinch on her ribs before finally getting it just right. She had never actually used any of her armor besides trying it on, but her father had been sure to fashion her a light set should the need ever arise. She huffed at the size change from the last time she had worn the piece six years ago when she was seventeen, before shrugging the thought away. She was larger than she was back then, primarily due to the muscle mass from working in the forge. Although she lamented not having the girlish figure of others in Valen at times, she took pride in her strength.

She regarded the extra plates in her bag, ones she had personally made in the previous months as a future gift for Irvine, and wondered when would be the right time to present them to him. As if her thoughts had summoned him, she looked up just as Irvine stepped around the trees, her expression shifting to surprise as he wore one of frustration. He carried his leather armor and shirt in one hand, naked to the waist save for the strap over his shoulder that carried his sword. As he approached, she started to speak, but noticed the fresh wound on his forearm. She started forward in a new panic, but he held his hand aloft towards her and shook his head.

"It's just a scratch." he said, grabbing his festival tunic and ripping it into strips. He then set his armor and weapon on the stone shelf and walked to the pond, submerging his arm and blood-soaked shirt in the water. Erika gasped at the sudden cloud of red in the crystal water, but Irvine waved her off again. "It's not all mine."

This panicked her even more.

"Not all yers? What kind o' answer is that?" she proclaimed, stomping over towards him.

He stood to face her directly as she came within a breath of him, flinching as she raised a fist in her customary punches, but she stopped.

Irvine put his right hand to her shoulder, trying to calm her. "It's fine, Erika. I'm fine."

She put her closed fist between them, gently thumping his bare chest. "Just don't be runnin' off without me anymore." she said, giving him a halfhearted smile and turning away. She tried to stifle the sudden tears in her eyes, putting one hand over her mouth and smoothing her hair back with the other. The thought of losing him, and her not being able to do anything to stop it, was too much to bear.

Irvine watched her as she strode off, looking down at his injured arm, and beginning to wrap it in the remnants of his festive tunic.

"Even when you're changing?" he asked aloud, trying to lighten the mood.

Erika replied with a laugh, trying to mask the lump in her throat as much as she could. "Just look away, ye silly duck."

7
Confusions and Nightmares

The forest was still. Leaves falling around the trunks and branches were the only sound throughout the area. Autumn was nearing its end already, signs of an early and harsh winter. The harvest had come just in time, though the celebration still ran in the city of Sildenfeld.

Out here, the noise of the merriment could not be heard. Only the silence that permeated the beautiful trees of the expansive Willow Wood Forest. The place she called home.

She crouched easily on a thick tree branch. Her dark hair cascaded around her face and danced around her grim set eyes. She wore light, padded armor with sections of mail pulled tightly to avoid sound. Her legs were bare from the thigh until her thick boots, though her skin was covered in markings the same white and orange colors of the forest. A tattered cloak wrapped her shoulders colored a deep green, its simple enchantment warming her comfortably.

Two shortswords hugged her hips on either side, and a quiver hung on her lower back. An intricately carved bow idly hanging from her lithe hand.

She barely breathed. Her form motionless as the air around her.

A brief flash of grey caught her eye suddenly, and she whipped into motion. In one fluid motion, she laid back off the side of the branch, and loosed a single arrow towards the movement. She landed on the forest floor in a crouch, silent and still as a cat.

Across the clearing, lay her quarry. A large wolf, with an ashen coat of fur. Its eyes lay open and lifeless now, but frothing liquid still clung to its mouth and jaw, dripping from its teeth. The ranger strode to it with a sway in her step, pulling the arrow quickly from its heart. She didn't recognize the other arrow that adorned the beast's opposite shoulder. The shaft had cracked from its last fall, though the other half was only a few steps away from where it had fallen. The ranger retrieved the broken arrow, observing the pale dove feathers that fletched the back end.

She whistled sharply, marking her position to her allies in the brush, so they could collect the infected creature.

She noticed the crimson on its teeth, mixing with the repulsive foam. A sigh escaped her thin lips as she stalked the path the creature had taken.

Another individual came down near her, male, but dressed similarly to her.

"And well done indeed, Teria. Your aim is impeccable as ever."

Teria refused to take her eyes from the path before her, maintaining a silence.

The man continued to press. "I can't help but wonder why all these poor creatures are turning up like this. It's almost as if something is deliberately doing it."

She sighed, turning to the man, digging the end of her bow into the trail she was tracking, so she would not lose it during the conversation she was loath to engage in.

"What of it, Farris?" she asked gruffly.

The man stepped back, though she knew not if it was to avoid her wrath or to ogle at her muscled legs. Either way wouldn't save him from a swift kick to the head.

"Mistress Varia would love to hear of your perverse gaze." she threatened with a roll of her eyes.

Farris took another step back, his gaze snapping up to her annoyed face. "Of course she wouldn't, she's much too busy for the likes of me."

Teria rolled her eyes again, nodding for him to get on with whatever his ploy was.

"My only thought is that you are one of the sharpest, and most beautiful, blades in the Willows." he paused a moment, as if expecting her to blush at the compliment.

She didn't.

He cleared his throat. "My point being, is that all of these creatures seem to be going rogue in very close proximity to the city. That, and I've begun to hear some whispers."

Teria raised an eyebrow at him, wondering if he would finally prove useful in his conniving ways.

"Perhaps we should take a closer look at the underbelly of the city?" he teased.

She sighed deeply. "My patrol is for another two days. Perhaps after then, and I'll indulge your whims."

His face lit up slightly, until she snapped back with a hand resting on one of her shortswords. "Or perhaps I'll just take a look myself. Shady individuals usually meet my blades."

Farris laughed nervously at her pointed remark, eyeing her as she walked away.

After a while she found the source of the wolf's bloodied jaw. A young woman who had been out hunting, her shirt soiled with blood from her ravaged throat, her quiver bearing several more arrows of the same dove feather fletching as the one in the wolf's shoulder. Teria screwed up her face in a scowl of anger. She only wished she could have caught wind of the rogue wolf sooner, so she could have possibly saved the girl's life.

An odd detail stood out to her though, the woman had obviously been thrashed about by the throat, but no more was done to her. The wolf had not made a meal of her, even after going through the trouble of killing her.

She searched the area, but found no conclusive evidence for the creature's behavior. Eventually she sighed with resignation, stepping back to the corpse with a brightly colored cloth, draping it over the woman's boot.

After marking the location for the investigative group, she started back. Farris's words rang in her mind suddenly. He had obviously found something within Sildenfeld. She just wondered if he were too busy playing his games to be of any actual help.

† †

The next leg of the companion's journey was silent, Irvine leading the two through the Mystholt. They passed the dead nocturne gryphon, as they continued through the wood, Irvine bowing his head to the fallen creature as he went.

Erika glanced between him and the slumped form, noticing the thick slice on its side, as well as the puncture through its breast. No stranger to weapons, and their capabilities, she mentally measured the size of the wounds and Irvine's blade, and figured this was the creature he had run into. She wanted to question him, but understood that he knew these woods far better than she, and had traveled them countless times.

"Should we bury it or somethin'?" she asked as they walked past the corpse.

"No need. Persena reclaims her kin quickly in the Mystholt. Less than two days and there will be little left than a skeleton." he explained.

Erika shuddered at the thought of the creatures that would make feasts of the dead beast, but understood the cycles of the Goddess of Nature. More worry over Irvine clouded her mind though, realizing the same would happen to him if he were to fall here. She clutched a hand to the top of her breastplate, and pulled at it slightly, swallowing the uncomfortable notion as best she could.

She knew she was probably being childish for feeling so protective and worried over him, but couldn't help it. After the disaster in Valen though, she couldn't bear to lose another so close to her.

Besides that, her mind kept wandering to the items she found in his bag, wondering if her father had given him the portrait, and if the pendant was meant for her. She hated to assume that it was, but given the evidence of the portrait, as well as the necklace being an emerald, it truly did seem that way.

Perhaps he meant to give it to me last night? she wondered, cursing the Daemon for ruining their evening.

She could barely take her eyes from his back as he led them through the brush, dodging his occasional backwards glances. Occasionally she did become distracted by the beauty of the area around them, commonly looking up at the perpetual cloud above them, and the thick trees that dotted the uneven landscape.

In the quiet, she could hear all manner of wildlife, birds calling and treetop rodents squeaking. The experience was surreal and amazing, but she was still wary of her surroundings, unsure of what other monstrous creatures might attack them.

She gripped her warhammer tightly, her metal gauntlets scraping against the metal handle, feeling a certain amount of unease at that notion, and refused to use the sling on her waist for the weapon. Looking up at Irvine as he crested an uphill slope, she wondered how he walked so casually with his sword sheathed. He did rest his hand on the hilt, though if it were a comfortable position for his wounded arm, or just a habitual walking position, she could not tell.

Thankfully the bleeding had seemed to stop on his arm, the tattered cloth still retaining some of its original color. The thought that perhaps she was overestimating the injury, and it had not been as bad as she originally believed, did cross her mind. She knew that blood had a tendency to cloud uncontrollably in water, and a small drop of the liquid could appear to be a tankard's worth under the right conditions. In addition, the sight of the gryphon had supported Irvine's dismissal of not all the blood being his.

Yet she could not help but worry over her companion's well-being. She shuddered under the thought that if he fell, unconscious or dying, she would not have the slightest clue as to where they needed to go next, regardless of if she could help him directly.

I'll have to keep 'im close, even if one o' us is changin' clothes. A smirk spread along lips as she considered the humorous thought, brightening her mood a little. Not that him changing clothes stopped her from peeking before. Her face reddened slightly, remembering his bare skin and muscled physique.

Moments later, Irvine looked over his shoulder for what was likely the tenth time, Erika perking up slightly, hoping he would say something, but his gaze was far past her. She wondered why he kept checking behind them, but figured it was likely just another habit of his travels.

Eventually he started picking up branches and loose pieces of foliage. She looked up at the misty sky to see that it had begun to change color, morphing from a milky white to a burning orange, likely the signs of dusk beginning. It was then that she started to feel the effects of the last day, realizing that neither she nor Irvine had actually ever slept since the night before the festival.

"We'll find a clearing over there." he said quietly, pointing to a thicket to their right. "We can make it out of the Mystholt by midday tomorrow at the latest."

She looked back to him, trying to give him an encouraging smile, but it faded as he continued retrieving materials for a fire, and didn't meet her gaze.

Had I upset him that much? she wondered to herself, though realizing she had become upset with him in her own right.

She clenched her fists slightly, giving the sky a determined look, but slumped her shoulders again, unsure of how to approach him or the situation.

Irvine cleared away the foliage from the small inlet, placing the kindling and branches he had collected in a small stone circle that had been there when they arrived. Erika stepped over to one of the handful of larger stones to sit on, removing her gauntlets, and pulling up her skirt slightly to brush dirt from the side of her leg. Irvine sighed as he searched through his satchel.

"Damn it all." he hissed. "Can't find my tinderbox."

He scanned the area around them. "Not many sparking stones through here either, it's the wrong geology." He ran his fingers through his dark hair, scratching his scalp and turning away.

Erika watched him carefully, reaching down when he turned away and focused into her fingers, producing small embers from her hand into the kindling and setting it ablaze. She flinched at the faint red markings beginning to appear at her fingertips, holding them close to her pack so Irvine wouldn't notice. Erika cleared her throat lightly, Irvine turning towards her with surprise.

He smirked and chuckled slightly. "Well, it's good that one of us had a tinderbox. Though I should expect as much from the blacksmith's daughter, I suppose."

Erika nodded with a somewhat nervous smile. "Aye, always ready to start a flame."

Irvine helped the fire grow before retrieving two small sacks from his satchel, handing one to Erika and opening one himself. Inside was a mixture of preserved nuts and dried meats. Erika suddenly felt herself craving a seared lamb chop with garlic and rosemary, with a side of mashed potatoes, but knew this was at least sustaining.

"I'll have to set some traps later to hopefully get some rabbits." he said idly as he glanced periodically towards Erika, who ate the food he gave her gladly, but with a slight hesitation.

He couldn't quite put his finger on why she was being so quiet, as she was normally quite talkative. He had expected her to continue asking him questions the further they journeyed out, yet she had maintained this silence since they had left the brook.

Did I say something to irritate her? he wondered, trying not to stare, but still wanting to observe her behavior through their small dinner. His face ran hot suddenly, when one of his glances met hers, both of them quickly turning away after a moment of eye contact. Every moment after felt like an eternity with her still remaining quiet.

"Are you doing alright?" he asked quietly.

She nodded in reply. "Much better now. Thanks to these boots, and being rid of that tight dress."

"Understandable. It did look nice on you though." he said with a slight smirk.

Their conversation fell short a moment. The noise of birds roosting nearby was the only thing breaking their silence.

Erika looked at the ground below him, wondering if he'd continue. She exhaled slightly when nothing came. "Ye looked rather dashing yerself. I liked the color." she said, motioning towards his shredded and stained tunic wrapped around his arm.

He raised his arm, looking over the bandage. "I guess the color is a little faded now." he remarked, chuckling slightly, causing Erika to laugh as well.

"I had a nice time with you." he said, quieting again.

"Aye." she smiled. "I did too. Thank ye fer the dance."

Irvine stood a moment later, replacing the ration pouch in his bag and retrieving a length of thin rope. Erika started to protest, but Irvine looked at her, smiling at her emerald eyes. "I'm not going far, just a couple yards or so, to set some traps. Might catch us a better meal for tomorrow."

Erika nodded reluctantly. "Just stay in eyesight?" she pleaded.

Irvine nodded back. "In eyesight."

He stepped off moments later, cutting off sections of the rope with a small dagger. Erika watched him walk away, and carefully leaned towards the still small flame of the campfire. When she was sure Irvine was still facing away, she moved her hand towards the fire and waved her fingers upwards, the flames rising eagerly, licking up onto more of the firewood.

Thankfully that encouragement of the flames did not spread the markings on her fingertips any. She worried over the thought of him discovering the heritage she shared with her father, but knew he would have to one day. She would develop the markings one way or another. A sigh escaped her lips, resolving to make that an issue for another day, despite staring at the faint red blotches on her fingertips.

A while later, Irvine returned, wiping his hands free of soil. "Well, I've only got one bedroll."

"Oh, we sharin' tonight?" Erika teased playfully.

He smirked at her. "Won't be that cold yet. You need the sleep more though, judging by your expression."

Erika put her hand to her face, feeling the droopiness of her features while glaring at him. "What're ye goin' to use then?"

"The ground around here is plenty soft, between the soil and the moss. I'll be fine."

He threw out the bedroll on her side of the fire and smoothed it out for her, before returning to the other side and nestling against a thick tree.

Darkness came quickly, the Mystholt turning almost pitch, with no stars or moons visible to light the area. Torch bugs flickered up in the fog occasionally, and strange fungi attached to the trees gave off an eerie blue glow.

Erika glanced cautiously around the suddenly new area, staring at the bioluminescent mushrooms and insects.

"Strange place at first, but we can rest in peace. Nothing will disturb us around here." he said, looking at her and smiling.

She seemed to take little comfort in this, removing her breastplate and rubbing her hand underneath her shirt where the armor had chafed against her. He gave her a concerned look as she scowled at her flesh, but she waved him off.

"Didn't ye say the jordhaks were nocturnal?" she asked as she laid down inside the bedroll, noticing that Irvine kept his leather armor on, and held his sword against his chest.

"They hunt off of the sound of footsteps, but they rarely hunt humans or elves though. Usually just deer or the like." Irvine said with a yawn as he laid back further.

Erika sighed softly, watching him through the fire as her eyes fell shut from exhaustion.

He closed his eyes a short while later, and slowly drifted into unconsciousness.

† †

He dreamt of a simpler time, when he was far younger, in a house that was not his uncle's. The daylight shone through windows, with thick rays that highlighted the dust in the air.

He looked around, seeing the fresh flowers on the window sill, wooden toys scattered around him and a constant ringing sound. He brought his hands to his ears, unable to rid himself of the droning. It dulled when he heard footsteps behind him. He turned, seeing a dark-haired woman above him. She was clad in a dull colored dress.

Her facial features were blurry, as if behind a thick veil, but Irvine felt no panic as she reached down and lifted him. He felt warmth against her breast, and a comfort at her lullaby, though it sounded muffled. A man joined her, with thick arms, calloused hands, and similarly dark hair, wearing a tarnished apron. One of those calloused hands reached out and touched his. The face of the man was also obscured by the strange veil, but still felt familiar and warm.

The ringing returned, he could see movement behind the fuzzy details of the faces, their mouths moving, but the droning obscured their words. The woman gently sat him back in the middle of the floor, both her and the man stepping back to the side of

67

the room. They seemed so close, yet so far away, and he felt panic at the absence of their touch.

A light flared up behind them, an orange glow flickering to life, but neither of the figures moved. They both stood eerily still, staring at him with heads cocked towards each other. Irvine focused in on the increasing light, realizing the flames as they spread to all sides of the room.

In the center of the blaze was a face. It was skeletal, with curving horns protruding from the forehead, jagged teeth making a twisted smile and maniacal laughter. The room was engulfed in the flames, the two figures burning, their clothing fading to ash and their flesh melting from their bones.

A crash echoed from behind him. He turned to see a massive hulk of a man, hair and beard red as the fire, as he stepped through the broken wall. The Smithmaster's face was clear as the summer sky, unobscured by the strange veil.

He was scooped up in the burly arms of the new figure, and lain over his muscular shoulder. He stared back at the man and the woman, their human forms stripped away, and their skeletons crumbling to dust. He felt his face become wet with tears, though he could not call out.

† †

Irvine jolted awake, a cold sweat engulfing his body.

He looked around, the firelight almost out but still giving a smoke cover. The woods around them were quiet, nothing within his immediate sight.

He turned back, seeing Erika's form under his bedroll, raising and lowering with her gentle breath. Her shining warhammer lay beside her, the head still tarnished with the black ash of the creature she killed in the town. Realizing his own heaving breath, he swallowed, and squeezed his eyes shut, trying to calm his unconscious panic.

A snap echoed from the woods, Irvine instinctively grabbing his sword handle, and wrenching the weapon free with a dull ring. Several moments passed, his blade held in an upwards guard towards the tree line. He could feel the muscles in his arms tensing with the rigorous position. His expression softened, eventually deciding that it was one of his traps being sprung by some unsuspecting creature. He glanced over as he lowered his sword, watching Erika roll over onto her back. He had worried he had woken her with his sudden action, but exhaled in relief when her eyes remained closed.

He sheathed his weapon quietly, sitting back down and crossing his legs. He could tell that sleep would elude him for the rest of the night, and instead focused on the surrounding area. He reached back for his satchel, rummaging through for a moment and sighed when he found the box containing the emerald pendant. He feared he may have lost it in the mad dash from Valen. After replacing it in his satchel, he retrieved the portrait of Erika.

He wondered what she would think if she knew that he kept the painting as a keepsake, and as a reminder of his home. He returned the portrait next to the jewelry box and then dug down to find a thicker wooden box from the bottom of the bag. He opened it, observing the various trinkets inside. Talons, claws, teeth, and other parts of creatures he had killed in the past.

He kissed the gryphon feather, and placed it carefully inside.

He looked down, regarding his injured arm. It burned, and itched, but he was used to the pain that came with a battle with an animal. He glanced back at Erika, remembering the expression she wore when she saw his injury. He pondered that moment for a while, concluding that it was partially because she had always defended him when they were children, and partially because they had to deliver the news to Sildenfeld.

Perhaps because I'm the only one she knows to be confirmed alive, he thought grimly. *Or because I'm the only one who knows the way.*

He turned his gaze back to the fire, thinking about the terrible things that fire had done in his life, and the continual reasons he feared the chaotic element. He envied Erika, for having such an intimate understanding with it, and regretted each time he declined Versal's offers to teach him. Maybe he could have moved past his fear, and seen Erika more often on top of that. Though there was no point in focusing on what was already past.

Thoughts of his uncle clawed at the back of his mind, but he did his best to resist them. He hated ignoring his uncle's fate, but knew that he had no time to mourn just yet. He adjusted around, nestling back against the tree trunk, to where he could keep an eye on the clearing, the outlying woods, and Erika's soundly sleeping form.

A smile parted his grim face at the sight of her, somewhat amused at how apprehensive she was about sleeping in the open, yet how deeply she slept now. The soft curve of her waist and hip were outlined by her blanket, rising and falling with her gentle breaths. It was soothing in a way. Such an aggressive woman at times, yet now she was so docile.

Gods, she's beautiful.

He couldn't help but stare at her.

Tomorrow would bring a longer journey still. He only hoped that the several days' time it took to get to their destination would be soon enough to warn the Region of the Daemon's arrival.

8
CANDLE

Teral stepped lightly through the Mystholt, looking around in wonderment at the strange haven of life that was held here. He was familiar with the jordhak that prowled the first section of the forest, despite its erratic behavior, but he was unfamiliar with the region as a whole.

He knew of the Mystholt, but never ventured through himself, preferring to stick to the roads that ran around the Seraphine Mountains instead of attempting to trek through them. He was surprised and somewhat impressed with the distance the runaways had made, surmising that at least one of them had some kind of experience either in moving through wilderness, or in the Mystholt specifically, though the latter likely accompanied the former if it were true. If he remembered the maps correctly, these woods let out into the belly of the Seraphine Mountains, meaning a rough journey for anyone passing through. Should his suspicion be correct however, one of these individuals was a courier, giving him somewhat of a disadvantage when it came to catching up with them.

Though if only one of them knows the path, then the other may slow them down. he thought to himself, smiling at the knowledge that his new abilities would be more than enough to run them down in the open.

"No rush at all." he mused aloud as he started to step into the damp wilderness, enjoying his time in the fantastical place.

What was a journey, if not to be enjoyed, after all?

Here he was far from the Daemonic monster that he had unleashed, and far from its wrath as well. Even if the specter could revoke the arcane prosthetic, he could think of no reason the Daemon would revoke it when he knew not where his 'servant' was located.

The more time it took to catch the pair meant the closer to Sildenfeld he would wind up as well. The thought of visiting the fair ruling city gave him grim satisfaction, in the prospect of finding the party responsible for giving out that bounty.

Revenge was not a common dish of Teral's taste, but he never enjoyed his meals cold. He resolved to find the one responsible quickly.

His eyes flashed around the area, and a dagger slung from his grasp, meeting its mark on a rabbit that would do well for a meal.

He wrenched the blade free of the carcass, and savored the thought of the same weapon ending the life of whoever tricked him into his predicament.

"Can't be too hard to find you, 'A.H.'." he muttered, feeling the note in his pocket.

† †

Irvine gently shook Erika's shoulder to wake her, smirking at her quirky grin at him before she raised her arms in a stretch.

"Ready to go?" he asked, shouldering his satchel and checking the fire was properly doused.

Erika looked up at him lazily as she slipped a boot over her foot. "Don't we need to be packin' everythin' again?"

Irvine smiled, placing a small cloth with cooked meat on it. "Already have. Here's some rabbit for breakfast too."

Erika slapped her hands to her cheeks to rouse herself quicker, happily biting into the fresh cooked meat. Irvine helped her pack the bedroll she used, and shortly after, they were off again. Irvine led the way more predominantly now, while Erika did her best to keep pace with him.

The towering trees of the Mystholt were eventually interrupted by a jagged fissure in the stone wall bordering the forest. The foliage and soil gave way to stone and gravel spilling forth from the imposing cave entrance. Irvine entered slowly after letting out a shrill whistle that echoed through the cavern system.

"What's the whistle fer?" Erika asked, removing her hands from her ears.

Irvine wrapped a thick tree branch in some excess of his festival tunic and used his tinderbox that he had finally found, to set the makeshift torch alight. "If there were any creatures or animals in the first section of this tunnel, the whistle would have spooked them, giving us an easier time through."

Erika nodded her understanding. "An' that works?"

Irvine chuckled. "Usually."

Erika stared at his back as he ventured further into the cave, muttering to herself. "Usually. Aye."

The tight quarters made Erika more uncomfortable than the forest before. She held her arms to her breast, trying to guard against the eerie chill that ran through, though her metal gauntlets hardly helped, while also desperately trying to avoid the dripping water that occasionally cascaded down from the ceiling.

Irvine had to stifle a laugh each time she squealed lightly when a drop landed on her head, or on the bare skin of her neck or shoulders. Erika's reflexive reaction to each laugh was a quick punch to the back of the shoulder, but despite the dull pain, he was still amused.

The side caverns and tunnels that they passed seemed to house unknown terrors within them, but Irvine held true to his path. It was almost as if he knew this particular cave better than their hometown, and Erika didn't doubt that he likely did.

In between her nervous glances, she looked at Irvine, and the torch he carried. "Can I ask ye a bit of a, personal question?" she asked cautiously.

Irvine shrugged and chuckled. "I don't see why not. Though you've known me since we were little, I figured you knew basically everything about me."

Erika's brow scrunched, pondering on the many journeys he had taken without her, and to the contents of his satchel in regards to that statement, but shook her head to rid herself of the distracting thought.

"I'm sure I don't know everythin' about ye." she started. "Though I was wonderin', an' I don't mean to pry, but aren't ye fer fearin' the flames?"

He slowed a bit, regarding the low burning torch in his hand. "Yeah. I do. Though I can manage with smaller ones like this and a campfire, say."

She nodded, reasoning out the rest. "But Papa's forge was more intimidatin'."

"Yeah." he said with a sigh. "That fire was a bit scarier if I'm honest. It heats metal to the point of it being malleable by normal people. I get nervous thinking about it, and what it could do to a person. Unreasonable, I know."

Erika looked down at her forearms, covered in metal plating, though she could count her own burn marks dotting nearly her entire body. "It's not so bad. Ye just have to be gentle with it."

Irvine smiled, enjoying the loving way she spoke of the forge. "I know. If I had just taken up your father's offer to apprentice, I may not fear the fire as much." he said in a mimicking kind of way, before slumping his shoulders slightly. "I'm alright though. I have an understanding with fire. I know to stay away from it, and I won't get burned."

She stared at his back, imagining the pained expression he was likely wearing, and fearing the sight of it. "Well, I'm proud o' ye."

"What for?" he asked, slightly turning his head towards her.

"Fer gettin' through the forest fire, and up to the mountainside. If ye hadn't been able to face yer fears there, we'd be dead in the town more 'an likely." she said, trying to sound encouraging.

"That was you mostly. I was still in daze and didn't really understand fully what was happening." he let out another chuckle. "I mean, some of the fires even seemed to move out of our way. That just shows how out of it I was."

Erika looked down at her open palm, a small ember forming in her grasp. She quickly doused it, knowing that it would spread the markings on her skin.

"Aye." she said quietly.

Irvine paused suddenly, putting his palm out towards Erika, listening intently. They could hear a light scratching sound, accompanied by high pitched mutterings from the tunnel ahead. He carefully stepped back towards her, bringing the torch down low and whispering. "How is your vision in the dark?"

She stared ahead, eyes widening to no avail. "Spent my whole life lookin' at fires an' hot metal, so not great."

Irvine nodded with a shrug. "Understandable. In that case, just stay behind me, and hang on to my shoulder strap. We're going to move forward very slowly."

Erika nodded absentmindedly, still focused on the noises. She put a hand up to her mouth to stop her unintentional squeal when the torchlight suddenly disappeared. Her eyes took a few moments to adjust, until finally she could see in front of them somewhat.

Odd, shouldn't it be dark as pitch in here now? she wondered, seeing a soft glow emanating from the corner in front of them. She held tightly onto Irvine's shoulder strap, feeling only some of his muscle movement against her fingers, due to the metal gauntlets she wore and his own leather armor, though she could feel when he moved forward slowly. They neared the corner, and she couldn't help but move her head closer to Irvine, standing on the tips of her toes and practically resting her chin on his shoulder to see.

In the next section of the cavern were three creatures, each coming to Irvine's waist in height, their features seeming rodent like, but also canine in their snouts. Their eyes were small and grey, nearly lifeless. Two crouched low, their slender legs bent inwards and huddling over a single deteriorated wax candle on the floor in the side of the tunnel. The third seemed to be berating them over something, in a fast-paced language she couldn't understand. He waved his arms wildly, despite none of them seeming to have the ability of sight.

Irvine took another careful step, quietly whispering.

"Kobolds. Thieving little creatures."

Erika looked up to his face, barely illuminated by the dim light of the candle, and was taken aback at his intense expression. He glanced back and forth, searching for something, seeming satisfied with what he did or didn't find.

Erika startled slightly as she heard the quiet metallic ring of Irvine's sword sliding from its scabbard. He put an arm back towards her, resting his hand on her thigh to stop her movement.

"Looks like there's only three." he said quietly. "I can take them on my own, but if one runs past me, I'll need you to take care of them, alright?"

Erika stared into his blue eyes, feeling her stomach sink with intimidation. She had never felt this way when her father scolded her even, but in that moment, Irvine seemed a wholly different person. She finally ripped her gaze from his aggressive demeanor and harshly brought herself back to the task at hand.

"Alright." she replied, grabbing her warhammer carefully, to avoid her gauntlet from making any noise against the metal handle despite the slight clink as it contacted.

Her breathing became shaky, as nervousness filled her body. She could feel her hands shaking violently with the prospect of battling these small creatures, and an unspeakable coldness filled her chest. She hesitantly let go of Irvine's shoulder strap with her other hand, hoping that he hadn't felt her incessant quivering, then crouched down to one knee, despite her shaking legs, and readied her weapon to her side. Irvine stepped forward carefully, fully unsheathing his blade and gave a long and low whistle, sounding as if a wind had blown through the cavern.

The kobolds stopped talking suddenly, their heads jolting in his direction. He made eye contact with each of them, though none of them seemed to notice, extending one leg back slightly and lowering his stance.

Erika blinked, and startled again, as he sprang into action. He dashed towards the creatures with his sword down low. The first kobold jumped back, able to at least see the sudden movement, giving a panicked scream as the blade tore across its chest, drawing a thick red splash of blood onto the stone wall.

The second jumped past the first and struck out towards Irvine. He leaned back, avoiding the claws by a few inches from his nose, and brought his weapon back into an uppercut, slicing the assailing kobold up the side. The creature grunted briefly, before the blade cut through the base of its jaw, and it slumped to the ground with a wet slap.

The third hesitated, stepping back slightly before Irvine rushed forward and bashed his fist into the creature's head, slamming it against the wall. He shook his hand from the hard impact, as the little beast crumpled down unceremoniously. As it sprawled, its foot kicked out and slung the candle across the cavern floor, extinguishing it with the force.

The last thing Erika saw before the light flashed out of existence was the first kobold with the wound on its chest dashing wildly towards her. She saw her chance and did her best to time the motion, swinging her hammer in a wide arc in case she missed the creature. She felt a dull impact against the haft of her weapon, but not enough for her to believe she hit its center mass. She heard a light thud behind her, and the sound of a blade exiting flesh from in front of her.

Less than a moment later, she heard the slapping footfalls of the creature running away from them.

"Damn it all!" she muttered to herself. "Irvine! I missed it!"

"Come towards me!" she heard him call out.

She started to run towards the voice, making it nearly to where she thought he was before her foot caught something below her and she tumbled to the ground, her warhammer slamming against the stone with a loud echoing crash.

She felt a hand on her back, before it reached under her arm firmly and helped her back to her feet. A light flashed, causing her to avert her eyes for fear of being blinded.

She looked up to see Irvine holding the candle upright looking flustered, but otherwise unharmed. He flashed her a quick smile, before turning his gaze to the direction they had come from.

Erika followed, her eyes widening at the sight of more than a score of the creatures all barreling towards them. The light of the flame reflecting off of their dull, unseeing eyes. She heard Irvine curse before lobbing the candle towards the horde and grabbing hold of her hand. She reached down and narrowly snatched her dropped weapon before feeling his momentum dragging her in the opposite direction. The candle flew into the mass of creatures, all of them collectively lunging for it, howling something that sounded almost like '*candle!*' excitedly.

She followed Irvine as best she could, guided only by his hand holding hers tightly.

Erika could feel the presence of the kobolds behind them. The exposed flesh of her legs under her skirt suddenly tingling with a strange sensation, like they were anticipating the claws scratching at them. She fought hard to keep those legs pumping below her, but nearly thought she could feel a jagged blade or claw nicking at the soft skin behind her knees. She tried her best not to squeal in fear, or to look back. Instead she focused on Irvine, and the firm grip he held on her hand.

The sound of the approaching creatures finally seemed to die out as they gained distance from them, but Irvine kept running. She saw a light ahead of them, gaining more confidence in her strides now that she could better see the ground below her feet. She glanced back, seeing several more of the kobolds still on their trail, but screeching as sunlight touched them, thin smoke rising from the burning flesh. The two eventually made it out of the tunnel, Irvine moving to the side and swinging Erika around towards him, putting their backs to the stone wall.

She took several deep breaths, trying to regain her composure, before looking out before them and gasping for air again at the sight of the open mountain range in front of them. The powerful wind gusting up and blowing her hair out of its tie, the auburn strands flying wildly around her face.

Her vision became blurry, darting around from the distant mountain peak across the pass from them, to the cliff side only a few feet away, to the grey overcast sky that seemed closer than it ever seemed before.

She could feel her chest heaving uncontrollably, but couldn't wrest compliance over her own lungs. Her knees buckled, and she slowly slid down the stone wall on her back, eventually coming to rest on the uneven ground. The wind howled and the air felt colder than the most biting of winters, everything around her seemed like an illusion, yet was painfully real in the most terrifying way. Irvine crouched next to her, though she could only make out his silhouette, she was completely numb to his touch, and despite the shape of his jaw moving, any words melted into the sound of the torrential winds. The only warmth she felt were the involuntary tears that melted away from her eyes and down her cheeks. She desperately wanted to scream, to release the lump that rose in her throat, but couldn't even choke out a whimper.

††

Merrick eventually was able to organize the meeting between the guards and the higher-ranking members of the town. Versal expected a few of the selected to be aggressive due to the shock of the situation, yet was still disappointed when he found it to be true. Even some of the more experienced guards had to be ushered away because they were too busy trying to assign blame over the situation to think of any viable solutions. Eventually, the discussion became as close to civil as the situation allowed, even after Versal himself had to step away due to several of the skeletal creatures wandering close to the hovel they found themselves in. The Smithmaster thanked the Gods for the creatures being as fragile as they were, yet they were still bolstered by their numbers. His fire powered punches laying more than a score of them low, their forms scattering into ash and fading in the winds, while more still wandered the empty field.

He took cover behind a burning boulder after crushing the skulls of two more, seeing a larger entity closer to the ruins of Valen. He peered over the blackened rock to confirm the sight, spotting the new creature that was much bigger than the specter that he and Feldran had battled in the square, though he knew it came from the same Circle of the Seven Hells. It bore a thick musculature, with cinders decorating its pitch flesh, and bony protrusions accentuating its forearms and spine. Only Wrath Daemons burned like these did, meaning that the original Daemon likely couldn't summon from other Circles just yet. He quickly made his way back to the small outpost of townsfolk, meeting Merrick soon after.

"We've come to a conclusion that our best bet for now is to make our way to the coastline, from there we may just be able to work our way around the mountains and into the neighboring valley." the young guard explained.

"Good. It'll be a rough journey, but I'm seein' none better." Versal replied. "We should 'urry and get 'eadin' that way though, I think the bastard's summoned some Lesser Daemon's to 'elp 'is cause."

Merrick's expression darkened. "Do you think, that it's starting a new Chaos Age?"

"Mortals were much weaker in the Chaos Age lad." Versal said assuredly. "We may not 'ave the Dragons or Angelus' to aid us, but we 'ave much more to fire back at 'em."

Merrick managed a weak smile, but nodded nonetheless, jogging off to help ready their next move.

9
Cliffside Terror

Irvine checked behind himself, making absolute sure that none of the kobolds had tried to brave the daylight to pursue them. Satisfied with his findings, he turned back to Erika.

She sat against the cool stone wall, clutching her warhammer to her breastplate, her breathing still erratic underneath, her grip tighter than a vice against the handle of her weapon. Irvine hadn't seen her blink since they had exited the cave, her eyes wide and darting around at their surroundings. He could see the shimmer of the endless tears flowing down her cheeks, further drying her eyes.

He grabbed hold of her shoulder and lightly shook her. "Erika, come on. Everything is alright." yet she still did not answer. He looked around in desperation, having no idea on how to break her from this panicked state. He retrieved a blanket from his pack, wrapping it around her as best he could, hoping that it would warm her from the heavily chilled mountain air. The updraft nearly flung the blanket from his hands, until he was finally able to wedge it behind her shoulders and under her thighs.

"Damn this wind." he muttered as his hair whipped around, stinging his eyes. He rubbed his hands on her shoulders and upper arms, trying to warm her still, but her gaze was still unfocused, and her breathing still erratic. Irvine felt lost, he had never seen her this terrified of anything, though he imagined this is what he must have looked like when they fled the town, and any other time he was uncomfortably close to a raging flame.

The notion gave him a sudden idea, realizing that focus is always what helped him through those trials. Any time he got too close to Versal's forge as a small child, the Smithmaster would command his attention. Any time he went numb during combat training with uncle Feldran, the elder guardsman would simply force him to focus on something nearby, usually their elderly cat laying in the window. When they fled the town, the only thing that kept him running was focusing on Erika, rather than the flames.

He took a deep breath, moving himself closer to her, and placing his hands on either side of her face. He moved his own face directly in front of hers, her wildly darting eyes eventually calming, and coming to contact with his.

"Erika." he said calmly. "Everything is alright."

She blinked once, her emerald orbs locked onto his, then blinked several more times, finally fighting back the dryness of her eyes.

"The kobolds are gone." Irvine continued. "They cannot follow us into the sunlight, even if it isn't direct."

She gave a jittering nod, her breathing slowly steadying, before she closed her eyes and lunged up towards him, snatching him into a tight embrace. He jumped up slightly, but was summarily wrenched back down by her force as she slammed her rump back down to the stone. The haft of her warhammer pressed against his collarbone uncomfortably, but he ignored it, focusing on her slowing exhales that warmed his neck. He closed his arms around her, gently stroking one hand down her waving auburn hair.

"You've never been on a mountain before, have you?" he asked.

She shook her head violently.

"Alright. We'll take it slow, but we do have a bit of a journey ahead of us." he said, trying to be as comforting as he could.

The mountain pass cutting through the Seraphine range was treacherous, though through the efforts of Irvine, and several other couriers he knew in the guild, a comprehensive system was constructed to aid those with the knowhow. Ropes, bridges, and pulleys were set up at particularly difficult junctions of the pass, and were maintained by each of the couriers each time they came through. Irvine treated this time no differently, mending any frayed rope, or marking loose boards with chalk for later repair. The only difference in this trek, as opposed to his previous ones, was his companion. He routinely made this journey alone, sometimes accompanied by another courier; their pace always maintained through the area nearly as fast as they would on a flat grassland field.

Erika was not an experienced courier though, and Irvine's normal pace was greatly slowed because of it. Due to that, he added several new tasks to his routine of maintenance on the path, grabbing hold of her when they moved through narrow cliff sides, supporting some of her weight when she dropped down rope ladders, and generally staying close to her. She seemed calmer now, but her breathing was still somewhat heavy. He noticed each time he looked at her, that her chest was still heaving up and down, worsening when she would begin to panic again. Periodically they had to stop, she would turn into the mountain side, or into him, avoiding the sight of the open range sprawling before them.

Irvine could think of several of his fellow guild members that would be put out by the inconvenience of having someone like her around, but he remembered his first time, and the first times of some of those same couriers.

The situation felt strange to him though, Erika had always been the one protecting him and he always saw her as a figure of infinite strength, alongside her father. Their muscled forms able to hammer their way through every trial that came before them. Now though, she seemed more vulnerable. It was jarring, but endearing at the same time. He only wished this somewhat intimate journey could have been under better circumstances.

Irvine tried to maintain a steady conversation with her the whole time, though it was mostly one-sided. He would explain the path or the systems the couriers had put into place, and tell her stories of his times going through the various Regions. Erika's replies were short grunts or simple nods, rarely uttering words. Her expression was a constant painting of stress and anxiety, focusing on whatever task was currently at hand. Her condition seemed to worsen any time he fell silent though, so he tried to keep the stories and explanations going, embellishing some of the details to lengthen some of the tales.

They stopped for a rest every so often, allowing Erika time to sit down and drink from either of their water skins, while Irvine scouted the next step, never straying too far from her. The only thing that troubled Irvine was the increased number of mountain wildlife that was normally holed up for the winter by now, or off in the lower ranges hunting. Multiple occasions came where their progress was halted because of a stray gryphon, either the common royal breed, or the carrion. The eagle and vulture-like beaks of each stained red with their last meals, but their behavior was odd and erratic, furthering Irvine's suspicions that the Daemon's arrival had upset some kind of natural balance. He also worried more over the figure he had seen dashing through the valley when they had entered the Mystholt, being as he had seen no sign of the mystery entity since that first sighting. He just hoped Erika didn't see him checking the path they had already traveled periodically, knowing that she had enough to worry about.

⇡⇡

The forest was a commotion of sound. Teria hated when this happened. The younger, inexperienced rangers bunching around the source of the chaos.

Her lithe form slipped between the crowd that shouldn't be there, while others of her guild bashed through roughly, barking orders for them all to return to their posts. Though few listened.

She finally arrived at the scene. The foliage turned a sickly copper color by the spatter that covered them, and several trees were painted as well. The medicinal crew worked in a frenzy while their patient screeched aloud with seething pain that jolted through him.

She knew this one. A newer ranger than she, but no Sapling by any means. She turned and glared at the actual Saplings that still crowded around. Her icy gaze doing much better to disperse them than the burlier men and women that barreled through with commands.

The young man spoke suddenly, albeit between labored breaths and grunts of pain.

"It was a coleptus."

Teria set her angled jaw firmly. She knew of one of their kind in the area, though she had never seen it herself, no reason to. The massive beetle creature had been cataloged as nesting somewhere nearby, but the notion that it attacked a human was unfathomable.

"Color?" she demanded almost more than asked.

He grunted as a tear cascaded down his face. "Green. Gods, I messed up, I didn't even see it."

This made Teria's face tighten even more. The creatures were known to defend themselves occasionally, but this one had apparently struck first.

With efficiency.

Her sharp eyes darted to the ground, scanning the grisly scene around them. A moment later, she began to follow the trail that was obvious of the heavy coleptus.

A hand met her slender shoulder, though she fought back immediately to the grip.

"What are you doing?" Selbor asked gruffly.

She eyed him with that same cold glare. "Going to find it."

"We need to regroup, possibly get Mistress Varia involved."

Teria scoffed. "She'll order it slain. Simple reasoning, I'm just expediting the process."

She wrenched free of the larger ranger's grip, and stormed off.

"Be careful!" Selbor called out to her. "Creatures are turning rogue all over! We don't know why!"

He sighed when he realized she was ignoring him, her lithe frame disappearing into the trees. He scratched his eyebrow, then turned to the fallen ranger. Selbor's muscled shoulders slumped when he saw the medics sitting back from the massive hole in the young man's side, and his empty, lifeless, eyes.

† †

Teral stepped through the cavern carefully. His new appendage lit his path better than a torch, though his eyes were more accustomed to darkness than most. After a ways through, he heard the irritating sounds of the cave's inhabitants. The canine heads jerking towards him when he came around the bend.

Several of the creatures uttered their wonderment at his fiery leg, "Candle..." they whispered eerily. He knew these diminutive creatures and their obsession with warm light sources that didn't burn them like the daylight. The only word they knew for any of those sources being 'candle'. Their sight was incredibly poor, bordering on fully blind, save for shadows and light.

"No candle for you." Teral called back threateningly, his daggers flashing into his hands, causing several of the beasts to startle at the ringing steel. A moment passed, Teral gritting his teeth and placing his blazing limb behind himself, pushing off a moment later.

In a flash of flame and an explosive *crack*, the thief was upon the first line of kobolds, his daggers easily finding the throats of the first two unlucky participants. He slammed their corpses to the stone floor, savagely wrenching the curved blades from their flesh backhanded and brought them inwards in a horizontal slash, severing the throats of two more. He pushed off from his crouched position dodging the strikes of three more of the beasts, using his still normal leg to adjust slightly, turning upside down onto the ceiling and reversing the motion. His blazing leg crashed down onto the skull of the middle one, the flames searing into the creature's flesh. He spun himself, pirouetting on the now dead kobold's melting cranium, slinging his daggers out and slicing the other two into death.

He couldn't help but grin at the effectiveness of his new power, and how quickly he had been able to master the use of it, at least one good thing had come of all this. He turned his gaze to the cavern ahead, the next dozen creatures cowering in fear at the sound of their dying kin, unsure of how to approach this terrifying new threat. He glanced to the side of the tunnel, seeing two kobolds, felled by a blade other than his own and an impact to the head. He also noticed a fresh wound on the chest of one of the corpses below him, grinning wider knowing that his quarry had indeed come this way.

"If you can understand me, then tell me true." he said to the huddling creatures ahead of him. "Where did the last people go?"

No reply came in words, but the still living kobolds held out shaking fingers, pointing towards where they knew the nearest exit to be, and the beginning of the mountain pass.

Teral nodded his thanks, and casually stepped with his boot heel clacking on the ground in time with his flamebound leg sizzling. The remaining creatures cowered as he passed, none making even a hint of a movement for their coveted flame.

† †

Erika had never felt such an intense fear over anything. Every time her gaze fell to the impossibly deep chasm to her right side, a chill ran down her spine, making her stomach turn in spirals and her vision to go blurry. She wanted to lay down and cry, wanted to just vomit and release the feeling in her gut. It took everything in her power to keep moving, focusing on each step and on Irvine's guidance.

She appreciated his constant talking, though she didn't actually hear most of his stories. Simply the sound of his voice was comforting. This all seemed so easy for him, each time they reached a rope ladder, he barely used any of the rungs, just deftly leaping down as if gravity had no real control over him. She on the other hand, had to hand her weapon down to Irvine, before carefully sliding over the edge backwards. As much embarrassment as it caused her, she insisted that Irvine put his hands on her rear to help her coming down the ladder, though her sinking stomach didn't allow her much time to dwell on it. Thankfully, Irvine didn't seem to react to the action much at all, simply continuing to the next task without so much as a word.

The bridges weren't much easier either, each one being a massive hurdle for her, but a casual step for him. She nearly had to crawl across the first few due to the terrible shaking of the apparatuses. Irvine was patient with her through all of it, though she felt terrible about the entire situation.

"Just put your heel in front of your toe, in the middle of the walkway." he would say, trying to help her not sway the bridge as much.

She had felt severely limited in the Mystholt, but now felt like an absolute burden now. *How quickly would he have gotten through all of this alone?* she wondered, biting back the tears that threatened to spill from her eyes at a moment's notice.

After what seemed like an eternity of ladders, bridges, ropes, and cliffs, her knees buckled below her. Her face felt hot while her guts danced around in her abdomen, the tears finally flowing free from the edges of her eyes.

Her mind raced in another panic, unsure of how much further she could go, but knowing that there was no option to turn back. Out of her blurry peripheral, she saw Irvine's form sit beside her, offering her his water skin. She almost reached for it, but was unsure if she could stomach it at the time. She turned over, falling onto her rump, crossing her arms over her knees and buried her face in them, trying to stifle the tears. She felt his hand on the back of her shoulder, taking comfort in the warmth, until she felt it shaking slightly. She looked up, wondering why he would be scared or crying, but instead found him laughing.

She stared at him incredulously, her cheeks still wet from the tears she couldn't suppress, as he placed his other hand over his mouth trying to stifle the laughter.

"Why in the Hells are ye laughin' at me?" she demanded with a growl, slapping his arm away harshly with one arm and wiping her face with the other.

He looked at her directly. "I'm not laughing at you, I'm laughing at the situation."

"What situation?" she asked, her anger rising steadily with her voice.

Irvine simply gestured to the edge of the cliff that they sat on, out to the rocky pass that lay a mere breadth away from them. Erika stared at the uneven ground, finding no more cliffs, and now noticing the lack of the wind from before. She choked out a laugh herself, feeling ridiculous for not noticing that they were almost to the ground level from the cliffs.

"You actually did really well." Irvine said after they both finished laughing.

Erika scoffed, finally taking a drink from the water skin. "I think that was suren' the worst I've ever done. At anythin'."

Irvine looked back up at the series of ropes and bridges that were barely visible from where they were. "I've seen worse on that pass."

"Has anyone ever fallen?" she asked absentmindedly, taking another drink. She looked over to him after several moments of silence, his expression suddenly dark. She immediately realized what she had brought to light. "Oh no, Irvine, I-"

He waved her off with his hand.

"It's alright." he said, shakily at first. "Accidents happen. I know that better than most. That's why I'm careful."

He stood up a moment later and leapt down the last drop, slowly walking out into the pass. Erika opened her mouth to say something, but couldn't find the words. She gripped at her bare arm with her gauntlet clad hand, irritated with herself for souring his mood. She watched him depart, finally coming to her senses and standing up to catch up to him. Her boots landed with a crunch on the gravel below her, happy to finally have solid ground all around her, with no empty air except that above her head.

Few hours remained in the day, meaning a place to camp for the night was needed for them. Irvine could have made it through the pass in less than half a day if he were alone, but he hadn't noticed quite how much Erika's first time through had slowed them. Though he was satisfied with having seen no sign of their possible pursuer.

He could only hope that the jordhak in the Mystholt had a new meal out of the scout, or perhaps they made a slip on the cliff side and met their rest in the canyon somewhere off to their side. He didn't hold much hope for that though, being if they were anyone who knew what they were doing, or at worst one of the Daemon's kin, those things likely weren't more than minor obstacles for them. The two made their way through the pass, Irvine informing Erika the remaining legs of their journey before arriving in Sildenfeld, including their current standing in the rocky pass.

"We've a while to go through this pass, likely the rest of the day. After that, is a short cavern, nowhere near the length of the tunnel from the Mystholt. No kobolds last I came through either. Then we have to travel westwards a bit to get to the bridge that crosses the river. After the bridge, we'll have a hike down the mountain to get to the fields that surround Sildenfeld, and finally we're there."

Erika nodded at each of the steps. "Where are we settin' down tonight?"

Irvine paused a moment. "That's just the thing to figure out. I made the mistake of not grabbing extra firewood to make camp tonight."

Erika stopped alongside him, lowering her face. "Because we should have already been through the pass." she reasoned.

Irvine looked over to her. "Normally, yes." he said, her expression darkening further.

"However." he continued quickly. "I still have enough rations to last us this night, then early tomorrow, once we get into the more forested area on the other side of the wall, we can get a fire going for cooking something fresh."

He patted her shoulder lightly. "Everything will be fine, Erika." before walking forwards again.

She found herself trailing after a while. Thoughts swimming through her head from the last day. She looked down at her palms, a small flame conjuring forth, Irvine's words echoing in her head.

'*I have an understanding with fire. I know to stay away from it, and I won't get burned.*'.

The thought brought anguish to her mind. The last thing she wanted was for him to stay away. His reaction to her father's display meaning he definitely did not know of their heritage. The worry over how he might react to it caused her face to screw up in a worried scowl even more.

She startled when Irvine called out to her, slamming her fist shut, and the flame dissipating quickly in a cloud of embers. She jogged lightly to catch up to him, finding the spot he was calling from. It was a small inlet between two halves of a massive fractured boulder, enough space for the two of them to lay abreast, but not allowing much room further than that.

"It's a bit tight, but it'll keep us hidden from the stray gryphons and anything else after dark." he said with a shrug.

Erika felt her face get slightly warm at the prospect. "Yeah, that'll work great." she said with a nervous smile.

Irvine didn't seem to notice the slight shakiness in her voice, as he swept his hands around the small hovel, evening the ground a bit. "Well, let's get settled for the evening. We can have an early start in the morning." he said.

She found herself staring at the small area they were to call home for the night. She settled her pack down while he moved around the boulder for another lay of the land.

"Last thing I wanted was fer 'im to stay away." she muttered with a smirk as she loosened her gauntlets.

Her overjoyed thoughts halted when she found the faint crimson lines across her palm where she had conjured the flames.

"Damn!" she hissed, before checking to make sure Irvine hadn't heard her. She scolded herself for picking now of all times to experiment with her heretical magic, as she tore a strip of cloth from her festival dress to wrap her hand in.

The gravel crunched underfoot as Irvine returned. "Is your hand alright?"

She nodded, trying not to panic. "Just a little scrape, don't ye worry yerself over it."

Her stomach turned in knots at the lie, but her fear over his reaction to the truth of her nature made her swallow it down.

10
Deceptions

Teral stepped through the quarry carefully. He found that the flames of his leg would dim somewhat when he used it less, so he focused on putting more effort into his other leg, reducing the light to a dull glow. It was an amusing time coming down the cliff side to get to the pass, simply dashing down, his powerful gift allowing him a cushioned landing to the farthest of falls.

There was a time when he would have been thankful for the bridges and ladders that had been set up through the treacherous walkways, but he found little use out of them, and an even faster time down the mountain with the blazing appendage. He tested the limits by increasing the height of his drops periodically, searching for a threshold to its capability, but finding none, at one point dropping nearly a full four stories of height with no repercussion or injury.

Now the challenge came in finding the couriers, the darkened pass seemed darker than the tunnel above, the light of the moons obscured by thick cloud covering. He worried somewhat that the escapees had already made it through the pass, though he also wondered if they were just spending the night with no fire.

The silence was palpable around him, he found himself having to focus on his breathing the same way he would if he were on a retrieval job in the city. Each footstep measured to muffle the crunching gravel and stone beneath him, stopping at intervals to listen for any sign of his targets.

Eventually, he heard something, a soft shuffling, sounding like a bedroll moving.

He followed the sound, finding a cleaved boulder with a small space between the two pieces, the sound coming from the inlet between. As he approached, he found exactly what he was looking for, a boy with leather armor and a longsword, and a girl with heavier metal armor and a warhammer. The two of them awkwardly shared a single bedroll for comfort on the stone floor.

He scowled lightly, as he deftly climbing to the top of one half of the boulder, peering down at them and observing their features. The two of them were still young, both likely in their twenties still, although the boy's armor had the kind of weathering that only real combat and wear could provide. He seemed a traveler, boots tarnished and worn, and a musculature befitting that of a journeyman, strong legs and back, with an added upper body strength that came with swordsmanship.

The girl on the other hand, her armor had a particular luster to it, with very little apparent use. Her boots were dirtied, but had a fresh coat of travel grime on them, with much less set in than the boy's. Her arms were incredibly thickened, likely a craftsman, with calloused hands and numerous scrapes and burn marks. He cocked his head to the side while looking at her sleeping form, her bright hair catching even the low moonlight of the overcast sky, Teral knew he had seen that same shade before.

The Ignis blood that Zyrxak spoke of, he realized.

Even in the little time that he had seen the burly man, he recognized the auburn hair, though the older man was heavily greying, and the facial features, coming to the conclusion that this girl must be his daughter.

"And what of the boy?" he wondered quietly. "Her lover perhaps?"

He peered closer at the young man, his face resting against the girl's shoulder. He searched his mind for any sort of answer, finally realizing at the sight of the emblem on his satchel, that he was a member of the Courier's Guild, a matching one on the chest piece of his leather armor.

"Explains the traveled appearance." he confirmed quietly to himself, and added with a slight pout to his lips. "Shame the girl can't keep up with your normal pace, you may have covered more ground before I caught up to you."

A curved dagger twirled through the air with a quiet ring, landing in the thief's open hand. Death was sometimes part of the job; it couldn't be helped. These two had to die, otherwise Teral would be first on Zyrxak's kill order. He lightly stepped down to awkwardly share their space, barely a breadth away from their faces, hovering the blade over their skin. He puzzled for a moment, wondering which he should kill first in case he botched the strike. He reasoned that the boy was likely more skilled in a full-on fight, so he should leave the girl for last.

He brought the blade down slowly, pressing the tip into the flesh of the boy's neck. He took a deep breath, knowing that this was never his forte. The blade pressed further, a small trickle of blood coming forth from the skin-deep wound, the metal was removed a moment later when the girl suddenly shifted, rolling over and laying on top of the boy. Teral jumped back, unsure if she had awoken or not, cursing himself when the boy started to stir, his eyes barely flickering open.

The thief panicked against his best judgment, applying pressure to his magic limb and dashing off quickly, the leg brightening for a short time. As he fled, he glanced back, seeing a smile on the girl's face. *Had she seen me?* he puzzled, sure she was asleep just a moment before.

He damned his negligible skill when it came to the killing arts, and took cover behind another boulder. Biding your time was as much a part of assassination as thieving, after all.

✝ ✝

Irvine's eyes opened slowly, looking down at Erika laying partially on top of him, one leg fully thrown completely over him, and her head resting on his upper chest as if he were the best pillow that ever existed.

He sighed in frustration at the realization that he had awoken in the middle of the night again. It seemed she was still soundly asleep atop him though. He could feel her skin under his hand where her tunic had raised slightly. She was warm, skin as soft as a cerotae calf. The scent of vanilla and jasmine from the festival had faded, replaced with a subtly sweet scent. He wanted to hold her closer, feel more of that soft skin and warmth. Once again, he found himself wishing they had been on this journey under better circumstances. Though he reasoned they would have brought two bedrolls if they hadn't been so rushed.

His warm thoughts were interrupted as he felt a wet sensation coming down his neck. He lifted his arm that wasn't lodged beneath Erika's form and wiped his fingers across his throat. His eyes widened when he saw the red stain on his skin, suddenly feeling the open puncture just under his jaw. His gaze flicked around wildly, and he was suddenly up in a rough motion looking for some sign of his assailant, wondering what had stopped them.

The movement and jostling brought a lazy groan from the young woman, as she started to stir. She slowly crawled onto all fours and looked towards Irvine with eyes still shut.

"Everythin' alright, Irvine?" she asked with a slur to her voice, her eyes struggling to open.

Irvine put a hand on her shoulder, careful not to touch her with the bloodstained one, and eased her back down to the bedroll.

"Yes, everything is fine, Erika." he lied, not wanting to panic her when she needed rest. "Just go back to sleep, I'm going to sit up for a while."

"Alright." she said with an odd smile as she instead crawled over and lay her head on his lap, apparently still not awake enough to fully recognize her surroundings. She sighed contentedly. "Ye're so warm, love."

Irvine's heart skipped at her words, partially in surprise at her not using her normal 'silly duck' for him, but more so at the allured tone. He quickly snapped back to the limited view of the pass from their concealed camp, tearing his attention away from Erika. Although, their rest area didn't feel very concealed any-more.

The rest of the night passed slowly and painfully. Irvine hardly even noticed the smith as she crawled further and further into his lap, muttering incoherently. He found himself focusing solely on their surroundings in a mad paranoia.

⚔

The darkness fell over the forest. The path of the colep-tus becoming increasingly deep as she traveled. Her singular goal distracting her from the memory of the young ranger's eyes. The eyes of someone who was being greeted by death.

She wasn't sure if he had actually succumbed to his wounds though. The healers of the Willow Rangers were just as capable as any clerical aids in the city.

Her bow came off her back as her sensitive ears caught a scraping sound. Her toes coming down before her heel to mini-mize the sound of her footfalls. She rounded a thick oak tree to find her target.

A massive coleptus, a deep green coloring flooding down its insect-like chitinous exterior. A single horn protruded from its thick head, stained in crimson.

She scowled at the uncommonly macabre sight, and began to draw the string of her weapon. The creature's behavior caused her pause though, and she found herself cocking her head to the side at the display.

The creature was boring its head into a tree repeatedly. The horn had already struck the tree in half, but the beetle was still continuously banging its head against the bark that it could reach. It was almost as if it was fighting some horrid sound that only it could hear.

Teria wiped the confusion from her angular face, making a note of the occurrence in her mind. She stepped forward another step, and loosed the arrow she had readied. It hit its mark immediately after, popping the tiny eye on the creature's right side, lodging into the cavity underneath.

It screeched loudly, Teria slinging her bow around over her shoulder, and pulling her short blades from their sheaths. She sprinted towards it, leaping over the creature's instinctive slam to the side that it was being attacked from. She twirled in the air, bringing both blades down and slashing across the insectoid armor. One glanced harmlessly off, while the other found purchase in the soft flesh between the plates.

The blade hooked into the firm tendons beneath, and whipped the ranger's lithe body around just as she wanted, allowing her to land both boots on the side of the creature. It bucked wildly, trying to rid itself of the threat, but Teria didn't let up.

Her first blade came in next to her second, and the coleptus' screeching became all the louder. She set her jaw firmly and started the grim task of separating the hilts of both weapons, cracking the shell of the creature open. Eventually, a large part of the fleshy interior of the creature's body was finally visible.

Teria tried to make all of her kills with the least amount of pain possible, but colepti tended to have such hard carapaces, that it made painless deaths near impossible.

The creature slowed, starting to drain its own stamina as it continually failed to remove the assailant. The ranger used the opportunity, and began ramming either blade into the muscle, one after another. Her body was repeatedly splashed with the dark violet gore of the creature until she finally hit the elusive nerve point in the interior, and the massive insect fell to the ground dead.

She stood a moment later after the twitching began to cease. Her breast heaved from the effort, while the blood dripped from her armor and down onto her bare legs.

Selbor broke into the clearing a moment later, his eyes widening at the grisly sight of her. "What happened?"

"I avenged our injured brother." she said in between labored breaths.

The male ranger's face darkened. "Teria, these creatures are not bandits or orks. They have no vendetta against anything. There's no avenging the fallen by them."

She hesitated, blood dripping down from her cheek as she stared at him.

"What do you mean, fallen?"

"He's dead, Teria. Passed soon after you stormed off to find his killer." he answered in a nearly scolding tone.

She threw her arms to the sides, which loudly slapped against her thighs. "Then all the better I killed the beast! Stop it before it does anything else malicious!"

Selbor looked as if he would strike her. "The beasts are not malicious, Teria! When will you learn this, you foolish girl?"

Teria groaned even louder as she replaced her blades in their sheaths, and wrenched her arrow from its head with a sickening squelch. She planted her bloodied hand on Selbor's chest and roughly shoved him to the side as she rushed past.

"That one was infected with something." she stated cryptically.

Selbor looked back to the corpse, wondering what she meant by 'infected'.

†† †

The morning came eventually. By then, Erika had lain completely over Irvine, causing him some happiness in his waking paranoia. Though he had other business to attend first. After the process of slipping out from underneath her, and depositing her onto the bedroll again, he stood to survey their camp. He donned his armor as quickly and quietly as he could, retrieving his sword and stepping away from the camp, making sure to keep an eye on the inlet where Erika still slept soundly. He looked over the quarry, finding no sign of anything besides the gryphons and other animals that made their way through.

He sighed again, wondering if he was overreacting, and the blood was simply from a sharp rock or twig. He rubbed the area of the wound lightly, careful not to disturb the first stages of healing, but trying to feel the wound itself as he made his way back to the sleeping Fjordling woman.

He stared at the ground on his return trip, stopping suddenly at the sight of a discolored portion of the gravel. The ground itself appeared scorched, but the small stones appeared as if someone had kicked off into a sprint. He followed the direction of it with his eyes, but raised an eyebrow when the next sign of a footprint was several yards away.

Irvine searched around the quarry again, surmising that whatever was out here was either incredibly tall, or incredibly fast, though he wagered it was the latter based on what he saw leaving Valen that night. He quickly made his way back to the camp, grabbing Erika's shoulder and lightly shaking her

"Erika, time to go." he said, trying to play off the urgency in his voice as them simply needing to get an early start.

She squinted her eyes open, unconsciously smiling at the sight of Irvine's face as she lifted her arms over her head in a stretch. "Mornin', Irvine." she said, still smiling. "Yer always up so early."

Irvine lightly regarded how endearing she was when she first awakened, and smiled. "And you sleep in incredibly late for a blacksmith. Come on, we don't have far to get out of the pass."

Erika's brow tightened at the slight jab, reaching out and lazily rapping her fist on his hip. Irvine barely noticed the playful strike though, still scanning the area periodically and frantically gathering his supplies, folding up his bedroll as soon as Erika rolled off of it.

She sat up, straightening her disheveled clothing with a grimace and looking at Irvine carefully. "What's gotten ye all agitated?" she asked.

Irvine paused a moment, trying to think up something other than their pursuer. "Nothing, just wanting to get out of the pass is all."

Erika raised an eyebrow. "Ye sure that's all? Nothin' happened last night or anythin' did it?"

"Well, you did roll on top of me in the middle of the night." he said with a chuckle.

Erika suddenly became more awake as her face flushed red. "I'm sorry! I wasn't meanin' to!"

Irvine waved her off. "You're fine Erika, I used to sleepwalk as a child, I understand not being able to control things like that. Go ahead and pack your things up, I don't want to get caught by any gryphons."

She nodded her understanding, face still reddened with embarrassment, as she started to dress for their next hike.

Erika trailed behind Irvine slightly, unable to look away from him. She wondered if he was upset with her due to his silence through the morning. Even if he wasn't, he was definitely agitated over something, she just didn't know what.

The pass was much easier to navigate than the cliffs, and Erika tried to make up for her multiple breakdowns on their descent by upping her own pace, overtaking Irvine at times, though she still flustered with embarrassment each time she took a wrong turn.

Irvine seemed amused for those short periods, but almost immediately went back to his intense silence. Erika avoided eye contact with him, seeing the same expression on his face as when he was about to attack the kobolds in the cave, the intense look of aggression. Each time she met his gaze though, it softened slightly, but she averted her eyes quickly, not wanting the militance to be directed at her for any reason.

"How much further?" she asked curiously.

Irvine took a moment to reply. "Not much. Just around the next bend."

Erika breathed a small sigh of relief, hoping that once they were out of this quarry, Irvine would relax some. Despite the urgent circumstances, she was enjoying this journey with him, and in a strange fashion wishing it could last longer. She could faintly remember laying atop him after waking just slightly in the night, her cheeks warming at the thought.

He turned around ahead of her, still keeping his pace, scanning the area as they crested a slight incline. Erika then noticed the wound on the underside of his jaw. "Irvine." she said cautiously.

He raised his eyebrows. "Hmm? What is it?"

Erika grabbed his arm and yanked him towards her. He put his hands up in defense. "What are you doing?"

She replied by grabbing his jaw roughly and turning it towards the sky, inspecting the puncture. "When were ye goin' to be tellin' me o' this?"

Irvine wrestled free of her grasp, placing his hand on her shoulder to distance himself slightly.

"It's fine." he said curtly.

"Fine?" she mocked, suddenly raising her voice. "Nothin' about that is fine, Irvine, yer injured!"

"It's just a scrape!" he said back, matching her tone. "I probably got it in my sleep last night on a rock or something!"

She raised her gauntlet, pointing with a metallic finger towards him. "That, is not a scrape from a rock! That is from a blade! Ye know who I was raised by, I'm fer knowin' a blade mark when I'm seein' one!"

Irvine sighed, turning his gaze away from her. In his motion, she glanced down and glimpsed a faded stain of red on his fingers.

Erika suddenly felt tears of anger welling up in her eyes. "Don't ye lie to me, Irvine."

"I didn't want to worry you." he replied, staring up at the overcast skies.

Erika felt her face get hot, but this time not from embarrassment. She threw her arms up in the air, desperately wanting to punch him. "Ye're worryin' me more when ye aren't tellin' me things, Irvine."

She stormed past him, her boots crunching in the gravel. Her stomach swam again, knowing that she wasn't telling him everything either. She looked to her hand, knowing that the crimson patterns painted her skin beneath the gauntlet.

Irvine turned his eyes to the sky again, unsure of what to do from here. Eventually deciding to just follow after her, while also giving her space. As they walked, Irvine tried to deduce if she was crying or cursing at him, though he figured it was likely a bit of both. They were in the last stretch of the pass now, nowhere to make any wrong turns, which he was immensely grateful for, fearing her wrath should he correct her path now.

Finally, they arrived at the stone wall that separated the pass from the neighboring forest on the exterior of the mountain, the opening seeming like a gate between worlds as the grey lifeless rock suddenly became green grass and swaying trees.

A short way forwards and they arrived at a massive stone dais, a rushing waterfall cascading underneath it, the trees around them making the stone cliff seem out of place in the otherwise green and brown landscape. Erika stepped tentatively to the edge of the stone, looking over at the waterfall not even a yard away. She closed her eyes, feeling the cool mist on her face, before turning around and staring at Irvine with a passive expression. Irvine met her gaze with an apologetic look, but couldn't find any words.

Erika smoothed her hair over her head. "When did it happen?"

"Last night." Irvine replied, his gaze shifting to the side to avoid her eyes.

"So, it wasn't one o' the creatures in the cave?"

"No. It happened when we were asleep, I awoke to find you rolled on top of me, and blood trickling down my neck." he hoped she would lighten a bit at the mention of her antics while asleep, but she seemed to ignore that part.

"An' ye didn't think to wake me when ye found an open gash on yer neck?" she continued, stepping forward slightly each time she spoke. Her voice sounding more pleading than scolding.

Irvine sighed again. "You did wake a little, but I wanted you to rest, yesterday was rough for you."

Erika was nearly in his face now, her voice shaking. "The cliffs would've been a far-off memory if I had found ye dead next to me, Irvine!"

Her gaze was intense, the aura of her emotions not allowing Irvine to break eye contact. He saw the tears still shimmering in her bright green eyes.

"What did this, Irvine?" she pleaded now, the liquid freely flowing from the corners of her eyes. "Who tried to hurt ye when we were asleep, and are they comin' back?"

Irvine shook his head. "I don't know. When we entered the Mystholt, I thought I saw something dashing across the field in our direction, but I didn't think it would catch up to us this quickly."

Her eyes widened even more. "Ye saw this thing when we were still on our home side? Why didn't ye say anything then?"

"Because I thought you had enough to deal with!" Irvine snapped. "We watched my uncle get turned to ash! We still don't know what happened to your father!"

"That doesn't mean ye have to be shieldin' me from information, Irvine! If somethin' is chasin' us, I'd rather be likin' to know!"

The sound of two hands clapping together echoed through the vale, interrupting their quarrel. Irvine quickly twisted around, his weapon tearing from its sheath. Across the stone dais from them was a hooded figure with a leg blazing in flame. The figure stretched his arms out in a presentational kind of way.

"I'm impressed!" he said. "I wasn't fully sure if you'd noticed me chasing you two."

Erika gripped her warhammer, her metal gauntlets scraping against the handle gratingly. "Who are ye?"

The man's arms dropped to his sides. "That's not really important anymore." he said almost solemnly. "All that matters now is survival. There's a Daemon on the loose."

"Yes, we've seen the horrific creature first hand. Though it appears you may have had a closer look." Irvine said, motioning his blade towards the man's leg.

He looked down at the burning appendage. "Indeed, it would seem so. Too late for regrets now though I'm afraid."

"You're human." Irvine tried to reason. "Why are you siding with that monster?"

The man removed a curved dagger from his cloak.

"I have no choice." he replied bluntly, angling the blade towards Irvine. "This would have been so much easier if I had just finished the job last night. Why did I back off when I had your head practically in my hands?"

Erika screamed in a rage, sprinting towards him with her warhammer bared to the side. Irvine calling out from behind her. "Erika! Stop!"

11
BATTLE IN THE VALE

The city of Sildenfeld was busy, but peaceful. The air was crisp with the northern winds flowing across the open fields around it, the outer wall doing little to keep the breeze out. Spirits seemed high, still hanging on to the revelry of the Harvest Festival, until the townsfolk saw Teria.

She stepped through the cobbled streets, her slender frame still covered in the dark gore of the coleptus. The liquid long dried across her face, arms, torso, and legs. She elicited many gasps of horror and disgust as she stormed through the city, directly for the house of the Willow Rangers.

She ignored them with a grimace.

Mistress Varia must be informed that the wildlife has become erratic, and that she must alter the ranger's patrols into a more defensive pattern.

Teria didn't know what was going on in the forest neighboring the city, which irritated her deeply. She considered the wilderness to be her true home, and hated that things had so suddenly gotten out of hand.

The ornate wooden building lay before her, its tall spires nearly equaling the center structure of Sildenfeld. She banged the doors open with her forceful approach, several of the young rangers, and even some older ones, startling at the cacophonous noise.

Whispers spread around the room like a wildfire at Teria's disheveled appearance, and she rolled her dark eyes, annoyed even further at the childlike behavior.

A short time later, and she similarly burst into the office of Varia Wyldsbane, the leader of the Willow Rangers. The aging woman still held a considerable beauty to her. She had a strong, feminine, physical appearance, amassing a confident air that always carried with her. Her long hair was a striking silver, with honorable gold leaves decorating it. Her slightly wrinkled face wore an expression of supreme annoyance at the incursion, but Teria hardly seemed fazed by her glare.

She stormed up to the desk, and the Mistress sat back comfortably in her chair.

"Greetings to you, Teria." she said calmly, which did slightly catch the young woman off guard. The smooth, deeper tone of the older woman's voice always seemed to strike her in such a way, making her feel like she was much smaller.

She clenched her fist in determination. "The forests are getting out of hand."

Varia didn't blink. "Yes, the reports have said as much. I hardly think you needed to barge in here to tell me this."

"We have a dead ranger!" Teria shouted, several younger eyes peeking inquisitively out of the grand hall outside. "A coleptus killed him unprovoked! What could possibly have driven such a peaceable creature to such insanity?"

"Perhaps a sickness of some kind?" Varia replied calmly, despite Teria's outbursts. "We will assign a dedicated force to discover the source of the creature's ailments. You think I don't know what goes on in my forest dear girl, but I do."

Teria recoiled at the sly remark.

"Now please, do me, everyone in the city, and most importantly yourself, a favor. Go upstairs, take off those filthy clothes, and take a nice long bath." the older woman said, leaning forward and taking up her pen again, looking down at the papers on her desk. "I'm sure you would prefer a nice cool brook in the forest, but the warmed water upstairs will help with the smell."

The young ranger took a slight step back, hating when the Mistress began to sound motherly, but she couldn't find the words to cut back at her.

She began to speak again, the Mistress seeming to hear the words trying to rise up from her breast. "We will find the issue, I assure you dear girl. I have a meeting with the council in a few hours, and I will be sure to deliver the news to Sárif. I am sure he will be able to aid us with his arcane means. And, I'm sure he can also help calm the public when it comes to a ranger stalking through the streets, covered in blood." the woman sighed deeply, looking away from Teria as she rose from her chair, setting her pen in its holder carefully.

Teria felt her face get hot at the statement, understanding her error in coming straight through the city before washing herself of her most recent battle.

Varia stepped past her, and placed her thin hand on her shoulder, despite the blood. "Next time, Teria, please do catalog more of the creature's behavior, before killing it."

"It was boring its head into a tree!" Teria tried to say in her defense, but the Mistress was already gone, leaving the young woman in the office. Her lips came together in a pout, feeling thoroughly like a child in the presence of the matronly woman.

"You underestimate the Mistress." a male voice came from beyond the door.

Teria angled her eyes downwards as Selbor turned around the corner. He scolded the gawking audience back to their business with a wave of his hand.

"I don't need your lectures." she said roughly.

He smirked, stepping lightly to her, and placing a hand on her back, ushering her from the room. "I will not give you one then. Now, let us get you in that bath, I'll get your armor to the cleaners."

Teria suppressed her groan, taking off her vambraces, weapons, and other easy to remove pieces and handing them to Selbor as they walked.

Once they arrived at the bathhouse, he stepped to the side of the screen door, still carrying most of her gear.

"Sorry for dirtying your breastplate." she said quietly, nodding to her handprint, barely visible on his chest.

"It's fine, Teria, it needed a good wash anyways. Now get in there and relax for a while." he replied, opening the sliding door slightly.

She made her way in, removing the rest of her clothes and handing it to him, her face still thoroughly annoyed. He tapped on the door lightly after taking her blood-soaked clothing, giving her a smile that was likely intended to be comforting. She stepped into the bathing room, watching the steam rising over the water.

"Let me know when Farris gets back." she called to him.

She could see his silhouette nod through the screen door after he closed it behind her. "I'll be sure not to tell him where you are, he'd probably try to take a peek."

Teria couldn't help but laugh. "More than likely, knowing the weasel. Still, he seems to know something, and you know how he is."

Selbor nodded again, and departed with heavy footfalls, leaving Teria standing inside the doorway. She sighed deeply, stretching her arms over her head and moving to the side where a fresh bucket of water awaited her. After thanking the water maid, she set to work scrubbing her front where the dark ichor of the creature had seeped down the front of her tunic.

† †

Irvine called for Erika to cease her charge towards their unknown assailant, but she didn't hear him, focused in on the person that had harmed him.

Her mind flashed briefly to when they were children, and a group of boys were shoving him around in an alley. Erika was naturally bigger at that age due to her Fjordling heritage, using that weight and strength to lay one of the boys out on the cobblestones. Her father had always scolded her for her bloody knuckles.

She fell back to that instinct to protect him against anyone who hurt him, except this time it wasn't just some bully in town, and they weren't kids.

This time it was a real enemy, one who had just confessed to a legitimate attempt on Irvine's life. This time it was completely unforgivable.

As she neared him, she swung her hammer in a wide arc, the man leaping over the strike and bringing a dagger around towards her shoulder. A loud ring cried out as Irvine deflected the blow away from Erika. She hadn't even noticed him behind her, but as she turned, she found the same aggressive expression again, only this time it was even more intense. Irvine grabbed the back of her tunic and pulled her roughly to the side, swinging his blade outwards towards their opponent, who stepped back out of range of the attack.

Erika saw an opportunity and swung her hammer outwards, using the momentum to swing her own body around Irvine and brought it down low to the assassin.

She audibly gasped in shock and pain when her strike was blown backwards, her feet knocked off balance and fell out from underneath her. The man had kicked the shaft of her hammer with his blazing leg, a loud cracking sound resounding at the impact and echoing across the vale.

Irvine slung his blade in an overhead arc, pulling it back when his opponent parried it and lunged in for an underhand stab. Their assailant used his dagger to deflect the second attack as well, the blades sparking lightly as they grated against each other. His eyes widened when Irvine's off hand came around in a hook, as he was barely able to dodge. Irvine grunted with each strike, trading blows with the more dexterous fighter. Irvine was used to fighting prolonged battles though, he felt confident in his own endurance, and ability to wear him down.

Erika pushed herself back up on her elbows, shaking her head to rid herself of the ringing sound in her ears. She cried out in pain as she ripped her crushed gauntlets from her hands. Her wrists and palms were deeply bruised from the impact. After a moment she gripped her warhammer again, gritting her teeth against the tender feeling in her fingers.

Irvine brought his blade around, forcing the assassin to duck, only to slash his own dagger out viscously. Irvine was barely able to dodge, taking a shallow cut to his side, before the quick man spun around him and kicked him in the side. Irvine fell to the ground, rolling with the impact and over onto his feet to focus on the man again, taking in the features of his face.

In again came their assailant again, his cunning blade scoring two more hits on Irvine's arm, inconsequential, but still drawing small splashes of blood that painted the stone below them. Irvine shoved his free arm out, bashing his forearm against the man's dagger arm twice in quick succession to ward off two more strikes, then flipping his own sword into a reverse grip, raising it upwards and ripping across his opponent's chest. The assassin backed away with haste though, lessening the slash.

"Damn, you're quick." Irvine muttered, whipping his free hand out to ward off the stinging pain from the cut across his forearm.

In came the man as he recovered, feinting his dagger out unsuccessfully, as Irvine knocked the true strike to the side with his backhanded blade, and punched his fist out savagely into the man's face.

"And you're annoyingly strong." he retorted, spitting a red glob from his lips.

Irvine ducked around the half-hearted strike of the man's unarmed fist, swinging his blade out from behind him. The man ducked again, backing away and throwing more weakening strikes towards Irvine. The courier caught the blade against his crossguard and wrenched it around, freeing it from the man's grip and throwing it off the side of the shelf.

A second dagger came free from under the man's cloak, swinging out to ward off another strike from Irvine, who hopped back for another attack. He brought his sword over in another arcing swing, the man slinging out another dagger, crossing the blades and catching Irvine's sword.

Irvine simply had to overpower him to send him sailing over the edge and down the waterfall like his first dagger. He pressed harder and harder, using every ounce of his strength and weight to continue the pressure. His body size was bigger than their attacker, and he felt he could use it to his advantage in forcing him over the edge of their arena. The man crouched lower and lower, seemingly unable to recover from the oppressive push.

The assassin's eyes widened when he saw Erika sprinting up to join in the battle. He lifted his leg slightly and slammed it into the stone, the blast punching him past Irvine's pressure and into the air. He arced over, landing nearly on the other side of their stone arena.

The assailant let out a curse, then shouted. "Enough of this game!" he crouched a moment later, readying both blades at his sides.

Irvine had seen the power in his flame covered leg, and was able to surmise what his gambit would be, yelling to his companion. "Erika! Move, now!"

She stood steadfast, her forearms and fists suddenly flashing into flame, her flesh turning black as obsidian with orange lines cracking down to her fingers. Irvine hesitated at the similar sight to what her father had done in the battle with the Daemon.

"Damn this bastard!" she screamed as her heat intensified up to her elbows.

Their opponent kicked off the ground and thrusted forward at a blinding speed. Erika resolved not to miss this time. Irvine began to run forward, convinced that Erika was his target. She swung her warhammer with a guttural cry as she heard the blast, the head smashing into his right shoulder.

She could hear and feel the bones shattering under the impact, but his momentum still carried him forwards and into Irvine, tackling him with his left shoulder and sending the two flying over the rushing waterfall.

The impact winded Irvine. The last thing he heard before being thrust under the cold water was Erika screaming his name.

PART TWO

My children are many, and my children are capable. Most of all I believe, is Teria. The young woman is beautiful, and extremely capable. Many more experienced than her would have issue in defeating the obstacles and adversaries that she finds herself locked into battle with on a daily basis.

This beautiful, and capable young woman is not without her faults though.

She is rash, and impatient. Despite those sharp and calm dark eyes, she holds an inner fire that boils her blood constantly. She is always ready to fight, and I worry that she does not know her own limitations. I fear that one day she will find an adversary that she cannot defeat, and she will fight that truth until her death. That, and her difficulty in social situations, are her two greatest weaknesses.

She fails to understand the nuances of people. She is human, but she reminds me more of the elves that I have met in my youth. With the exception of Sárif and his partner, as well as gaia elves; most elves are distant and quiet in my experience, and most aash are distrustful of any outsiders. The demeanor of sol always shows a confidence that seems to border on hubris at times, and both seem to have a degree of difficulty in speaking to others who are not elf in blood.

She is an inquisitive young woman, and I applaud that, but she needs to slow down, and enjoy life more. Perhaps she will find a friend, and will learn to see things in a way other than through the eyes of a ranger.

Despite her cold attitude, I believe a warm heart beats in that young woman's breast. I only hope she learns to listen to it.

-Varia Wyldsbane, Mistress of the Willow Rangers

12
DETERMINATION

Versal and the archers watched over the open field, watching for any of the Daemon's thralls. They all bordered the caravan of civilians, Versal tossing a veritable missile of condensed flame or the archers raining arrows any time one of the skeletal creatures came in too close.

It was a slow journey, but he took solace in seeing how much progress they had already made from the doomed town. He occasionally paused, looking at the still smoldering visage of the buildings, wishing that he could have done more to stop the Daemon.

Merrick reported in to him periodically with any news from the caravan or sightings of larger Daemons, which caused them to alter their course. Each time, Versal explained that he was not the commanding officer, but after a while he stopped trying to convince the boy of the new order, understanding that he just needed some semblance of structure to keep moving forward with sanity.

The land itself gradually became less and less scorched the further they journeyed from the town, grass and foliage becoming more and more regular again, and with that change, less Daemons were seen. Though the guards and Versal found themselves lunging at any stray shadows or shapes that bore even the slightest resemblance to the creatures.

Not long after leaving the desecrated area, they arrived at the shoreline, several small docks and shacks lining the water. Versal remembered arriving at these same docks just over twenty years previously, a single pack over his shoulder, and a small child cradled in his massive elbow. He reminisced over the memory, Feldran met him at the dock, smiling with that horribly bushy moustache, and holding Erika to give him a chance to rest. Feldran himself had become an uncle to a small boy, and thus was no stranger to a child. His daughter slept easily for the first time that day, no more traveling, and no more danger. Unfortunately, a tragedy had struck the town only a handful of years later when Feldran's sister perished in their home caught ablaze fire, along with her husband.

He wondered how many trials she and Irvine had encountered since they departed, regretting not being able to protect her. Though he was impossibly glad he had broken into the burning building when he had, and been able to save the young Irvine. The boy had been screaming at the top of his lungs, sitting in the same room as the burning body of his mother. He knew that fractured memories of that night were the source of his fear regarding fire.

"Irvine is a capable lad. Feldran raised 'im well." he said aloud to himself as he looked over the horizon of ocean.

Merrick stepped beside him, looking to him curiously. "I didn't mean to eavesdrop or anything, but did you mention Irvine just now?"

Versal glanced down to him, happy that he was speaking of anything other than one of his reports. "Aye. I assume ye know 'im?"

"I do." the young guard said, scratching at the back of his head. "Though I'm afraid I may have been less than friendly to him when we were children."

The Smithmaster raised an eyebrow. "I assume ye were one of the ones me daughter bloodied 'er knuckles on?"

Merrick swallowed nervously. "No, that would be the ones I used to spend my time with though. I was the first to run."

The smith chuckled at that.

"What's yer interest in Irvine then?"

"I just." the young man began, seemingly unsure of his own words. "I wonder if I was part of the reason that Irvine took the job of a courier, and took all of those long treks away from Valen."

Versal sighed, placing a hand on the guard's much smaller shoulder. "Not to make ye feel guilty, but aye, I believe ye were. Though that means I likely have a reason to thank ye."

Merrick looked up to the massive man. "Why?"

"Erika is out there right now with Irvine. Warnin' the world of the Daemon's arrival. An' because of all those long treks, he is more prepared than anyone to protect me little girl."

Merrick stifled a laugh. "I mean no offense, but I never thought Erika would need protection from anyone."

Versal chuckled. "Aye, she is a tough one. Though she's never journeyed much farther than where we are now since she was a wee thing. So, I do fear fer her in that reasonin'."

"Well, I know how accomplished Irvine became because of the things we did to him. And though I regret all of it, and wish I could be friends with him now, I am glad that he's with her. They can protect each other." Merrick added with a hopeful grin.

Versal nodded. "When he gets back, ye should talk to 'im. I think ye'd be surprised at how forgivin' he can be. He loved 'is town, and the people in it."

"Perhaps. I will be glad to see him again, after this is all over." Merrick said, smiling at Versal as he stepped off to the front of the caravan again.

Shortly after, they met with the guards in the watchtower that kept vigil over the coastline, filling them in on what had transpired.

"I'll stay here for now, and make sure the Daemon doesn't pursue you." offered Maurin, the young woman that had been there for the last shift. She was a lean thing, muscled and stern, though still young. "If I see anything coming, I'll make my way to you. I was the fastest runner in training."

None could dissuade her, and simply thanked her for her dutiful task, and continued along the coast at the base of the mountains.

† †

Erika lay on her stomach, peering over the edge of the waterfall and the stone shelf. Stray tears joining the cascading river, as she struggled with the concept that she may never see Irvine again.

She had no idea how far down this waterfall went, nor what lay at the bottom. Images of blood covered rocks and floating corpses flashed through her mind, causing more tears to fall each time she imagined them.

Several moments passed before Erika eventually crawled back and away from the edge of the stone. She rolled over on her back, trying to focus on regaining control over her shaky breathing, but her vision was blurry. Each breath coming in a labored gasp, as if she had the wind knocked from her lungs. The world seemed to drown in the unbelievable sinking feeling that plagued her.

She hated how she had been on this journey, seeing herself as pitiful and useless, slowing down Irvine's pace and bringing their progress to a halt now.

If I hadn't been here, he would never have been caught by the assassin. she thought.

Blame and guilt filled her head, believing herself to be the one that killed her best friend. Eventually she wrestled control over her thoughts, slamming her fist down into the stone, her flesh exploding into obsidian again with the rage that she felt towards the assailant.

She raised her arm, staring at her transformed limb, wishing she had as much control as her father. Perhaps then, she could have fought off the man better. Though the sight reminded her that she was not helpless, her eyes eventually drying and her expression turning to one of determination.

She focused on the things that Irvine had taught her in their short time traveling through the wilderness, breaking down each task she would need to do. First, she would make her way to the bridge he had told her about, then follow the declining ridge to the base of the waterfall and confirm the fate of the two, even if it broke her. After that, she would continue on and finish the journey to Sildenfeld.

"Even if Irvine is gone, there's still a Daemon." she choked out between her slowing breaths and the lump in her throat.

She retrieved her warhammer, and stuffed her broken gauntlets into her pack before making her way up the ridge, following the river to where she hoped the bridge would be. Focusing on each step as she walked quickly through the forest. The sound of the raging waterfall died out with each stride she took.

She held her weapon tightly against her breastplate, despite the bruising in her hands, wishing more than anything to see Irvine again.

† †

Irvine slowly awoke, feeling the cold rushing water around him. He pushed an arm behind himself, and dragged himself more onto the shore beside the river. His body felt horribly bruised and sore. The stinging of cuts and scrapes ringing out across parts of his body, but he sat up nonetheless.

The water was deep just under the waterfall, but very shallow downstream, rocks and pebbles covering the bottom and digging into his hands. He coughed, choking liquid from his lungs onto his chest, taking a moment to rid himself from the uncomfortable feeling.

Looking around, he saw the crumpled form of his assailant, still unconscious or perhaps dead on the opposite side of the stream.

His sword was missing, possibly lodged somewhere in the waterfall, or carried further downstream. The daggers of his opponent were nearby though. Irvine made a point to retrieve the weapons before making his way over to the man.

He rolled over his body, confirming the steady but shallow breathing. He searched his torso and legs, taking several other daggers and small knives from his person, reducing the chance of him getting another chance at his life. Lastly, he found a small piece of parchment from his pocket.

The thought of ending the man's life crossed through Irvine's mind, but he shook his head quickly.

I am not him. I am not a killer. he resolved.

He glanced down at the powerful leg that had caused the fall, heatless flames surrounding the exposed bone of his leg, with no foot remaining. The sight caused Irvine to wince slightly. Although he noticed they flickered out when exposed to the running water below them. Irvine decided to leave him partially in the water, hoping that if he did awake, the water would weaken him at least.

He stood, looking upstream to the waterfall that met its end several yards away from him, the top of the fall was much farther above though. He suspected that this was actually a second waterfall and the original one that he fell down was even further above and out of sight. Otherwise, he would be hurting quite a bit more.

Erika would be appalled if she knew how many waterfalls I had fallen over. he thought with slight amusement.

He let out a heavy sigh a moment later, walking upstream at the hope that his blade would be somewhere close by, but was disappointed by the lack of evidence that it was still in the area. As he walked, he checked into his satchel, and confirming all the contents still remained inside. The portrait of Erika bearing some extra wear to it, but still discernible. His other, more practical, supplies still lay inside relatively unharmed.

Moments later, the man groaned as he awakened, Irvine turning towards him with a stern expression. The groaning continued, and worsened in tone as the man began to feel the pain in his shoulder, gradually turning into a string of curses.

Irvine quickly made his way to him, and pressed his boot into the unbroken shoulder, forcing him back to the ground with no leverage to fight back with the injured appendage.

"Who are you?" Irvine asked firmly.

The man laughed through his obvious pain. "It doesn't matter anymore. You can kill me here and now, makes no difference."

"Why is that?"

"The Daemon will finish the job if you don't. He bears no love, even for me."

"So, he sent you to assassinate us? Gave you that special leg to give you an easier time?"

The man laughed, though it came more as a wheeze. "I am no assassin, only a thief. This leg was less a gift and more a mercy."

Irvine cocked his head in confusion.

The thief continued. "I was hired to destroy a magic cage. Only I assumed the cage held hordes of treasure, little did I know that monster was inside."

"You did this?" Irvine screamed, pressing his foot down harder and increasing the pained groans of the man.

"Not intentionally, boy!" he screamed back. "I was tricked! Look at the paper in my pocket."

"This paper?" Irvine asked, flicking the parchment out and unfolding it. His eyes squinting as he read the bounty through still bleary eyes.

"No details of the complex besides cryptic clues on how to break the seal. High reward which I have already kicked myself over. I was foolish to believe it, but I took the bait. This, 'A.H.' got the better of me." he explained.

"And now my uncle, and countless more are dead because of your actions." Irvine continued for him in a low tone.

"My intentions were purely of avarice," he said, Irvine flashing him a sharp expression, to which he replied quickly. "And I know that excuses nothing! But know that it was never my intention to release that, thing, on our world."

Irvine slowly removed his boot, allowing the thief to sit up and cradle his wounded arm. "That girl of yours destroyed my shoulder." he said with a light chuckle.

"She is not mine, but yes, she did. I'll have to remember to commend her on a job well done for that." Irvine retorted back.

"Not yours, eh? Could have fooled me with how close she was to you last-" the thief began, trailing off.

Irvine didn't hear him though. He glanced up and noticed a cave entrance on the underside of the mountain that they had fallen from, partially obscured by the waterfall. He found himself drawn to it, a strange orange glow emanating from the interior in pulses, despite the light of day.

He could hear the injured man behind him still talking, but absorbed none of his words, all of his attention focused on the entrance in front of him.

Inside was a short bend, leading into a cavern with a perfectly rectangular stone pedestal directly in the middle of the chamber. The pedestal was the source of the pulsating glow, the smooth top alighting every few moments in a bright light. Irvine approached cautiously, but a strange feeling compelled him closer, as if a voice was pleading him closer.

He suddenly found himself directly before it, his hand placed upon the smooth surface. The heat of it surprised him, though he could not will himself to remove his hand. Images flashed through his mind, strange humanoid individuals with wings of fire and lightning, with scaled armor that seemed almost organic.

Horrific creatures of flame, and ice, and poison.

Mythical Dragons flying overhead and the winged people fighting alongside them.

Clashes of epic proportions, legions of armies as far as the eye could see, all fighting in endless tides.

The last thing he saw was the cave that he currently stood in from the outside, two figures in white and gold robes entering, and one bearing the scaled raiment behind them. The armored one stepped forward within the cavern where he now stood, the firelight shimmering off his crimson scaled armor and his pale underlying skin. Eventually placing the tip of his impressive spear on the ground, the stone pedestal formed and rose under it, slowly swallowing the weapon. The figure did not let go however, his form lighting into bright flame as the other two figures chanted in a language unknown to Irvine.

The warrior's scales and flesh began to turn to fire, though he did not seem in pain, an expression of grim determination from what Irvine could see underneath his jagged helm of scales. His form scattered into embers, floating into the stone pedestal. At the last moment before fading fully, he turned and looked directly at Irvine

"Fate has chosen you. Calamity approaches with the Daemon's return. Our power is yours."

The vision flashed out of existence a moment later, Irvine looking down to find the pedestal gone and a burning sensation in his palm. Outside, the sun was not to be seen. The shadows of the trees played in the wrong direction.

Morning had come.

The thief was gone, and Irvine stood there alone, and wondering how he had missed an entire night.

↑ ↑

Erika crossed the solid wood bridge that spanned across the river, the construction thankfully much sturdier than the ones she had to cross in the mountain pass. She couldn't help but appreciate the craftsmanship in the ornate carvings of the railing on either side, as well as the beautiful colors that decorated it, even if they were somewhat faded.

Afterwards, she followed the river as closely as she could, always keeping it in eyesight at the least. Eventually she found the large waterfall that Irvine had fallen from, the stone shelf several yards over her head.

She followed the land as far as she could, finding a steep drop-off neighboring the cascading water. The height was intimidating, but nothing near what she had already been through, even if Irvine wasn't here to help her this time.

She took a breath, retrieving the excess rope that Irvine had given her and tied off the end to a nearby tree trunk. She then tied small knots in the length of the rope, giving herself a length of holds before tossing the loose end over the cliff side. She rested her warhammer on the sling fashioned into the bottom of her pack, making sure it was secure, before taking another deep breath and slowly lowering her feet over the edge.

She held tightly to the rope, angling her body backwards and securing her feet onto the side of the cliff, then slowly began to walk backwards. She measured each step, making sure that her footing was secure, before taking another. She looked directly to the wall in front of her, each time she dared to look down, her breathing became erratic and she had to pause for a while before regaining her composure. Even with her hard earned callouses from forging, the rope still dug into her bruised and numbing palms, causing a burning sensation unlike any flame she had touched, but she gritted her teeth against it and continued on. A stone gave way from her left foot as she stepped down, causing her legs to split apart with a sudden striking pain. Her warhammer slipped from her back and clattered to the ground below her. She loudly cursed at her own lack of flexibility as she dangled from the rope by her arms alone, her thickened muscles starting to shake, unused to this kind of strain.

She kicked her legs out again, gaining new footing on the wall and started again, eventually reaching the bottom of the cliff. She fell to the ground and laid back, resting every aching limb from the short journey down and laughing at how terrible she seemed to be at all of this. She could swing a hammer for hours on end, but one short trek down a waterfall, and she was more exhausted than she'd ever felt in her entire life.

She couldn't help but admire Irvine more for being able to do this kind of thing regularly. Sitting up again, she looked back to the river as it steadied from the fall, before cascading into a second waterfall several yards out. She rolled her eyes and groaned, realizing that she would have another cliff to traverse. She retrieved her warhammer and peered over the next waterfall on all fours. She could see a shallow section littered in rocks and pebbles in the area below the next waterfall.

She held her breath, waiting to see a corpse crushed onto the stones, but found none. Next, she looked straight down where the waterfall ended directly, and saw the shape of their assailant, walking onto the dry land next to the stream, shaking water from one hand and cradling the other.

She screamed a curse out at him in rage, nearly tossing herself from the cliff to land on top of him. He responded by looking up at her and then dashing off with haste into the forest. She took some pride in seeing him favoring the arm that she had struck, satisfied that she had at least disabled him somewhat, but cursed again as he disappeared from sight.

She retrieved the end of the rope, tying more knots and slinging it over the next cliff, taking another deep breath before climbing down the next section. She took it slower after testing to make sure it was still tightly secured at the top where she began, measuring each step more carefully.

No slips this time, and less sudden striking pain. she instructed herself mentally, doing her best to imagine Irvine's voice. Although the biting of the rope and the strenuous exertion still plagued her slightly. She could only admire Irvine's strength in these journeys.

She found herself admiring a lot of things about him. His striking blue eyes danced in low torchlight in her imagination. His handsome features appearing in perfect clarity.

Tears again welled in her eyes at the thought of never seeing him again. She truly had enjoyed this journey with him, and wished she could have spent more time with him.

She felt foolish and childish in all the memories of scolding him through the years, and she realized that even through those harsh treatments, he always came back. Erika liked to think that he came back to her.

Her inner fire burned all the brighter with those feelings.

13
FEAR OF THE UNKNOWN

Wildlife across the region has begun to act erratically? And are we doing anything about that?" the man with the puffy cheeks said loudly.

The one with the red coat retorted aggressively. "All the more reason to heighten the walls!"

The thin woman yelled back. "Higher walls are no way to welcome allies!"

The system of individuals shouting at one another continued, Sárif Vlësk rubbing his eyes gently, while his mind drifted elsewhere.

His long and thin pointed ears felt chilled in the late autumn air, as a light breeze flowed through the outdoor meeting area. His seven-foot stature lifted him much higher than any of the others around the great table, even while sitting, and his golden hair drifted across his face slightly in that breeze. His large, angular amber eyes drifted to daydreaming as the others droned on.

He wondered if his old friends Feldran and Versal would allow for a visit soon, but dismissed the thought when he considered the political structure of Sildenfeld, and the slim likelihood that anyone would be willing to see him leave for a few weeks' worth of time.

"If a Daemon had been resurrected, the Angelus would strike them down instantly." the man to his left suddenly shouted, violently rousing Sárif from his trance.

"And if the Angelus have abandoned us?" Mortan asked with widened eyes.

Sárif groaned internally, realizing that the talk of Daemons was begun by Mortan, a former priest who had abandoned the temples himself, and now spoke of the higher beings abandoning them. Sárif wasn't overtly religious himself, though he still found Mortan a hypocrite in his objections. He had voted the aging man off of the council. A shame that he was in the minority for some reason.

The regal sol elf leaned forward in his chair, raising his voice for the first time during this discussion.

"In the unlikely event that a Daemon has been resurrected, we will send scouts to all of the known Consecrations, with caution, to confirm that they still lay dormant. Should we discover one has been awakened, we will mobilize the Arcanist Guild to start on barriers, and enlist the temples to attempt at rousing the Angelus. Even if they do not answer the calls of the clerics, we do possess the necessary might to neutralize a Daemon's presence." The room fell silent from the ongoing arguments, every member focusing on the charismatic elf.

He spread his arms wide in his showmanship. "We have come far from our days in the Daemon War. No longer are we a weak civilization, we have the means to stand against any threat now."

The representing clergywoman, Tarina, stood as well. "As the Angelus intended!" she said, supporting Sárif's words. "We were entrusted with these lands, and have gained the spirit and strength to defend them!"

"Thank you for the sermon." General Atrosby said sarcastically, pulling his chiseled face from his palm. "Nonetheless,

Mortan is afraid of nothing. The chances of a Daemon's return are less than slim, no one even knows how to end the Consecrations, let alone where thousands of them are."

Mistress Varia, the leader of the Willow Rangers stood in a calm demeanor, her silver hair dancing around her face. "Precisely. The creatures of the lands are behaving strangely yes, but my children are well equipped to deal with them. None shall breach the walls of our city, and we will find the source of their ailments. On that note, I should be returning to my work."

She turned sharply and started out of the room, her forest colored cloak trailing behind her. The meeting running in circles had obviously become tiring to her, and none of the other members could blame her.

Sárif smiled warmly at the remaining council. "Ever vigilant it seems. On that note, let us adjourn this meeting, and return to our duties to Sildenfeld." he said, clapping his hands together. Varia had inquired him to investigate another matter, and this mindless debate over nothing was dragging on far too long.

He was answered with murmurings around the circular table, as the members began to shuffle out of the chamber, and waved to the last few as they exited and closed the doors.

He took a large breath of relief at the sudden silence, looking up to the clouding sky above, past the wooden canopy decorated with vines and green foliage. He much preferred the open air of this meeting room, rather than the confined spaces further into the hall.

He sat back in his chair again, observing the lack of birds that normally permeated this area, and wondering at the similar situation in his personal sanctum, where he kept a steady supply of seeds for the finches. Perhaps there was merit to the former priest's callings of Daemons, or at least some disruption in the natural order of things. More investigation would be required in this matter.

He retrieved a piece of parchment and a quill from his bag, continuing the letter he had begun earlier that day, informing

Feldran of the goings-on in the last few days, as well as asking him of any strange occurrences on that side of the Seraphine mountains. He hoped Irvine would stop by on an errand soon, and he would be able to send the message back with the young man.

The elf pondered a moment, and mused aloud. "The Harvest Festival should have just happened. I wonder if Irvine danced with Versal's young girl."

† †

Erika's breathing became erratic again, searching around the small dale frantically. She witnessed their assailant leaving the area, but there was no sign of Irvine.

She had held some hope that Irvine was alive down here when she saw the man leaving on both feet, but when she was nearly down the cliff, she realized that he may have finished his work on Irvine and left him somewhere with a fresh blade wound to his throat.

She had dropped down the rest of the length of rope, sending a sharp pain through her legs from the impact, but the panic overpowered the pain. The water splashed chaotically around her, soaking into her clothes as she paced back and forth through the stream, her eyes darting around for anything that hinted towards his presence.

She could no longer tell if her face was wet from tears or the river, but her mind raced for any possible answer as to where he could have ended up. She ran to the waterfall, placing a hand on the cold wall to its left side and looking behind it, the water cascading over her head in what would have been a refreshing jolt.

As she leaned forwards to try and see into the deeper water directly below the falls, her hand slipped on the wall, sending her tumbling in. She regained her composure a moment later, kicking to the surface and gasping for air.

She threw her pack onto the shore and took a deep breath, diving under the water and opening her eyes as best she could. The darkness under the water clouded her vision, and made for a difficult search.

She became frustrated with the conditions, focusing her energy as she had before, her arms blazing to life and running obsidian again. The orange magma-like lines cracking down her bare arms and powerful open flames blasting forward, causing the water around her to boil and sting at her neck and face, but the light allowed for a temporary flash in the dark waters for her to confirm nothing to be under the surface. She crawled back onto the shoreline, her chest heaving and sucking down the air around her.

The skin reddened where she was burned, steam crawling off of the damp flesh. She blinked heavily, ridding her eyes of the water from the stream. She sat up shortly after, cupping her hands and throwing cold water onto the burns.

Looking down, she realized that she had immolated more than she had ever done before. Her already sleeveless tunic was singed just past the shoulders, telling her that she had successfully immolated to that height on her appendages. This gave her a small smile, happy that she was finding some control over her power, though she wondered if it was just the panic that allowed her the extra boost in flames.

She also took note of the gently curving crimson lines across her skin, similar to her father's but not yet full. Always she had been careful to relegate her power to just encouraging outward flames to grow or shrink, but never had she flushed any part of her body like that before.

She sat back, looking around again and taking some comfort in that she hadn't found any sign of Irvine, living or dead, which gave her hope that he had already moved on and still very much alive.

Retrieving her pack and holding her warhammer ready in case her enemy or any aggressive wildlife came at her, she started off northwards. She remembered the direction that she and Irvine were headed originally, maintaining hope that she could catch up with Irvine soon. She whipped her hair, slinging the soaked in water about, and wringed her skirt as well as she could. The dampness on her legs underneath the skirt nipped from the cold winds blowing through the trees. She forced herself to imagine Irvine's face and felt optimistic to see that wonderful sight again.

† †

Irvine stepped back over the stream, noticing the prints in the soft sediment from the thief, and where he had escaped to.

He looked closer, seeing another set of steps that were too small to be his, concluding that it was likely Erika passing through. He looked up to the cliffs, finding the lengths of rope running down each wall, and smiled knowing that she had learned something from him. Though he wondered how she didn't discover his whereabouts in the cave, knowing that she would have turned over every stone in the area looking for him. He found his answer when he looked back to the entrance behind the waterfall and discovered a flat stone wall.

He cocked his head to the side in confusion, jogging back to it and placing both hands on the wall, feeling the cool stone and grainy water droplets that permeated the surface, yet no opening appeared.

The cave had vanished, no trace of it remained, not even a crack in the rock. He stared at his hand, feeling the warmth in it subside. He didn't know what had happened, but knew he couldn't dwell on it now.

Searching over the area, he saw where Erika had been, and finally found the path she had taken outwards. He shouldered his satchel, and started out in the direction of his companion's path. He wanted to catch up to Erika as quickly as possible, though his pace was slowed by his still bruised musculature from the tumble down the waterfall, as well as a newly noticed twinge in his left leg that caused a him slight limp.

He also noticed the path of the thief, though thankfully it was in a different direction than his companion. He had no desire

134

to pursue the man, his lack of a familiar weapon making him a bit more unnerved than he would normally be, though he had confidence the daggers would do just fine should he need them.

After testing the balance of the daggers, he wrapped the blades in the remaining cloth of his festival tunic, and replaced the make-shift bandage on his left arm, the wound still fresh, but at least clean. Satisfied that he had prepared adequately, he set off, following the path of his auburn-haired companion through the forest.

† †

Teria waited impatiently for Mistress Varia to arrive. Her dark hair still slightly damp from the bath she had taken to rid herself of her last battle. It had taken much longer than she'd hoped to scrape the dried gore from her legs, and they still shone a bright red from the scrubbing in the darkening light of day.

Varia finally arrived, Teria having half a mind to berate her for making her wait, but thinking otherwise when she considered the sour expression the older woman wore.

"Fools. The lot of them." she said harshly, walking past the younger woman, who instinctively knew to follow close.

"They cannot cease their arguing for more than a breath, and they expect things to happen in this city." she sighed deeply. "This is why I prefer the woods."

Teria smirked, amused slightly by the similarity in their thoughts. "So, what is our next move?"

Varia turned to regard her slightly. "Ah, so the bath did help your mood."

The young ranger rolled her eyes at the remark, eliciting a chuckle from her Mistress.

"Don't be so high and mighty dear girl. To answer your inquiry, we will be increasing our patrols around the city. No creatures are to be allowed near it, and we must investigate their ailments. Sárif is going to look into occurrences across the

Sildenfeld region's towns and villages for anything strange, and perhaps send a message to the Myrefell and Sylvanna regions in inquiry of strange happenings there as well."

Teria pondered a moment, remembering what another ranger had mentioned to her.

"Farris had mentioned something." she began.

"Ah, my favorite weasel." Varia commented sardonically.

Teria smirked slightly at their shared nickname, but continued when the woman nodded to her. "He had mentioned hearing about something in the 'underbelly of the city'. As if he knew something was amiss inside the walls to cause the creatures to go berserk."

The older woman thought a moment, placing her hand on Teria's shoulder. "Thank you for sharing this with me dear girl. I'll bring in Farris immediately, and persuade him to tell me more. In the meantime, I need your sharp eyes outside the walls tonight."

Teria nodded, thankful for something to do. She hated just waiting in the city. The bath and meal were plenty rest for her, now she needed to get back to work.

14
CRUSHING JAWS

The open valley was barely illuminated by the light of the moons, the fields a far stretch from any official roads, and still covered in tall grass that whipped at the thighs of any traveler. Erika winced every time a reed snapped up and struck her thighs.

A normal walking pace was greatly slowed by the foliage, but she managed to trudge through with some haste. Her breathing was heavy for what seemed like the thousandth time after leaving her home, though nearly every time before was due to her concern for her companion or fear of travel conditions.

This time however, it was fear for her own life, as she ran across the thick grassy hills. The tips of the blades stinging her legs through the fabric and ripped holes of her skirt, while others caught on her boots and ripped free of the earth. She didn't dare look back at the creature that was chasing her, fearing that it would only make the monster closer than she believed it to be.

The massive scaled creature the size of an ox barreled after her with reckless abandon, keeping its less-than-stellar vision on the fleeing girl. She had recognized the deep-toned trill from the Mystholt, remembering that Irvine had said the jordhak creatures were more active at night, but didn't realize how close the beast was before it launched from the ground tossing her several yards away. Her landing gave her a shock through her hip as she tried to save her bruised hands. She recovered and saw the creature looking around seeming confused. Assuming that its eyesight wasn't great, she started off as quietly as she could, though it snapped to her when she let out an involuntary gasp after her hip issued a twinge of pain that radiated through her waist and thigh.

Now she seemed to be outrunning the creature for the most part, its poor vision causing it to stumble periodically and slow down, giving Erika the time she needed to distance herself from it. She could see the buildings and spires bordered by a tall stone wall in the distance, praying that it was Sildenfeld, but simultaneously happy for any civilization that could offer a respite and a safe place to heal.

Suddenly, she felt a lack of resistance, the grass no longer nipping at her legs, and she realized that she was in an open field that was cleaned of the outlying foliage. She didn't feel she had the time to survey and confirm if this was soon to be a farm plot or otherwise, and instead focused on her steps, careful to not put too much force on her pained leg.

Her eyes went wide when she heard the low trilling call of the jordhak, followed by a loud crashing sound, knowing that the creature had gone underground. She halted her progress, remembering that these beasts hunted using sound when they lay under the earth. Looking around the area, she couldn't see any sign of it anywhere, though she knew it must be nearby.

She heard a voice suddenly call out to her, turning and seeing several cloaked figures in the distance, she smiled in relief, glad to see others nearby, but then realized that she was putting them in danger by bringing the hungry jordhak closer. She waved her arms to them, trying to get them to stop, but the four individuals continued in her direction.

"I don't want to lose anyone else." she said quietly to herself, despite not knowing the four figures. She bared her warhammer and tossed her pack as hard as she could towards the approaching people, before screaming out at the top of her lungs and smashing the head of the hammer into the ground below her.

She felt the rumble beneath her feet, turning to the figures and waving them off, each of them retrieving a bow from their backs and nocking arrows. She moved to dodge, but wasn't fast enough, the creature bursting forth from the ground and engulfing her midsection between its jaws. Her breast plate prevented the creature from clamping down with full force, but she felt several of the large teeth punching through the armor and into her chest and into her waist unobstructed.

She let out a sharp gasp of pain as arrows whistled through the night air, several bouncing off of the creature's armored hide, others lodging between the plates and into the soft flesh of the beast. It began to gallop, Erika's legs and head bouncing uncomfortably with each stride. She raised her warhammer with her left arm that hung free of the maw, attempting to bring it down on its back, but she lost her grip mid-swing, the weapon tossing from her hand and bouncing harmlessly off of the creature's back.

Her eyes went wide, gasping for air as she felt the jaws tighten over her torso, she felt warm liquid flooding down her neck, her side, and leg. Her vision started to fade. For a moment, the world went black, the sound of the creature's footfalls and breathing started to drown.

She could feel the warmth of its breath around her growing colder and the air around them held a similar chill. Her flesh felt more frigid than she felt in the water earlier that day, but somewhere inside, she felt a spark.

In the darkness, two burning eyes stared at her.

Urging her to fight.

A creature, like a fox in a wildfire, staring at her through a vast blackness.

Burn it to ashes.

A flame roared to life and she sucked in a massive breath of air, her vision returned in sharp clarity, the creature letting out another trill, this one sounding pained. She instinctively brought her free arm down, driving the bottom of her fist into the beast's forehead, the obsidian colored appendage causing a large scorch mark to strike across the grey scaled plates.

The grip around her loosened, and she was able to wrench herself free. Her legs felt numb, but she felt her arms and torso with more precision than she had ever felt before.

She didn't notice that she had successfully immolated her entire upper body. Obsidian skin with scattered orange lines running down to her waist, rising up over her chest, and back. Her entire face blackened with glowing eyes of magma. Her normally fiery hair blazing upwards in a very living and powerful flame, and her fists amplified with the energy of the flame within her.
She raised herself up and out of the jordhak's mouth, striking her fists down in rapid succession, the force of each blast cracking the beast's natural armor and crushing into its flesh underneath.

She felt a rage in every strike, every pummel, and every slam that halted the creature's rushing pace and pounded it into the ground.

Incinerate it.

She wrenched herself from the dead creature's maw, and stood weakly, her legs not fully answering to her call. She looked down at her form, realizing the new level of power that she had suddenly attained, an adrenaline filled grin of satisfaction crossing her face at the discovery.

A moment later though, her strength fell. Her body returned to soft, pale flesh. The crimson lines on her arms thickened, and dim new ones suddenly formed on her midriff up to her neck and her face.

She fell to her knees, the figures from before finally catching up to her.

"Gods the armor is hot, get it off!" one said, as if from a league away from her.

She felt hands tentatively touching her flesh like one would a tea kettle that may still be scalding. Two straps of her crushed breastplate came loose, allowing her to breathe in again. The cool night air rushed over her bare breast, her tunic turned to ash in the jordhak's mouth.

"We need to get her to Valk." said a feminine voice. "He's the best at treating bruising and internal damage."

Erika tried to look around but her vision fully faded, as she drifted into unconsciousness.

†⸝

Teria held her bowstring taut, ready to sling an arrow at any other creatures in the vicinity. The jordhak was obviously very dead, but with the wildlife acting as strange as it was, she wouldn't be surprised to see another creature on the horizon, attracted to the commotion.

She glanced back, relaxing after a few moments and staring at the young woman who had just fallen into unconsciousness.

"What the Hells was that?" she asked, her dark eyes drawn to the woman's strange tattoos that decorated her naked flesh as Selbor pressed rags into her bleeding wounds.

"Likely an Elementia blood." Selbor grunted as he lifted the muscular woman in his arms. "Ignis, to be more precise."

Teria scowled slightly. "Can't say I'm read on that one. Usually spent more time on Daemonology and the history of the Chaos Age myself."

The older ranger scoffed. "Of course you did. You always did like dead things."

She scowled harder, following him to Sildenfeld as the other two jogged away to retrieve the woman's pack.

"Elementia bloods are exactly what they sound like." he explained, trying to hold the injured woman steady as he walked. "They control one of the elements, usually a hereditary thing. As they use their abilities, they develop these markings."

Teria leaned around his broad shoulder at the woman, observing the tattoos again, with closer scrutiny. "Think she meant to burn all her clothes above her waist?

"I don't think she meant to burn anything." he replied with emphasis. "Adrenaline probably prompted the transformation. She might be young enough to not have even known of her heritage, or just hadn't used it much at least. The way the tomes always described it, it usually happens by accident or in extreme circumstances, especially if it skips a generation. Not that we know anything about her parents"

Teria looked back to the mutilated jordhak.

Definitely extreme. she thought.

† †

Zyrxak glided to the arcane circle he had formed nearby the stone pedestal that carried the thick tome. The thralls throwing several corpses into the center, the blood oozing from their bodies and filling the lines of the circle. The runes began to glow an eerie red, as the forms of the dead slowly heated. Their clothing burned to ash, while their flesh burned and melted into the ritual. Their bones soon snapped and exuded a foul smoke as they cracked into nothingness.

The circle opened up, the stone vanishing, replaced by a dark ooze that seemed to steal the light from the surrounding area.

A massive claw protruded from the portal, grasping the edge and digging into the stone bordering the pit. The creature pulled itself up, revealing a hideous head with a jackal-like snout, jagged teeth and bone exposed to the open air. Large ram-like horns curled back from behind the burning yellow coals that lay where its eye sockets were in its grotesque skull. Only the bony skull lay bare, the rest of its torso was wrapped in thick muscle tissue that sparked eternal embers. Its cloven hooves stepped out of the portal and it stood, towering over the floating specter, looking around at its new surroundings.

A moment later, it bent its knee, bowing low before its summoner. Zyrxak clapped his skeletal hands together in a disturbing applause.

"You appear as mighty as ever Xarvix." the specter said in his hissing voice.

The impossibly muscular Daemon stood tall again, turning its head to peer into the second story window of a nearby building. "The Hells are much kinder to our kin than the eternal prisons. Though they are not so eternal judging by your presence here before me."

"Indeed. It seems we may have allies that are sympathetic to our cause in this realm after all. Allies that are able to break the Consecrations."

Xarvix turned to the specter inquisitively. "Who are these allies you speak of?"

Zyrxak shrugged. "Alas, I know not. Although I fail to see their importance at our present time."

"What is it you would ask of me then, Elder?" the muscular Daemon seemed to have some contempt in his tone.

Zyrxak ignored it, as he pointed with a skeletal hand to the north. "Across those mountains lay a settlement far larger and formidable than this one. Messengers were dispatched to warn them of my coming, and I do not possess the confidence that my releaser holds the conviction to end them, nor do I possess the hubris to believe that I can take this settlement alone."

Zyrxak grinned maliciously, remembering the man who had so readily divulged the information of the settlement. The destination of the escapees becoming obvious with that knowledge.

How delicious that human's soul had been.

Xarvix turned to the mountains. "Understood. I will crush the humans underfoot. Long may thy reign, Elder Zyrxak."

The beastly creature began walking towards the mountains, each step leaving a lingering flame in his wake. Zyrxak chuckled slightly, ecstatic that he would finally be able to focus on his own strength now, and not have to concern himself with the escaped humans. The specter's gaze drifted to the sea that lay in the west, its fingers clicking together in a joyful expression. Even that band of humans couldn't possibly be a bother for him now.

A thrall brought another human to him, dragging them by the leg. Zyrxak leaned down and retrieved the appendage from the slave, and raised the human in the air. He opened his jaw and sucked the little life left from the pitiful creature, their scream drowning as their essence vacated their body and entered the maw of the Daemon.

How delicious these souls were indeed.

† †

Irvine arrived in the city of Sildenfeld. It was much grander than Valen, with more stonework buildings, and wider streets that seemed to go on for miles. A hard wind blew overhead, billowing the dark green standards that bore the city's symbol of the Bundled Arrows.

He walked around, twisting in circles and gazing at the busy streets around him. Soldiers donning armor, workmen sharpening weapons and fletching arrows.

The entire city appearing to be readying itself for war. The tone of the streets was of intense unease, whispers and murmurs spreading through about a second Daemon War, and the ramifications of such an event. Irvine searched around, puzzling over the situation, wondering if someone else had escaped Valen and warned the city ahead of him. Bells echoed out from the temples in unison, sending a deep resonance that rattled his bones throughout the city. He stared at the nearest tower, muttering to himself. "Those are warning chimes, why are they ringing at the same time?"

He suddenly heard a voice from behind him, low and gruff. "Won't do them any good. The Angelus are done with this realm."

Irvine turned sharply, looking for the man that had just spoke to him, finding no one closer than ten feet to him. He shook his head and blamed his lack of sleep the previous night for his possible delirium, as he continued closer to the Hall of Choice.

"Irvine!" he heard a voice cry out, this time familiar, ahead of him. He looked up to the balcony of the Hall, seeing Sárif Vlësk waving to him from atop the second floor.

He waved back. "Good morrow to you! I come bearing grim news from Valen!"

The sol elf's face darkened. "I am aware, though it seems the news has preceded you. Come, I will fill you in on the details inside."

Irvine nodded and made his way into the great hall, the doors opened by attendants, as several soldiers followed a large bearded man with decorative armor out of the building. Irvine turned to watch them pass, recognizing General Atrosby. The older man stared at Irvine harshly, though Irvine didn't see a need to avert his gaze from the uniformed soldier. A roll of thunder rang out in the distance as he passed. Irvine snapped out of his idle gawking, and excused himself into the building, thanking the attendants.

Sárif took Irvine in a warm embrace, not uncharacteristic of the elf, though this one was different. The mage lay his cheek atop Irvine's head, both hands gripping his back tightly. "I am sorry to hear about your uncle, Irvine." he said as he released the young man.

Irvine's expression turned sour. "I am sorry too, Master Sárif. I know he was an old friend of yours."

The elf nodded. "No word on Versal?"

"I did not personally witness him fall, so I still hold hope that he is aiding in the continued evacuation. If I may ask, who informed you of the Daemon?" he asked.

Sárif smiled. "Versal's daughter, and to my understanding a good friend of yours, Erika."

Irvine's expression lightened dramatically. "She's here? When did she arrive? What happen-"

Sárif held up a thin finger to halt his questions. "Very late last evening, she was badly injured but very alive. I visited her several hours before sunrise and she told me of the entire ordeal. Thankfully one of our most skilled clerics, Master Valk, was able to heal her with haste. Though her endurance expired quickly, and she fell into a rest not long after."

He could see Irvine's increased breathing, and could practically hear his racing heartbeat. "I will take you to her. You should know before you see her though, she was nearly killed by a jordhak, and her injuries show that. The sight may be a shock."

Irvine swallowed the lump in his throat. "No, I would very much like to see her."

Sárif nodded gently with a smile. "Very well then."

As they started out of the hall, Irvine looked to the elf, who began to chuckle lightly, Irvine meeting him with a confused expression.

"I apologize." he began, stifling his laughter. "I hadn't realized just how smitten you were with her from your uncle's letters alone."

"I can't say if she feels the same." he stammered, his face flushing red.

The elf gave him a knowing look and a sly smirk.

15
DRACONIC INTERVENTION

The smell of lavender and honey filled the air. A gentle breeze drifting through and rustling the tapestries and vines that decorated the walls. Men and women dressed in white moved to and fro attending to the few individuals that lay in beds through the hall.

Erika's eyes opened slowly, the hazing blue sky above greeting her with its cool glow. She barely remembered the night before after her battle against the jordhak. She somewhat recalled that she had told a sol elf, whom she didn't know, about the Daemon in Valen, but was unsure of what all had transpired. The individual was incredibly bright visually, having golden hair and deep amber eyes.

She wondered if it truly had been the night before that she had successfully immolated her upper torso, or if it was several nights in the past. It certainly felt as if she was asleep for an extended period of time. She glanced around the room, seeing the nurses moving around and attending to the other sick or wounded further into the infirmary. Each of them clad in white garb, patterned white bandannas holding back their hair, which framed their faces in an almost angelic light. She looked down, seeing herself dressed in a loose-fitting white shirt, with what felt like a soft skirt over her legs under her blankets. Her upper torso was wrapped in thick bandages from her collarbones all the way down to her sternum.

She attempted to brace her arms behind herself, pushing herself up, but gasped from the pain of the puncture wound in her right shoulder and promptly fell back into the bed. A nurse rushed over quickly, urging her to be more careful, but assisted her in sitting upright. Erika asked her where she was, and how long she had been there, the woman giving her a warm smile and explained.

"You're in the city of Sildenfeld, Temple of Phanel, you arrived here late last night. The Willow Rangers delivered you here. You took quite the beating it seems." she said, reaching out and tenderly placing her lithe fingers on Erika's shoulder. She winced slightly expecting a twinge of pain, but a warm sensation radiated from her hand, soothing the pain in her muscle.

Erika looked down at the bandage, slightly stained in crimson. "What did ye do?" she asked.

"I possess the ability to cast minor healing spells. I am no true cleric, but I can ease pain and hasten the natural process." she said with a smile. "Do be careful though miss. You have several worse wounds than that lower down on your torso. Your armor could not stop all of the creature that attacked you."

Erika returned the smile, thanking her for her help, before the nurse excused herself and left her bedside. She looked up to the sky above the open rafters of the building she sat in, appreciating the respite, but itching to return to her feet and find Irvine.

† †

A short time later, Irvine followed Sárif through the doors of the medical wing in the Temple of Phanel, the sol elf holding out his arm in a guiding gesture. He followed the path and found Erika sitting on one of the hospital beds, staring to the open sky.

His eyes widened, and tears began to well in his eyes, as he saw the stained bandages covering her upper chest underneath the wide collar of her shirt. She sat peacefully, eyes drowsy and wandering, her hands resting gently in her lap. Her thick, muscular arms similarly wrapped in bandaging halfway down to her elbows. Past the wraps, curious red markings decorated her skin, covering the flesh all the way to her fingertips, like those of her father, but different. Her auburn hair draped past her shoulders, giving a sharp contrast to the loose white shirt she wore, along with the same markings on her face and neck, though these were much fainter.

Irvine's eyes continued to dampen, though no tears fell. She had never looked more beautiful to him than that moment, though she also seemed more vulnerable than he could have ever imagined. Her head slowly moved towards him, her eyes becoming more alert as she saw his battered form, caked in dust and grime. Their eyes met, each of them failing to utter the first words.

Sárif glanced between the two with a smirk, clapping Irvine on the shoulder and whispering in his ear. "I believe she feels the same."

The graceful elf promptly glided from the room, the door closing gently behind him.

The rest of the world seemed to drift away around Irvine, all that remained was her in front of him. They had only been apart for a short time, but it seemed like he hadn't seen her for an eternity.

She raised her arms slightly, smiling warmly. "Ye'll have to come to me. I can't move much."

Irvine broke out in a laugh, as he walked forward to sit on the side of the bed, wrapping his arms around her in a gentle embrace. He could feel her breath on his neck, her hair tickling his nose, and her hands gently stroking along his back. He felt a sudden wetness on his shoulder, knowing that he wasn't the only one losing tears.

"I thought I'd lost ye." she said in a shaky voice.

"I thought the same, after Sárif said you had a close call with a jordhak." he replied as calmly as possible, though he realized it wasn't very calm at all.

She laughed. "Aye, stubborn bastard he was."

She pulled away from him and wiped her hands across her face. "Got 'im in the end though."

Irvine crossed his arms. "I see you used some of my tricks to get down the waterfall too."

"I'm glad ye taught me. Not sure what I would've done after ye fell." she said, fidgeting with her hands slightly. "What happened with the assassin?"

He shook his head. "He was no assassin. Simply a thief who was in the wrong place at the wrong time. I don't think he's any threat to us now though." he retrieved the weapons from his satchel and set them at the foot of the bed.

She laughed at the display. "Aye, I doubt those spindly little arms o' his could do much without a weapon. I could take 'im, even now." she lifted her arm and flexed slightly, wincing at the pain.

Irvine put his hand on her arm, gently gesturing her to put it back down.

"I'm sure you could." he said with a smile. "You should rest up though. I'm sure Sildenfeld could use a talented blacksmith in the coming days."

He eyed the strange markings on her arms, Erika's eyes flashing at the recognition. Irvine found himself putting his fingers to her cheek, tracing the fainter lines that ran along her cheekbones.

She grabbed his hand lightly, running her calloused fingers over his skin. The touch was rough, but he never wanted it to stop.

"I'll explain everythin' later, alright?" she nearly whispered.

He gripped her hands back before standing. "I'm going to go see if I can help in any way."

She nodded hesitantly, but held his grip as he turned away, pulling him back and gesturing for him to come closer. He leaned in and she planted a kiss on his cheek whispering lightly to him. "Just be careful Irvine. Please. I can't be losin' ye again."

He nodded back to her and squeezed her hand gently.

"Get some rest." he said with a smile, then departed from the room. He lightly touched the spot on his cheek where her soft lips had touched.

As he left the temple, he glanced into the small storage room next door to the infirmary. The attendant sat in a small wooden chair next to a desk, reading a thin book. Irvine searched around for a moment, eventually spotting Erika's bag, and the heavily damaged breastplate resting atop it. The metal was bent inwards, with two holes lining up with the stains in Erika's bandaging.

Irvine winced at the sight, the same voice from before, calling from behind him. "The elf did say she was nearly killed. She was lucky to survive that."

Irvine twisted around at the sound, once again finding no one.

"Sir?" he heard from the storage room, turning around to find the attendant looking at him confused. "Can I help you with something?"

He shook his head. "No. Thank you. I was just looking to make sure my friend's belongings were here." he pointed to the bag and armor.

"Ah, yes, the red-haired girl. Judging from the damage, I'd say she was lucky to survive that." the man said.

Irvine squinted, unsure of the situation suddenly. "Indeed. Thank you, please let the clerics know to contact me if she needs anything."

151

He nodded. "Will do. Shall I put you down as her spouse, mister?"

"Columval." he answered. "Irvine Columval. Not spouse though."

"I'll just put you as the spouse, it'll put you on the first word." he said, scribbling down Irvine's name on a parchment.

"Right. I'll be back later." he said with a resigned sigh, and waved to the attendant as he made his way out of the temple and into the streets of Sildenfeld.

Shortly after, he found Sárif speaking with a solider he didn't recognize, the two discussing something that seemed important. Irvine paused for a moment, the elf catching his eye and finishing his conversation quickly. He stepped over after patting the soldier on the shoulder and smiled at the young man. "I trust the young lady was ecstatic to see you?"

Irvine rubbed his cheek lightly. "Yeah, you could say that. I was wondering, two things actually."

The tall elf raised an eyebrow, his angled eyes widening. "Anything I can help with, just let me know."

"Actually, I was wondering if there was anything I could help with, but also, if anyone knew where the battle happened with the jordhak last night?" he asked tentatively.

The voice called again. "I'm interested to see as well. Curious what she did to it, after what it did to her."

Irvine spun around in response, Sárif giving him a confused look. "Everything alright, Irvine?"

"Yes, sorry. Just hearing things, I think. Nerves are getting to me probably." he replied.

"I see. Well don't push yourself too hard, and let me know if you require aid with anything, please. I'll retrieve a ranger to take you to the battle site." he started to turn and walk away, but paused a moment. "Irvine. Do not go if you are not comfortable with it. It is never easy to see things like that."

The courier nodded. "I know. I'll be fine. Thank you for your concern though."

The elf smiled at him, holding a finger in the air for him to wait there, and stepped off to find a ranger to guide him.

† †

It was a decent distance from the city walls to where the chaos began. Soil and sediment scattered around the area, stray traces of crimson in the trampled grass. The female ranger that escorted him stood a distance back from him. He recognized her sharp, angular face from a previous experience, but couldn't say they had become fully acquainted.

"I doubt I need to tell you who the blood belonged to." she said in a monotone that surprised him, considering the normal friendliness of her order.

He did not reply, but grimaced at the amount of the dried ichor that remained in the jordhak's path. Following through, he found a massive section of the grass that was scorched, nearly to ash, several yards from that, he saw the crumpled form of the beast itself.

Stray arrows protruded from the corpse, several broken. As Irvine approached, he looked down, observing the grass blades that were scorched along the path. The body itself was also burned all along the front side. The hard skull was completely caved in from what seemed to be a bludgeoning weapon, though it didn't match the head of her warhammer. The traces of this great fire suddenly caused his heart rate to accelerate, and he felt a sweat brimming on his brow. He thought back to the last moments in their fight with the thief in the forest, of how her forearms took on the same smoldering obsidian as her father's torso during the battle with the Daemon.

She said she would explain later. he thought to himself, a nervousness filling him that he couldn't explain.

He searched around the area, tracing the path of the jordhak backwards, wondering where her warhammer lay now, being as he didn't see it with her belongings at the temple. He strode a distance, nearly to the taller grass again, and finally spotted the metal of the haft reflecting the sunlight.

He retrieved the weapon, glancing over it and admired the weight of it, when the voice returned yet again. "The beast was not killed with this weapon."

Irvine didn't bother turning around this time.

"My thoughts exactly." he said cautiously. "So how did the jordhak sustain such massive trauma to the head, when it possesses such a thick natural armor that many ork tribes dare to hunt the beasts for?"

"The scorch marks around the wound suggest an Ignis blood." the voice replied.

Irvine shook his head in disbelief at his conversation with seemingly nothing. "And what is an Ignis blood, O great voice in my head?"

He glanced back to the dark haired ranger, hoping that she couldn't hear his conversation with the thin air around him. He was relieved to see her looking out at their broader surroundings, gripping her bow and nervously fingering at the bowstring.

A chuckle sounded out. "If you know not of Elementia blood, nor of who I am, then it seems much of the past has been lost to this world."

Irvine squinted, looking around for an answer to this strange situation he found himself in. "Would you like to educate me then?"

"Frankly? No. However if you are to be our vessel, then I suppose it cannot be avoided."

The word 'vessel' stuck out in Irvine's mind, his eyes flashing to his hand. He turned his back to the ranger, the voice chuckling again. "It seems you are a clever one at least."

He slumped his shoulders. "So, am I talking to the one from the cave?"

"You're talking to a Dragoon of the Daemon War boy. Show some damned respect." the voice called out, a ribbon of orange light drifting away from his hand and swirling in the air a few feet from him. A moment later, a humanoid figure appeared before him, much of his body covered in crimson scaled armor, the same as the vision that he had seen. Irvine glanced back to the ranger, prompting the new individual to put out a hand. "Ease your nerves, she cannot see me. Though I'd wager an order of rangers may actually remember my kind."

Irvine couldn't make out any details of the figure's features, hidden behind the helmet that encompassed his face, but he bore an intimidating stature, reminiscent of a solider.

"I am a Dragoon from an age long past, and you are our vessel." the man said bluntly.

"You keep saying 'our'. What do you mean?" Irvine replied with matching tone.

"How prevalent is magic in this age?"

Irvine raised an eyebrow. "Mages are rare, save for Distoll, and the academy there. Clerics use holy spells of the Gods."

The man scoffed. "So, you know little of the old magics then."

"I suppose, but what does that have to do with anything?" Irvine said defensively.

The scaled man held up his arm, a long, jagged lance flaring to life in a show of flames and into his waiting grip, causing Irvine to recoil. "Dragoons are bonded with the soul of a Dragon. The Dragon was named Arcera, the Flame Dancer. My name as a human was Jarthrak. Together we are Arce"Thrak."

Irvine marveled at the weapon, and the Dragoon

"Now is the part where you name yourself." Arce"Thrak said with a degree of annoyance.

"Irvine Columval." he said nervously.

The Dragoon nodded. "Irvine Columval. You have now been bonded with Arce"Thrak the Dancer. Take this power forth, and use it to slay the Daemons that walk your world."

Irvine glanced back up suddenly. "Me? I'm no soldier, how can I do anything against those monsters?"

"You possess the power of two of the greatest warriors of the Daemon War. We now pass that power to you. Destiny brought you to my chamber of waiting, and destiny will see you through to the death of the foul beasts that have returned once more. I shall guide you to the best of my ability." Arce'Thrak said, holding the great spear out to Irvine.

Irvine began to reach for the weapon, as flames began to erupt from it. Dancing around his and Arce'Thrak's forms. He fell back in panic suddenly, his primal fear of flame returning with extreme potency.

The visage of the Dragoon fell away.

The ranger rushed over to him, a look of concern on her face. "Are you alright?"

"I'm fine." Irvine replied, his voice shaking from his racing heartbeat. His consciousness had briefly escaped him when he was suddenly enveloped in those flames, returning him to that dreadful night so long ago.

The ranger lifted him back up to standing and placed her hand on his back, ushering him towards the city. He paused a moment, to retrieve Erika's warhammer, his gaze falling to his hand once he had picked up her weapon again. A warmth permeated his palm and a cold sweat began to envelop him.

The woman impatiently urged him onwards, insisting that he see a cleric as soon as possible. Irvine looked back at the dead jordhak, its skull crushed inwards, and imagined the amount of power needed to achieve such a feat. He felt himself starting to shake, his affectionate feelings for Erika suddenly clouded by the fear of what she had never told him.

16
PRIMAL FEAR

Irvine walked back into the temple infirmary, this time being entered as a patient.

He saw the ranger he was with speaking to one of the clerics, surely informing him of his panic in the fields. He hardly thought all this was necessary. He tried to talk to any of the nurses, but all of them hushed him promptly. He was redressed in the customary white clothing of the temple, his traveling gear taken to the storage room.

Shortly after, he found himself in the hall, several beds down and across from Erika, who wore a distressed expression at the display. She was unable to garner any attention to inquire of the situation though.

Irvine avoided her eyes, shamefully, but also somewhat fearfully. His gaze locked onto the markings that were so similar to her father's. Visions of the flames surrounding the Smithmaster's torso, and Erika's arms engulfed his head. Rationality wanted nothing more than to listen to Erika's explanation, but the fear of the primordial element forced him to distance himself.

His discovery in the field had taken time to set in, his thoughts distracted by the ghost of the Dragoon. Though after the revelation of the fiery power that was offered to him, as well as the realization that a similar power had felled the jordhak, the understanding of the situation began to weigh on him fully.

It seemed to him, that Erika had been hiding something, though he still didn't understand what exactly that was. Two nurses began an examination of him, checking his eyes and ears, testing his reflexiveness and muscle strength, as well as overall responsiveness.

One did the physical examinations, while the other scribbled loudly on a parchment backed by a wooden tablet. The scratching sound of the quill tip on the wood under the paper bore into Irvine's mind, amplifying the confusing thoughts and feelings that he was already experiencing.

He suddenly heard the teasing names of the children back home. 'Firestarter' and 'flamemaker' being the prominent two. Their teasing calls echoing in his head, at the notion that he started the fire that claimed his own parent's lives. How could they have believed that? What child would do such a thing?

He noticed Erika, arched forward in her bed and calling out, her face wincing in pain as she leaned forward, until another nurse went to her and quieted her, though she didn't seem comforted by her words.

Finally, the examination was finished, and the two nurses sat him back in the bed, covering him and urging him to stay put for the time being.

He could hear Erika's voice, pleading his attention over and over. He stared at the sheets in front of him, trying to find the words to respond to her, though none came. His mouth gaped open, all sound failing to emit from his throat, no matter his efforts.

Her voice started to sound shaky, and he wondered if she had started crying. Guilt washed over him, his emotions locked in a chaotic stalemate of wanting to assure her that everything was fine, yet also fighting with the fear of the aftermath he had witnessed. He felt like he was a child again, freshly rescued from the burning building that had destroyed everything close to him, unable to do or say anything. His chest started to ache with an intense pain. He reached a hand upwards and pressed it hard to his breast, hoping that the pressure would help subside the feeling.

Erika finally gained the attention of another nurse, though Irvine couldn't hear their conversation past the ringing in his ears. The same cleric from the hallway, a stocky man with a clean shaven face, drew a curtain in front of his bed. His last glimpse of Erika saw her with wide eyes and a wet face, an expression of apology and some shame washing over her.

The man exhaled deeply through his wide nose, turning and laying Irvine down fully. He began running his hands across Irvine's body, issuing his own examination of him, checking each of the more fresh scars on his torso and legs, placing his fingers on his wrist to find his heartbeat and forcing his eyelids open as he peered deep into them. He called for fresh bandages a moment later, and carefully wrapped his more recent wound on his forearm from the gryphon. After he finished not long after, he motioned for Irvine to sit back up again, and pulled up a small stool to sit beside him.

"My name is Valk, I'm the head cleric of this temple. Tell me, what happened in the field?" he began in a deep, but gentle voice.

Irvine swallowed nervously, the ringing in his ears starting to subside at the voice, but his body continuing to sweat and shake. "I was investigating the creature that attacked my friend."

The man pointed his thumb over his shoulder. "The Fjordling girl?"

He nodded, swallowing again.

"I see." the cleric began again. "I was actually about to see her next. See if I can accelerate the healing of those wounds she has. Quite the nasty experience it seems she had."

Irvine nodded again, unsure of what to say.

"So, Teria, the ranger that escorted you, she informed me that you searched the ground of the battle, finding the warhammer that the girl had dropped along the way, and shortly after, collapsed into the grass, nearly unresponsive."

"Yes. I'm not sure what happened." Irvine said nervously, partially lying.

The man raised an eyebrow. "I think you know more about what happened than you're telling me young one."

He tried to wipe the sweat from his face, but more quickly replaced it. "I don't know how to explain it."

"What is your opinion of fire, young one?" the cleric asked, retrieving a candle from the table and holding it up in front of Irvine, who responded by recoiling slightly. The man grunted in a manner that seemed like he had already come to a conclusion. "You fear it then?"

"Normally, small flames like this do not bother me." Irvine replied, still avoiding the tiny light.

The candle holder clicked against the wood table as the man replaced it. "And what did happen to the creature in the field?"

Irvine stared off into the curtain, flashes of the scorched corpse spinning through his mind. "Its skull was caved in. Some massive force had slammed into it, burning it in the process."

"And what is it that you think did this to the jordhak?"

Irvine's gaze focused on the curtain in front of him where he knew Erika to be on the other side. The cleric followed his gaze, exhaling again. "You would be correct."

The words made Irvine's stomach plummet, though he knew it already, hearing someone else say it made it more real suddenly.

"You need to speak with her of this yourself. Though to explain lightly, magic is a chaotic thing that comes from the realm around us, and beyond us. Clerics like myself are blessed with divine magic of the Gods, allowing us to treat the sick and dying, through increasingly complex prayers and hymns. The most common arcane magics come from the essence of our world, the more dangerous varieties from the realm of Daemons and others, making it a risky practice all in all. Although there is another type of magic in our world, that is less known, among others that is." he explained, Irvine looking back to him as he paused a moment. "Elementia blood, or elemental magic, is not of the Daemon realm, nor the Gods above, but is something in bloodlines. There are people born with the power to control one of the four prime elements: earth, water, fire, and air."

Irvine spoke again. "She is of the fire bloodline then?"

The cleric nodded. "An Ignis blood as they are called specifically. To be completely honest, I am somewhat surprised that such a widely traveled courier had not heard of this magic."

It was Irvine's turn to make a deep exhale this time, his nerves finally coming back under his control.

"Your name is written as her spouse." the man said with some surprise.

Irvine shook his head in response. "The attendant at the locker wrote that, saying it would put me as first contact if her condition changed at all."

"I see." the cleric said, nodding with a slight chuckle. "If it is any consolation, her condition will do nothing but improve I assure you."

After Irvine didn't reply, Valk continued his perceptions. "I assume you have some emotion towards her though."

Irvine managed a small smirk. "It seems everyone knows that except for her and I."

The man chuckled in response. "She asked about you constantly. 'Where is Irvine' she would say 'He should have arrived before me'. Though it seems she still beat you to our fair city."

Irvine felt his fingers fiddling. "It seems so."

"Is it because of this?" he asked, bringing his thick fingers to Irvine's palm. "I can tell there's a magic presence here. One that shouldn't exist."

Irvine looked up to the man's face, a seriousness pervading his deep eyes.

Valk sighed when he failed to reply. "Very well. You don't have to tell me about it."

The cleric began to draw the curtains back again. "You should really talk to her. She has done nothing wrong by being what she is, but she likely feels at fault for keeping this from you. Give her a chance to explain and reconcile this matter quickly, lest it damage your relationship more."

Irvine nodded, the cleric stepping out of the hallway and speaking to a nurse on his way out. Irvine looked back, Erika's face was buried in her knees. She looked up from the dampened sheets, and made full eye contact with Irvine.

He gave her a smile, as warm as he could muster, mouthing to her. *Everything is alright.*

She smiled back, wiping the tears from her cheeks and nodding back. Irvine laid back in his bed, closing his eyes and trying to clear his head.

Erika remained upright, refusing to break her gaze from his form. She resolved to explain everything to him as soon as she could. Her heart felt like it had cracked when he refused to look at her before, and she never wanted to experience that feeling again. Her eyes opened a little further, the feelings she had for the courier setting in even deeper. Everything had changed so much in the last days, but he was the one thing that had remained the same, and she vowed to keep it that way. She sat back, resting against the headboard behind her, and continued to watch him rest. She stared at his face, still shimmering from the nervous sweat that he had been experiencing.

I love him. she thought to herself suddenly, though she couldn't bring herself to say it out loud.

The late afternoon air had begun to darken slightly, as thick grey clouds continually grew overhead. A rolling thunder echoed through the city, sending a chill down her spine.

† †

The hallways creaked slightly with the changing of the wind. The house had been built long ago, though it had a certain ancient beauty to it that Sárif had enjoyed since he had first laid eyes on it, back when he, Feldran, and Versal had first visited this city so many long years ago. He walked through the long hallway, hands clasped behind his back, and pondered the situation before him.

"Stress does not look particularly good on you." a voice called out from a doorway to his left.

Sárif paused. "Yet I have willingly entered myself into the game of politics in our fair city."

F'Skar, the dark skinned aash elf stepped forward into the dim and waning sunlight, taking Sárif's hands in his. His ebon skin drastically contrasted with his short cut, ivory hair. His red on black eyes gleamed in the reflections of the windows. He wore a flowing robe of silver, equally contrasting with his skin in the same way, the sleeves falling open to reveal his slight arms more used to painting than any physical labor. He stood only slightly shorter than Sárif's tall stature, though his weak musculature caused him a smaller frame.

"I suppose it is a good thing that I love you for your sense of humor then." he said, gently patting Sárif's cheek.

The two shared a laugh at that remark. Sárif admiring the smooth skin of his mate's lithe fingers. "Troubling times await us."

"When in an era of peace, the smallest changes feel like troubling times." F'Skar mused.

"Yet the change now lies in the form of a Daemon resurrected by Gods know what." the golden-haired sol elf said with a sigh.

The aash began walking down the hallway, Sárif keeping pace alongside him. The leisurely steps a common thing for their daily conversations.

"Perhaps things are not as dire as they seem though." he began, attempting to calm his golden skinned counterpart. "Perhaps the beast still lays weak from its imprisonment, and all it will take is one fell swoop to rid the world of it again."

"I envy your optimism my love. Unfortunately, I fear it will take more than a simple 'fell swoop' to defeat this foe."

The roll of thunder rumbled through the house, creating eerie echoes that made F'Skar shiver slightly. "Whatever it takes. We will prevail. We are stronger than we ever have been."

"Peace breeds complacency though." Sárif said dryly.

"Peace breeds hope, for a return to peace." F'Skar replied curtly.

The golden-haired elf smiled, bringing his brow to his mate's, enjoying the last light the day had to offer.

† †

Teria tapped her foot on the pavement, once again impatient for what was to come.

The waning light of day always seemed to drag on forever to her. She wished the sun would just vacate the sky quickly, and leave the cooler light of the moons to do their duty.

She much preferred the night. She preferred the relative darkness that her perceptive eyes could navigate better than most. She preferred staying out of sight. Away from the civilians of the city, and content with her own company. Granted the night usually meant most of those civilians were tucked away in their beds, and couldn't bother her anyhow.

The chill air of the autumn breeze fell past her cloaked form, hood pulled over her dark hair. She rested her right hand on the top limb of her bow, in similar fashion to a cane, her other hand resting on her hip between the scabbard of her left side blade and the quiver that hung from the back of her belt. Despite her relaxed appearance, her muscles were taut, ready to whip the bow upwards and loose an arrow at anything that dared come near her.

She prided herself on being an unflinching sentry when needed. Yet she still flinched when her partner revealed himself. The thin ranger clicked his tongue annoyingly. "Shame. No lady of such beauty should be alone on such an equally beautiful evening."

Teria slumped after her initial reaction. "Why are we here, Farris?"

"Because Mistress Varia specifically requested me." he answered with a hint of satisfaction.

The young woman rolled her eyes at him, unbelieving of how any ranger could possibly be so smug. Especially when he held information that likely held extreme importance given the current circumstances.

"You are aware of the news I assume."

Farris bowed low. "You would be assuming correctly."

He quickly righted his posture, though his customary slouch held, and held a grim expression on his snake-like face. "I won't pretend to be pleased about it though."

Teria regarded his tone curiously as he continued. "I know how you and the other rangers see me, as a revolting weasel who is good for little more than messages and curt remarks."

The woman nodded her assent, unable and unwilling to stop the weasel in his confession.

"Yet, I am still a Willow Ranger, and the presence of a Daemon poses a threat to the balance I have sworn to protect, as have you."

The two stood in silence for a long moment, Teria slightly taken aback at Farris' sudden change.

He eventually spoke again. "I have learned the error in my ways. My coyness with information has led to serious trouble with the entire world, and I have already volunteered to accept my fate from the Mistress."

Teria followed him as he began walking to the west, his boots landing silently on the cobbled stone beneath them.

"I had known of an unsavory group of individuals in the city. Not the thieves' guild mind you, but a different one. One that is almost more concealed than the elusive former."

Farris slinked around corners, and swiveled his head almost nervously, but Teria recognized it as his own form of alertness. She couldn't help but be a slight bit impressed by his perceptive eyes, avoiding every gaze that befell them while also speaking in controlled bursts for fear of listening onlookers.

"I do not know their full agenda, or operation, as I had only just begun investigating them on my off-time in the city. I suspected something was strange about them, but I was too casual in my approach, and now I believe they are responsible for releasing that Daemon on Valen."

Teria's dark eyes widened, and she upped her pace to walk abreast with the roguish man. "What are you saying, Farris?"

He stopped suddenly, and for the first time that she had ever known, he made full eye contact with her. Strangely it made her feel more uneasy than when he was ogling her legs.

"I know who they are Teria. Daemonologists. Worse yet, a full-blown cult." he said darkly.

Teria nearly fell backwards at his statement. *How could a cult still exist?*

"The last of the Abyss Seekers were eliminated nearly three decades ago, and no cults remained after them. Even if a group was planning to release a Daemon, it would be for selfish reasons, perhaps a ploy to gain renown in their own twisted way. Surely the plot simply failed, and the foolish party was eliminated by the very Daemon they sought to slay or enslave." she argued.

"The things I have heard dispute that theory, Teria. As loath as I am to say it." Farris' eyes began darting again.

She suddenly began thinking about the courier that she had escorted outside the city. Her keen ears had heard him talking to himself, but she couldn't discern the importance of that, if there was any.

"Point is, we need to find their operation, and shut it down quickly. I'm not foolish enough to think that you and your impeccable aim could fell them all, or even the both of us together." he continued, snapping Teria back to the task at hand. "The Willows need to know, but carefully. I don't want this cult catching any wind of this."

† †

The sun had fully set, and the darkness had begun pervading the space around them. They made their way to a rooftop and were discussing where to start, Farris informing her of the possible whereabouts he had heard.

He motioned to the western edge of the city, the largely ruined sector of the city that had befallen a great fire many years ago, and unfortunately never recovered. Many of its buildings still stood, dilapidated and unused, and warily referred to as the 'Burn Ward' by the locals. Everyone always thought they were unused, save for by spirits during Shadesfall perhaps.

"The burned section is largely avoided due to a multitude of ghost stories, and a general distaste for the, frankly ugly, sight. Making it the perfect outpost for an unsavory lot." Farris explained further.

"Or, it could just be another hideout of the general thieves' guild? What makes you think there's anything special about it?" she shrugged.

Farris sighed. "Because I have an informant in the thieves' guild, and he blatantly told me that there are no operations out of the Burn Ward."

Teria raised a thin eyebrow. "Does Varia know about this?"

"No." he replied curtly.

It was her turn to sigh now, and she made sure it was drawn out enough for him to get the hint. "So where are you wanting to begin?"

Farris settled back slightly, and pointed off to the western area, and began to speak.

Teria put a finger up to him when a glint of light caught her peripheral. Her eyes went wide and her jaw locked at the sight. Farris followed suit shortly after.

A massive shape climbed over the mountains, engulfed fully in raging flames. It leapt down to the lower altitudes, the flame growing brighter as it landed with an echoing crash.

"I don't think that's a good sign." Farris uttered quickly.

Teria had no time to agree. A flash of light flared outwards, and a blink later, the city shook with a massive explosion against its walls. The flaming creature made its way onto the grassy hill that bordered the mountains, and overlooked the city.

The two rangers recovered from the shockwave of the impact, and quickly started back to the south plaza.

"Your cult will have to wait it seems." Teria said grimly, still staring at what could only be a Daemon threatening her home.

17
ASSAULT ON SILDENFELD

The alarm bells rang. First a sound from the southernmost watch-tower, followed by another, and another, and another, until finally the entire city echoed with the sounds of bells.

The soldiers rushed to don their armor and strap their weapons to their sides.

The rangers filled their quivers and tightened their bow-strings.

The civilians evacuated to the temples for safe harbor.

Irvine awoke with a start at the sound. He had heard them only once before, several years ago when a tribe of orks had attacked the city while he stayed after a delivery. He had aided the military by acting as a scout, helping to the successful repelling of the enemy forces. It had been a stressful time, and Irvine learned to treat the orkish people with more care in the future. Their strength was staggering, and Irvine was still amazed by them.

Though this time was different.

This time, the bells sounded louder, more erratic, more panicked.

He leapt to his feet, throwing his sheets off of himself and starting out of the medical wing. Erika awoke slowly, protesting at his departure.

Irvine quickly stepped back to her side, kneeling down beside her bed.

"Stay here. You still have to recover from the healing magic, so whatever is happening, I need you to stay here." he said, fixing his eyes on hers with a deadly seriousness.

She nodded slowly, the display waking her significantly. "What's going on? Are ye alright?"

"I'm fine now, I'm sorry for earlier. Something is attacking though. Those bells are the alarms across the city, used to alert the guard and military forces. I'm going to try and help." he explained.

Erika shook her head. "No, ye have to be safe too!"

He took her hands in his. "I will be, don't worry."

Erika gripped his hands tightly, resisting his effort to leave, but losing her hold when her shoulder flashed with a devastatingly sharp pain.

"Just come back." she pleaded quietly, fighting back her tears at the physical pain, as well as the thought of him leaving her again.

Irvine nodded, laying her back on the bed and dashing out of the hallway.

†⊦

The attendant was missing, Irvine bouncing on his toes impatiently, looking around for a sign of anyone to retrieve his belongings from the small room. After finding no one he groaned in annoyance, deftly leaping over the counter. He winced at his sore muscles, but recovered and skipped over to his satchel. He quickly stripped out of the temple clothing and dressed in his traveling gear, prioritizing haste over privacy.

He startled at the sound of clattering objects behind him, turning to find Erika, who accidentally knocked the decorative items from the countertop. He started to protest her being out of bed, but she cut him off. "My bag, in the bottom, take the armor!"

Irvine gave her a confused look, but obeyed, grabbing her pack and digging through her various supplies. Eventually he found a metal half breastplate much like her own, along with bracers and greaves.

He looked back at her. "This isn't your backup? Will it fit me?"

She shook her head, her face reddening slightly. "It's yers. I made it for ye. Planned on givin' it to ye when yer birthday came around, but obviously I didn't get the chance. Thought it'd be a good thing to grab before we ran from Valen though."

"Thank you." he said, admiring the craftsmanship he had come to expect from her work, but snapped back to reality and started to fix the pieces over his arms and boots. He pointed a stern finger at her. "You get back to your bed."

She nodded, still using the counter to support her lethargy, but smiled at the sight of him strapping the armor to his chest.

Still, she worried over what the night would bring.

††

The first sounds Irvine could hear were the same that he had heard that last night in Valen, screaming and the roaring of flames. Civilians rushed past him, making for a rough wade towards the exterior of the city.

He eventually arrived at the large wall that separated the buildings from the open world around the city, and was met by a solid hand slamming into his chest. He stumbled back, looking up to the solider that had halted him.

"You don't need to be here, boy." he said in a gruff tone.

"I can help, I'm a courier, just give me a weapon and I can scout the outskirts of whatever force is coming towards us." Irvine replied.

The soldier seemed to hesitate, glancing around as if he were waiting for Irvine's parents to come and claim him.

Irvine grew irritated. He felt an impulse suddenly, jabbing quickly at the man's shoulder. "There's important things to be doing right now!"

The solider turned back to him with an infuriated expression, looking as if he were ready to throttle Irvine. That anger faded quickly though, when he looked up to find Sárif stepping behind Irvine and placing his hand on the courier's shoulder.

"To your post man." he said calmly, but firmly. The soldier giving a hesitant, but obedient salute and returning to his company. The elf turned Irvine around. "Are you well?"

"Well enough to help with whatever is happening."

"I'm glad to have you then. Here." Sárif said, handing Irvine a small stone with a hole bored through it, a slight vibration emanating from the smooth object.

"It's a sending stone, I have the paired one, so just speak into it and I'll hear you."

"Where am I going?" Irvine asked

"Westwards and southwards, around the bulk of the enemy, we need eyes on whether or not there's more than one Daemon."

"It is here?" he asked, somewhat panicked. Sárif held up a hand to calm him.

"Not the specter that attacked Valen, this is something different, but we need to make sure he's alone before we launch a counterattack, which is where you come in."

Irvine nodded his understanding, accepting a sword from the smith apprentice that was handing out weapons to the militia that were reinforcing the city walls. Irvine had to reroute though when he found a section of the wall completely blown to pieces, workers moving furiously to get a barricade up.

The fields burned around the feet of the eerie walking skeletons that Irvine recognized from the attack on his home.

He did his best to distance himself from the memories, not wanting to revisit them at such an inopportune time. He dashed alongside the wall, quickly and quietly, hearing the thin whistle of arrows flying through the air, followed by the dull thuds of them meeting their targets.

He occasionally found stray thralls clawing uselessly at the walls. He was careful to avoid their gaze, before efficiently slashing through the base of their necks, felling them as fast as he could. He found it odd that even the ones that appeared more flesh-like didn't bleed.

Eventually he felt that he was far enough away from the bulk of the opposing force and started out towards the enemy lines to the south.

He dashed as fast as his legs could carry him across the fields. The tall grass allowed for decent cover anytime one of the creatures came near after he reached it, though it did make for slower progress. He spoke into the stone periodically to report his progress, though he felt somewhat foolish at first. Sárif speaking back to him eased the oddity of the experience though, showing Irvine that the device did work, and proving its usefulness, especially when the elf would warn him of nearby monsters that he hadn't seen in time. Enchanting objects was a kind of hobby for the sol elf, and he had an incredible talent for it, often enchanting weapons or armor. The process was expensive and taxing though, having a monetary requirement in the form of supplies that fueled the enchanting itself, as well as the mental focus required to do so.

After a while he began to hear the sounds of real battle, coming from the hole in the walls far behind him, as the soldiers began to pour out with their war cries and singing steel. He took some measure of comfort in knowing that it would likely relieve some of the pressure on him as he made his way around the opposing force.

†♱

Erika stared at the hallway that Irvine had run down, partially wishing he would come back around that corner. She wasn't actually disappointed when he didn't. It only fueled her own urgency.

She looked around, taking note of the nurses attending to the waking patients as the sounds of chaos erupted from the city outside. She took her chance, crawling roughly over the counter and slowly walking to her own belongings in the room.

The cleric had healed her wounds nearly fully, but the shock of the injuries still remained, the man assuring her that the scars would stay for the rest of her life. She had shown him all of the scars on her arms and other places on her body from her work in the forge, telling him that she didn't mind scars, though he still seemed worried about her.

"These scars are not occupational. These are from a dangerous situation that could have claimed your life. Some dwell on them and go mad." he had warned. "Just make sure you seek help from loved ones and professionals if you need it."

She took a breath, grabbing her pack and unloading her clothing. In similar fashion to Irvine not long before, she tore the loose white shirt over her head and dropped the skirt, valuing expediency over privacy. She paused a moment, regarding the new tunic that was neatly folded into her belongings, her memory flashing back to the night she had arrived in the city and the swift end her previous tunic had met. She wasn't sure how she had attained such a sudden surge in power from her innate magic, and wasn't sure if she could do it again. Doubt started to fill her mind, and she worried if she could even help Irvine, or if she'd be a detriment to him like before.

She shook her head, pulling the new tunic down over her head and her old tattered grey skirt around her waist. Once she had her boots on, she grabbed her warhammer with some protest in her shoulder and made her way back out of the room.

Outside she found the streets nearly empty, the sounds of battle ringing out from the south gates. The smell of burning wood and grass wafting heavily through the air.

She started making her way towards the gates as quickly as she could, finding more strength in her legs as she covered more ground, thankful for the healing that the cleric and nurses had done for her.

She tried to stretch her shoulders out and rid herself of the stiffness from the injuries, wincing as she twisted about. She laughed to herself slightly, seeing the irony in her telling Irvine not to do anything too risky, and here she was making an escape from the hospital.

The night was cold, the chilled breeze working its way underneath her clothing and into the fresh scars below, causing them to ache more, though it wasn't enough to stop her from the task at hand.

Eventually, she found her way to the walls surrounding the city, grabbing a spare full breastplate from one of the stockpiles that was unattended, and strapped it onto her body, wincing again as it constricted down on her sore spots and pinched in several fleshy areas under her arms. She was so used to her own armor that was more form fitted to her, wearing a generic piece made her uncomfortable due to how loose it was over her. She wondered how it fit on the average soldiers, being as her muscular frame was nearly as large as the men she saw nearby who bolstered the defense of the city.

She made a detour around the soldiers, making her way to the next gate to the east where there was less of a presence of guards and fighters, but some still keeping watch for enemies.

A guard held his hand up to her. "Halt! No civilians are permitted outside the walls at this time."

"Good, I'm not a civilian." she said, tapping a knuckle on his armored chest as she passed.

He grabbed her by the arm, though he struggled to stop her strong pace. "Ma'am, I'm sorry, but I cannot allow you past these gates."

She stared at him, her green eyes lighting up with annoyance. A moment later, the guard recoiled with a pained gasp, his hand sizzling as if he had placed it on a hot stove. Erika glanced down at her arm, placing her own hand over the darkening spot of her flesh to hide her unintentional immolation. The other guards moved in quickly to inspect what had just transpired.

"What in the Hells did you do to me?" the man yelled at her, the others grabbing him before he could draw his weapon.

"Sir, she's a just a girl." they said, attempting to calm him. Though he seemed far from calm. Erika glanced around the area, her eyes flashing back to the open gateway where she found a large gap in the guards, large enough for her to get through. The man she had unintentionally burned wrestled free of the others, finally wrenching his blade from its scabbard with a metallic screech.

"You are not leaving those gates!" he said, still infuriated. "Your life ends out there, it'll be on my head!"

Erika backed up towards the gate, her eyes locked on the aggressive guard. She could feel her time and her options dwindling quickly. In a panic, she held up her left arm towards him, arching her fingers upwards in a claw as she willed the arm to flush into flames. The embers exploding from her flesh caused all of the guards to jump back.

"I'm needin' to get out there, he needs my help." she growled back at the guard.

"You're a Daemon!" he shouted in a sudden panic, charging forward with his weapon raised.

Erika reacted, lunging forwards and grabbing the blade in her burning hand. She felt the sting of the edge digging into her palm, but it failed to cut all the way through. She twisted her body like she had seen Irvine do in his fight against the thief, throwing the sword from the guard's weakening grip and reversed her momentum, slamming her palm into the breastplate of his armor. The impact sent him flying several feet backwards, the display stunning the other guards for a moment. Erika saw her chance, sprinting out of the gateway and into the burning fields. She could hear the heavy metal gate dropping behind her as she ran, barring her from the city.

† †

Irvine crouched behind a solitary tree in the grassy field. The creature ahead of him was, in a way, more terrifying than the one that had attacked his home and killed his uncle.

This one was massive. Blackened, burning muscle wrapped around its frame, exuding smoke and embers by just standing there. Its skeletal head twitching back and forth as if it were surveying the battle in front of it, its teeth appearing to be curled into a sickening smile. Irvine leaned back against the tree and spoke into the magic stone, informing Sárif of what he had found.

"Irvine, do not engage that creature!" the elf called back, though louder than Irvine had expected.

A crack of lighting resounded past the Daemon's head as its gaze snapped to the tree Irvine hid behind.

"I see this realm still has rats." the monster spat, Irvine's eyes widening at the realization that he had been discovered.

He heard a loud crunching sound, like twine being snapped a thousand times, followed by the sound of something hurtling through the air. Irvine instinctively leaped to the side, rolling as he landed. A massive ball of earth crushed the tree into the ground and scattered back into the grass. He looked back to the monster, meeting its glowing eyes instantly.

Irvine hissed a curse, and muttered into the stone. "Don't exactly have a choice." before dropping it into his belt pouch.

He drew his blade, standing before the Daemon as his heart raced.

He had no plan, no method to defeat a monster like this. He wondered if he could even get close with its constant burning state, as his internal fear began to claw at the back of his mind, making him break into a sudden cold sweat.

"There you are little one." it laughed, sending a chill down Irvine's spine.

"I am Xarvix, the Scorned!" it called to him proudly.

Irvine thought back to his experience with the Dragoon spirit in the field, wondering if he should introduce himself as well. The Daemon seemed to care little though, as it suddenly charged forwards, kicking up massive amounts of earth with its cloven hooves as it launched.

Irvine felt a heat across his face and back as he leapt to the side again, the monster careening past him. It spun on its hooves, halting its momentum surprisingly fast for its size, and faced him again.

"Spry one you are! Are you able to retaliate?" he asked, sounding genuinely curious.

Irvine barely made it back to his feet with his shaking legs, thinking that the creature charged similarly to the bovine tauruni people. Another crack of lighting flashed to the side, causing Irvine to flinch from his thoughts.

He felt an impact on his chest, knocking the wind out of him as he flew backwards and landed in the burnt ash that lay in the once-grassy field. He opened his eyes to the sky that suddenly opened up in a torrent of falling waters, like the heavens were weeping at the display before them.

The swell drenched him instantly, stinging at his eyes, and gagging his throat.

The dull ring in his ears faded, the sound of the rain echoed around him, alongside the heavy footfalls of the creature stalking towards him.

He sat up with some difficulty, letting out a string of coughs that sent a thick mixture of blood, rainwater, and saliva down his chin.

The Daemon seemed to be enjoying himself, casually strolling towards him as he cracked his knuckles menacingly. Irvine stood slowly, regaining his breath and balance, wiping the red liquid from his face.

He reached into his pouch, hoping to call back to Sárif while the creature stalled, but found crumbled gravel in the bottom of the leather pocket. He rolled his eyes at his damned luck, wondering when or if anyone would come to help him. The sounds of the distant battle barely audible through the drowning rain, singing ill tides for the expediency of any reinforcements.

"I actually expected this world to be different. A different landscape. More or less trees, higher or lower mountains." the Daemon said, twisting around and raising his arms to gesture around himself. "Different than when we and the Dragons walked this earth. Different than when the Angelus rained razors upon my brethren. Different than when the Titans still roamed."

"Must bring a tear to your eye, reminiscing like that." Irvine replied, biting back his uncontrollable fear of this massive and intense adversary.

"Nearly!" Xarvix laughed, waving his arm out towards the spires of Sildenfeld. "Though you humans are the same as you ever were. Weak of stature, and short of life. Though I see that ambition has still never failed you. Your cities are larger, your population grown exponentially. Likely due to the absence of the Angelus though, you can now breed freely."

Irvine raised an eyebrow in confusion. "What are you talking about?"

"Do you not know?" the Daemon said, turning to Irvine with a surprised tone. "The laws the Angelus forced upon you mortals? They limited your numbers. They feared your kind, though I know not why."

Irvine stared at the creature, trying to measure if he was lying to him as the stories said of Daemons, or if he actually spoke truthfully.

"You know not what started the Daemon War?" he asked. "Tell me, small one. Is it not better to live under an iron crown of power absolute with freedom understood, than to live under a guise of false leaders and ideals?"

"I'm afraid I don't understand your question, Daemon." Irvine replied plainly.

The Daemon hissed. "The Angelus lied to your kind boy! My kin bled for you!"

Irvine flinched as the creature's tone rose into a low rumbling scream, his fists pounding against his chest each time he spoke of his fellow Daemons.

"Bah! Sick irony that you believe their damned lies all this time later!"

"Your kin destroys the innocent!" Irvine yelled back, gripping the handle of his weapon till his knuckles ran white. "My home was razed by your kind! For no reason other than amusement!"

"Zyrxak claimed your settlement, that much is true." the beast said, his tone lowering again. "You must ask yourself something though. Which is the lesser of two evils?"

"And you believe your kind to be the lesser evil?" Irvine asked, skeptically.

"I suppose the world did choose its favor already." the Daemon growled in response, casting a sidelong look at the ground below him, before snapping back to Irvine with a puff of air out of its nasal cavity. "Time to die little one!"

Irvine grounded his feet as the creature bellowed a great roar at him, the sound echoing in his ears and his bones long after it had finished.

Xarvix dropped to all fours, charging him with a relentless aggression. Irvine steeled his nerves, trying to ignore the blazing flames licking at the rain around the monster's shoulders, and ground his boots into the mud.

At the last moment, he spun. Moving out of the path of the Daemon, and swinging his weapon downwards with all his strength. The resulting impact felt like striking a stone wall, the metal skirting off of the hardened flesh with a piercing ring.

He turned to face his opponent again, another crack of lightning illuminating the resulting cut that he had made in the Daemon's side. Orange ichor dripped from the shallow wound. A claw reached down, gathering a drop of the liquid and brought it to the Daemon's face. A long black tongue snaked out from behind the jagged teeth, curling around the finger and lapping at its own lifeblood.

Irvine swallowed hard at the disturbing sight, but gritted his teeth.

He bleeds, he can die. he repeated in his mind.

The beast began to turn back to him again, but paused a moment, turning towards the city as if some drastic change had happened. Irvine followed his gaze, his eyes widening as he found what the Daemon had noticed. Erika standing in the rain, her soaked hair sticking to her face and neck as she stared at the creature before her, emerald eyes wide and unblinking.

Irvine's stomach fell, failing to choke out a scream as the Daemon stepped towards her.

† †

Erika stood, partway between relief and terror at the Daemon standing before her that was distinctly not the one that had attacked Valen.

Her eyes drifted across the thing's muscular body, spotting the small wound just below his left ribs. She regarded the intimidating aura that flooded from the creature, and glanced to her companion. The breastplate she had personally made for him was scorched and dented from an obvious impact. Blood stained his chin and the front of his armor over the black marks.

Her jaw set firmly.

She sprinted forward, determined not to be helpless, determined to be the one to save Irvine from this monster. The creature widened its stance, seemingly welcoming the assault. Irvine dashed forward as well, hissing another curse.

She held her hammer in her left hand, swinging her right arm as she ran. The Daemon raised its right fist in the air and punched out straight towards her. She screamed at the top of her lungs, immolating her arms to her shoulders and meeting the beast's fist with her own.

A shockwave of heat blasted through the air, slowing Irvine's progress by nearly knocking him from his feet. Erika twisted around the massive fist, grabbing her warhammer with both hands as she skipped forward and slammed it into the Daemon's knee. It buckled forward at the powerful strike, groaning in pain while also chuckling in eerie amusement.

"Finally! Xarvix gets a real fight!" he shouted. "The boy was beginning to bore me!"

He swung his left claw around, Erika reversing her warhammer and bashing the Daemon's swipe away. The two began a close-quartered brawl of sheer strength.

She dodged two strikes and brought her hammer in for another slam, while also parrying the Daemon's massive claws and fists at every other opportunity. Her rage and emotions carried her through the battle, though she knew in the back of her mind that it wouldn't last forever.

Irvine stared at the battle, trying to keep track of Erika's movements, dreading the moment that her boot slipped in the mud, or the Daemon was able to slip a strike past her defense.

He took an opportunity as soon as it arose, dashing forward and kicking off the back of Xarvix's legs, climbing up onto his shoulders. The flames flickered up towards him, causing images of his burning home to flash through his mind, the image of his mother and father's flesh melting from their bones. He forced the memories away, focusing on the flashes of red hair below him, the beautiful Fjordling woman that was desperately fighting a battle that no one person could hope to win.

He reversed the sword in his left hand, gripping the pommel with his right and driving it downwards towards the base of the Daemon's neck. A slight movement put him just off target, plunging the blade into the shoulder just off from the spine, the beast howling a graveled scream. A claw reached back, grabbing Irvine and throwing him off of his back. The blade remained in the creature's flesh though, orange blood oozing from the wound.

Erika called out to Irvine as he flew over her head, but knew she couldn't afford to check on him now. She used the distraction, raising the hammer's head into an uppercut under the Daemon's chin, knocking the massive creature onto his back with an earthshaking slam.

She leapt onto its chest, heaving the hammer over her head and striking it downwards at Xarvix's skull, as if piling a stake into the ground. Each arcing strike was met with a guttural cry from the Ignis woman, and ended with the sound of iron on bone. Over and over it crashed down, Erika taking grim satisfaction in the cracks that began to form in the ivory surface.

Finally, the burning yellow eyes seemed to blink out of existence, and the Daemon's body fell limp underneath her. She tossed her head, slinging the wet hair from her face as her chest heaved with labored breath. The warhammer nearly slipped from her weakening grasp, but she held it with all determination as she slid off of the Daemon's body.

She turned away, calling out to her companion again as she walked into the darkening rain. "Irvine! Are ye alright?"

A groan answered her. "I'm fine, just be caref-"

The words caught in his throat with a choking breath. "Erika! Turn Around!"

Blazing flames illuminated the field from behind her. Erika moved to turn, but was cut short.

Xarvix raked his claw across her back drawing a pained scream from her lungs as she hurtled forward and onto the ground. The breastplate straps caught on the claws and wrenched from her body, talon-like fingers digging deep into her flesh, and flinging the ill-fitted armor from her. The Daemon rose, gripping his head with his other hand and laughing into the falling rain.

Irvine's eyes went wide, the spray of crimson was a deep red, one that her hair had no hope to match, the sight causing his guts to turn in knots as a scream finally escaped his lungs.

The Daemon's smug victory quickly faded, his gaze turning to the young man with an expression of horror.

In a hail of scattered dirt and earth, a visage of a gigantic Dragon of raging flame shot from Irvine's form, driving its massive front claws down with a murderous intent, spreading its wings in a fantastical display that lit the night like the sun.

"No! That's not possible!" Xarvix screamed as the Dragon flew towards him.

Irvine did not see the display, his eyes locked onto the monster in front of him with a hatred that he had never felt. The visage of the Dragon melted into Irvine's form and he felt a warm presence in his hand, the jagged spear of the warrior roaring to life in his hand.

"You are a Dragoon Knight?" Xarvix asked incredulously.

"We, are a Dragoon Knight." Arce'Thrak proclaimed, proudly standing behind Irvine's shoulder with arms crossed. His form clad in the thick armor that looked to be made of dragon scales, two fiery wings jutting from his back, twitching with an excitement.

The Daemon let out another roar, beginning a hard sprint forward with claws bared in desperation. Irvine felt a tap on his shoulder.

"Fly." the knight whispered.

The wings pumped behind him, thrusting his body forward at a staggering speed.

Xarvix couldn't retaliate in time.

He brought the lance to his side and with a guided aim, impaled Xarvix's skull between his burning eyes. Irvine's boots landed hard on the Daemon's clavicles as he crushed the weapon further into the monster's cranium.

A gurgling screech echoed through the field, deafening the soldiers that were just then cresting the hill of the battle. They gawked at the display before them, shielding their eyes from the blinding light of flame that enveloped Irvine and the Daemon's form.

Cracks burst all along Xarvix's muscled body, his orange blood flowing freely from the wounds as the light became brighter and brighter.

Xarvix's time was at an end. His body exploding outwards in a column of fire that stretched upwards into the sky, halting the rain around them with its shockwave, and boring a deep crater into the earth below.

Irvine was thrown to the ground next to Erika, his vision fading as he reached his hand towards hers, steam rising from his flesh. She lay motionless, in a pool of crimson that rippled as the rain began again.

18
Recouperations

The column of flame was visible across the mountain range and into the valley that the ruins of Valen resided in. Zyrxak glanced up at the display, his glowing eyes narrowing as a low rumble resonated from his rib cage.

"That damned imbecile!" he screamed aloud after a moment, gripping another passing thrall by the head and squeezing until its skull shattered onto the ground below in a rain of muck, the skeleton body crumbling to the ground unceremoniously before turning to ash.

He had meant for Xarvix to be a distraction to the neighboring city, but hadn't expected him to fall this quickly.

As the light that marked the Greater Daemon's grave faded, Zyrxak snapped back to his temporary home. He regarded the last of the corpses on the heated stone dais, the final remnants of the bones crushing into ash under the heat.

Staying in this ruined settlement would be folly.

He would soon have to either pursue the runaway civilians of this town quickly, or make his way elsewhere. He knew that even if the messengers hadn't told the neighboring settlement of his presence, the attack by Xarvix would be an obvious tell.

"Time to get the lay of the land then." he muttered to himself, blasting a geyser of energy beneath himself to propel his form upwards, high above the ruined rooftops. His gaze lingered in the direction that the refugees had gone, before he spun around, looking to broaden his options.

Finally, his senses fixated on another town, just barely smaller than the one he had already taken with relative ease.

"Unlikely that two neighbors would both have Elementia blood of considerable strength." he reasoned aloud. "Time for more."

† †

"The Greater, Xarvix, is dead madam. It seems Zyrxak sent him as a probing force, though I doubt he expected this to happen." the hooded figure spoke quietly. The room was illuminated by dim candlelight, smelling of incense and burning herbs, though all of it had a foul odor. A grey-haired woman with wrinkled skin raised her hand from the back of the room.

"Zyrxak is cunning enough. He will find an alternative soon enough." her sutured eyes furrowed slightly. "Then again. Perhaps he could use some assistance. Provide a distraction in the coming days. Do your best to make it a crippling one."

The hooded individual bowed low, stepping out of the chamber and closing the thick wooden door behind them.

The woman took a deep breath, sucking in the heavy smoke that permeated the room, exhaling again after a moment. Her fingers ran across a wooden plank, a single thick fingernail digging into the grain and carving a rune into its surface. Blood ran down her finger each time she pulled away, and stained the wood where she had carved. She smiled eerily as she finished, seemingly unbothered by the wounds. The sigil came alight with a sickening green glow. She set it aside, atop the pile of other materials she had carved various sigils into.

She stood on shaking legs and supported her weight on a cane, stepping towards the doorway of the chamber, deciding that it was time for her to see for herself how much damage the Daemon had wrought in his short siege.

† †

Teria stared at the pair, still unconscious. The same young woman she had been too late to save from the jordhak, and the same young man she had escorted to the creature's corpse. So many strange occurrences, all involving these two.

They were obviously acquainted at the very least. That much was obvious at his request to see the site of her battle so quickly after arriving in the city. She'd met him before, but couldn't quite place his name out of all the Couriers she'd worked with in the past.

The woman was completely unknown to her though. She knew that she was an Ignis blood, from Selbor's explanation when she arrived, but had little to go off of besides that. She found herself drawn to the woman though, and those intricate markings that had darkened even more on the bare flesh of her arms since last she had seen her. Deep crimson fingers stretching over her clavicles and up towards her neck where they became more transparent. Even Teria had to admit, she was a beautiful woman, and the faint markings that outlined her face and jaw seemed to elevate her appeal.

"How are you this morning Teria?" Valk spoke beside her suddenly, causing the young woman to startle slightly.

She grimaced at the fact that he was among the few that was able to consistently surprise her, and he wasn't even a ranger.

Her eyes glanced to the priest. His eyes appeared sunken, and his hair seemed even more tattered with grey than she had remembered.

He looked incredibly tired.

"I'm fine. Thank you." she replied after a moment.

The much older man smiled warmly, his eyes squinting nearly shut as he gave her shoulder a firm but gentle pat.

"Thank you for taking the time to bring these two back to me. I'm afraid I hadn't quite finished healing the girl, and the boy was in here for the psychological reasons as you know." he explained, seeing the curious look in the ranger's eyes.

"What are their names?" she asked, her voice barely audible in a hushed whisper.

Valk smirked slightly. "Irvine, and Erika. They come from our gentle town of Valen to the south. That is where the talk of Daemons has originated. It is by their bravery that we know of this crisis at all."

Teria nodded, taking care to etch the names in her memory.

Farris came in from outside the temple and stepped to her side a moment later, quietly speaking as if to no one at all. "I did some digging while you held off the assault."

Valk seemed to step away, but Teria could tell he was still listening as he shuffled various medicines around on a small cart.

"I think I have more information, but I'm in agreeance with your sentiment before. We should inform Mistress Varia."

The young woman noticed Valk's head turn slightly at the Mistress's name.

Farris continued. "This organization is bigger than I had thought, and my informants are genuinely frightened of them. We need help."

She nodded to the wiry ranger, and he deftly stepped away without a sound. The priest quickly took his place as Teria still watched the two, fast asleep.

"She's doing well." she answered to the unasked question. "Still has a portrait of you in her office."

The cleric scoffed slightly. "Always hated that thing. Hated standing still for it too, but Sárif insisted on it for 'posterity'."

"Mistress Varia still treasures it." she interrupted, causing Valk to stutter slightly. His jaw set in a grimace shortly after.

"You really should go see her." she said, before turning with a deliberate flourish of her green cloak that was identical to the one her Mistress wore.

Valk watched her leave, his shoulders slumping with a drawn out sigh.

† †

Mist hung low around the walls of Sildenfeld, the early morning light causing an eerie glow all around. The southern gates bore scorch marks across them, the massive breach in the wall standing as a poignant reminder of what had transpired the previous night.

The massive sphere of flame had rammed into the wall, and resounded through the whole of the city. Sárif stood solemnly, looking at the broken and shattered stone from the outside. He could hear the commander of the guards screaming at the watchman assigned to the south tower last night, and the fact that they hadn't rung the bell until after the fireball had impacted the wall.

He couldn't help but smirk nervously at the situation. On one hand, the city was not even close to being overrun, and the casualties were just over a score, a far cry from what they could have been. Yet he knew how terrible things could have gotten had the Daemon pressed further.

He wondered why the beast didn't though, why it hadn't just charged the city itself. He glanced around at the fog that obscured the field from his view, nearly expecting another Daemon to burst forth and attack them all unawares. He shuddered at the thought, tugging on the coat that wrapped over his shoulders, though it did little to warm him during the grim time. The squelch of mud underfoot caused the elf to startle, turning around to find an elderly woman in deep purple robes stepping towards him, leaning heavily on a crooked cane. Only her face below her nose was visible due to the ornate mask she wore over her eyes.

Sárif bowed low, and scowled slightly as he did. "Madame Mipha. A delight to see you."

"And you as well Master Vlësk." she said with a curtsy that she seemed to struggle with.

"What brings you out to this gate on this early morning?" the sol elf asked, raising an eyebrow at the sudden appearance of the soothsayer, and hoping his disdain for her didn't bleed into his tone too much.

"I had heard the Daemon attacking the city in the night. I wished to see the damage for myself."

Sárif grimaced at her comment, wondering how she could truly 'see' anything with nothing in the way of eye holes in her decorative mask that may have well been a blindfold. Still, he gestured out to the fields. "Indeed. The creature itself was luckily slain on the hill just that way. By a young man and his companion no less, so nothing to truly worry about I say."

Madame Mipha scoffed, causing another raised eyebrow from the elf. "Luck is entirely right in that case. What of the two? Are they still among the living?"

"Yes. They are." he said with a resolve. "Both reside in the medical wing in the Temple of Phanel."

The soothsayer stalked the edge of the wall, running her wrinkled and decrepit hand along the jagged and broken stones. "I see. I'll be sure to pay them a visit. I am curious how they managed to fell such a monstrous foe."

Sárif looked at her bloodstained index finger curiously as he crossed his arms over his chest. "I'd say the young man was plenty capable. He's a Courier, and as such, faces plenty of errant threats along his treacherous routes."

"Errant threats do not tear city walls asunder, you as a mage of your ilk should know that well." she replied, almost threateningly. "These kinds of magics are much more than errant threats as you say, but rather weapons, ripe for destruction."

"Indeed. I know my particular flavor of arcana more than most." Sárif said flatly, quickly turning away. "If you'll excuse me Madame, I have other business to attend to."

She turned her head over her shoulder slightly. "Politics are sure to be daunting at a time like this. Do let me know if you require any assistance."

Sárif managed only a half smile back at her wide and broken grin, as he back stepped through the hole in the wall. Once she was out of eyesight he spun hard on his heel, his robes flying wildly from his waist as he upped his pace into the city. He found himself shuddering again, as he nearly always did after an encounter with that woman. Each conversation he had ever had with her felt like she was withholding information from him, like she knew a thousand things he could never comprehend. He hated talking to her for that reason, and as such, avoided her plenty. His pace quickened as he stepped further into the city limits, making a direct route for the Temple of Phanel as quickly as he could, and damning himself for divulging any information to one he trusted so little.

She would have found out eventually in any case. he thought.

On his way, he set up a grapevine of soldiers and rangers patrolling the city, and asked them to inform him immediately of Mipha's movements.

If anyone knew more than they should, it was her.

Sárif never liked when people knew more than him.

⸸

Irvine dreamed of flame.
Flames of life, not of death.

Their heat seemed subsided towards him, parting from the path that he walked.

Before him, was a massive creature of red scales, bright orange stripes lining her great shoulders and chest.

A Dragon.

He could feel her hot breath cascading past him as he stared at her in awe.

Beside the great wyrm, was a man, handsome in features. His dark hair was pulled back in a tight wrap that fell down past his shoulders, a beard holding neat and trimmed to his wedge chin.

The Dragon's voice resounded in his mind, gentle and kind. "I am Arcera, the Flame Dancer."

Similarly, the man spoke. It was a more familiar voice, deep and graveled. "I am Jarthrak, the bonded warrior of the Flame Dancer."

The Dragon stepped over Jarthrak, the two speaking in unison. "We are warriors of the Daemon War. Lost and forgotten to time, until such an event that a Daemon or Angelus may walk your world again. That time is now, and you are our destined vessel. You are the carrier of the last Crimson Spear. You now wield our power, the bond between Dragon and Man. Use it well, and destroy the invaders that walk this world."

Irvine looked down to his hand, the lance forming in a flourish of bright orange flame and embers. He held it aloft, admiring the size and shape, the jagged yet smooth nature of the weapon drew him in. Something in his mind settled as he regarded the weapon.

He no longer felt fear of the flames. Not like he used to.

"This lance bears the power to slay both Daemon and Angelus for eternity. As well as the power to seal them in a far-off realm known only to Dragons and few others, use this only in dire times." Arcera stated.

Jarthrak continued. "There may be a time when you find that everything you know and believe in is challenged. We were betrayed once, and we paid a heavy price for it. Trust in your instincts, and be the vessel you were destined to be."

Irvine opened his mouth as if to ask a question, but the dream faded. The flames flickered away, and the sight of the knight and Dragon blinked from existence as he fell through the world, and into the black void below.

† †

Irvine awoke with a start, sucking in a thick breath of air. The cool breeze of the familiar medical hall ran across his bare chest. It was daytime now, the leaves of autumn falling around the open ceiling of the hall from the thick oaks that hung over them. He looked to the bed next to him, seeing Erika laying on her front with nothing but new bandaging covering her torso from neck to waist. She sat up on her arms with some difficulty.

"Are ye alright? Ye were sleepin' soundly, then all of a sudden ye jolted awake." she asked with a concerned expression.

Irvine's gaze drifted to her back, none of her skin visible through the bandaging, but he could see the edges of the wounds she had sustained, staining the white cloth a deep red.

"I'm fine, just an odd dream is all. Are you alright?" he replied, turning his vision back to her green eyes framed in the faint crimson markings.

She smiled warmly. "Aye, I'm fine. It's painful to lay on my back, so they have me on my stomach while I rest. How're yer injuries? Ye took a nasty blow to the chest just before I got there. Lucky ye were wearing the armor I made for ye."

Irvine regarded his chest, noting the heavy bruising along his ribs. "It's sore, but I think I'm alright besides that."

"Damned right!" a shout rang out from in front of them, Valk crossing his arms with an infuriated look as he stomped to the end of their beds.

"I swear, the two of you are bound for death if you keep this up! Took four straight hours to make sure none of your ribs

194

stayed broken!" he yelled, pointing a wide finger at Irvine. "It's a wonder you were able to keep fighting. Must have had an astonishing amount of adrenaline pumping through your veins."

Erika chuckled quietly as she could, wincing at the slight pain it caused her, but startled when the man shouted again. "And you! Sneaking out of the hall before your previous wounds were fully healed! I was attempting to heal them as well as I could and leave you with minor scars, but those will be deep and very noticeable for the rest of your life!"

Erika bowed her head slightly, Irvine raising a hand to interrupt. "If I may, there were no attendants or nurses in the hall last night, where was everyone?"

"Attending to the wounded from the attack." the man said grimly. "Seven people were killed in the initial strike against the wall. Seventeen more died of lingering injuries, the last of them passed this morning."

Irvine lowered his gaze, Erika gently laying back down and hugged her pillow tightly to her breast, partly hiding her face in it to avoid the scolding priest.

"There were plenty more injured." the cleric continued. "Though I reckon it would have been much worse if the two of you hadn't killed the Daemon. There was an overwhelming horde of the skeletal creatures holding back our forces, so's to why you didn't receive any reinforcements till you'd already killed the thing."

Irvine nodded. "I understand. Sárif told me not to engage the Daemon, but he spotted me, I was left with little choice."

"Nothing to apologize for boy." Valk said, turning his attention to the Fjordling. "You, however young lady, do have something to apologize for."

Irvine's eyes snapped back and forth between the cleric, and Erika, who buried her face in her pillow even deeper.

"What happened? What did she do?" he asked nervously.

"She scalded a soldier's hand. He came in much later with heavy burns, and trauma to the chest." he said, motioning to a figure laying in a bed on the other side of the hall.

Erika's voice sounded out, though it was muffled by the pillow. "I didn't mean to."

"Did you mean to crack his ribs through his cuirass?" Valk retorted. "He started kicking and screaming when he saw you laying here, calling for 'The Daemon's head.'. Sound familiar?"

Erika nodded slowly. "I heard him when he came in." "Then you can apologize to him too. And explain what happened."

The suddenly intimidating man started to step away, calling back over his shoulder. "As soon as you're walking!"

After the cleric had left, Irvine looked up to the grey skies again. Turning towards the figure that Valk had motioned towards, then back to Erika, still buried in her pillow. He reached out with a heavy lean, placing his hand on her shoulder, and ran his fingers along her bandaged skin.

Her eye peeked out slightly, wet with tears. "I didn't mean to."

"I know." Irvine nodded.

"I had to help ye." she said, stifling a choke from her throat.

He removed his hand, but still leaned towards her. "How did you know where I was?"

"Ye had told us about a time ye worked as a scout fer Sildenfeld, I figured it might've been similar this time. I just never realized how much ye risked yer life when ye went away." her voice showing an obvious concern and sadness.

Irvine sat back in his bed. "Well, thank you. You did save me."

She took some pride in the statement, unable to contain her smile.

He paused a moment, trying to work out the next words. "You have some powerful magic."

Erika suddenly felt her heart skip, before beating faster, her breathing becoming erratic, worsening only by Irvine's sudden silence.

He shifted slightly. "Why did you never tell me about it?"

It took her several moments to find words to reply. "Papa told me about yer fear of fire when we were little. I always wished ye would apprentice with him, but knew ye couldn't. My fire didn't develop till I was fourteen, and Papa warned me to be careful around ye. Ye started bein' a courier a few years after that, and each time ye came back, I feared I'd lose control, and scare ye or worse. Feared ye'd leave and never come back. So, I bottled it fer a long time. I also knew that if I used it like Papa, it'd paint me with the markin's, and you'd probably question it too, an' I never would have an answer fer ye."

Irvine fell silent again, Erika felt an urge to scream into her pillow, convinced that he would never talk to her again after this.

Several moments passed before he found the words. "You were always my reason to come back."

She felt her heart nearly stop, she turned her head, seeing him staring at the foot of his bed as he spoke. "I considered staying here, or one of the other neighboring towns. To get away from the memories of the burning house, and the bullies who were convinced that I was the one who started it. But then I would never see you again. That's what kept me coming back."

"Would ye have come back if ye knew about my magic?" she asked quietly, afraid of the possible answer.

"I'd like to think so. It's not like you burned my family's home. And you're still you, Erika." he paused, thinking about the previous day. "Though I admit, when the realization of your abilities set in while I was inspecting the jordhak you fought, I didn't know how to feel."

She moved more of her face towards him. "How do ye feel now?"

"I feel like I'm glad you came with me." he replied, turning towards her with a smile.

She suddenly felt her face get hot, butterflies swimming in her gut as their eyes met. She smiled back and reached her hand out, grabbing his in hers and squeezing gently. "How long have ye had the portrait?"

Irvine turned red this time, starting to pull away, but Erika kept her grip on his hand. "I'm not upset about it, just curious."

"Around a year and a half. Your father gave it to me actually."

Erika's eyes widened, her face flushing further.

"He said that I needed to come back, that I was all you had."

She giggled slightly, wincing again at the pain in her back. "Aye, he was kinda right. Didn't have many friends besides ye."

"I didn't either. You were all I had as well. Now you really are all I have." he said, squeezing her hand back. Erika looked up at him, his gaze looking to the sky. A light rain had begun again over them, though the drops fell harmlessly away high over their heads as if on glass. She glanced up towards it to the best of her ability with the position she lay in, marveling at the sight of the water moving away from them.

"There's a magical barrier over the entire city. Keeps inclement weather out, which allows for a lot of the buildings to have open air ceilings like this." Irvine explained.

He smiled at her look of wonderment as the rain was washed away. A moment later, Sárif stepped hurriedly into the hall, jolting the two from their moment of silence, his golden hair disheveled around his face caked in stale sweat.

"What happened with the Daemon?" he asked with a stern look. "How did you kill it? I saw the tattoos on Erika's arms, was it her Ignis power?"

"I was able to fend 'im off, but Irvine landed the killin' blow, I was nearly unconscious for the last part o' the battle." she said, shaking her head as she gestured to her back with her thumb.

Sárif bowed his head. "I apologize, I did not mean any rudeness. Though I do need to know how the beast was finally killed."

"Likely due to this one." Valk said, approaching from behind the elf, gesturing to Irvine. "I had a hunch about the magic I felt from him. He holds the power of a Dragoon. Another forgotten magic."

Irvine sat still, looking back and forth between the stunned elf and the cleric. "Did none of the soldiers see the Dragon?"

He was met with confused expressions, both looking to each other with shrugs.

Irvine explained the battle to them, interjecting in the tale of how he had found the stone pedestal in the cave behind the waterfall. Erika added her confusion over the statement, and he explained the disappearance of the chamber after he had left. He continued with the conversations he had with Arce'Thrak, and how the Dragon made of flame had come to his aid in the battle with the Daemon, finally allowing him to strike the fatal blow.

Sárif took the tale in relative stride, rapping his fist into his open palm. "You may be our hope for a swift end to this catastrophe."

"Vlësk!" the cleric groaned loudly, before lowering his voice to a hush when a nearby nurse scolded him. "Don't place that kind of a burden on the boy. If he truly is a vessel, then yes, we will need him in the coming battle, but don't make him believe it's solely his duty to save us all."

The elf hung his head, his uncharacteristically messy golden hair draping down over his face. "Indeed. I apologize. Though I do need you to be careful, both of you. Madame

Mipha, the soothsayer seemed to know something regarding the two of you."

Valk scoffed at the name. "That old hag can't possibly know anything about them."

"Unless she does!" he pleaded. "It never hurts to be careful Irvine, watch your back. I don't know how these Daemons returned to our world with such force, but I fear Mipha knows more than she's telling me. She holds a position of power in this city by reputation alone, and when she acts curiously about anything, grim happenings usually follow. I fear she saw the two of you in a vision, meaning that you both could be in danger."

Erika sat up. "Master Valk, would ye mind tryin' to heal me a bit faster?"

"You'll be left with worse scars if I don't let your body take its time, Erika." he warned.

She stared at the deep scars on Irvine's back and sides, nodding her affirmation. "Scars are a small price to pay if I can help Irvine stay safe."

The cleric nodded, stepping over to her bedside and drawing the curtains. He looked to Irvine one last time. "She'll likely make sounds of pain. Healing is no easy thing for anyone. Trust in me though, I know what I'm doing, so give her privacy while we work at this."

Irvine nodded, smiling at Erika before the curtain was drawn completely closed. She gave him a determined look that seemed expecting of the uncomfortable experience already.

"I'll be careful Sárif. I promise. I'd like to accompany the troupe on the way back to Valen though, I want to help reclaim my home." Irvine said, looking up at the elf who had always been like another uncle to him.

The elf nodded, placing a hand on his shoulder before leaving.

Irvine was then left to the open-air hall, with only the sound of Valk's quiet prayers, and Erika's pained grunts and gasps.

19
RUMORS AND TRAGEDY

Teral stepped lightly through the hallways, keeping his hood low, and his cloak covering his leg. Despite the midday light, he could still avoid the majority of the temple staff. He could hear groans and slight screams of pain coming from one bed obscured by a curtain, the voice feminine and familiar.

Next to it was the young man he had taken over the waterfall. He stepped through the entryway quietly, his right arm hanging limply at his side, the shoulder still useless to him. He carefully eyed the young man's face, appearing as if he was sleeping, though the thief knew better. He dropped a coiled note on the foot of the bed, before pressing off on his leg, leaping through the open ceiling and out of sight.

The rafters were a much more comfortable place, but he knew he couldn't be complacent. He deftly made his way across to the adjacent rooftop, before a sound stopped him in his tracks.

"You really should get that arm looked at friend." the sly voice said, almost teasingly.

Teral turned with a frown. "Yet you know I can't go see a cleric with my leg like this. They ask too many questions."

Farris stepped out of the shadow. "And why not your home? Surely the guild has a healer?"

"Raven Mitrios asks even more questions." the thief said through gritted teeth.

The wiry ranger smirked. "Then you are in quite the predicament, friend. Perhaps I could put in good word for you with Mistress Varia, and maybe the rangers could heal you. Not as good as any right and proper cleric mind you, but still something."

"What do you want?"

Farris' smile disappeared in an instant. "You found the source of the Daemons, the Abyssal Hand. I commend you on this, but unfortunately, I need more, friend."

"I don't have any more, ranger." Teral said with a shrug. "Perhaps you should find a new informant."

"I already have other informants, friend, though perhaps you could help me in other ways."

The thief scowled further each time the shifty man said 'friend', but knew that with his injury, this one could easily remove him from every equation.

"What do you have in mind?"

"Simple." another ranger stepped from the shadows, a hand gently resting on the hilt of the blade on her hip. "Just kill any of the members that try anything against Sárif Vlësk or the cleric Valk."

Teral eyed her dark eyes, knowing the visage of death in them. He set his jaw firmly, grinding his teeth at how easily he had been cornered.

"Very well. The Abyssal Hand shall not touch them."

He started to turn, but paused, throwing a wrapped sword to the rangers. "Must've forgotten to give that back to the courier. Tell him that he was right."

Teria looked over the blade and nodded to the thief.

† †

Irvine opened his eyes, gently letting go of the dagger underneath his pillow. He winced each time Erika gasped, and despite the comforting words of the cleric, he knew she was undergoing continual waves of intense pain. He leaned over and picked up the parchment, slipping off the tie that kept it coiled and opened it. His eyes squinted at the scrawled writing, like it had been scratched with the writer's off hand.

The surviving townsfolk move north along the coastline, safe and well. Be wary of the Abyssal Hand, they move quickly.

Valk slid the curtains back at Irvine's quiet call, and took the note from him. Irvine glanced at Erika's naked back. The claw marks forming an imposing scar from her left shoulder to her right hip. Her skin was drenched in a thick sweat from the accelerated healing process. Her torso rising and falling with a gentle but heavy breath, seemingly thankful for the respite. She writhed back and forth, seeking some kind of comfort, and making Irvine wince at her pain when she moved too much.

"I'll inform Sárif and the rangers that they were right to expect this thief of yours." he said with a grimness.

Irvine stared at Erika, who again had her face buried in her pillow, causing a sadness to wash over him. "I just hope he realizes how much damage he's done."

Valk nodded quietly, looking back to the young woman and gently wiping the moisture from her skin with a small towel. He reached to the ground and produced a small flask, taking a deep draw from it, and looked back to Irvine.

"More work to be done. Try and rest young one." he said as he drew the curtains, and began his low prayers again.

Erika's pained gasping followed soon after, and Irvine wondered how he could possibly sleep while knowing the pain she was in.

† †

Teria, Farris, and Selbor slipped into a back alley behind the Willow Ranger Hall, Teria having stowed the courier's sword in her personal belongings, and Farris having talked Selbor into aiding them. The wiry ranger regarded the two with amusement as they adjusted their disguises.

Teria wore a wig of red with a civilian's dress and shawl. Selbor was fitted into am ill-fitting tunic and trousers, which to Farris' surprise, made him appear slightly smaller in stature. The two of them looked incredibly unhappy and uncomfortable, and Farris could barely contain his laughter at their expense.

Farris had everything planned out. Rumors spread among the underground that a courier and a woman with red hair had felled the Daemon from the night before, and were to be celebrating their victory with a night on the town. Some of the best sightseeing spots in the city were of course, scarcely patrolled, and young lovers often enjoyed the private places away from the rest of the world.

His rumor mill had traveled fast, and two of his informants that had never met gave him nearly the identical story. So, if the Abyssal Hand truly was making to revive Daemons, then it only made sense for them to remove the two responsible for killing one.

The two to be used as bait had plenty of qualms about this, but Farris encouraged them to no end. He told them that their disguises were fine, especially once the evening began to fall, and individual features were harder to pick out. Though he did warn them, the rumor did include the two young Daemon killers to be happily involved, and that a slight bit of affection may be in order to tempt any would-be assassins.

This brought Selbor to nearly striking the roguish man, but he assured him that it was all for the good of the city.

They finally came to their area of operation. A large bridge that spanned the open market of the city, though the market itself was largely closed for the day. The sunset in the distance made for quite the romantic scene over the skyline, the bordering fields, and finally the valley that met the sea.

Farris only wished he could freeze this moment, to use as convenient blackmail against the two Willow Rangers that quite possibly hated him the most. His post on a nearby rooftop was rather comfortable, though he lamented in not being able to hear his bait's conversation. He hoped they were selling it enough.

What does it matter if the assassins can't hear you professing your love to one another? he thought as he slipped a piece of a stale biscuit into his mouth.

His internal thoughts were interrupted as he noticed the two lean into each other, as if to share a long and heartfelt kiss. Farris nearly had to slap himself to stifle his entertained laughter. Though the thick wig and hood obscured the act, he wondered if they were actually following through with it.

A flash of movement came from the side, and his eyes darted. Farris' bow came upward and the nocked arrow slid back with the string silently. The dark figure came from behind Teria on the bridge, Farris genuinely wondering if she noticed him.

Of course she noticed him, she notices everything.

He held his aim carefully through the long moments as the individual wandered closer.

Just a passerby? he wondered as he watched them from over the broad arrow head.

All thoughts of innocence vanished when a silhouetted blade appeared in his hand. The disappearance of the sun was accompanied by the silent whisper of Farris' bow releasing its arrow.

††

F'Skar casually stepped through the open halls of his home. The building was in pristine condition thanks to the efforts of Sárif, and he was truly impressed and proud of his mate for it. The evening sunlight cast beautiful shadows through the great windows in its final moments.

He wiped the remnants of his latest painting from his dark hands on a small cloth, content with the work he had done that day. Despite the onslaught of a Daemon, life still continued, and due to the efforts of his sol counterpart and the young two that had killed the beast, life had continued still. He knew that they could accomplish anything, and even the Daemon that attacked Valen would soon fall. All would be put right in the world soon enough.

He paused near a portrait he had painted many years before, of his mother and father from the Shalti tribe so far away. His father's muscular bare chest showing the scars of his life, and his mother's sparse clothing worn and faded. Their faces, similarly, seemed cracked by the wear of time. He wondered if they truly looked that way when he had painted it, or if the painting itself had faded. Their crimson on black eyes followed him with sadness, and he had learned to expect that expression.

His kin were much different than he. An existence solely contained to the dark forest centers, and an existence that thrived on self-sufficiency. He had found himself much different than them at an early age. He was much weaker than them from the start, and had difficulty learning the ways of their people. His hair always stayed short, despite the proud manes of silver that other aash elves wore. Worse still, his flesh became cold, and thus he was forced to cover himself thickly despite the normally minimal clothing of the hot skinned aash elves. His bones became brittle, and he could not keep up with their incredible pace for fear of seriously injuring himself.

He figured himself doomed to a life of suffering, or an early death. Until Sárif came. The sol elf and his companions had stumbled upon the rare sight of the elusive aash elves when he was still an adventuring mage, and F'Skar found himself attached to the regal looking elf. It seemed Sárif had found a liking in the younger male as well, and had eventually come back after his journeying days were done. He offered a comfortable home and a chance to pursue an enriched life.

F'Skar found it hard to decline, and his tribe's approval surprisingly easy to come by. He found himself in this beautiful home not long after. The last time he had seen his parents, he gave them a portrait of himself, that he had painted with the aid of a mirror, to remember him by, and asked to paint them as well. He had successfully captured their intimidating gaze, and felt all the more pride for it. They had long ago returned to nature, though he felt at peace with that notion.

He also thought of his eldest sister, many years ago named M'Tara, and the Shalti tribe's newest shaman. Surely, she was the wisest they would ever know. She also helped care for their nephew and niece, F'Skal and F'Lessa.

He could still remember his last letter from his middle sister, J'Shala, detailing that the two young ones had chosen to take F' as their family name. They apparently had told her that they 'wished to be warm for uncle F'Skar'. He wondered how his sister's mate J'Kahn had reacted. He was a strong aash, though F'Skar feared over his drinking games.

He hoped he could see his nephew and niece soon. They could always make him smile. They were both in adulthood by now, and had likely received their dusting. He had regretted not being there for their ceremony, but still held some sadness of not being able to have his own due to his illness.

Though he did miss them from time to time, Sárif was plenty happiness for him, and he wouldn't trade that for anything.

His musings were cut short with a flash of lightning and a roll of thunder. Another thing that continually haunted him. The rain normally was simply a passing thing for the aash, their hot skin making for an easy resistance to the cold rains, but F'Skar was forced to hide under their hanging shelters or hollowed trees, for fear of freezing to death. Even in this house, the rain still made him shudder.

"Your paintings are rather well done." an unknown voice said from the hallway behind him.

He shuddered even further, knowing that Sárif was still in the city on business.

"Thank you for your kind words." he replied as calmly as he could, slowly turning to the intruder. "And whom do I have the pleasure of entertaining?"

The robed individual wore an expression of sadness on his tattooed face. One that F'Skar knew too well.

The expression of one who was resigned to his death.

The man sighed. "My name doesn't matter anymore. Perhaps I could just admire your art until we are done?"

F'Skar was caught off guard by his passiveness, and found himself lightly stepping towards him.

"Would you like to try your hand?" he offered, wanting to defuse the situation if he could.

The man shook his head slowly, the fringes of his hood dancing slightly. He raised his hand, trembling as it began to show glowing fissures. "I'm afraid my hands shake too much. I wouldn't be much good at it."

The aash elf sighed as the man's face began to crack and tear, showing lines of bright orange flame and cinders. He met the elf's gaze, and smiled sadly.

"Perhaps we'll find more luck in the next life." F'Skar mused with the stranger.

† †

Erika and Irvine were sitting across from each other in their beds, enjoying each other's company and conversation. The young woman's healing treatment had finally been finished after several hours, and while her wounds were still incredibly sore, she was sitting up and wearing no bandages. Irvine similarly was taking his time, favoring the ribs that had been damaged, but the healing had saved him from weeks of repair. Both of them were in more casual clothing, Irvine wearing a comfortable tunic and trousers, and Erika returned to her customary skirt and sleeveless shirt.

The markings on her arms were fully displayed, Irvine glancing to them from time to time.

"Perhaps we should go speak to your friend?" he asked lightly.

Erika glanced back into the hallway at the man lying in his bed, reading a small book to pass the time. She made a face slightly, but tried not to complain. She knew it was her fault he was in here, but still dreaded how he would react at seeing her again.

"Perhaps." she resigned with a sigh, standing from her comfortable bed.

Irvine stepped behind her, placing a hand on her back, both to comfort and urge her forwards. The man tried to focus on his reading, ignoring the approaching two, but found it a futile effort.

"What do you want?" he asked gruffly.

Erika did her best not to spit back a retort, swallowing hard and startling when Irvine gave her a gentle tap on her lower back.

"To apologize." she said with a sigh. "It was wrong o' me to strike ye like I did, and I feel awful about it."

The guard watched her with a furrowed brow, taking in her words.

"I know ye were just doin' yer job, and tryin' to protect my safety, but I did need to go help my friend here." she said, holding out a hand towards Irvine.

The man sighed, replacing his bookmark in the pages and setting it to the side. He sat up more, with some difficulty, and made more solid eye contact with the young woman. "Given the situation. I understand your haste and panic."

Erika brightened slightly, but was shut down by his continuing words.

"However, I still believe that you should have stayed inside the walls. You don't seem a fighter, and if you had died out there, it would have been my fault."

Erika started to protest, but Irvine put his hand on her shoulder, calming her with a look.

"Your wounds already fill me with guilt." the guard said, motioning to her bed where he had clearly been able to hear her healing ordeal. "So, I ask that you try and be more careful in the future. I apologize for losing my own sanity for a time, and calling you a Daemon. I simply did not understand your abilities, and I was fearful given the timing."

She began to explain herself, but he held up a hand to stop her. "Valk already filled me in. I may not have ever heard of an Ignis blood before, but I understand the concept."

His expression became distant for a moment, and Erika struggled to find the words to continue, until he finally spoke again. "My name is Orlan. And I accept your apology, on the condition that you accept mine."

"I'm Erika. That's incredibly kind o' ye." she replied. "Though, ye have no reason to be apologizin' yerself Orlan. The fault is in my own actions."

Orlan shook his head with a smirk. "Don't place all the blame on yourself. Just be safe, and try to help the next guard understand a little quicker and with less intimidation tactics."

Erika felt her face flush, nodding all the same and bowing to the young guard. "May ye have a quick recovery."

Before Orlan could reply, the two were thrown from their feet with a sudden tremor through the temple. Erika fell to the empty bed behind her, and Irvine fell awkwardly on his rump. The two spotted Valk sprinting with a purpose from the building, and quickly gave chase, after wishing Orlan farewell.

The cleric gave them both a look, still continuing his hurried pace. "The two of you will probably have to find new lodgings for the night. From the sound of that, I'll need the beds."

Irvine nodded grimly, Erika glancing between the two with a worried expression.

†ꞁ

The robed man stalked the young couple, believing them to be lost in each other's lips, and therefore becoming all the easier to kill. Such an easy way to please his Madam. Yet all that was interrupted when he felt a sharp pain in his left knee. The quiet echo of blood spattering onto the cobbled stone was the only sound around them, until he fell to his other knee with a pained groan.

The woman spun, wrenching two small swords from hidden scabbards under her long shawl, the man shortly behind her with an axe to bear. She kicked the assailant in the chest after slapping his weapon to the side. Selbor rushed around him and brought the axe to his throat.

Farris landed to the side and sauntered towards them. "What did I tell you, easy as that!"

Teria sheathed one blade and ripped the wig from her head with a scowl. "Feels strange, you being right for once." she said as she picked out the small pins that held her natural hair up.

The robed man stared at her as her natural dark hair fell back around her shoulders. "It was all a trick?"

"The whole time. You picked the wrong side." Selbor said gruffly before he punched the man on the back of the neck, knocking him into unconsciousness.

The three stood over the unmoving assailant. Selbor started to allow himself a smile, until a cacophonous blast emitted through the air, and a shockwave threw them from their feet.

† †

The scene was one of complete destruction. Several buildings fallen to ruin. Others were cracked open like eggshells by the blast. Flames lit the night, and alarm bells rang through the air. Rain came in another full downpour, and though none made it through the magical barrier over the city, they seemed to be tears of the Gods. Teria and Farris worked to evacuate townsfolk

from the rubble. Selbor and a score of other rangers joined them
after he had deposited their newly acquired asset at the dungeons
and called for aid in the Guild Hall. Irvine, Erika, and Valk arrived at the site shortly after. The cleric immediately went to work,
assigning roles to the survivors still well enough to work, and es-
tablishing a checkpoint for the wounded on the way to his temple
and others across the city.

Irvine searched the scorched ruins, Erika clinging to his
arm with eyes wide. She tried not to look at the unmoving bodies,
but found her gaze drawn to them all the same. Irvine gently led
them to where the center of the explosion had occurred.

He knew the place much too well.

It was Sárif's home, still glowing in embers. The sol elf
was atop the destruction, frantically digging through the heavy
stones. His normally clean hands bloodied and blackened from
the effort. His golden hair changed to a dull orange as it matted to
his face from sweat and tears. His amber eyes glowed wildly in the
firelight around him, and every so often he screamed a name.

Irvine started to step forward, Erika still clinging to him,
when Sárif stood up. The elf traced a sigil in the air with his
wounded fingers, and a purple glow shot down his arm and
through his fingers, blowing a section of stonework to the side with
a massive force. It landed with a crash, and Sárif fell to his knees
again, dragging what he was looking for from the new hole in the
rubble.

Erika gasped at the sight, and Irvine could feel her warm
tears on his sleeved arm. He stared at the display with eyes wide,
and stinging from the ash that flew around them. The body he
held was an aash elf that Irvine had met only a handful of times,
but knew well enough.

F'Skar lay limp in the sol elf's arms. His entire chest was
ripped open, half his face torn off, and the other blackened with
soot. The contrast of the golden elf against the dark-skinned body
was made all the more haunting by the former's howls of agony

and despair. He lifted him further, Irvine wincing at the sight of his severed left arm and hanging legs.

He urged Erika to stay back, as he climbed the mound of destruction, and reached a hand tentatively towards Sárif. "Master Sárif," he said calmly as he could. "I'm sorry." The mage whirled on him, causing him to startle at the expression of pure rage on his face. His face akin to a wild animal backed into a corner, as his hair flared a wild purple color, mirroring his emotions. "F'Skar implored me to always see the best in everyone. He helped me calm my own inner turmoil that lashed out at everyone around me, but no more." he said as he stood slowly, trying to wipe his bloody and shaking hands on a cloth to no avail. "They took him from me, and now they will all pay dearly."

"Sárif, I know it doesn't mean much coming from me, but recklessness will only cause more problems." Irvine said, trying to calm the elf.

"Thank you for your words, Irvine. It does mean plenty, you are a trusted individual, and I value everything you say. You have lost as well, and you know how it feels."

He turned to the young courier. "I have no intention of being reckless though. Relentless, yes, but not reckless. Go rest Irvine, you will have an early morning tomorrow to start your hunt for the Daemon that killed your uncle. I've already made arrangements for a force to accompany you back to your home."

"But I can help here." Irvine pleaded.

"No. You bear the weapon able to slay that monster. I bear the abilities to track down these people. The Abyssal Hand, as I know them to be called. They will not survive, I assure you."

Irvine backed away slowly, the intensity in Sárif's bright eyes encouraged him to back down. He understood Sárif, and that he was determined to avenge his loved one. He knew no one would be able to stand in his way.

Valk stepped behind Erika, who had fallen to her knees. Her eyes streamed tears at the scene, and despite never meeting Sárif's partner, she knew how much pain he must be in. The cleric tucked a hand under her arm and gently brought her to her feet. She looked to him, her hair matted to her face and neck from her own sweat and tears, and her green eyes reddened from the ash in the air. He nodded slowly, and forced a small leather sack into her hands.

"Go to the *Silver Mare*. It's an inn on the other side of town. Get a room for you and Irvine with this." he tapped the coin pouch. "We'll get this all sorted out."

She hesitantly nodded, stepping away with some difficulty towards his directions. She looked back to Irvine and Sárif, and hoped against her sensibilities, that no more death would come before her.

† †

Irvine stepped into the small room in the *Silver Mare Inn*, Erika greeting him with a tackling embrace. He was taken aback at first, but understood how she felt. How akin to the beginning of their journey this felt like. She had stripped off most of her clothes in favor of a loose fitting grey shirt that fell to the middle of her thighs, seemingly only waiting on him to turn in for the night.

"I only got one room." she said nervously. "I didn't want to be takin' too much space, if any o' the people that lost their homes came here too."

"It's fine Erika, I understand completely." he replied, placing all of their belongings in the corner of the room, and starting to unpack his bedroll onto the floor beside the bed.

"I'm heading out for Valen tomorrow." he said grimly.

He winced at her panicked expression. "Sárif set up an offensive force to attack the Daemon, but they need my help."

"And yer fer thinkin' that I'm stayin' here?" she retorted, her voice raising slightly as she stomped closer to him.

"It's going to be dangerous Erika." he said, trying to calm her.

"This whole journey's been dangerous, Irvine! I'm not leavin' ye to fight a Daemon alone! I'm comin' with ye!"

She laid back in the bed in a strangely aggressive manner, staring at Irvine with a look of bewilderment. He held his hands up in defense, and conceded to her. He continued shuffling about slightly, preparing for bed after she had already pulled the coverings tight over herself. Less to sleep though, and more for hiding her own emotions.

She knew her hope of no more death would go unanswered.

Part Three

I retired from my travels and adventures alongside Feldran and Versal many years ago. Our days of fighting Daemons and monsters were over, and our hunger for danger sufficiently satiated. We all settled down. Feldran in his hometown to work as a guardsman, and protect his younger sister's new family. Versal returning to the northlands of Máðir, and their imposing cliffs and fjords.

I settled not in my homeland of Tarkal, but in a frequent city of our travels, Sildenfeld. The city was beautiful, and I had especially fallen in love with a particular manor on the edge of the city that I was able to purchase with a portion of my well-earned adventuring coin.

I moved there with my chosen mate, F'Skar. An aash elf that I had become involved in a wonderful friendship with during our travels. He was a weak elf, and was doted on by his tribe, but I felt I could offer him a better life. He readily accepted, as did his tribe. Though I still wonder if it were for the betterment of his life, or so they could resume their normal lives themselves. It mattered not though, for we were happy together. He was truly my better half.

It seems that the chaotic lives of adventurers never end though. It always catches up with us. Versal lost his wife and *people to something that is still unknown to me, and was forced to travel across the continent with a small babe tucked in his arm.* He *arrived in the Sildenfeld Region not long after and attempted another new start, only for Feldran's sister to perish in a horrible fire only a few short years later, the cause of which is also unknown to me. She and her husband were lost, but her child was saved, to be raised by Feldran.*

Finally, a Daemon attacked, and now my friend is lost to me forever. Just as I thought things had reached their worst, F'Skar was taken from me as well.

Mercy is not in the nature of fate when it comes it adventurers, it seems. Fate has much crueler things in store for us. I only hope our children will live to see better days.

-Sárif Vlësk, Former Council Leader of Sildenfeld.

20
Slaughter and Jealousy

Erika awoke slowly, her head fuzzy from the restless night's sleep. Sounds of clinking metal and shuffling feet wafted in from outside, along with the familiar smell of burning coal. The window let in a cool morning breeze, causing her to pull the covers further over her body with a shudder.

She found herself laying on the bedroll beside the bed, but Irvine was not next to her. She felt her face get warmer as she looked up at him, though he didn't seem to take notice of her. He stood next to the wooden table at the end of the room, facing the foot of the bed, his focus directed at tightening the straps on the half breastplate she had given him. The scorch marks and heavy denting from the previous battle still lingered on the once shining metal. He appeared to be ready to leave at a moment's notice, sword on his hip and boots on his feet. He wore a grim expression, but lightened somewhat once he finally made eye contact with her.

"Is it time to go already?" she asked with a deep yawn.

He nodded. "Soon, yes. I didn't want to wake you by getting up, but I couldn't sleep."

She sat up slightly, saddened over the previous night's conversation. She would have greatly preferred the simple awkwardness of waking up directly next to him to the grim task of traveling back to their destroyed home.

Irvine opened a map on the bare bed, Erika standing and holding the missing covers over her body as she felt her loose shirt riding up to her waist. As he studied the route they would be taking to return to Valen, she moved away. He started to look back at her, but quickly turned when she began changing to her day clothes. He tried to force the image of the massive scar on her naked back from his mind, but still found himself glancing repeatedly at her. The markings of her magic were still unfinished on her muscular torso, only interrupted by the three thick lines of the scar. He shook his head and returned his gaze to the map, informing her that they would be taking the long route around the mountains due to the large force they would be traveling with. The ravine and Mystholt would be too treacherous for such a mass of soldiers. This garnered no quarrel from Erika, who was in no hurry to return to the cliffs that petrified her. She lifted up her crushed breastplate, rubbing the places where the jordhak teeth had punctured through.

"Your father made that for you right?" Irvine asked when he found her clothed again.

She looked to him with a somber expression. "Aye. I suppose it did me well, savin' me from the jordhak an' all."

"Indeed. Remind me to thank him when we see him again." he said, looking back to the map. "I don't know what I would've done if I had lost you."

Erika took pause at his words, bringing her fingers up to her shoulder where the tooth had punctured through the armor and into her flesh, fidgeting with the healed wound. The scar was rough, and tingled at her touch, the feeling deadened in the area. She thought back to the last time she had seen her father, nearly his entire body immolated as he rushed in to fight the Daemon during their escape. She hoped they would see him again, but she was unsure if he survived the battle.

She gathered the rest of her belongings and placed them inside her pack, turning to Irvine. "I'm goin' to the smithy down the street, see if I can't borrow a few tools to bang this back into shape." she said, holding up the marred breastplate. "I'll see ye soon, alright?"

Irvine nodded, smiling as she started to leave. She paused at the door, quietly staring at his back for a long while as he resumed preparing. She let out a silent sigh, trying not to think about what could have been. There seemed to be no time for those thoughts now.

† †

The dripping of water and the foul smell of a damp underground chamber filled the nostrils, acrid and stinging. The man awoke slowly, a single light illuminating the dark room. He sat in a simple wooden chair, his hands tied behind the backrest of the seat. Metal bars were in front of him, wet stone walls on every other side including overhead. His vision became clearer over time, the room, and his situation starting to come into focus. The air was cold on his smooth, hairless head, and his robes were soaked with moisture.

He startled when the gate in the middle of the bars creaked open, echoing through the unseen complex beyond him. Several guardsmen stood outside the cell with pikes. A tall, gaunt looking sol elf stepping into the small chamber with him. The elf's hair was matted with mud and spare traces of crimson, also wet from the damp underground. His bright amber eyes stared at the ground, moving very little. His hands were bandaged with red stains peeking through the soiled white cloth. The man recognized this elf as Sárif Vlësk. The high-ranking councilman had been a thorn in his organization's side for all the years he had been in the city, enacting heavier security, and removing a certain board member that they had planted there several months before his arrival.

"The Abyssal Hand." the elf began, slowly and quietly. "Who are they?"

The man regained his composure to some measure, clenching his jaw shut.

Sárif sighed. "Silence will not save you. Though I will not kill you. I will get my answers though, one way or another.

As the elf turned, the man saw a chance and began a quiet chant, focusing the energy on the elf and the guards outside. Sárif spun quickly, and before the man could react, slammed a pair of metal tongs into his mouth, gripping his tongue and ceasing its movement.

"Hm." Sárif muttered as he saw a chip of tooth fall from the man's mouth.

"Curses will not do you well here. I have done plenty of research into the darker of the religious magics, and while I do not practice them, I do recognize the signs of them. You may have a speech deficit after this." he said casually, pulling the tongue out of his mouth and placing the sharp point of a thin metal rod in the center of the pink muscle, pressing gently at first on the opposite end.

The man screamed as best he could, but Sárif didn't let up, a trickle of blood beginning to seep forth and onto the dark stone floor. Several moments later, the elf turned, letting go of the tongue and metal rod, the sharp object falling from his mouth and tearing a small portion from his flesh.

"You're a damned maniac!" he shouted with a slight impediment to his speech, wincing at the pain in his mouth. He desperately looked past the demented elf to the guards outside, but found no salvation in them. They both held strong, jaws set, and eyes forward.

"Ah! So, you do possess speech." Sárif remarked. "Let's start with your name. Real or fake I hardly care. I'm simply looking for something to call you, unless you'd prefer me choose a name for you, that might be childish though."

"Gelran." he said, biting down on his tongue to distract the pain.

"Gelran then." the elf repeated, clapping his hands together and continuing in a sardonic facade. "How wonderful to make your acquaintance, I'm Sárif, as I'm sure you know. Now, to business. You had attacked a couple of my associates last night, to ill results it seems. I would like to know why."

The man spat a globule of blood at Sárif's face, splatters staining his faded golden hair further, and began screaming. "You set them up! It was a trap for me, I know how it works. Get the information to my people about who killed the Daemon, then set a trap when we try and get rid of them! I'm right, aren't I?"

Sárif whipped the blood from his annoyed face, focusing his willpower in a broad area and flicking his ring finger outwards. A loud concussive blast sounded out, sending Gelran flying into the back wall. The wooden back of the chair splintered against the stone, the remaining seat falling sideways and taking its captive with it, his smooth head slamming against the ground, drawing a new fountain of crimson.

"I believe you fail to see the point of this encounter, Gelran." he said. "I am interviewing you, not the other way around. What our plan was, holds little significance now."

The man shook his head of the intense ringing sound that resulted from the aggressive arcane spell. He rested his head on the cold stone below him, the temperature helping to numb the pain only slightly. The elf stalked back and forth in the small room, wringing his hands together. It unnerved Gelran, how he didn't look at him, even once, as if he was treating this all like a game.

"I will get my answers. I have all eternity to spend in here with you." the elf said in a dark monotone. "I, quite literally, have nothing better to do. So, I'd recommend getting comfortable. It'll likely be a long day for you."

† †

Versal stepped alongside the coastline, his boots pounding on the damp rocks as he walked, careful of his footing on the wave struck stones. He looked behind him, taking a sigh of relief that they hadn't seen any Daemons since they had made it around the Seraphine mountains. Their biggest problems had been people falling from the rocks and scraping their knees or spraining their ankles. Trivial issues, but incredibly slowing for such a large group of inexperienced travelers.

He remembered a similar journey through worse terrain with a small babe from many years prior, thankful that their youngest members now were at least of walking age. Merrick was his main source of conversation, the young guardsman asking him about their destination, or his travels before settling in Valen. The old smith was happy to oblige the man, but found himself digging up past experiences that he'd rather leave buried, though at no fault of Merrick. He left out the reasons of why fighting Daemons was not a new experience, or why he had fled from his home in the fjords with Erika. He gladly told him the tales of when they had saved a forest of dryads from a poison, and when he had singlehandedly beaten a band of orks in a fistfight, seven to one. The young man seemed enchanted and encouraged by the stories, though Versal couldn't help but wonder if he actually believed them.

Eventually they found the opposite end of the mountains, arriving in the neighboring valley that held the city of Sildenfeld. Versal's vision wasn't what it used to be, and he could barely make out the edges of the exterior wall. Eventually, he found what appeared to be a large force leaving the city, heading in a curving path, eastwards towards the opposite pass around the mountains. Long spears and flags were held high in their march, bearing the crest of Sildenfeld, the Bundled Arrows.

"Stronger together." he said quietly, echoing the city motto. A smile broadened his face, assuming that Irvine and Erika had made it to the city, and that the force was being dispatched to deal with the Daemon incursion. Merrick stepped beside him with a spyglass, peering through it at the mass.

"Looks like soldiers. You think they're going to fight that monster?" he asked.

"Aye, likely." the large man replied. "I'd wager our couriers made it to the city too, meanin' that we'll see yer friends soon enough."

Merrick's eyes fell slightly. "I only hope they're both alright. I'd much rather make amends for my behavior as a child to them in person."

Versal placed his meaty hand on his shoulder. "I'm sure they'll be happy to see ye too Merrick. I doubt they hold the angered emotions ye believe them to."

"Perhaps." he said with a smile, patting the smith on the back lightly and walking back to their group. Versal looked on, barely making out the section of burned field at the top of the hill leading into the mountains to the south of the city.

† †

The coolness of autumn was quickly being replaced by the cold of winter. The leaves seemed to be falling faster and the clouds shifted by the hour in eerie winds that the elders said spoke of ill tidings. The small village of Feldsbar stood on though, through all of these strange changes in weather. The lake had not yet frozen over, and the harvest had been efficiently stored away for later use. Everything was as it should be, until the dawn came.

The day began with the bright light of burning buildings, first the houses to the north, followed quickly by the storefronts and eventually the storehouse. People ran through the streets screaming, attempting to find shelter or save loved ones after being forced from their burning homes. Spare glimpses were caught of the spectral creature that drifted through the collapsing buildings. The jagged crimson armor stained with spattering of a deeper red. The only thing accompanying the horrifying creature, was the shrill laughter, echoing through the fields.

Guard and militia opposed him, though their blades made less and less impact as his rampage continued. Bodies fell to the stone in charred husks, their clothing and flesh burned away, life force drained and strength stolen. Zyrxak's hunger still far from satiated.

The village of Feldsbar burned that day. Daylight had barely begun licking the edges of the settlement before it was nothing but a ruin of stone and wood.

Zyrxak drifted through the village slowly, eagerly peering through each of the destroyed doors and windows. His bent stature looking like a ravenous predator stalking through a thick forest, hunting the last few rabbits it knew to be there. His bony fingers audibly clacked against the charred stones, an eerie echo ringing through the ruined buildings. He paused a moment, hearing a slight sound. His horned head cocked to the side as he leaned over the broken wall of a nearby building, a woman sitting just under the shattered wood. The wall began to sizzle with Zyrxak's errant heat, the woman looking up at him and screaming briefly as his hand met her. His jaw clicked up and down as her corpse slumped to the side, his senses tingling at the flavor of terror. He much more enjoyed hunting through the settlements himself, regretting his method with the previous town, blatant assault was so uncouth.

He grunted slightly, knowing that the Minor Daemons had surely stolen lives from him, and had things gone more poorly, his crusade would have ended in the same matter as Xarvix the Idiot. His new title in death seemed much more fitting. He arrived at the center of the village, and grinned madly. "No more need for tomes, I'll reduce you all to bones."

He lowered in the air, planting both hands on the stone cobble below, speaking Daemonic words that seemed to cut the air around him. The ground turned black, a blight covering the stonework as small particles began to float from the dark magic. He had summoned creatures from his previous dominion of the Seven Hells before, but now it was high time to begin a full-scale invasion. That, and fodder never hurt his own chances of survival in the coming battles.

He shuddered as a chill blew through the air and through his bones. His teeth ground together with a horrible noise, the notion that the Angelus could return irritating him slightly.

"Those damned birds. Need to keep their noses out of my business." he hissed more to himself than anyone else.

"Gods strike you down, monster!" a shout rang out.

Zyrxak lurched slightly as an impact met his spine. He turned slowly, the wood axe falling from the void between his bones with a loud clatter. A young man stood in front of him, a look of horror painted his face. The specter imagined that face was full of bravery just a moment ago, but it had faded quickly when his attack fell useless. He backed slowly, tripping over an uneven stone, the specter lunging forward and grabbing him by the throat before he landed.

"The Gods have nothing to do with me." Zyrxak growled as tears streamed down the human's face. This was the one thing he disliked about his hunts, the ones who are so full of false bravado that they believe themselves a savior. "Yet you all fall to ash." he said lightly, responding to his own thoughts as the charred body fell to the ground with a multitude of snaps.

That one at least distracted him from his errant thoughts of his eternal foes. The winged creatures he and the other Daemons had battled those generations ago were nowhere to be found, while he was free to dominate the realm. None could stand before him. Even the Dragons had vanished.

† †

Irvine stepped through the streets that were packed with soldiers readying their belongings and mounts. All conversation was halted as he passed, the air becoming filled with stares and quiet murmurs. He could only make out spare words, speaking of 'Daemon Slayer' and 'Fire Bringer'. He frowned, realizing that the nicknames of his childhood had somehow come full circle again, though this time in a more positive light at least. Senior officers hushed their subordinates and called for a return to work though, granting him a slight respite at the gossip over his battle on the hill.

He scanned the mass of men in shining armor, searching for one with more ornamentation, General Atrosby, the leader of the force that he was to accompany. He proved a difficult man to keep track of though, his strong legs carrying him throughout the grounds, checking on every nook and cranny of his forward forces, and eluding Irvine every step of the way.

He found the massive caravan already beginning its trek from the city when he came to the walls. General Atrosby sat atop his black mare at the edge of the gate, overseeing the exodus of soldiers as they filed out of the walls and into the fields. Irvine fought his way through to the imposing man, clearing his throat as he approached.

"Greetings, General." he said respectfully.

"And to you, Courier." the general replied curtly.

Irvine raised his eyebrows, taking a deep breath before beginning to speak again, Atrosby quickly cutting him off.

"I understand that you possess a powerful weapon boy. Do not think that it gives you free accolades in my presence."

Irvine felt his temper start to rise. "I understand sir, I-"

"My men speak of your battle with the Daemon as if it were a myth from some child's story. I have only heard second hand of your deeds, and as such have no respect for you until you prove your worth." he continued, making sure Irvine couldn't get in a single word. "We are leaving now, as you can surely see. Whether you and your maid are with us, is entirely up to you. We will not slow for you."

The way the soldier addressed Erika made Irvine's blood boil, wanting nothing more than to punch the pompous man from his saddle, though he knew it would be a sore mistake. Before he could recompose himself, the general clicked his tongue and kicked his legs, spurring his horse onwards and outside the city walls, leaving Irvine in a small cloud of dust.

So much for making a good first impression. he thought to himself.

"He's arrogant and rash, but he hasn't failed the city yet." a feminine voice called from behind him. Irvine turned to find a familiar face in the ranger that escorted him from the city to the site of Erika's battle. She held out both arms, carrying two cloaks of a dull grey color, and Irvine's own sword, gifted to him by his uncle. "More rain will fall on the journey."

Irvine gladly took them, though he offered a confused expression at the return of his familiar weapon. "Am I to assume you are coming with us?"

She nodded, showing no indication of an explanation for his sword. "Mistress Varia wishes there to be a certain amount of presence from the Willows in the expedition, though she is staying behind to ensure the security of the city."

"The rangers are always a welcome sight." Irvine said with a smile. "Your guild has saved me more times than I can count on my treks through the forests."

She chuckled slightly, eyeing him slyly. "As long as you don't pass out on us again."

"Right. Sorry about that." Irvine said, scratching the back of his head.

She laughed again, slapping her palm on his back and starting to walk away, brushing her dark hair from her face while glancing at something over his shoulder. "No need to apologize. Just don't die on us!"

Irvine watched her leave, put off slightly by her dark sense of humor. He sidestepped in pain as he was struck again from the side, turning to find a grinning Erika.

"Who's yer friend?" she asked.

He rubbed his side where she jabbed him. "She's the Willow Ranger that took me to the place where you fought the jordhak."

She nodded, watching the woman walking away with more of a hip sway than Erika thought she could ever muster. She scratched her cheek slightly, staring at her until she disappeared into the crowd. "I look forward to meetin' her sometime."

"Well, she's coming on the trip with us, so you'll probably get the chance." he said, holding out the second cloak to her. "She also gave us these, apparently it'll rain more."

Erika took the cloth, draping it over her shoulders and pulling the hood over her auburn hair. Irvine watched as she did, her emerald eyes flashing in the low light, framed by the darker hood. He looked back to his own cloak when she glanced up at him, while she squinted at him suspiciously, wondering what he was thinking to no avail.

Eventually, she slapped his shoulder with the back of her hand. "I was able to repair my armor a bit." she said, pointing at the half breastplate she wore, now back into its original shape with a rough patch over each of the holes the jordhak had made. He smiled at her, though she found it to look forced.

Erika glanced to the armor he wore over his chest, heavily dented from the Daemon's fist. She kicked herself mentally, for not taking his piece to repair as well.

"Come on, we'd better get our supplies secured and start moving. Don't want to get left behind." he said, putting his hand on her back and ushering her forwards.

† †

Teria watched the two as they moved from the crowd, her jaw chewing absently on a piece of dried meat. *What is it that intrigues me so much about them?* she wondered.

She hadn't felt the same when talking to Irvine alone, but as soon as the Fjordling appeared, she found herself compelled to leave.

She thought back to Varia speaking to her several weeks ago. 'You need to work on your people skills, Teria. If you never learn to deal with other humans, you'll be alone in the forests forever.'

What's so bad about being alone in the forest? she thought. The forests were peaceful, and away from the complicated creatures that were human and elf, but more importantly, away from these conflicted emotions.

"Why the long face?" a snakish voice asked beside her. She didn't even startle this time though, so engrossed in her own thoughts. This caused a raised eyebrow from Farris.

He nudged her side cautiously with a finger, wanting to avoid a strike if possible, but she stood unmoving even after his prodding. He let out a sigh, and followed her gaze to the young pair walking further into the market.

"How are you so good with people?" she said finally, catching her companion off guard.

He hesitated, unsure of how to respond, especially when she seemed so serious about the question. "I suppose it just comes with experience." he replied, sounding more like a question than an answer.

Teria simply stared at the stalls that the two had disappeared around, her jaw set, causing Farris to balk even further at her lack of a retort to his confused reply.

Farris simply stood with her, leaning against the wall in silence while watching her.

He was good with people, yes, but only recently people had begun to actually want to be around him. He was used to being the weasel that everyone groaned over when he showed his face, but she almost sounded happy for his presence just now. He stared at her face as she crouched down comfortably, her dark eyes locked on that same corner as if she would shoot it at a moment's notice. Her features were normally intense, but never so vulnerable looking. Her expression looked as if she were concerned and waiting for something, as if an unknown force would strike her, and she was certain that it would come from that corner specifically.

He sighed again, but she didn't seem to notice him at all. He decided he would just watch over her for now. The Abyssal Hand was out of his jurisdiction at this point, and they wouldn't likely have to deal with Daemons for days at least. So instead, he decided Teria would be his charge. He began his own breakfast, glancing back to her worried looking face between bites.

† †

The journey away from the city was much slower than their pace coming to Sildenfeld. Erika tried to focus less on the ground covered, and more on the ground below her, the rough road made rougher by the large mass of soldiers and horses and carts in front of her. Softened by the heavy rain in the past days, and more so by the steady drizzle that permeated many hours of the journey, becoming more uneven and slippery as they walked. Irvine had to catch her balance on multiple occasions, much to her idle embarrassment.

Her emotions were swimming the entire way, sharing a tent with Irvine for each night, though being little help pitching and tearing down the shelter. Added in was the ranger woman called Teria, who seemed to be watching their every move, though she couldn't tell if she was looking at her or Irvine more.

She was used to stares, her auburn hair and pale complexion being a wellspring for attention since she was a child, though when she would meet those stares, they would look away quickly out of shame for being caught. This ranger though, made full eye contact with her on multiple occasions, narrowing her eyes at Erika, and making her feel uncomfortable in a strange flip of the situation. She couldn't tell why she was paying so much attention to them, though her emotions got the best of her on several occasions, wondering if she had taken a liking to Irvine.

She found herself looking at Irvine more and more, especially after she had met Teria officially. Neither of them made any mentions of their exchanges across the crowds when she had finally introduced herself, being the picture of formality towards Erika, but seeming much more casual in her conversation with Irvine. He seemed oblivious to the situation though, frustrating Erika more in his thick head.

Perhaps it's just my imagination. she thought to herself, trying not to dwell on her thoughts. Instead she focused on her time with Irvine, and learning the travel skills as best she could. Irvine had begun training her to fight at her request as well, finding his expertise in weapons to be incredible. Though she made them, she knew not how to use many of them. Over the course of the journey, he taught her to use a sword, dagger, and even how to implement her own warhammer with better efficiency and skill. She realized how many of her battles had been fought with her raw strength and pure luck so far. The thrall in the beginning only fell so easily because she managed to land a solid hit on its head, and it was already a fragile creature to begin with. The Mystholt was a completely solo effort by Irvine, especially the cave afterwards where she managed to only trip a single kobold with the haft of her hammer. Then the jordhak in the field nearly killed her, though Irvine did try to console her, saying that jordhaks were difficult beasts for seasoned travelers. Finally, the Daemon was only staggered because of Irvine's sword jammed in its shoulder, and nearly killed her in a single strike afterwards.

She also found herself trying not to look at her own naked torso when she changed clothes. The sight of the patches in her armor succeeded in making her annoyed, but the actual scarred wounds on her chest and midriff caused her to seethe in anger. In these times of frustration, she found herself involuntarily shedding tears, causing even more negative emotions to flood her senses.

She was tired of crying. Tired of being too weak to protect Irvine like she used to. She used to feel as if she could win any fight, but this journey had done more to solidify her own weaknesses than anything else. Irvine seemed sympathetic to her, though she avoided him when she found the tears falling freely.

Occasionally, Teria would stop by, but this caused her to become even more angered. She began to see Teria as a better woman, as a better version of her. The ranger was so strong of will and body, but in a different way than Erika. She could easily lift one of the anvils from her father's shop, or hammer for hours on end at a stubborn chunk of metal. Yet, this woman seemed able to march for hours, unhindered by rough terrain, and her casual demeanor seemed able to spring into action in the blink of an eye.

She worried that Irvine would be more attracted to the ranger, and have her become a traveling companion once the crisis was over. Erika feared she would resume work at a blacksmith, and lose Irvine to the lithe curves of this woman forever.

She knew these concerns to be juvenile, and mused that Irvine was still the same shy boy she always knew when it came to the opposite sex, but the thoughts still persisted. She began to eye the ranger with contempt for much of the day, her time occupied by little more than annoyance and frustration.

21
Experience

Farris sat against a tree on a hill, overlooking the roadway and the bulk of the traveling force, while shaving his fingernails with a small cleaning knife. Teria stalked to him with stomping footfalls that almost seemed to make her entire body tremor. He regarded her with a smirk, knowing that her seeming frustration was with the traveling pair that had come from the other side of the Seraphine Mountains.

She threw her arms to the sides when she made eye contact with him, puffing out her cheeks and groaning slightly. "I don't know what I'm doing wrong!"

He smirked even wider, continually amused by her coming to him for advice. If someone had told his past self that the beautiful and stoic Teria would be running after him and begging for help on social interactions, he would have laughed in their face.

"I'm not sure you're doing anything wrong dearie." he said with as much genuine emotion as he could muster. This didn't seem to convince her though. She glared at him, and clenched her fists in a way that seemed most unthreatening to him.

"I'm not making any headway with Erika! She still looks at me like I'm trying to kill her or something!" she complained, tossing her arms in the air, only for her hands to slap against her bare thighs and smear her camouflaging paint that she had just applied.

Farris leaned to the side slightly, eyeing the auburn-haired woman sparring with the young man that she traveled with. Her movements were incredibly blocky, and the weight of the hammerhead seemed to dictate each of her body movements, despite her arms looking like they could command the direction of an earthquake. The courier was obviously much more experienced with weapons than she was, as he should with his occupation in mind, but even Farris had a hard time not wincing when he slapped the back of her thigh with the flat of his blade after easily dodging a swing.

"So, let me see if I fully understand." Farris began, still preferring to watch the one-sided match over Teria's flustered face. "You want to be friends with the girl?"

He didn't see her, but Teria rolled her eyes at him, or perhaps at no one in particular. "I don't know what I want! I was trying to get better with people, and not come off as a conceited bitch!"

Farris snapped back to her, holding up a finger. "Now wait just a moment! You're not conceited."

He stood a moment later, Teria realizing the point of his verbal jab and holding herself back from slamming him back to the ground. Farris brushed off his rump of the dust and dirt and put both hands on his hips.

"From what I can see, and what I have observed." he began, Teria hanging on his every word. "She sees you as competition."

Teria nearly fell over, her eyes widened and she found her gaze flashing from the two sparring down below, and the insane ranger that stood before her. "What do you mean she sees me as competition? Look at her, she's so slow, and her strikes are obvious before she even starts to move! And do not even get me started on that footwork!"

Farris laughed. A loud, guttural laugh that caused everyone in the vicinity to stare at the two, including the sparring travelers that were the focus of their conversation. Many cocked their heads, and lingered, wondering what the joke was. Teria flustered, pulling the hood of her cloak up tight over her forehead and turning away from all of them. Eventually, his laughter subsided, and he brought a finger up to wipe away the tear that had formed in his left eye at the act.

"The fact that you think I'm meaning combat is such a testament to your entire life." he said, with no shortage of sarcasm. Before she could retort, he looked her dead in the eye with a sardonic grin. "She sees you as competition for the boy!"

Teria balked at his display, looking back and forth between him and their topic again. "What do you mean, for the boy? Irvine? What could I possibly compete for with her in that field?"

Now it was Farris that nearly fall over, not even able muster a laugh this time. "For his affection, Teria!" he said as loud as he dared.

Teria took a step back, while the roguish ranger continued. "She is obviously interested in him, romantically! From the looks of it, she's only begun her attempt at garnering his attention in a way that goes beyond friendship, and then here you come along with your swaying hips and shapely legs, and start talking to him like he's been your friend for years!"

The young woman looked as if she'd just been impaled through the gut with fifteen jagged pikes. "I never intended to-"

"Intentions only go so far dearie." Farris interrupted, finding himself to sound almost parental. "I'm only telling you how she sees things. I understand that the interactions feel more natural with him, and that's because he's a traveled man, and a courier to boot, meaning he's dealt with all kinds of characters far stranger than you."

Teria was still too shocked to recognize his verbal jab. "The girl on the other hand, it seems like this is her first real time leaving her small town, so the only people she's ever interacted with, lived there, besides the occasional traveler stopping for supplies. Though I'd wager, even with that relative isolation, she's got more experience with other people than you!" Farris allowed himself a chuckle at the notion.

Teria stood with her mouth agape, unable to find words to retort her companion. Her mind swam, remembering every interaction she'd had with the two up until that evening, and she realized the full truth of his words.

"Next, you're going to ask me how to fix it all, aren't you?" Farris baited, a pompous grin spreading his thin cheeks. Teria didn't give him the satisfaction, but grabbed her elbow with her opposite arm and gingerly nodded. Farris mused at how much like a nervous little girl this dangerous woman looked like in that moment.

"Try and speak to her, and only her. The more you interact with Irvine, the more she will think you're trying to strip him naked in your tent." he said, making her expression even more incredulous.

"Maybe help her with those things you pointed out as her flaws in her combat skills. Perhaps another teacher could help her a bit, and we are technically marching towards a fight with a Daemon, so I'm sure it couldn't hurt."

"How am I supposed to get her alone though?" Teria asked, watching the two as they drank from waterskins and started packing for the night. "She's practically tied to his hip. Wherever he goes, she follows."

Farris shrugged, not willing to give her all the answers. A moment later, a young soldier came past them, the wily ranger snatching his shoulder and demanding to know what was happening.

"Nothing urgent sir." the young man said. "The general requests the presence of Irvine Columval at the head of the convoy to discuss the Daemon."

At that, the messenger was down the hill and pulling Irvine to the side. Farris had to contain his laughter, nudging Teria's back with his elbow.

"Looks like you'll get your chance there, dearie."

† †

Erika barely slept that night. She couldn't hear what the messenger had said to Irvine, but thinking on it kept her mind swimming. Alternatively, the ranger girl caused her emotions to swirl, still seething in anger every time she pictured that feminine form and her sauntering walk. She found herself looking in Irvine's direction, barely able to make out his gentle breathing in the dimmed light of the moons from beyond their tent. She had thought that they had grown closer than ever before in their short time healing at the temple, sharing meals and conversation. It made her happy just thinking about it, and she wished nothing more than to return to that. She loved just spending time with him, though it was somewhat dampened when he acted more as teacher than friend, telling her every tiny thing she was doing wrong with her fighting. Even sleeping in the same small space as him became less of a sterling experience, when they were surrounded by so many others outside the thin walls of the tent. She almost wished they were traveling alone again, and often thought back to their comparatively short time traveling through the wilderness. Being alone with him was such a wonderful experience and part of her wished she could just immolate and burn everything else away besides him.

Eventually, the night passed, and she found Irvine up at his customary hour. She watched him change into his day clothes, though he likely thought she was asleep. He strapped his sword to his side, and adjusted his armor pieces, and wore an expression of sadness. It seemed he was dreading whatever he was asked to do. As he turned, she closed her eyes quickly, feigning sleep. He crouched down next to her and shook her shoulder lightly. She almost didn't answer, simply in the hope to feel his hand against her skin for a little longer. Reluctantly, she opened her eyes in a slow fashion, trying her best to act as if she hadn't been awake all night.

"I have to go see General Atrosby." he said, nearly in a whisper. "Teria and the other rangers are nearby if you need anything, alright?"

Erika nearly scoffed when he said her name, figuring she'd rather leave her to struggle behind the convoy than to help her keep up. Nonetheless, she nodded lazily, leaning up and tightly embracing him before he departed from the tent and ventured into the morning mist.

She sat up as soon as he left, already wishing he hadn't. She knew she should probably be productive though, and started her own morning ritual. She took her time changing, taking extra time to rub the healing salve that Valk had given her on her scars, though unable to reach most of the claw mark on her back. After that, she rubbed her sore legs, both from the walking, and the spots that Irvine seemed too eager to slap with his blade during their sparring. She knew it was to point out her poor footing, but the light bruises on her thighs made her rather him target some other spot.

I only wish I could have a hot bath on the road. she mused as she stepped into the early morning light, still mostly illuminated by the bright moons above, and stretched her arms over her head. Most of the camp was already buzzing, and preparing for the day's march. She fished the leather strip she kept from inside her boot and tied her thick hair behind her head in a loose tail, and began setting to work herself.

She struggled some with the tent, but through the teachings of Irvine, was able to pack it up well enough to fit onto the cart with the rest of the night supplies. She grinned at her work, however much later it had been, and started back to her now more private spot in the encampment.

Her relative happiness at the isolation and her self-sufficiency, was summarily ruined when she heard a low feminine voice from behind her.

"Where'd Irvine go so early?"

Erika turned on her heel, putting a fist on her hip and angling a leg to the side in a common display of resistance she used on her father or unruly customers. "Wouldn't ye like to know?"

Teria's bouncing pace was slowed suddenly by the remark, and a sadness seemed to drift over her angular face. Erika tried to hide her confusion to no avail.

"I'm alright actually. It's his business, I don't need to know necessarily." she conceded.

Erika narrowed her eyes and started to turn back to her belongings, but Teria didn't leave.

"I was wondering, Erika." she began, causing the Fjordling to turn slowly. "Would you mind if I gave you a bit of advice with your fighting?"

An eyebrow shot up on Erika's face, showing her confusion even more poignantly. "What do ye mean?"

Teria shuffled her muscled legs slightly, and seemed scared to look her in the eye. "I was just meaning, that maybe it would help you if you heard some advice from another person, besides just Irvine. Not that Irvine has been teaching you wrong or anything."

"Irvine's been teachin' me just fine, ranger." she responded aggressively. "What can ye teach me that he can't?"

"To use this, for starters." she said, holding out her bow, and then moving to the shortswords on her hips. "I can spar with you too, show you what it's like to fight a faster opponent."

Erika resisted the urge to question her about the comparison, but accepted in the end, figuring any help she could get might lessen the bruises. Much to her surprise though, the next hour was filled with valuable information about how she carried herself in a fight. Teria manually moved Erika's legs to show her the more proper stance to fight someone, though she grunted in pain when the ranger's sharp fingers dug into a bruise, causing her to recoil at first. After her trepidation though, Teria pointed out each of the bruises that she had found through her skirt and explained why Irvine had hit her there, Erika absorbing each word with some idle contempt for the woman.

She explained that Irvine wasn't like any of the soldiers, and likely relied on exploiting weaknesses to win most of his fights. Erika wanted to disagree, being one to witness his battle with the thief after the mountain pass, but saw the logic in her observations nonetheless.

Still though, she was beaten in the sparring matches with her, just the same as Irvine. She groaned as Teria tapped her hip with one of her shortswords, dropping her warhammer to the side and retying her hair for the thousandth time.

"Tying your hair back over and over won't make you any better at this, sweetheart." she said.

Erika eyed her with annoyance, removing the leather thong from her strip and wrapping it around her thick hair. "It's a habit when I get frustrated. Don't be callin' me sweetheart either."

Teria reddened slightly. "I'm sorry, I didn't mean to."

"It's fine. Let's just get on with it."

The ranger set back into a ready stance, and moved slowly. "Now, just as I showed you, these routines will help in the long run."

Erika set her jaw, and did her best to mimic the movements. Even through her chagrin, she had to admit Teria knew what she was talking about. She tried to keep in mind her previous usage of her warhammer, using her considerable strength to alter its trajectory when needed, and to use its weight to her advantage when it came to moving fluidly.

Eventually the caravan began moving again, but Teria remained by her side, seemingly trying to start conversations with her, and smiling each time they met eyes. Erika began to wonder if she had thought wrong of this woman, but still required more time to judge her fully.

† ⊦

Versal stepped into the walls of Sildenfeld for the first time since he was nearly half his current age. The guards welcomed the refugees of Valen with open arms and supplies. Fresh clean clothes were given to all, along with blankets and food for the weary group. A familiar face soon greeted the smith, as Sárif stepped roughly through the streets, which came off as odd to Versal as the elf usually seemed to glide, causing him to think that something was seriously wrong.

"It is good to see you, old friend." the golden-haired elf said quietly as they watched the rest of the refugees slowly move into the temples.

"What's wrong Sárif?" he asked briskly, not wanting the mage to avoid the topic of his disheveled appearance.

He smiled weakly in response. "There's a Daemon in the world, we're in a troubled time."

Versal's face darkened. "There's more ye're not tellin' me."

"Indeed. I should have figured I wouldn't be able to hide anything from you." he sighed. "My mate is dead."

The smith placed his large hand on Sárif's shoulder. "That's never easy to be goin' through. How can I 'elp?"

The elf started to protest, but the Fjordling refused to hear a word of it. Rest wouldn't come easy when he knew that a friend was in need. Sárif expediently explained as much as he could, the involvement of the Abyssal Hand in releasing the Daemon, as well as their recent attacks in the city. They started walking carefully through the streets, the sol elf informing Versal that his daughter and her companion had arrived in the city, but had just recently set out with the forward force back to Valen. The

242

smith expressed some discomfort in his daughter accompanying the military, though he trusted Irvine to look after her. Sárif also told him the tales of Erika's battle with the jordhak, as well as their successful destruction of the Daemon that attacked the city.

At this, Versal was surprised, but proud and impressed at his daughter at the same time. She had always been shy of her own power despite it being such a useful tool in their occupation. He always figured it was because of Irvine's intense fear of fire that she didn't use it, avoiding anything that would cause her markings to set in.

The two arrived at Sárif's destroyed home when he told him more of the Abyssal Hand, and the words of Madame Mipha. Versal's face souring at the mention of the soothsayer, never having complete trust in the woman. The two had met her many years ago when traveling with Feldran and the rest of their old band. The Fjordling had always been wary of her, due to a poor history with the elders from his homeland. The two discussed the little knowledge they had, as well as Sárif's hostage from the organization, prompting a grim smile from Versal, who volunteered to gain more information from him.

† †

The drainage tunnels below the city of Sildenfeld smelled of rot and refuse. The chilled air above causing this darker world to feel much more comfortable than it would be during the summer, but still not comfortable by any means. The leader of the Abyssal Hand stalked between these throughways, her nose turning up at the foul smell while her cane and footsteps made light taps in the low standing water beneath her. Her plans had only worked partially, causing her a certain degree of disdain. Indeed, the aash elf that assisted that damned councilman was dead, the explosion having rocked the entire city to its core. The boy that was the vessel for the Dragoon was still alive though, other members informing her that an Ignis blood was with him. She cursed under her breath, cursed Sárif for not mentioning the fact that the city's savior was accompanied by a woman of that primordial strength, and cursed the fact that they both represented a power that could destroy her work.

"Pure magic of the Primordials." she muttered aloud, with a degree of envy. "Wasted on a child ignorant to the world."

She had her own Elementia blood that she had recruited a short time ago, but he was not in any way interested in destroying the Daemons. Quite the opposite, he seemed ready for another Daemon War, and a chance to flex his innate abilities.

She wondered if this Ignis, that she heard tell of, had any relation to the Fjordling the sol elf used to travel with many years prior. In any case, she had much information to gather, and dire punishment to dole out to those failures that still dared to suck air from this world. A time later, she arrived at her destination, waving her bony fingers in the air with arcane energy swirling around them. The doorway opened, granting her access to the somehow darker tunnels beneath the Hall of Choice.

Shortly after, two guards gave her a respectful salute. "Afternoon Madame Mipha. What can we do for you?"

She smiled wide as she hobbled towards them on her cane. "Oh nothing, dear boys. Look at you two, so strapping in your armor."

The two shuffled slightly, unsure of why the soothsayer had appeared before them. Neither noticed her hand movement as she clutched her cane, rubbing incredibly small runes in the wood as they lit in a dull purple glow. The man on the left quickly clutched his throat, thick green slime washing from his open mouth as he let out a muffled scream. The other bent down to him in response, shaking his shoulder and attempting to turn him over, but was met with a thin dagger just under his jaw.

The two let out sickening gurgles before falling totally silent. Mipha retrieved the keys from the belt of the first guard, unlocking the cell they stood in front of. The man inside was bruised and blooded, his eyes slowly opening to her. She clicked her tongue and shook her head as she stepped closer.

"A shame you had to go through this." she said quietly.

He could muster no reply besides his scream that was cut short only a moment after it began.

† †

Sárif led Versal down the dark hallways of the dungeon below the hall. The smith shuddered at his memories of this place, following a grave misunderstanding during their first visit to the city. The elf explained the dismal amount of information he had been able to glean from their captive, besides the confirmation that the Abyssal Hand had indeed been responsible for releasing the Daemon, as well as the fact that their main force lay somewhere in the city. Versal grunted, determined to get as much information as they needed, especially knowing this man had a mind to hurt his daughter, even if he had only met a decoy instead.

They paused a moment, Sárif holding a hand outwards to the large man to halt him. His sharp ears twitching slightly as he listened down the hallway. Versal saw what caught his attention. There was a hand laying on the ground just barely peeking from around the corner that they were nearing, a slight sheen of crimson surrounding it.

He noticed Sárif making hand motions, as a thin light of arcane energy surrounded him. The smith similarly prepared, setting his jaw, and willing his body to heat as they waited.

Moments passed, until they finally heard the clicking of wood against the stone floor. A hunched woman stepped from behind the corner, carefully avoiding the bodies that laid out on the ground. She wore a mask over her eyes, her wrinkled mouth distorted into a wicked grin that faded ever so slightly when she glanced up to find the two facing her, despite her apparent lack of sight.

"Damn." she said, loud enough to echo through the silence that hung over the hallway.

Versal's torso burst into flames, his flesh turning black as obsidian with the cracking lines of fiery energy webbing around his body. "I always knew ye were crooked, Mipha!" he shouted, hurling a blast of energy towards her.

She waved her cane in front of her, a transparent silvery shield appearing to cover her small frame. The fiery missile exploded around her and scorched the stone walls and ceiling. She snapped her fingers, three small orbs of light appearing before her, lingering for a moment before shooting out towards the pair. Sárif stepped to the side, waving his right hand in a protective ward that sent the bolts careening off to the sides, whipping his left out in a second gesture that blasted a powerful beam through the smokescreen caused by Mipha's attack. The elf smiled cruelly when he heard her scream in pain, Versal moving past his shoulder and slamming both fists into the cold stone below, sending a shockwave of heat outwards. Sárif followed behind the heatwave as it cleared the smoke, but scowled at the disappearance of the soothsayer.

Versal's intimidating stature stalked down the hall, his hair and beard blazing in a bright flame that illuminated the path in front of them, his expression souring as he found the two dead guards, as well as the dead prisoner. He dropped his immolation, shaking his head as he took in the sight of the man they had captured, his clothing and skin turned to a foul smelling sludge, and his flesh following soon after. His form melted slowly with an acidic substance that slowly dripped from him.

"Ain't gettin' anythin' from this one." he called back to Sárif.

The elf followed after him, his face darkening considerably. "Fortunately, we have more information from our encounter than we likely would have gotten from him. You and Feldran were right to have such distrust in the woman."

Versal nodded. "Aye. Not like ye were friends with the old crone though."

Sárif glanced down to the fallen guardsmen. "No. But I didn't think she was capable of this."

He was met with a large hand slapping him on the back. "I didn't either. Now we know though. Let's go find 'er."

22

Roadside Attack

Erika's latest journey had taken a strange turn. Instead of Irvine, the one that she considered her rock in this convoy back to her home, she found the ranger that she had previously thought herself at odds with. The two walked side by side, Erika finding herself commonly glancing at the woman, who stood nearly a foot shorter than the Fjordling. Her slight frame hid a terrifying resolve though, and Erika found each sparring match with her to be more intimidating than with Irvine.

While they were walking, Erika was surprised to find the ranger talking nearly endlessly. Some was about her life as a ranger and her comrades, some stories telling of an irritating example named Farris, while other times she seemed to be talking about nothing at all.

Erika herself found the words to drown out periodically, her face screwing up in a scowl when she thought on their closing proximity to their home, and wondered what horrors could await them.

"Worried about getting home?" she heard suddenly, looking down to find the angular, beautiful face of Teria. Though she was surprised to see it filled with concern.

She nodded tentatively in response. "I'm not sure what to be expectin'. The last time I was seein' this monster was such a blur."

Teria thought for a moment, and quieted her voice. "From what I've heard, this is an Elder Daemon. Essentially one of the leaders of their kind."

This didn't comfort Erika, and she resisted the urge to trip the woman, though she figured those quick legs that were used to tree roots, would be able to recover quickly if she faltered at all.

"I'm honestly trying to inform you and help you understand what is going on." Teria said in defense, as if she could hear the young woman's thoughts. "It is my understanding that this Daemon escaped from a Consecration, a holy prison basically. If that's true, it may not have regained its full strength yet."

Erika scowled again. "How is that fer helpin' me? That monster was terrifyin' and stronger than anythin' I've ever seen. Yer sayin' it could be even more powerful?"

Teria held up her hands to calm her. "I know, I'm sorry. I was trying to offer some hope, in that it may have not regained much strength yet, and we may have a decent chance of ending this quickly."

Erika started to reply, but was interrupted by a sudden cacophony of shouts and screams.

† †

Sárif and Versal sat across from each other in the grand hall. The spare moonslight peeking through and bathing the two in the cool glow, though the overcast skies brought a chill breeze with them. The two pored over documents detailing Madame Mipha. Versal's eyes began to glaze over, the words starting to bleed into one another. He threw the papers on the table and leaned back in his chair.

"Damn these pages. How do ye work like this, elf?" he asked, running his thick hands through his grey hair, the faint auburn tinge flashing in the light.

Sárif glanced up towards him with a slight grin. "More so, how do you keep a successful business with your poor reading skills."

Versal glared at him. "Cause deception ain't a common thing in me business. Me clients are trusted."

"How very lucky you are to possess such a friendly customer base." Sárif said sardonically.

Versal stood, starting to pace around the room, scratching across the crimson patterns on his forearms. As he aged, the magic seemed to cause light tingling in his flesh where the lines lay on him.

"Your daughter is beginning to develop those." the elf said, gesturing at the tattoos that he knew were caused by the smith's elemental abilities.

He turned to his friend with a surprised look. "Is she? Does Irvine know about 'em?"

"I should say so. She's used it to great effect against the Daemon they fought, and the jordhak she had a run in with before entering the city. Irvine had a bit of a shock with the latter when he had discovered it, but had been together nearly constantly after they killed the Daemon."

He nodded slowly. "I'm glad 'e took it well. The two of us worried 'e would fear 'er, and me, if 'e knew about our abilities."

"Doesn't seem to have stopped his feelings for her." Sárif said absently as he returned to the parchments.

Versal found himself thinking more on those words than the issue at hand. Thoughts of having Irvine for a son-in-law filled his skull. It wasn't the worst thought in the world, especially since he himself had offered up Erika as a reason for Irvine to keep coming home after his journeys. Just the thought of his daughter in wedding robes made his emotions turn knots though.

Silence filled the room, save for the spare hoots of an owl above the open ceiling room and the eerie howling of the wind as it passed through the hallways. Versal paced back and forth, a common habit of his and Erika's when faced with an issue. Sárif continued skimming through the documents that detailed Mipha's career as a soothsayer in the city. He steamed over the situation, knowing that few people in the city would believe him of Mipha's betrayal, save for Master Valk, and possibly General Atrosby though he was already long from the city on his campaign towards Valen.

Even Varia would be hard pressed to pursue her without concrete evidence further than hearsay. he thought with annoyance.

He slammed his thin hands on the table, angered at her absolutely spotless records. Versal startled at the sudden sound, turning towards him with a sympathetic look.

Before either could speak though, the door opened with a slow creak, both occupants turning to the newcomer. The robed figure stepped slowly in, the slumped forms of the guards outside signifying the mysterious man's intent. Two wickedly curved swords glimmered in the light as they gently drifted from beneath the cloth, runes covered the flat of the blades. Sárif stood, tracing his fingers in the air as a glowing arcane energy surrounded his form in an arcane ward. Versal grounded his thick boots, cracking his knuckles as his flesh began to heat, the air filling with errant steam.

"Ye've come t' the wrong place 'ere, lad." the barrel-chested smith growled.

The assailant's blades snapped to a horizontal position, slashing outwards and sending a thin line of force through the air, rocketing towards the two. It flashed across Sárif's arcane shield harmlessly, Versal immolating his left arm and reaching his palm up to block. He grunted in pain as the ribbon successfully opened a wound in his hand, despite his hardened obsidian flesh. Crimson fluid flowed freely from the cut, boiling on his skin.

"They've got a nice trick there, elf!" he shouted out in warning, though Sárif's counterattack was interrupted by the figure dropping his blades a prompt moment later.

The man gagged as a stream of blood poured from his gaping mouth, his eyes rolling back and his form slumping unceremoniously to the ground. A figure in dark leather stood behind the corpse, a stained dagger blade held where the base of the dead man's neck was, though his other arm hung limply to the side. His left leg burned in a magical flame just below his knee, a smile flashing from beneath his hood.

"Maybe I should have been an assassin after all." he said quietly, then called to the confused two with a smile. "Greetings. Perhaps I can be of some assistance. Free of charge!"

† †

Teria rushed away from Erika, who started to jog after her, but to no avail. She was joined by four more rangers, Farris and Selbor among them. They reached the edge of the convoy to find a burning form, batting soldiers away with abandon. Standing on two legs that looked akin to a goat's, and bearing a pair of ram-like horns like Xarvix and Zyrxak. The Daemon roared at the group. The soldiers preoccupied with getting their wounded out of the fray.

Teria slung her bow around and let fly her arrows at blinding speed, caring more to distract the creature than to seriously harm it. Her guildmates dashed forward around the barrage that she and the male ranger beside her provided.

Selbor bared his axes and began hacking at the back of the creature's legs, alternating with their fifth member, and her sword strike. Farris brought two thin blades from his cloak and dove in between the two's attacks. His wicked blades dove in deftly, severing tendons in the Daemon's joints, spewing a thick orange ichor from the deep gouges.

Teria slowed her attacks, starting to aim with more precision and blinding the creature with arrow shafts that blasted into its eye sockets.

A short time later the Daemon fell to the ground, the ember infused body beginning to darken and crumple into ash.

Atrosby barreled through the crowd shortly after, barking orders to his gawking soldiers and berating the lookouts for failing to notice the creature before it was on top of them.

Teria made eye contact with Irvine as he stalked the perimeter of the convoy, following his gaze to the landscape behind her. She recognized his perceptiveness, seeing how easy an ambush would be with the rocky landscape around them. Atrosby had obviously seen the error, and would likely double the lookout from then onwards.

Unfortunately, the caravan had paid for the mistake. Nearly a score of soldiers lay unmoving, with only a handful still groaning over bludgeoning injuries. War had not been waged in decades on this continent, the Regions reaching peaceful negotiations, and even border disputes ceasing to be relevant. No one was accustomed to wartime anymore.

Erika found Teria soon after the dust had settled, her chest heaving from the exertion it took to simply get through the crowd.

"What was that?" she asked the ranger incredulously, staring at the melting corpse.

Teria took a deep breath, and began collecting her arrows that were still intact, cleaning each one and replacing it into the quiver at the back of her waist. Erika followed her, and helped retrieve them.

"That, was a dredge. Daemonic servant that was more footsoldier than anything else in the Daemon War."

Erika screwed up her face in a scowl, staring at the form, nearly fully turned to ash. "That was a footman?"

Teria nodded grimly. "Granted, that doesn't say much about the Elder's strength. These weren't hard for it to summon. The Greater that you and Irvine battled on the hill probably took a lot out of it though."

Erika's face darkened, feeling the tears that tried to break from her eyes. The thought that Irvine's uncle had fought such a creature, and had perished after pestering the thing as much as he did. It didn't bode well for the fate of her father, though she knew she couldn't give up hope.

Irvine appeared next to them a moment later, putting his hand on Erika's shoulder. "Are you alright?"

The Fjordling nodded, smiling at him. Teria moved away while they spoke, feeling awkward after what Farris had told her. Soon after they shared a brief embrace, the courier was jogging around the caravan back to the general at the front.

Teria and Erika began helping the soldiers in burying the fallen in the earth nearby the road. It wasn't much, but they all hoped it would be well enough to keep the souls at rest when the grim Shadesfall season came. The annual reverence of the dead would begin in less than a week when the month of Hallowden began. Erika realized the amount of time it had been since they had fled, nearly a fortnight already, and how close her birth month had come already. With that thought, she gave the fallen soldiers all the more respect, burying their forms gently and reciting quiet parting words.

The two of them sat back after finishing, neither speaking for quite a while. The convoy began moving back into formation again, slowly carrying on from the sudden stop in their journey. The two looked up from the graves to the mountains above, scraping the sky with their harsh points. A light, drizzling rain had started again, wetting Erika's face and adding more to her negative emotions.

"I'd like to apologize." Teria said slowly, drawing a side-long glance from Erika. The ranger took a long while to continue, but Erika didn't prod her, seeing that this was a difficult thing for her to express. "It came to my understanding that you may see me as a rival for Irvine's affections."

Erika began stammering a rebuttal, her face becoming hot and her thoughts swimming for a reply. Teria continued before she could though. "I honestly never had any interest in Irvine. He is a valuable asset to the upcoming battle, and I know he's already proven himself to be a good fighter."

Erika's skin cooled slightly, as she listened to what seemed to be the most heartfelt thing this ranger had ever said. "I never had any friends really, growing up as a ranger, I always distanced myself from other people, and focused more on my duties. You and him were interesting though, for some reason I can't explain. I honestly just wanted to actually be friends with someone that wasn't a ranger."

She turned to face Erika, a vulnerable expression spreading across her face, as if looking to her for some kind of answer. Erika smiled, no longer seeing the ranger as someone to be hostile towards. "I'd be happy to be yer friend, Teria."

This seemed to evoke a happiness in the ranger that she had never felt. A single tear dropped from her dark eyes, only to be hastily wiped away by her hand. She stood a moment later, offering a hand to Erika, and the two started off with the convoy.

Behind one of the boulders, Farris smiled warmly. Happy to have been of some help.

23
THE CALM

The dawn of their final day of travel came with an orange glow. The light filled the landscape in the outskirts of the valley. The clouds had at last shifted, taking the rain with them and leaving the company with an exceptionally beautiful morning. Few spirits were lifted with the weather change though, as the realization of the decreasing distance between them, and what promised to be a challenging adversary at the least, became more apparent. Erika started her own day, tearing down her tent with the aid of Teria, who had volunteered to spend the night just outside of it.

A feeling of dread had washed over her, and she had found sleep elusive in the night. A pain began in her chest, and her stomach twisted in knots. Her mind raced with the possible outcomes of the coming battle, each one more negative and terrible than the last. As Teria helped her pack up, she seemed to be able to sense her unease. She tried making casual conversation, as Farris had advised, with the dual intent of distracting her new friend, as well as getting to know her more.

The ranger seemed surprised when she told her that she was not actually in a committed relationship with Irvine besides their close friendship.

"You two seem so close though. He's never made an advancement?" she asked in disbelief.

Erika smiled in her memories. "Just time spent honestly. He'd never made any kind o' flirts or anythin' that I noticed. We did go to the Harvest Festival together, though the Daemon attacked and ruined all that."

Teria's face seemed to sour, but brightened as Erika continued.

"Although, he did have an emerald pendant in his satchel." Erika said. The ranger gave her a sly smirk, to which she stammered to reply. "I wasn't tryin' to sneak through 'is things, it just fell out."

"Right, and I didn't mean to shoot Farris in the ass with my practice bow when we were still Saplings." she replied with a cackle. "Emerald though, matches your eyes. I bet that's what he had in mind."

Erika felt herself blushing slightly at the thought. "Just don't tell 'im I know about it."

Teria nodded quickly, happy to seal away the knowledge.

⚔

Irvine's last full day of marching was much less enjoyable, spent alongside General Atrosby as he had been for the last several. The attack by the Daemonic dredge had been a wake-up call for the seasoned solider as to just what they were fighting. It seemed this sudden sobering caused him to seek out Irvine's advice as one of the few among them who had not only seen their target, but had actually slain one of its more powerful kin. Irvine did his best to answer any question that arose from the gruff man, though he didn't pretend to have all the answers he was seeking.

He was met with grunts and grimaces each time his answer consisted of 'I don't know.' or 'I wasn't around long enough to find out.' though he seemed mostly satisfied with the information given, however scarce it may be. He attempted on multiple times to point Atrosby to the rangers, who seemed to be more knowledgeable about the Daemons than him.

He replied curtly though, saying. "I already know the hierarchy of the damned creatures."

He occasionally glanced behind them at the convoy, able to spot Erika's tell-tale auburn hair in the sea of grey and black cloaks. He worried about leaving her behind with the large group, though Atrosby firmly commanded him to stick close. He was comforted only by Teria being close by her, and further more by the fact that they seemed to be getting along much better now. He didn't know what they were speaking about, but they seemed to be genuinely enjoying each other's company. He smiled at that, glad that they had become friends.

The day passed uneventfully, their final encampment of the journey being a scant league from the edge of Valen. The sun dipped below the buildings, highlighting the bare frames of the majority of them, some buildings burned away completely. The large cracks lining the crater the Daemon had created no longer glowed, but were now blackened and solid, giving the ruins an even more ominous appearance. As the convoy set up camp outside of the town, with strict orders to keep low light to avoid any attention, Irvine scanned the area with a spyglass.

"It looks empty. I don't even see any movement." he said darkly, stowing his glass and crossing his arms.

Atrosby grunted. "Perhaps its dormant. We'll leave a constant watch throughout the night to ensure no surprises."

He began to turn away, pausing as he met Irvine's grim expression. He cleared his throat and shuffled his left foot slightly. "Are you alright, son?"

Irvine nodded slowly, trying to speak positively. "Just nerves most likely. Let's make sure we kill the bastard."

Atrosby thought back to the talk Sárif had with him, informing him of Irvine's full involvement, and his uncle's fate. He had hoped he wouldn't join the company, and wait in Sildenfeld, but he also knew that they needed his weapon if they were going to have any kind of good chance at killing the monstrosity they would soon face.

He placed a hand on the courier's shoulder. "Get some sleep. You'll need it for the battle ahead."

Irvine nodded, but stood for a while longer. He stared at the charred husk that was once Valen, remembering his life spent in that place, and all the people who were gone now.

The smoke of Valen was long dispersed, and the neighboring village of Feldsbar that lay to their southeast, was too far past its own destruction for anyone in the company to notice.

† †

"Then the girl shattered my shoulder. After that, the boy and I had a chat, and I was on my merry way after he disappeared. I figured I was far enough away from the Daemon that I wouldn't receive any immediate repercussions, so I decided to come get some revenge against the people that hired me into that damned contract. Ah!" Teral jerked as Valk wrapped another layer of bandage over the brace on his shoulder.

"Stop your moving!" the man shouted, echoing through the halls. "Else you won't move this shoulder ever again."

The thief made a face at the wound, glancing back to the two he was speaking with. The Ignis blood leaned his massive frame over the back of the chair he sat on, a smile widening on his marked face. The sol elf sat, looking regal as sols were oft to do, in another chair, though his unkempt and darkened hair, tinged with red, spoke against his calm demeanor. The head of the Willow Rangers stood coolly to the side, though she seemed to be glancing at Valk more than anything.

"Yes, your daughter has one Hells of a swing." Teral said, regarding the proud father that he had just confessed his initial murderous intent to. "That aside, I have obtained a fair amount of information about this Abyssal Hand organization. Including the fact that they have been summoning Daemons for years. This is just the first time that they were able to hit a big one."

Sárif put his hand to his chin, his eyes distant as if lost in thought. Versal adjusted in his backwards seat. "Yer tellin' me that these bastards 'ave been around for a good long while? Just 'ow many Daemons 'ave they let loose?"

"Likely several of the ones we battled a long while ago." the elf answered absently. "Seems you and Feldran were correct in suspecting the old woman for something sinister."

"Bah! It's not that we suspected 'er fer nothin', we were just spooked by 'er, that's all." he replied in his boisterous manner, throwing his massive hands around with his words, and making Teral flinch more than a little.

"Only this time it seems the Daemon is an Elder of the Circle of Wrath." Valk piped up suddenly, drawing a grimace from Teral as he tightened the bandage.

"You two fought ones from Lust and Avarice if I remember correctly?" he said, nodding towards Sárif and Versal, and trying to avoid the sharp gaze of the willow woman.

The two nodded in response, Sárif speaking calmly. "Among others, yes."

Teral's jaw fell agape. "You've fought Daemons before? I had always thought they were dormant for hundreds of years, until I inadvertently released Zyrxak."

"For good reason. If the world knew that we were still under near constant threat from the Hells, they would panic. The world would be in anarchy. The peace we've all enjoyed would be shattered. Churches would be ostracized at best, if not outright attacked for promises which the people would then deem falsehoods." Varia explained grimly.

Sárif continued for her. "Our world would be thrust into the very wars we fought to end. All because the Angelus' haven't been heard from since the end of the Daemon War. They are the crutch that much of our society hangs on and hopes for. We still have no knowledge of where they truly went."

Valk sat upright in a jerk, as if he had suddenly realized something, Varia appearing as if she wanted to move to him.

"What is it, healer?" Teral asked cautiously, fearing for his injured shoulder.

He shook his head, waving off Varia. "Nothing. I'll have to remember to look into something, but it's no matter for now. Sit back! I'm going to start healing you more, you may feel some discomfort."

The cleric began to speak words under his breath, not fully understandable, but it sounded like sweet whispers, like wind through grassy reeds. Light emitted from his thick hands and flooded into Teral's body. He winced at the feeling, but kept his attention on the two he was trying to gain the trust of.

"So, in short. Ye released one of the most powerful Daemons in recorded history, helped burn down me home and caused the death of a close friend. Then ye hunted me daughter and her best friend, nearly killed 'im, and tackled 'im down a waterfall. Not 'afore me daughter gave ye a right wallop!" the slight boast did not go unnoticed. "Then ye came 'ere to 'elp dismantle the people that 'ired ye fer the job."

Teral stared at the barrel-chested man, intimidated by his size even when sitting, doubly so knowing the fiery power he held in that massive frame. "Yeah. That just about covers it."

"Then why in the bloody rivers should we trust ye!" Versal shouted, bursting from his chair and flinging it a foot in front of him, the thief slinking further into his own chair, to the violent correction of the cleric.

"He has given us information we did not previously have." Sárif said, putting a thin hand on the man's shoulder. "Plus, he warned all of us of the Abyssal Hand, albeit in a cryptic manner. And perhaps a bit late."

The room fell silent, Valk eventually pulling away and slapping the thief on the thigh.

"Huzzah, you're healed." he said sardonically, causing Varia to smirk. Valk looked to her and managed a small smile.

Teral stretched his mended shoulder and grimaced at the cleric.

"In all seriousness though, take it easy. Even with magic, wounds leave effects on the body. Don't go overdoing it, or I won't be able to help you."

He briskly gathered his supplies. "Now, if you'll all excuse me, I have something to look into. I'll inform you should I discover anything helpful."

Sárif nodded his head as he bowed to them. Versal started to protest, but was cut short by the elf's outstretched hand. Varia stalked out of the room shortly after, winking at Sárif and Versal, and trailed after Valk.

Silence returned again, Versal assuming a stature of frustration and Sárif one of intense contemplation. Teral sat nervously staring at the two, doing everything in his power not to fidget his fingers. He did that when he was exceptionally nervous, and in a strange irony, this was the most nerve-wracking situation he had been in these stressful days.

"If you give me a day, less even, I can find where they live. We can all go knock on their door together." he reasoned out to the silent watchers. "There is no apology for what I've done, but I want to help bring down the people who did this."

"Ye're one of the people who did this!" Versal replied coldly.

"A life of servitude then!" the thief quickly shot back. "Dear smith, I've considered myself dead already. That Daemon trapped me to his beck and call, but now that I've escaped him, I am free of his will. I do not know if this power will disappear when he is slain though."

The two regarded the ever-flaming leg of their conversation partner.

"Let me help while I still can. I fear that is all I can do until my mobility is stolen permanently."

"Engage your methods then." Sárif said, this time eliciting no quarrel from Versal. "Find the home of the Abyssal Hand. Dawn tomorrow we will attack and destroy their organization. We've wasted enough time against this unseen foe as is."

The two grimaced in unison at the days' time between discovering Mipha and the present conversation.

"I will oblige to your request." Teral said dutifully. "The Abyssal Hand will not see the light of tomorrow's sun."

Moments later he disappeared from the room, leaving the two companions to their own machinations.

"He's the only way I see forward." Sárif said, answering Versal's unsaid complaint.

"He tried to kill me daughter." the smith reasoned quietly.

Sárif turned to him, anger and death in his darkened eyes. "Haven't we all done things we regret?"

† †

The nighttime wind blew eerily on the ridge overlooking the ruins of Valen. The army of Sildenfeld and the allied forces camped nearly halfway between the same ridge and the town. Two figures stood there facing the force's rear, unaffected by the breeze. Zyrxak's exterior was cooled to a dull grey, ash falling off of his form with every twitching movement. Next to him was a lithe form, humanoid in silhouette, but his face bore a hideous smiling mouth of jagged teeth, two horns curling from his forehead around the back of his head, angling upwards just slightly before their sharp points. His body seemed bare, save for thin wrapping around his hips that appeared as spider webs. His sharp red eyes darted along the line of soldiers unbeknownst of their arrival.

"I'm actually rather impressed in their speed." Zyrxak muttered in a growl.

"So many toys to play with." the second figure giggled in sickening glee.

The specter regarded his new companion. "Do leave me some fun, Vayex."

"Why of course, Elder." the lanky Daemon replied, mocking a curtsy with a nonexistent skirt. "I only ask for a few playthings. Come, Gryvax."

A thick bubbling sludge popped next to him in acknowledgment. A faint visage of a face curled in the oily tar substance, grinning madly.

Vayex knelt slightly, running his sharp tipped fingers through the slime. "Hungry, aren't you my sweet?"

"Have your fun." Zyrxak began, interrupting the two and looking up at the dark skies. "I shall join you at dawn. I wish to take the full measure of this army."

"Nervous that an Angelus might come to ruin the festivities?" Vayex asked, with a hint of toxic sarcasm.

Zyrxak turned slowly, his horrific skull twisting on his spine with cracks and creaks, flames beginning to lick from between his teeth. Vayex suddenly wore an expression of fear, cowering back and expecting a strike to befall him. Though none came.

"The Angelus were never long for this world. Take care whatever slew Xarvix does not fell you, Daemon of Lust." the specter warned antagonistically.

"As you wish, Elder Daemon of Wrath. We eagerly await your attack at dawn." the small one said, caressing a hand on Zyrxak's lower jaw affectionately, though a hint of fear still twisted his thin lips. The sludge beside him popped again in reply.

"Such a gluttonous girl tonight, Gryvax. Come, let us find you some flesh to enjoy."

Vayex's thin spider-like legs carried him silently into the night, the sludge following him with a slower pace, leaving dead grass and foliage behind, sucked dry of any nutrients and life it once had. Zyrxak allowed himself a grin, his twisted jagged teeth grinding together.

Soon this world would be weighed, and found wanting.

††

"Quiet night." Atrosby commented, if only to break the silence of their camp.

Irvine glanced up at him, chewing on his nightly ration, and decided to forego a reply.

"What do you suppose caused this Daemon's arrival?" he continued. "We were just having an argument at the Hall about the erratic wildlife and weather changes. I suppose this is the reason after all. I thought Morton was spouting drivel about the Angelus abandoning us. I now think it could be true."

Irvine rolled his eyes, assuming that Atrosby was deliberately not speaking about the thief that had released Zyrxak in front of him, even though Irvine was the first to know about it. He hated dealing with high-ranking military officers, often skipping jobs from them due to all their bureaucratic attitudes. Irvine didn't mention what Xarvix had spoken about on the hill outside Sildenfeld, or Arce'Thrak's cryptic words. Those graveled words echoed in his mind now. He never thought much about Angelus or Daemons before, but since one had appeared, he now found himself dwelling on the events of the Daemon War. None of it could be helped though. The mortal races had such a small role in the ancient war, they may as well have been bystanders watching titans fight to the death, the fate of their entire world hanging in the balance.

"Do you think we need the help of the Angelus?" Irvine asked quietly.

The general paused a moment. "I am not sure. Truly. I would like nothing more than to think that we can handle our own world, but now I have my doubts."

"Do you think that wise?"

Atrosby's gaze snapped back to the courier as he pulled from his waterskin, his contemplative notions vanished as he suddenly felt a challenge from the young man. Though doubt gripped the back of his mind.

"Right." Irvine said passively after waiting for a reply.

"How dare you presume to know more than me. I am your superior, you are merely a courier." Irvine mocked at the general, causing the incredulous stares of many nearby with his raised voice. Irvine had grown so tired of the soldier's high and mighty attitude that he ceased to fear any punishment he would dole out.

Atrosby began to raise his voice in his throat, but paused again, his gaze lowering. "And yet you carry the one weapon that can haul our sorry asses back to peace."

Irvine turned to him again, confused.

"I know how I sound. I'm not going to question your impersonation. Though I must commend your gall." he said, managing a small smirk. "Not many men would have the bravery, or stupidity, to insult me like that directly."

"A shame that so many hide their true feelings." the courier prodded again, beginning to sharpen his sword.

The general shot him an incredulous look. "And now twice. I'm beginning to like you."

Irvine smirked and met his gaze. "Likely an unhealthy way to make friends, basing it on insults."

Atrosby openly smiled now. "A soldier's life is rarely healthy lad. Though a scrawny errand boy would hardly know."

He grunted at the young man's silent nod, as if he was accepting the comment. No reply came to further their strange back and forth though. Atrosby's head falling back to his own blade that he polished carefully, his eyes glancing back to linger at the courier.

Irvine sighed after the obvious nudging to resume. "General, there is no shortage of things I would love to call you, and I am sure none would truly offend you. Just the same, I was teased as a young boy, saying I was the one who burned down his own home with his parents still inside."

Atrosby's expression turned to concern.

"False, I assure you." Irvine resumed, holding up a hand. "Nonetheless, there is nothing you can say to offend me either. I cannot say I enjoy this game of yours."

He sighed. "My apologies. I agree it is kind of a sick game in theory. We used to engage in insult contests when I was a footman. I confess I miss those times, and you reminded me of them just now. Thank you for that."

"Where are those men you played this game with then?" Irvine asked

A sullen expression came over him. "Dead for the most part. Peace is not as satisfying as it seems, when you look back at what it cost to get there."

"I see. I'm sorry for your loss." Irvine replied sympathetically.

"War never apologizes. Neither should you." he said, meeting his eyes. "You never knew them, I hardly expect your pity. I'm sure you've seen your share of death too. As much as I talk, I know couriers haven't the easiest of jobs."

Irvine nodded in response. "You know we have a saying about death?"

Atrosby looked back at him curiously. Irvine spoke without looking away from his weapon. "It's the courier farewell. 'May death find you alive.' Doesn't always work out that way though."

The old soldier nodded slowly, then turned away again after a moment, resuming his work on his own weapon in silence.

† †

Teria sat carefully by Erika, giving her a fresh canteen of water to drink from. She absently touched a slight hand to the Ignis markings that covered her arms thickly, admiring their crimson shade. Erika started to jerk her hand back, but Teria stopped her.

"Nothing to be ashamed of, Erika." the ranger scolded lightly. "I think they're a beautiful addition to your appearance."

Erika reddened slightly, still unsure of how to take the compliment. She was used to giving those she was more friendly with a light punch in response to such comments about her appearance, though she knew Teria could thrash her if she did.

"So, what was Irvine like as a child?" she asked suddenly, putting her hand up at Erika's questioning gaze. "I don't plan on sleeping tonight. We're too near the enemy. I am simply making conversation."

Erika drank from the bottle quickly, coughing to clear her airway. "He was a quiet boy. Not very outgoin'. Used to get picked on by the other children after 'is home burned. Lost 'is mum and da in the fire."

Teria hung her head slightly, listening to the tale that she hardly expected to be somber.

"Moved in with his uncle, an old friend o' Papa's. He raised him like his own son. I always beat up the other boys that accused 'im of startin' the flames." she continued, the ranger stifling a laugh. "He always had a fear of fire after that. Only rarely did he come into my father's forge, and when he did, he'd stare at the flames like they'd jump at 'im."

"Is that why you're apprehensive about your Elementia markings?" she asked

"My papa has 'em real thick, all over his body, an' on his face too." she answered, gesturing to the light markings that had begun on her own face and neck. "I knew he used to fight a lot when he was younger. He would teach me to use my own abilities too, but I always feared how Irvine would react to his closest friend burstin' into flames. So, I avoided usin' it beyond just encouragin' the forge here and there. Not enough to brand me with the markin's."

The ranger laughed more openly this time. "I can see your concern, but I don't think you give him enough credit. He's a courier after all. Sure, he may have those mental scars, and he may have closed off a bit after he found out what you did to that jordhak, but he is adaptable. All couriers have to be. Just learn to control your magic, that's the important part."

Erika nodded quietly, sipping at the canteen more.

Teria's head darted up suddenly. "Did you hear that?"

Erika stared at her for a moment before glancing around, the ranger setting her bottle to the side and putting a hand on her bow. She raised in a low crouch, scanning the sea of soldiers around them. Erika felt her heart begin to beat violently in her chest, instinctively grabbing her warhammer laying by her side.

Teria nocked an arrow and drew the string back halfway, raising slightly more. Erika could see her eyes focusing, her entire demeanor akin to a bird of prey locking on to its quarry. The ranger scowled, then exhaled sharply. Erika didn't see the arrow leave the bow, but she heard the sharp sound of it hitting flesh. She followed her gaze, a solider just beginning to fall in the distance, his blade raised over a resting comrade.

"Teria..." Erika breathed in horror, but the ranger stood quickly, shouting a call to the rest of the force.

"Enemies among us! To arms! Watch for any not acting themselves!"

24
The Storm

Atrosby cursed under his breath, leaping onto his horse and leaving much of his kit behind, simply taking his shield and blade. Irvine darted to his feet as well, quickly calling to the general. "I'll try and get a vantage point!"

The gruff man nodded in reply. "Watch your step, courier!"

Irvine spent the next minutes damning their luck, and their choices. Of course they would be assailed in the pre-dawn hours, they were fighting a Daemon, not another mortal force. His legs pumped furiously, his heart rising in his throat.

Where is Erika? was the repeating thought in his mind, though he knew he had no time to seek her.

He raced around the occupying force, trying to ignore the horrifying sights that he found. Soldiers rising to strike their brothers, their eyes cold and lifeless. He knew not what was happening, but the sight disturbed him deeply. He slowed a moment as a corpse fell in front of him, a sudden arrow slicing across Irvine's cheekbone and gouging through the neck of another man. The soldier fell with gouts of crimson falling down his side from the severed artery, a single ranger beginning to nock another arrow. His eyes pleaded to Irvine.

"Move, courier! I cannot stop my movements!" he shouted as the second arrow loosed and flew towards Irvine's head.

He narrowly dodged to the side, the fletching drawing more blood on his neck. "What is happening?" he called back.

"I'm being controlled by some-"

His voice was cut short as his body twisted horribly while his head stayed still, the bones in his neck making awful snapping sounds as the body continued, his arm slinging a third arrow into the visor of an approaching soldier by the sheer force of the arm whipping it around. The ranger's lifeless stare affixed to the ground between him and Irvine, blood fountaining where shards of his vertebrae had splintered through his neck.

Irvine's face contorted into a terrified expression, realizing that a new kind enemy was upon them as a shrill laughter encompassed the battlefield. His eyes scanned around for the creature, but suddenly found his boots encompassed by a dark ooze.

A disembodied female voice, low and bubbling spoke to him, laughing uncontrollably with glee. "You's is the ones the masters talkses abouts. You's ours next meals!"

✝ ✝

The catacombs under the temple of Phanel seemed to be constantly damp. The smell was a gagging musk that came from years of the tunnels being closed off with no contact with fresh air. Valk wore a cloth over his face, a precaution against the dusty interior that threatened to block his lungs. He hated coming down here, like most in his station, the environment was plenty enough to stop them from exploring the long-derelict archives. The torch he carried illuminated the thousands of slots in the walls, housing the remains of honored warriors from the ancient wars. He shuddered slightly at one of the ghastly skeletal faces that stared at him with a gaping mouth devoid of flesh. Mothers told their children not to wander at night when close to the month of Hallowden, lest the walking dead snatch them up in a gambit for new life. It had been quite a long time since Valk had been told any of those stories, even longer since he actually believed them, but these graves still caused a nervousness in him that he couldn't explain. The maze continued on, though he knew his way around due to a venture many years prior, and he eventually found his way to the chamber he sought.

He took the time to begin lighting each of the torches that hung from the sconces on the walls, the room gradually brightening as he went. As he circumvented the cylindrical chamber, he peered with narrow eyes at the paintings on the walls, their faded nature not betraying any of their detail.

Daemons, Angelus, and Dragons. All participating in the wars that were collectively called the Daemon Wars in their current age. Valk suspected that was due to the Daemons being perceived as the more antagonistic force of the ancient conflict. He walked slowly around the room a second time, searching for a specific fresco he had seen those many years ago when his mentor had brought him here.

He received several lashings that day, his master informing him that his questioning was heretical. Though he held the highest station in the temple, Valk didn't possess the same blind devotion that his master did. He still questioned everything, even now. He arrived at the scene of the final battle that shook the world and moons, banishing the remaining Daemons and Angelus from the world, while the Dragons retreated to their unknown homes far from the reach of mortals. He raised an eyebrow when he came to his senses fully, realizing that the next scene was not the beginning. He clicked his tongue in annoyance at his long-passed mentor, and his ignorance to this painting that did not reflect any recorded historical event.

"No memories here, eh Phanel?" he said quietly, looking up as if he were to garner a reply from the God of Memory.

The painting itself was split in two. On the right side, lay a city with towering monuments and a powerful wall. The city was not unlike his home of Sildenfeld. Above the towers and buildings was the visage of a six-fingered hand, the paint used was a pitch black, seeming to suck the light from the surrounding wall. His eyes narrowed further, the mentioning of the organization called the Abyssal Hand is what prompted his journey down to these catacombs, and now his trek appeared fruitful.

The second side of the painting, bore the likeness of a smaller town, though the buildings lay in a husk, seemingly burned. An army was in a large circle around three combatants. One a Daemon, skeletal and horrific. The next, a Dragoon, nearly forgotten from folklore and history entirely, bearing a great flaming spear and jagged armor. The last, was a figure clad in gold and silver, with three pairs of feathered wings that protruded outwards imposingly, an Angelus.

Valk grunted uncomfortably.

"Prophecies of a forgotten age to all but Phanel. How much history has been forgotten out of sheer ignorance of the truth?" he wondered aloud.

"Much I would assume." a ragged voice replied, the elderly woman stepping down the steps, her cane clicking against the stone below.

Valk sighed quietly to himself. "It is quite late for a woman of your age to be out and about Madame Mipha."

The laughter that followed sounded like glass shards being dragged across a stone wall. "I think you'll find that with age, one requires less sleep, and therefore is awake earlier each day."

The cleric glanced towards her, counting the fingers on her bare hands, which were customarily covered. "And pray tell elder, why are you here this particularly early day?"

Mipha held her left hand up, as if answering an unspoken question, bearing a sixth finger. "I believe we both know why, my dear cleric." she stepped forward with a confidence that unnerved Valk. "It is a shame when one learns too much for their own good. Though I think not much time remains in any case. One of the great Dreadnaughts will soon appear, and we will resume the war that we have ignored for this past epoch."

Valk's eyes flashed to the mural depicting the Angelus battling the Daemon, and Dragoon, before returning to his adversary quickly. "And what of the Abyssal Hand?"

She grinned a broken tooth smile. "The Abyssal Hand-"

"Will die!" came a sudden shout from higher up the stairs, a bolt of magic energy shooting through Mipha's shoulder as she threw herself to the side, avoiding a killing blow. Her elderly form slamming to the ground with a pitiful sound. Sárif stalked down the stairs with a look of hatred and anger burning in his eyes.

⸸ ⸸

The thief Teral and the Ignis blood Versal approached the large building at the western edge of the city. In the heart of the burned portion of Sildenfeld, the once storage warehouse had long been thought forgotten and abandoned, yet the information that Teral had gathered spoke otherwise. The two paused, watching for any movement in or around the structure.

Versal eyed his companion nearly more than their target. "So, what made ye change yer allegiances? Really?"

"I suppose that girl of yours just knocked some sense into me." he replied sarcastically, smirking at his jest.

The massive man rapped his shoulder with a closed fist. "I don't trust ye, thief."

"Nor should you." he affirmed as he rubbed his freshly healed shoulder. "We all have things that we regret though. I am simply attempting to make amends as best I can, though I know my offense is far beyond any."

The smith watched him, Teral not making eye contact for the short conversation. Versal allowed the smaller man to go first, following a short distance behind as they made their way into the storehouse.

Inside was a veritable maze. Corridors and walls erected sometime after the construction of the building, twisting through the walls in a deliberate attempt to confuse any who entered. The two stepped forward carefully before the door shut suddenly behind them. They both clearly heard the lock slamming down from the outside and realized they were now trapped here. The only light being provided was Teral's leg, emitting a soft orange glow around them. The sound of steel ringing against steel caused both of them to shudder.

Teral drew two curved daggers from his cloak, while Versal cracked his knuckles and ignited his flesh in a blast of heat and light.

"That is impressive." the thief said, sizing up his companion. "Never thought I'd actually meet an Elementia blood, only heard scattered tales. I thought people like you were myths."

"Less talkin', more fightin'." the smith said gruffly, his voice amplified by the full torso immolation. He balled his hands together, producing a flame and slinging it down the hallway like a stone. The fireball slamming into the chest of a black robed individual who had just begun to draw his weapon.

Teral deftly twisted and crouched, bringing his dagger around and into the belly of another who meant to flank them. Versal turned to the wall and took a half step back.

"Damn their games. My rules now." he said, slamming both palms into the wall beside them. Teral shielded his eyes with his elbow as the flash of light rang out just before the sound of the blast. He grinned at the massive man's handiwork, and heartily chased after him, quickly slashing through the cultists that meant to corner them.

⸸ ⸸

Erika followed Teria in her mad dash.

Screams echoed from all around.

Bodies fell at her feet.

Warm liquid spattered and dripped down her bare arms.

The ranger in front of her made a weaving path, loosing arrows whenever she saw a threat, and wrenching them from the bodies as they passed.

Erika's mind was a blur, unable to fully comprehend what was happening, she knew not what or who to strike at. Though Teria had a sort of sense about her, able to know when and where an attack would happen, and was able to deftly avoid it, following with a counterattack.

Erika eventually broke off from her companion, unable to follow her any further as her stamina reached its limit. She found her way outside of the hoard of soldiers, finding a kind of peace at the edge of the battle. Her chest heaved and her heart felt ready to burst as she put a hand to her breast, trying to calm herself. Her breastplate felt tight suddenly, constricting. She scanned hurriedly through the battlefield looking for a sign of anything comprehensive in the chaos that ensued before her. Eventually she found an alien shape, a tall and lithe figure striding through the ranks in a kind of dance, his legs long were pointed, akin to a spider's, his fingers elongated into visceral blades. His hair blacker than night, and his glowing red eyes surrounded by a black substance that seemed to drip from his high cheekbones. Gleaming horns shone in the moonlight as he danced, smiling a jagged toothed smile. Each soldier he touched suddenly fell limp and began striking at his neighbor.

"Teria!" she screamed, her voice cracking midway through the name.

She wanted to call again, but the creature stopped mid step, head snapping unnaturally in her direction. The sight of the thing unnerved Erika, like something from a nightmare come to life, and there was nothing she could do to fight back.

Her heart pounded in her ribcage, and she felt a sudden pain in her stomach. A fear gripped her mind as her eyes stared wide into the crimson orbs of the monster before her. Tears streamed down her face in an uncontrolled river. The Daemon flashed from sight, then suddenly appeared beside her, a suppressed exhale of terror escaping her lips.

"Are you the one who slew Xarvix?" it asked, a coyness twisting its almost feminine voice. "I am Vayex. I believe you'll find me much more fun than those Wrath Daemons."

Erika felt the monster's cold hands running down her side and hips, sharp fingers edging underneath the waist of her skirt. A chill ran up her spine at the touch.

"Don't you want to have some fun, little one?" it whispered in her ear, the voice dripping like oil.

A hiss ran through the air, Erika's eyes widening suddenly as she felt the arrow toss her hair to the side. The creature slumped to the ground, the shaft protruding from its lithe neck. She regained control over her body and leapt away from the thing, her muscles shivering as she did.

Teria ran to her side. "I heard your call, don't worry. It's a Greater Lust Daemon."

"Someone's read a few books." the voice called from below them. The creature's torso raised from the ground in an unnatural movement as the tips of his thin legs planted into the soft soil, lifting the rest of his body in a sickening motion. He reached a hand up and wrenched the arrow from his neck. A deep crimson liquid, darker than any mortal blood, spilled forth from the wound and stained the side of the thin, web-like clothing that hugged the Daemon's form.

"Erika! I need you!" Teria said firmly, nocking another arrow and holding two more in her drawing hand.

Erika's mind swam, torn between the fear of this creature before her and the knowledge that her friend needed help. A dull pain started in her shoulder, and her eyes flashed to the source, realizing that Teria had just struck her.

"At least one of my rangers is already dead." she said with a lump in her throat, pleading to Erika. She was shocked by the look of panic in the ranger's eyes, and lifted her warhammer in a defensive posture.

"And there you go, ruining my fun." Vayex growled in a rasping voice very much unlike his previous words. He emitted a screech that pierced the ears of all around, and as he did, three scores of men turned limply to the battle, stumbling forward as if drawn by strings. "Come my puppets! Come and kill these insolent girls!"

Erika never took her eyes from the creature, though she felt more in control again. She called to the ranger. "Ye said yer cloak was magic, right?"

Teria called back her affirmation. Erika clenched her jaw and willed her body temperature to rise. Her arms blazed to life in a flash of light, consuming her flesh into the immolation. She called for her friend to get down and watched the flood of adversaries that launched towards them. She raised her arms up, the immolation crawling down her torso to her waist and up her neck to engulf her head. Her tunic under her breastplate flashed to cinders as she screamed aloud, slamming both fists as hard as she could manage into the ground below her.

⸸ ⸸

Irvine stared at the black ooze that surrounded him, covering the ground in a radius around him. He was starkly reminded of a tar pit he and a group of couriers had discovered in Myrefell to the south, though that was not sentient as this was. He attempted to raise his feet, but found himself restrained by the creature. A gout of sludge leaped upwards and gripped at his left leg, just above his knee. It dripped down slowly with a hiss, Irvine looking on in horror, as it melted away his boot, pant leg, and skin.

"No's! Yous can'ts leaves!" the gurgling voice said again. "We's loves yous, and yous's tastes!"

He grimaced at the sound of its voice, as well as the stinging pain of the bare flesh and muscle of his leg. He tried swinging
his blade downwards in quick slashes which seemed to part it like
a liquid, but failed to damage it. All around him, the battle raged
further, while any soldiers that came close were suddenly swallowed by the entity, disappearing as if pulled into a bottomless
chasm, while nothing but a scream cut short pervaded the night
further.

"You kill them so quickly, why?" he found himself asking
the monster, confused as to why it was taking the creature so long
to consume him.

A laugh came, drowning and horrid. "Theys is plain!
Yous is tasty!"

Irvine groaned, just his luck to be the one the gluttonous
creature savors. He struggled more, seeing little else he could do,
before falling and catching himself with his right hand, in turn becoming caught in the muck as well. His crouched position gave
him little strength extra though, as he sunk his hand further trying
to free his feet, and his feet further trying to free his hand. He
could feel the flesh melting from the hand that was engulfed in the
thing.

"What are you?" he asked, trying to block out the pain
that nearly caused him to pass out.

"Daemon of Gluttony, Gryvax." the feminine voice replied. "Elder Daemon of Wrath Zyrxak chooses us, to be his
aids!"

Irvine paused, showing no signs of resistance, he could
see the light of dawn beginning to shine from just beyond the horizon. The creature complained at his sudden lack of energy,
pleading him to struggle more.

He thought on the futility of everything around him.

The Daemons were once again attacking their world, and
they truly did not seem powerful enough to fight back against
them. Zyrxak had not even appeared, and yet pandemonium had
broken around them.

C. STEPHEN HICKS

One side saw the soldiers fighting amongst themselves, General Atrosby doing his best to simply aid the ones that still lived.

The other saw Irvine and other soldiers being consumed by this slime-like Daemon. Irvine took a deep breath, then threw his sword to the side. The weapon landed some ways away from the battle, and he called at the top of his lungs. "Arce'Thrak! Your aid is needed!"

A blinding flash of flame burst from his chest, bathing the battlefield in a sudden light. Fighting stopped for a moment as the entire field stared in awe at the sight. Another explosion of fire suddenly occurred further off, but Irvine hadn't the time to wonder at its source.

The creature below him seemed to shrink slightly, and he used the opportunity to free his hand once again, the appendage up to his wrist reduced to the bare muscle and tendons, the bones of his fingers terrifyingly white. He reached his good hand into the air and accepted the spear from his ghostly companion, who bore an expression of pure resolve. Atrosby watched as the scene played out, now dismounted and blade bloodied from his men who had become puppets. A stern expression across his hardened face.

A breath later, the sun peeked from the horizon, bathing the valley in light as Irvine gripped the lance and continued its momentum downwards, plunging it deep into the Daemonic ooze that held him. The flames of the Draconic energy enveloping him in the jagged crimson armor given to him by the Dragoon Knight. The Daemon's scream pierced the battlefield as it began to shrink, its area of influence showing bare ground devoid of all life.

Moments later a female shape lay writhing on the ground, her form in constant jerking motion as the ooze moved to try and escape the blazing spear jammed into her navel, but to no avail. The creature's human looking features stretched and elongated weirdly in her attempts to flee. With a final twist of the blade, the scream ended and the corpse melted with a dark column of energy flowing into the open sky above, marking the end of Gryvax.

Atrosby approached Irvine, staring at his armor covered form. The intimidating armor bore the likeness of a Dragon, and for the first time, he truly appreciated the power that Irvine had inherited. Irvine was simply glad that the spirit had covered his stripped leg and hand in scales, protecting them from the environment. Atrosby's viewing was cut short however, as he felt the temperature suddenly raise to sweltering heights. He turned and raised his shield before him towards the source of the overwhelming power, the thick metal shield absorbing the energy but turning to ash in his hand, the excess still burning the armor on his arm.

The skeletal specter rose into the air from his landing, raising his arms upwards and cackling. The skies darkened and the sunlight was dimmed as clouds enveloped over the force that opposed them.

"Welcome, Dragoon Knight!" Zyrxak proclaimed. "To the end of everything you fought to protect!"

25
Hell

Mipha laughed as she engaged from both sides, sending wave after wave of energy towards the man and elf. Sárif calmly deflected each of the bolts, firing back with his own simple invocations, but unable to score a hit between the ferocity of her attacks.

Valk fared similarly as he blocked the dark magic with a divine shield he had conjured, attempting to move closer to her for a physical strike. He gripped the thick club he usually hid under his robes, waiting for an opportunity to close the distance.

The old woman watched as they approached, sidestepping Valk's attempted slam and pushing him towards his friend with a wave of energy. Sárif's arcane defenses began to falter from her barrage of missiles.

"Come now, I'm just a little old woman." she teased. "Can't either of you keep up?"

She cackled again as she launched a thousand blades of violet magic towards the two in a blinding barrage, the two holding fast against her black magic. The old woman grunted in pain though, as an arrow sprouted from her shoulder, interrupting the attacks. Valk couldn't help but grin at the tell-tale white fletching of the arrow, calling back up the stairs. "Wonderful of you to join us, Varia!"

The woman laughed behind him. "As if I'd leave you to die, love!"

Mipha groaned as she snapped the arrow in two, throwing the back half to the ground and moving with surprising haste to the back side of a pillar.

"So glad to see you two on speaking terms again, but we do have other things to deal with right now." Sárif said through gritted teeth, his hair flashing wild shades of red in his anger.

Varia tapped him on the shoulder, readying another arrow and nodding her readiness. Valk shook his head, amazed that it had only taken the end of the peaceful times to get him to talk to the ranger woman again.

† †

Versal and Teral dashed through the complex, Versal making a new doorway whenever their path seemed limited. Teral laughed heartily at the irony of his position, but engaged each combatant with a deadly seriousness. Once a wall exploded, he would launch himself forward, felling groups of the black robed cultists with his whirling blades and momentum. Versal similarly launched individuals towards the ceiling like children's toys being fired from a cannon. Shrapnel rained around them from the broken ceiling, and both knew this needed to be over quickly. Versal's continual renovations were compromising the supports of the building.

They regrouped again and started through a new walkway, stopped short when Teral put his arm past the massive frame of his ally. Versal halted abruptly, careful not to burn the man with his body.

"Do you hear that?" the thief said, putting a finger up to his ear.

A whistle resounded through the hallway to their right, a wave of pressure forcing both of them back and dampening both of their flames, ending in a resounding crash against the wall. Teral peeked around the corner gingerly, narrowly avoiding the next strike, which appeared to be an arrow made of a contained wind gale. The force was so great inside the object, it lit the area dimly, before disappearing into a wisp of smoke.

"Ventus blood." Versal said with a measure of contempt, grinding his teeth together.

Teral rolled his eyes and groaned. "Another Elementia blood? I thought you people were rare."

"We are." the smith grunted.

More of the Abyssal Hand members began to appear around them, Teral bringing his blades to bear. "I'll leave the wind to you then." he said as he flashed away and began tearing into the oncoming members. His daggers whirling around him in a storm of pain and death. Even those a distance away weren't safe, as smaller blades flung from the spinning rogue, meeting their targets with visceral accuracy.

Versal moved into the hallway, watching another shockwave of wind approaching him. He forced his body to heat further, causing the oncoming air to lose momentum and drift upwards. Far in front of him, he could see the Ventus blood, his light blue tattoos glowing from below his dark robes.

Versal glanced upwards, gauging the height of the building as his opponent made for another bolt of contained wind.

"Damn it all." he muttered, clenching his body and flushing fully into flame.

The massive smith slammed his fists into the ground, causing a small explosion that rocked either wall away from him, taking several of the Abyssal Hand with them. The force catapulted him into the air, where the Ventus blood couldn't hope to get a clean shot with the intense heat surrounding him.

As he came in to his landing, his opponent waved his arms away from himself, transforming his body into a whirlwind of air. The billowing robes flung into a spiral and then upwards towards Versal, who burned them to ash in an instant. He landed and spread his arms outwards, heating the air around him. The thin man returned to his physical form, knowing that he would lose control if he flew too high from the hot air. He stood naked before the still immolated smith, who flashed before him baring a wide smile of magma.

"Neat trick. Almost worked fer ye." he growled, crushing his fist upwards under the Ventus blood's chest.

In an instant, the building rocked in the ensuing shockwave. Teral dug his fiery heel into the ground to maintain his spot in the warehouse as it exploded around him. Moments later, he and Versal were the only remaining individuals standing in the ruins of the warehouse.

Teral laughed nervously at the abrupt end to the battle, and the smoking legs that remained of the Ventus blood. "Godsdamn, I am glad I'm not fighting you."

The large man met him with a scowl, as he returned to his physical form, his clothes completely burned away. His flesh steamed from the exertion as his markings dimmed to crimson from their bright red glow. "No answers here."

"Do you want to steal some clothes off these bastards?" the thief asked, looking at the smith's bare backside.

Versal shook his head. "No time fer that, I'd just burn 'em again."

Teral shrugged and jogged after the powerful man.

† †

Teria felt the surge of heat, even through the enchantment of her cloak, the oppressive energy threatened to throw her a distance away from where she crouched down. When she recovered, she caught a glimpse of Irvine destroying another Daemon, but flashed back to Erika. The Fjordling's clothing was burned away from her torso where the sudden immolation had blasted from, leaving her tattered grey skirt smoking from the blast and her breastplate scalded clean by the flame. The markings that painted across her skin dimmed as the power faded from them, covering her torso and face more clearly now after the massive exertion of power.

Her chest heaved beneath the armor, and her hair lay disheveled across her face. Her strength gave out as her arms slowly returned to their pale skinned complexion, and she fell to her knees exhausted. The controlled soldiers were scattered across the battlefield in droves, but the Daemon began to rise again. Now though, he shook from the injuries he had surely sustained.

Teria nodded her thanks to Erika. "I'll take it from here, you did well."

She drew her bow again, and dashed forward at a blinding speed. The Daemon was barely back on his spider legs before arrows assailed him in rapid succession, three piercing his form and protruding like ugly spikes, and the others serving as a distraction. He screeched as the ranger flashed behind him, throwing her bow to the side and bringing her blades to bear, slamming both into his spine. Deep wine-colored ichor splashed across her from his dark flesh.

"You irritate me, wretch!" he screamed, turning and slinging his wrist downwards towards her, but she wasn't there.

In and out she sprinted, tirelessly as she slashed and stabbed at the Daemon, Vayex barely able to counter her strikes with his blade-like fingers. She vanished as soon as he mounted a counter, and was upon him again just as quickly from a different direction. His strength outmatched her in a direct contest, and she knew that well, playing her advantage of movement and comprehension of their surroundings. She scoffed at herself, having spoken about Irvine's reliance on weaknesses as if it were a bad thing. Varia would have given her a lecture had she heard that comment. The small strikes she took to her cheeks and arms were nothing more than shallow cuts, and weren't nearly enough to stop her.

The Daemon seemed panicked for a time, unable to keep track of the ranger's movements as she danced in and out of melee with him. His sharp fingers dripped with the crimson that he drew from her flesh, but his own wounds were much more grievous.

His claws seemed too busy, crossing over to block one blade strike, while her twin weapon came from below and jabbed at his legs or hips. The war of attrition seemed to be rapidly coming to an end.

She seemed to shout from multiple directions at once, taunting the creature. "Your time is over, Daemon!"

Erika flinched at the grin that spread across the creature's face. She tried to call out for her friend, but failed to choke out a whisper. She knew something was wrong, but her entire body was weak from the exertion of heat that she had produced. Her muscles felt like they were melting from her bones, and she couldn't even find the strength to stand. She could only watch as the battle played out.

"Never attack a spider on his web." Vayex warned in a calm tone as she appeared in the air above him, a thin thread flashing upwards and surrounding her, wrapping around her right leg nearly at her hip. The Daemon crossed two fingers, the thread taut on the tips and flashing in the early sunlight. Erika could see it now, spreading across the field and wrapping around every single body that lay around them. With the subtle movement, the wire tightened around Teria's thigh in a flash, slicing easily through her flesh and drawing a wide-eyed expression of horror across her face.

The burning feeling in Erika's face cooled by the tears streaming down her cheeks as she watched helplessly. Teria's momentum carried her over Vayex, her right leg severing from her body in a spray of crimson, showering the Daemon as he raised his arms outwards.

She crumpled to the ground a moment later, unmoving. Vayex began to cackle.

Erika called out a haggard scream from her spent throat, her emotions blazing wildly.

The voice seemed to come from all around her, though only she could hear it.

Burn it to cinders.

Vayex's laughter cut short as he stared at her.

Her arms flashed into immolation once more, crawling and extending past her shoulders and enveloping her entire torso down to her waist. Her auburn hair blazed to life in a vibrant orange flame, her eyes burning with a magma that dripped like tears from her face. She rose with renewed vigor, as the threads covering the battlefield burst into flames from the sheer heat around her. Vayex gasped in surprise as the flame extended across his entire web, burning the threads to ash.

Destroy this monstrosity. Incinerate it until no ashes remain.

The Ignis blood rose, fists clenched around her great warhammer, staring at the Daemon before her. Vayex flinched when she stomped her foot down, immolating it for just a blink, and propelling her to the Daemon at a blinding pace.

† †

Irvine spoke loudly and clearly, his voice ringing with Arce'Thrak's in unison, though he was not in control of the words. "Your punishment will follow shortly, Zyrxak."

Atrosby stared at the two, the raw power radiating from the Daemon was oppressive, as if a volcanic heat wave flowed outward from the specter.

"I shall join you in your battle, Irvine!" he proclaimed, swallowing his reservations. "I feel this beast has had enough time to walk our world."

"Your world, ripe for the taking!" the Daemon replied, a sardonic emphasis on the first word. His skeletal hands blazed in a hellish flame rising past his forearms, slashing both arms outward in an opening offensive.

Irvine slammed the butt of the spear into the ground, launching his body in the air over the horizontal slash of energy, while Atrosby sprinted forward and ducked underneath. The two advanced on the creature with haste, Irvine coming from on high and the general staying lower to the ground. The Daemon found the lance driving across his ribs with a spray of sparking energy leaving a small chip on the exposed bone. Irvine's eyes flashed behind the visor of the helm in surprise as Zyrxak snatched the shaft of his weapon and hefted him up into the air.

"Why so surprised? Is it because I do not bleed?" he taunted, slamming the Dragoon vessel into the scorched earth beneath them.

Atrosby's strike rang true, skirting across the armor that guarded the Daemon's hip but striking effectively into his lower ribs on the opposite side of Irvine's attack. He lurched forward, groaning in pain at the realization of the enchantment that empowered the soldier's blade, the intricate runes glowing along the steel with an enthusiasm. The monster turned to him and struck out with his sharp hands, slicing the general's face when he failed to gauge the speed of the creature. The soldier went on the defensive then, batting aside every savage blow thrown at him.

Zyrxak lurched again, finding the dragon lance tearing into him from behind, gripping the weapon again in an attempt to throw his assailant away the same as before.

"You may not bleed, but you still feel pain!" Irvine shouted, eliciting a hiss and arcing strike from his adversary.

The stalemate continued for what seemed an eternity. Irvine holding strong due to the power of the lance and the Dragoon abilities, but Atrosby began to falter in his endurance, damning his age and complacency in their time of peace. Zyrxak seemed to grow stronger as the battle wore on though, each attack he seemed to welcome with a relish in his sickening laughter. His flames intensified and Atrosby found his exposed skin beginning to scald from the heat.

Irvine paused, favoring his injured leg, as he heard the voice of the Dragoon Knight in his mind. A tone of urgency twisted his normally calm demeanor.

"Another entity approaches. The general needs to vacate the battle."

Before he could call out to his companion, Irvine watched as Atrosby's blade was batted to the side, and the Daemon lunged forward, grabbing him by the collar of his breastplate.

† †

Vayex felt pain. His form bounced across the ground several yards from his web. He choked his own lifeblood from his throat in a splashing vomit as he stood on uneasy legs. He stared down at his once beautiful body, crushed in the middle by the strike that launched him and lacerated by the ranger's blades. He reached his hand downwards, touching the scorch marks that stretched from the more detrimental wound, his appendages shaking at the effort. Time seemed to slow for the Daemon, fear gripped him, the fear of death. He glanced upwards at the sight of Zyrxak furiously battling the Dragoon Knight and smiled weakly.

"My best to you, my beloved master." he whispered in a rasping curdle.

Another flash came from the battlefield, and he looked to it, seeing the flaming haired woman stalking towards him, the threads of his web burning openly above the field behind her, casting a bright light in the early morning glow. In her flaming eyes, he saw hatred, and death itself. He shrieked in horror; the sound cut short by the warhammer separating his head from his shoulders.

He felt no pain after that.

Erika stood, chest heaving, gripping the weapon from just under the head and midway down the haft. Her immolation faded from her body, her hair slinging over her face. The skin of her arms, torso and face covered in the curving crimson markings, darkening as the power faded. All of them beautifully wrapped around her, marking her as a true Elementia blood. She could feel the presence of the wildfire fox that she had seen before, watching the battle as it played out. The voice was comforting, like a mother's.

Rest now, my child. You will yet be needed.

The Daemon's body seemed to separate into crimson threads and fly into a column stretching into the skies, colored the same as the creature's blood.

She fell to her knees, the chill of the air a welcome comfort to her naked flesh as she wrenched the scalding breastplate from her torso. Her muscles were still burning from her earlier expulsion of energy. She breathed deeply, and fell back onto the ground, frustrated as she watched the struggle with the Daemon that burned her home. Teria screamed in pain from behind her, tying her belt as tight as she could manage around the short amount of leg that remained on her right side. Erika crawled to her, barely supporting her upper half as she lit her hand with her magic, pressing it against the wound. Teria's scream of agony at the cauterization attracted what was left of the medical unit of their convoy, all of them scrambling to gather their supplies and recruiting nearby soldiers to check the bodies scattered around for signs of life.

Many still gawked at the unearthly battle that raged before them. Zyrxak easily trading blows with Irvine and Atrosby. Erika cradled Teria's torso in her arms after the medics had covered both of them with blankets. The ranger sobbed and groaned in an effort to stifle the pain, pressing her face into the soft skin of Erika's stomach. Erika simply watched on, hoping desperately for Irvine to finish it quickly. She couldn't handle any more bloodshed this day.

The battle paused before them, a new light sparking in the sky. Golden and pure, as a figure emerged from the overcast skies.

↑↑

Valk and Sárif fell limply behind one pillar, Varia crouching behind another not far from them. She tied a cloth wrap around a newly opened wound on her upper arm, using her teeth to tighten it. She exchanged a look with Valk, assuring him that she was alright, seeming more concerned with his own condition. He looked down, seeing the blood flowing freely down his hand and staining the handle of his maul. Sárif seemed out of breath, likely nearing the end of his arcane limit.

"Come now, you'll all outlive me." Mipha taunted, pausing her barrage and likely tending to her own wounds. "All of you just walk away and pretend nothing happened here. Let the changes happen, maybe after my time comes, you can try to reset the pieces where you like them instead."

Valk watched Varia grit her teeth and call out. "I care for the wellbeing of my children Mipha, and I worry that you threaten that!"

The priest smiled, knowing that when the ranger woman brought her 'children' into the mix, she was unmovable. She brushed her silver hair from her face and nodded to the two.

"All of this is a game to you then?" Sárif called back after nodding back to her. "A pastime for your old age?"

Mipha cackled again. "But of course! I always felt your distaste for me. From the first time your little troupe came through my city! Though I must admit, I never expected you to find a seat on the council."

"I'm full of surprises, Madame." he called again, tracing a sigil in the air, and moving around the pillar with a clap of his hands.

Valk and Varia followed suit, allowing Sárif to be their diversion. A bright light flashed outwards from his wounded hands, hoping to blind the elder woman with its glow.

The two rushed around and brought out their weapons, Varia drawing a thin curved sword, and Valk baring his maul. The two engaged in a kind of dance, trading blows onto the cult leader, though she seemed to be able to predict their movements. She did not rely on sight after all, and Sárif's gambit had to trick her into thinking it was an attack.

"The Abyssal Hand does not die with me!" she shouted, throwing the two into the wall with a purple force of energy. "Time to end this charade."

She drove her sharp fingers into herself, drawing thick gouts of blood as she separated her ribcage.

"I give myself to the Abyss, and all of its primordial horrors! Rend these fools from existence, and return us to the time before all!"

Her form began to bubble weirdly, and tear. Bones audibly snapped as she completed her last hex, and began the transformation that ushered in her new age of terror.

26
ANGELIC INTERVENTION

The skies above the battle erupted into blinding light. The shining beacon drifting through the clouds as if a thousand burning suns now lit the world below. The struggling ceased as all looked up in amazement, wonder, and horror.

Zyrxak's cackling laughter was replaced with a screech of anger. Irvine and Atrosby glanced to him in confusion.

"That's all you damned creatures know! Isn't it?" the specter howled. "Never can you fight your own battles! You must call to your false idols!"

All around them, the battle erupted into shafts of light, striking the ground like a thousand piercing blades. The sudden silence was replaced with the agonizing screams of the soldiers being rent into pieces by the powerful blasts. Irvine glanced to see Erika carrying the battered form of Teria, barely managing a limping jog away from the sudden violence, another ranger rushing over to help them.

A voice boomed around them, deep and baritone. "Mortals are frail, Daemon. You must give them the pity they deserve."

"Wystaea." the Daemon hissed in a tone of pure hatred.

The voice chuckled, sending vibrations through the ground. "I see your imprisonment in the consecration has not dulled your memory, Zyrxak."

Zyrxak's skeletal hands snapped outwards, crimson energy flowing to him from the shredded corpses of the soldiers around him, as well as the places of the two fallen Daemons. He raised his palms upwards, guiding the ribbons up to his jagged maw, and sucking the force inwards. His form suddenly began to shift, growing in size to the dismay of his two previous opponents who began to dash to the side of the field. Zyrxak's skeletal form wrapped in sinewy muscle, tying eagerly around each bone, each finger, in a horrible dance of the macabre.

Wystaea breached the cloud cover, a remarkable figure of shining gold armor with six, purely white, feathered wings sprouting from his back. He carried a massive executioner's sword, ending in a rounded tip, the crossguard shining more brilliantly than even his armor. Behind his winged visor, two gleaming golden eyes stared at the Daemon intently. As he witnessed the Daemon's gambit, his form crashed to the ground with an explosion of earth. His blade arced out in a horrid path, cleaving a score of the few soldiers still standing into halves. Screams erupted again, but were cut short in anguishing retches as the bodies erupted into ash.

Farris had just gotten Erika and Teria to a safe distance, Selbor aiding the medics in bandaging Teria's stumped leg.

The roguish man had just begun to run back when he was thrown from his feet by the impact of the Angelus. Once he was back up again, he spotted one of the rangers that had come with them. The younger female ranger was frantically sprinting towards him, and he rushed forward, grabbing her right hand and pulling her towards him. He hadn't realized the proximity of the Angelus though, and felt the sharp rush of air that followed the great being's blade swing. He felt warm liquid rushing down his face where the just the wind had sliced slantwise across his nose.

A moment later, he realized that not all the blood was his, when the ranger woman's torso separated in a slice from her right shoulder to just above her left hip. He had successfully grabbed her hand, but was horrified when her upper torso and left arm did not follow.

He looked from the lifeless girl's eyes to the Angelus with terror in his own, feeling an intense pang of guilt washing over him, over not having pursued the Abyssal Hand sooner. A moment later, the girl's body melted into ash, her hand crumbling through Farris' fingers. He felt rage, horror, and anguish, as he watched her face fade away.

"By the Gods." Atrosby muttered, his face bleeding profusely from the laceration he sustained from Zyrxak, one eye closed from the wound and the draining blood. He heaved himself upwards from his kneel and slashed his blade through the air towards the new combatant. "Angelus! What in the Hells are you doing?"

The imposing warrior from above glanced towards him after another devastating swing of his weapon. "You are blind human. This monstrosity leeches the life force from your warriors to feed his strength." he began, motioning to the Daemon still strapping in layers of new muscle and flesh.

Atrosby's one good eye widened. "And they are better off flayed by your blade? When the chance to flee still exists?"

"Better to be flayed than consumed." the Angelus replied. "For the greater good."

Irvine had heard enough.

He dug his heels and launched himself, propelling his body with the Dragon's fire. He first slammed into Zyrxak's chest, interrupting his strengthening ritual. As the Daemon fell backwards with the great lance protruding from his now muscled chest, Irvine watched the Angelus complete another swing, and thrust himself to his new target. The knowledge of the power flowed into him from the spirit of the Dragoon, as well as the accuracy of a trained hand. Wystaea lurched forward as Irvine's boots slammed onto his upper back, driving the lance between the collar and base of his helm.

"What good are you if you don't defend them from the Daemon?" he screamed aloud. "They all had families! Loved ones! Friends!"

The Angelus groaned from the pain. "They have no choice. Entering combat with a Daemon leads to consumption and nothing more. Their fate has been sealed."

"Damn your fate!" Irvine cried as he wrenched the handle to the side, jumping downwards to use his weight to drag the blade across what he imagined to be the creature's neck. Wystaea grabbed at the handle, trying to slow its progress, but the surface of the metal burned his armored hand in an audible sizzle, gaining nothing more than a grunt of pain and annoyance.

"You are a warrior out of time, Dragoon." he crooned, grasping at the wound as what appeared to be tangible liquid light seeped from his wound and between his fingers. "Your kind have no place here."

"Neither do yours!" Zyrxak cried as he slammed into the Angelus's side, sending him crashing to the ground in a fiery blast. His red flesh strained in the impact, tendons snapping with every slam of his fists. Muscle fibers tore off of him as he continued his assault.

"Now you see the truth Irvine." he heard Arce'Thrak say from somewhere beside him. "Daemons and Angelus have always battled. Though neither had a good and true vision for humanity. Dragons were our saviors. The Angelus are nothing, save for lies. I am saddened to see your world's worship of them."

Irvine's right arm twitched painfully where he had gripped the lance with his barely hanging flesh. He turned to look at Erika, who was walking back to the battle weakly, gripping a blanket around her torso.

The sight of her brought warm, stinging tears to his eyes.

"Is there a way we can end this quickly?" he asked.

Arce'Thrak paused. "An incantation on the handle of the lance. Used only in hopeless situations."

Irvine glanced to the gleaming pole drenched in crimson. *Is that my blood?* he wondered, knowing Erika would be mortified at the volume of viscous liquid. *It must be. I'm the only one who bleeds red.*

A glowing series of runes lit at Arce'Thrak's mention.

"Ward of Sealing" he called it, sadness tinging his voice as he explained the effects.

He looked back to Erika. She had stumbled and fallen, but screamed as she lifted her warhammer again. Her beautiful auburn hair, matted and dirty from the battle. The blanket drifted free of her naked torso slightly, and Irvine looked curiously at the crimson tattoos that flowed across her sides and midriff. They were much like her father's, but still unique to her.

"Gods, she is beautiful." he said somberly, pulling the jagged Dragoon helm from his head and cradling it in his fleshless hand.

"That she is." Arce'Thrak agreed.

Irvine could feel a warm touch on his shoulder

He smiled at her, as she began to scream again, trying her hardest not to fall to her knees.

"I'll leave the rest to you, General!" he called.

† †

Bones cracked and rearranged, flesh tore and merged, cackles mixed with pained grunts. Valk and Varia picked each other up from the wall, as Sárif stared at the old woman's form, snapping and popping into something massive and terrible.

Valk grabbed Sárif by the collar of his robe, muttering a prayer and telling Sárif to flee as hard as his long legs would allow. A flash of light ensued, Varia leading them up the stairs and into the street beside the hidden entrance under the temple of Phanel. Just then, Mipha's enlarging form cracked the stone pillars that held the chamber aloft, sending sections of stone and rubble crashing to the ground.

"We cannot fight her. We need to find the smith and the thief." the priest said, with a degree of nervousness in his voice.

Sárif nodded, catching his breath as he watched the underground complex start to crumble under the monstrosity that he could barely see through the smoke and dust.

A short while later, the three broke the surface, sucking in the fresh morning air as well as they could, barely able to keep up the pace of their younger days. They each looked about in horror as townsfolk started filling the streets around them, investigating the cacophonous sounds as the early sun began lighting the sky in purple hues.

Varia was already at work, commanding the citizens to vacate the area, while simultaneously rallying the guard to assemble a fighting force. Quickly enough, they saw dark shapes move through the alleys. More of Mipha's underlings ready to aid in her mad quest.

Sárif was thrown from his feet by a sudden blow, landing several yards away, having not seen the swinging appendage of the monster that had attacked him. Mipha's transformed body surfaced through the ground, creating a massive crater that sunk entire sections of the temple. Valk muttered another prayer and readied himself for the next stage in their battle.

Sárif recovered in time to dodge a cascading blade that sparked off the stone street, he drew a sigil in the air, and an assailant was blown into a building. The impact bent his form impossibly backwards and snapped his spine with a resounding sound that caused the other attackers to pause briefly. Sárif threw his hands to his sides, readying a set of spells to launch at his new opponents, but was relieved of the fight when two standing close together fell to the ground to Teral's blades, and another was incinerated by Versal's flames.

The fully immolated Ignis blood stepped forward with steps that cracked the stones under his feet from the sheer heat. "What in the blazin' Hells is that thing?"

"No time, just kill it." Sárif grunted as he loosed a spell at the horrible visage of exposed flesh and torn muscle. Stained white feathered wings jutted out of the fleshy mass, fluttering weakly as they fell and were quickly replaced by the ever-growing horror. Mipha's voice was a distorted screech of pain as the eldritch power consumed her. Valk couldn't help but feel a certain amount of pity for the elderly woman, but was quickly reconciled when he considered the suffering she had caused, and the chaos she threatened now if she wasn't quelled.

Buildings crumbled around them, townsfolk running from the chaos, screaming in terror, as the guards attempted to evacuate them while also fending off the remaining Abyssal Hand members from another side.

Sárif flung a barrage of spells, though his pace weakened as his endurance drained. The damage made marks across the creature, but dwindled in their potency.

Valk continued to pray to Phanel, ghostly flames and bolts of energy sparking off the amalgamation. He noted that it seemed to be a melding of spirits, both Daemon and Angelus, but was transforming into something else entirely.

Versal threw more and more bolts of flame into the exterior, scorching the flesh and burning it away, only to be replaced by more in its constant regeneration.

Varia held off the Abyssal Hand members that approached, trying to silence their defense. Her bow seemed to fire multiple arrows at once with her speed, each striking with deadly accuracy.

Teral stood by, cutting down any of the fanatics that broke through the guardsmen and the ranger woman. He kept trying to find a way to assist the dwindling defense he stood by.

Sárif fell to one knee as he let loose a massive energy spike that blew through the center of the mass. The thief did a double take as his keenly perceptive eyes caught a small object in the center. A skull, solitary and clean, quickly reclaimed by the monster and sucked back into the mass.

"There!" he shouted. "Focus your magic on the center!"

The artillery complied, blasting all their forces simultaneously into the revolting creature, and exposing the white skull that lay floating within.

Teral jumped back, knowing he had no time to hesitate, using his enchanted leg to rocket himself into the gaping hole in the creature, wrapping his arms around the skull as the flesh compounded back into itself. None of the warriors were fast enough to stop him.

Inside, Teral looked back on himself, as if time stood still.

Raven Mitrios would be furious with me. he thought, picturing the Sildenfeld thieves' guild master.

The thief laughed aloud as he heard the old man's scolding voice. *'Never jump into a hole you don't know you can come out of.'*

He moved his flaming appendage atop of the floating skull as he cackled, focusing his energy, and blasting through it with every ounce of force he could manage.

Maybe those two will find happiness.

The three outside took pause, staring at the rampaging monster as it flailed aimlessly for a moment more, before jolting into a still position. Varia reached a lull in the oncoming cultist force, and looked on as well.

A final inhuman, gurgling scream resounded out. The fleshy mass melting into the ground and turning to dust a moment later. The center revealed Mipha's skull, smashed into splintered pieces, and the crushed body of Teral the thief.

Valk fell to the ground beside him, screaming his prayers aloud. Nothing would rouse his form though. Eventually Varia made her way to him, the Abyssal Hand in full retreat now that their gambit was destroyed. She gently lifted the priest in her arms and held him in her matronly grasp.

"Nothing more you can do." she whispered gently. "Allow him a hero's death."

Sárif and Versal watched him and steeled their own resolve. Teral had saved them from Mipha's chaos.

27
SACRIFICE

General Atrosby ran to Irvine's side, as the Dragoon's vessel dropped his jagged helm to the side. "What's the plan?" he asked resolutely.

Irvine blinked hard, tears being forced down his cheeks, but drying quickly in the heat that surrounded him. The clash of Angelus and Daemon before them sent earth and foliage into the air. Shockwaves resounded with each strike they made, scattering the fallen forces and widening the arena of their world-shattering struggle.

He couldn't believe where he stood. Merely a handful of days prior and he was dancing the night away with his love whom he hadn't told his true feelings.

Now he believed he never would be able to tell her.

"Atrosby." he called with a shaking voice.

The general answered with a nod.

"In my pack, there's a small box. A gift I had bought before all of this. Make sure she receives that." he stated grimly, motioning to Erika, still struggling to keep her footing.

"Give it to her yourself, boy!" Atrosby's eyes narrowed. "Let me do it! Give me the lance! Whatever final gambit you have, let me do it. I have nothing left here."

The solitary figure of Arce'Thrak shook his head darkly. "There can be only one vessel. I am sorry, Irvine."

"Vengeance for my uncle." he replied with a violent determination. "And for the lives burned by that monster."

Atrosby couldn't understand the depth of Irvine's hatred. The courier knew.

Zyrxak was the one who destroyed their lives and their world as they knew it. After a spark of recognition earlier of the horned skull that marked the Daemon's visage. He realized why it was painfully familiar to him. He had seen it the night his home burned, though his fear of fire had blinded him to the truth of the culprit. That source of his family's destruction, of his lifelong dread, was here before him now.

Though it meant abandoning his life, and those he cared for, he knew he had to. Irvine planted his feet in the softened ground below him, angling the lance downwards and watched the titans as they battled, timing them.

Atrosby saluted him, blood running down his face from his wound. "Your battle will be remembered Irvine. On my grandfather's blade. No one will forget your story."

"Just remember my request." Irvine said, finding his voice again.

Irvine watched as the combatants broke away from each other, then slammed the lance down, engaging the dragon's fire within it. He wasn't sure if the blast or Erika's scream were louder. Both sent a pain through his chest.

His trajectory landed him on the Angelus's cuirass, jamming the blade deep into the seam between the collar and the helmet. Zyrxak's momentum carried him forward and Irvine wrenched the pole of the lance into his pathway. The Daemon impaled his skull on the shaft in his blinded rage. Both of them shuddered as the runes lit with a fiery orange glow. Irvine looked down and found a cascade of crimson falling from his own breast-plate, in a wound that he hadn't recognized, and had only opened further with his gambit. The world became fuzzy, and a light shone from the lance.

A flash ensued, Zyrxak muttering something to Irvine that he couldn't quite hear.

Atrosby, Erika, and the remaining onlookers blinked.

The next moment, the Daemon, and Irvine, had vanished.

The battlefield lay bare, with the crumpled corpse of the Angelus littering the desolated and scorched field, his head separated from his shoulders, before melting entirely into an otherworldly light. The ground was wet with the blood of the fallen, and another downpour of rain that began in the silence.

Erika fell to her knees, eyes wide at the scene before her.

Atrosby quietly stepped across the field, and handed her the discarded helmet of the Dragoon.

She clutched it to her breast, her anguished scream echoing through the rain around them. Eventually, the helm fell to ash in her grasp.

† †

The journey back to Sildenfeld was quiet. Every wagon that was sent with them was piled with the dead that were actually recoverable. General Atrosby personally carried Teria most of the way. Her wound was staunched with some difficulty by the field medics, but she was expected to make a full recovery, save for her missing leg, which lay on one of the wagons. A couple younger clerics still held out hope that it could still be saved, but the more experienced ones just shook their heads somberly when posed the same question.

Erika carried her bag and Irvine's satchel as if her life depended on it. It had taken the better part of the first day for Atrosby to convince her to move from Irvine's final stand. He

305

brought her Irvine's satchel, handing her one of his spare tunics from inside to dress in. He couldn't bear to fulfill Irvine's last request of him.

Many soldiers of the remaining company made their way to Atrosby, all asking the same question.

"Was it a victory?"

The general would simply adjust his grip on the wounded ranger, then blink a few times and clear his throat.

He couldn't find an answer.

This did little to console the men and women who lost friends and family on that field.

It seemed to console Erika even less.

†††

After their arrival in Sildenfeld, the company was met with solemnity. Those who had witnessed the damage wrought by the Abyssal Hand alone, knew that the company had seen far worse. The horseshoes and boots on the cobblestone were the only sound besides those who wept for the fallen. The night was filled with funeral pyres, including one for Teral. Raven Mitrios, the leader of the thieves' guild in the Region, even came with a large procession and offered his condolences to all in attendance, apologizing for Teral's mistakes.

Teria looked to Farris from her seat not far off. The roguish ranger stood, silent, with a sad look across his bandaged face. Still, she knew that he had told Mitrios of Teral, and his full involvement.

Merrick stood by Erika, as she refused to light a pyre for Irvine.

She called back to something one of the surviving rangers had spoken of. A sealing ritual that the Dragoons were fabled to possess, banishing the user and target to a place unknown. She insisted that the courier survived, and anyone who tried to console her was met with a look of pure rage and determination. Even her father had difficulty approaching her the first days, though she was happy to see him well. The Courier's Guild members in the Region agreed with her as well, saying resolutely. "If his Courier Tags have not been retrieved, Irvine is considered 'missing', not 'deceased'."

Erika took some vindication in their words, and promises to spread her name through their ranks in the case they discover anything.

Valk was not seen for some time, as he was busy with tending to the wounded, along with the other clerics that inhabited the temples. A caravan soon followed word of the incident, filled with healers from across the countryside, all coming to aid the recovery efforts.

The world became clouded, and rain fell often, though blocked by Sildenfeld's protective ward. The month of Hallowden brought the solemn time of Shadesfall, and the respect for the dead was all that existed in the city. Erika's birthday passed in that month, though she refused to celebrate her twenty-fourth year, even Teria being unable to convince her to do so with a box of pastries from the ranger's favorite bakery.

Eventually the rain turned to snow, as the winter set in deeply. The land painted white, and the skies perpetually grey.

However, the sun finally emerged, and the world brightened once again.

Epilogue

My daughter has become a powerful woman. An Ignis blood, just like myself, and her mother. Though I daresay she is fast approaching a level of ability far exceeding my own.

She must now leave.

Though it pains me to say, I cannot stop her. Irvine has left this world, and she believes she can find the answers, and a way to regain him. I can't say I don't believe her. I have to have faith in my daughter's judgment and instinct.

She will find him, this I know.

For now, I will enjoy the last of my time with her, and help Sárif to rebuild. Erika will find her way, and I wait anxiously for her return.

Erika, I love you more than any father has ever loved a daughter, and I know you can achieve your goals.

-Versal Ildherre, Smithmaster of Sildenfeld.

Twenty-Seventh Day of Fonsifal, Year 1127

The breeze of the approaching summer blew silently through the fields and streets of Sildenfeld. Craftsmen, nobles, and families stepped through the streets, enjoying the warmer weather. Windows hung open and wildflowers bloomed, releasing sweet aromas into the air around them.

Erika stood in the open window, staring at the deep crimson patterns that had formed to run across her muscular, pale skinned arms. She followed the magic runes enveloping her lithe calloused fingers, moving up her arm and running under her shirt, and mirroring on the other side. The markings continued unseen under her clothing, from her chest and back to her midriff, marking where her immolations had touched, stopping only at her waist, and becoming fainter in the dark scar she bore on her back, as well as the frontside where the jordhak teeth had penetrated.

"They look rather beautiful on you." Teria said with a warm smile as she wheeled her moving chair towards her. Her previous rugged leather armor and forest colored cloak was replaced with a bright dress, accentuating the body still more used to combat than to civilian life. The long skirt flowed downwards, hugging near to her hips but concealing her missing leg. Her dark hair lay braided over her left shoulder, ornamental gold leaves decorating the tight knots. Erika had learned they were symbols of honor among the Willow Rangers, for the injured and for the heroes.

"Thank ye." she said quietly. "Yer lookin' rather beautiful yerself, Teria."

The former ranger moved either wheel in opposite directions, mocking a twirl as best she could. "Your father said he'd try and fashion a false leg for me, so I might walk again, even if for short times."

Erika smiled. "I'm glad he's found a place here."

Teria frowned. "But you haven't."

"I know he's still out there. He never gave up on me, now I can't give up on him." she said slowly.

Teria brought a hand up to stop the tears she hated to show. "Come back and see me, alright?"

Erika leaned down and took her in a tight embrace, Teria kissing her lovingly on the cheek. The Ignis woman turned, her grey skirt dancing around her legs as she moved away.

"Wait! Take this." Teria called out, handing her a folded cloak of deep green. "I want you to have it."

Erika looked at her long and hard, Teria waving her hand in front of her face. "I already spoke with Mistress Varia. She practically sees you as one of her children at this point."

"Thank ye, Teria. I'll treasure it always. Take care o' yerself." she said, clasping Teria's hands in hers and then making her way from the room.

⚔⚔

Saying goodbye to her father proved more difficult, though in the end he understood her drive and her need to begin her pilgrimage.

"Any leads yet?" he asked.

"North!" came a call from the side, Valk standing with both hands on his hips, Varia smiling at her from beside him. "Legends say the Dragons reside in the Fjordlands."

"Or perhaps farther." Varia added.

Versal made a face. "The 'ome of our people. Be careful, ye hear?"

Erika nodded, her father nearly crushing her in his traditional bear hug. He turned and handed her a new half breastplate, much like her old one.

"Brand new, an' enchanted by Sárif 'imself. Fire resistant so ye don't 'ave to strip it off after usin' yer magic, and it should have extra protection on top o' that." he said with a beaming smile at the handiwork.

"Seems I'm getting lots o' gifts today, and they're all clothes." she laughed.

"Hope you don't mind another." came a smoother voice from behind her.

She turned to find the slender frame of Sárif, dressed in much more casual clothing than his regular formal robes. He held out a beautifully embroidered red and gold cloth. It had some wear to it, but none sacrificed the visual appeal of it.

"F'Skar's favorite scarf, made by his tribe. I believe he would have wanted you to have it, especially since you are going northward. Perhaps you can garner the aid of his aash brethren that still live that way. Do be careful though, as we have not tracked down the surviving members of the Abyssal Hand, nor do we know if they still lurk across the continent, biding their time."

Erika graciously accepted the scarf and neatly tucked it into Irvine's satchel, nodding her understanding at his warning.

She glanced back at him. "No one happens to have a portrait o' Irvine, do they?"

Versal laughed heartily. "Nah, I'm afraid the paintin' 'e 'ad o' ye was the only one o' the two o' ye we've still got. Anythin' else was burned back 'ome."

She smiled grimly but giggled at her father's boisterous laugh all the same. She bid them all farewell and started out of the city. She passed the multitude of buildings, the high wall and the many people she had grown accustomed to seeing each day.

Teria smiled sadly at her from the window as she went, waving her slender hand to her as she walked northwards. All around she was given well-wishes and fond farewells. She was regarded as a hero to the city, and all of them were sad to see her go.

She stood atop the first hill bordering the settlement, pausing to don the armor her father had given her, stretching her arms out slightly to adjust the fit, then slung Teria's cloak over her shoulders. The enchantment set to work instantly, cooling her body to a comfortable temperature in the warmer sun of the season. She smiled at the brisk wind that swirled around her, throwing her auburn hair up around her face. Her emerald eyes turned northwards.

Her destination lay in Máðir, the land of the fjords, and the land of her heritage.

She took a deep breath, securing her warhammer in its sling behind her thighs, along with Irvine's sword on the side of her inherited satchel.

A long road awaited her.

↑ ↑

In another realm, a landscape of dust and stone changed in constant, violent winds. Crimson and orange lightning cracked from the ever-morphing clouds overhead. Dark blots of dust and grime flew in an eternal whirlwind across the jagged landscape.

A figure wrapped in broken crimson armor awoke with a deep inhale, leading into severe choking and retching as the dust entered his lungs. He turned over and vomited into the sands, purging his system of the alien substances. He winced at the pain of his right hand, exposed nerves blaring underneath the thick gauntlet.

"Impressive power from one so young." a grating voice said from not far off.

The figure turned with an expression of horror in his recognition of the voice.

Zyrxak sat idly on a nearby stone. The specter turned towards the armored figure, his skull cracked and shattered. His left horn was completely missing, a jagged hole replacing where it once was and meeting the eye socket underneath. The normally glowing left eye was dark and lifeless. His bones appeared worn and dark, opposing his shining white appearance from before.

"You thought you'd seen the last of me." he said with a sick grin.

The figure nodded as he slumped into a sitting position with favor to his left leg, sinking into the sand slightly.

The Daemon's ribcage rose and fell, making a sound like a sigh, while the dust flowed through his teeth and ribs. "Now we are both stuck somewhere in the Sands of Conflict."

The figure now stood, sand and dust falling from between the armor plates. "And why aren't you attacking me?"

Now Zyrxak laughed a painful, grinding sound that escaped his jagged teeth. "You are in a sorry state Dragoon. Though I have not enough power left to even hope to win in combat with you. That, and I believe I will soon die."

His skeletal hand rose to meet the large hole in his skull, fingering at it slightly, and recoiling when a small chip of bone fell away and turned to ash in the violent winds.

"How do I leave this place?"

Zyrxak shrugged in defeat. "Ask your lance, Dragoon. Only the Dragons knew the properties of this place."

"You mistake me, Daemon. I'm no true Dragoon."

"I mistake nothing." the voice raised, interrupting his conversation partner. "I know you now boy. I know your rage. Your kin fell to my attempt at an escape."

The figure clenched his good fist at the angering memory, now so painfully clear to him.

"You are a vessel of one of the Dragoon Knights from long before. I was so consumed by hubris, and fear for the Angelus to return, I had not even considered the thought of the Dragon men leaving safeguards after the war ended." the Daemon made another sighing noise. "What is your true name boy?"

The figure had some pause, wondering at the wisdom of divulging his name to a Daemon. He struggled for only a moment, then answered. "Irvine."

The Daemon's jagged teeth seemed to spread into a smile, causing more shards of bone to break away. "Always a pleasure to know the name of those who have bested you."

The winds howled louder still.

Erika Ildherre

Erika is a Fjordling woman of twenty-three, who lives with her father, Versal, in the town of Valen. She apprenticed with him as a blacksmith for most of her life, and has quickly approached his level of skill in the craft. Her bloodline carries Ignis magic, allowing her a degree of control over the element of fire, and the ability to immolate her body in flames. She is nervous to use this ability though, due to her best friend Irvine's aversion to fire. Her father is the one who passed down this magic to her, and has used it extensively in his own life, as shown in the thick crimson markings that cover his body. Erika wishes to explore her innate abilities more, but knows that it will mark her in a similar way, and wishes to avoid the possible conflict with Irvine over it. She is very inexperienced to the world outside Valen, as she has never left the valley it resides in. She was carried by her father all the way there as an infant, after being forced to flee their homeland of Máðir, where her mother was killed.

IRVINE COLUMVAL

Irvine is a Meridian man of twenty-four, and is an experienced courier across the continent of Patrias and its various Regions. His mother and father's lives were claimed by an intense fire that destroyed their home, though Irvine was barely old enough to remember it. Even still, the event has left a mark on his psyche, and has caused a deep rooted fear of fire in him. After he was rescued from the blaze that tore down his family's home, he was taken in by his uncle, Feldran, who was the guard captain of Valen at the time. Irvine was relentlessly bullied by many of the other children in Valen, after a rumor had spread that he was the one who had started the fire. Erika was among the few that came to his defense over the topic. After coming of age, he applied to become a courier, hoping that it would help him to distance himself from the trauma of his hometown, but could never bring himself to leave permanently.

Teria

Teria is a twenty-five year old Patrian woman. She is a member of Sildenfeld's Willow Rangers, who protect the borders of many settlements in the Region, as well as hunting game to be sold into them. She is a focused warrior and keen hunter, who becomes easily irritated with other people regardless of their race. Her closest comrades, Selbor and Farris, are the only two that she could reasonably call her friends, though she has a tentative relationship with the latter and his antics. Teria prefers to spend as much of her time in the wilderness as possible, believing that she is much more suited to hunting wildlife and helping to rout threats such as goblins, rather than keeping a watch on Sildenfeld's closer borders.

AFTERWORD

All my life I have loved stories. I can remember revisiting many of my favorites as a child, and even now as an adult, I continually return to those special ones that I love.

For many years, I have also created my own stories, though mostly for my own benefit. An outlet for a creative drive.

Some time back though, I started writing the story you hold in your hands now.

Sundering, is the first in the Ignis Trilogy, and the first foray into the world of Fædin, specifically in the continent of Patrias, and the Regions found within.

This world is quite special to me, from the time that I have spent in it, which at this point is quite a lot. A part of me, I feel, lives in Fædin with Erika, Irvine, Teria, Farris, and all the rest that will be met in the future.

I hope this was an enjoyable stay in this world, and I hope you will join me in Odyssey.

For now, thank you for reading my book. You have truly made my dreams come true, and I cannot thank you enough for that.

May Death find you alive,
- C. Stephen Hicks

Special thanks as well, to the beta readers:

Jaycee
Becky
Joanie
Juleen
Davin
Lisa
Patsy
Trinity

Without you, this story would not have been possible.

About the Author

Christopher Stephen Hicks lives in the ever-expanding Houston, Texas. He is joined in daily adventures by his wife Jaycee, their corgi Misa, and their multitude of cats: Tesla, Maxwell, Vierna, and Guenhwyvar.

When not writing, he is reading, watching shows or movies, or playing games to explore even more fantastical worlds.

Sundering is his debut novel in the *Ignis* series.

Milton Keynes UK
Ingram Content Group UK Ltd.
UKHW012240050124
435526UK00004B/300